P9-DEP-124

The MAIL ORDER Bride's Secret

LINDA BRODAY

sourcebooks
casablanca

Published by Sourcebooks Casablanca, an imprint of Sourcebooks
P.O. Box 4410, Naperville, Illinois 60567-4410
(630) 961-3900
sourcebooks.com

Printed and bound in Canada.
MBP 10 9 8 7 6 5 4 3 2 1

Also by Linda Broday

Dedicated to Sarah Mason Stipp, a dear cousin and avid romance reader. Enjoy the fruits of your labor and the rest you so richly deserve. If only I could laugh with you one more time.

One

Darkness closed around Melanie Dunbar as a clock somewhere beyond the stone wall gonged eight times. The honeysuckle-scented night breeze blowing in through the barred window wasn't that cold, but with fear added to the mix, it chilled her to the bone. Shivering, she put an arm around her sister Ava and pulled the one blanket they shared around them.

"I'm so scared, Melanie." Ava's whisper was loud in the quiet stillness. "And hungry."

The sheriff had long since locked up and left, not bothering to feed them.

"I know. Me too." Melanie hugged her sister tighter. Though they were twins, Ava had never been as strong or sturdy. In fact, she'd been sickly most of her life. "Try to think of something pleasant. Remember that time when we were girls and Mac left us with Grandmother?"

"She was real nice. I wish we could've stayed there longer." Ava laid her head on Melanie's shoulder and fingered the silver locket around her neck. "It was one of the few times I felt loved—really loved. I wish Mama hadn't died when we were born."

"Things would've been different. She wouldn't have let Mac drag us from pillar to post."

Melanie had no misconceptions about their father. Mac—a gambler, a con man, a cheat. And he'd started their lessons in the art of trickery and sleight of hand over fifteen years ago, only they'd never done anything but run an honest game at the tables. They both had skill at counting cards and found enjoyment in besting other players the right way. Anyone could cheat. That didn't take finesse. But to be the best took much more than deceit.

Now, the sheriff of Canadian, Texas, had arrested them for carrying fraudulent bank notes that Mac had thrust on them.

And the rat had disappeared into the wind, leaving them to take the fall.

Melanie silently called him every vile name she could think of. She should've been more careful, but Mac had been charming and for once had seemed to truly care about their welfare.

Damn! He'd conned them just like he did everyone else.

"What are we going to do?" Ava voiced the same question running through Melanie's head.

"I'll figure something out."

"I can't go to prison. Please don't let them send me to that horrible place," Ava begged.

"I won't," she promised, knowing she couldn't very well stop the law.

Twenty years of hard labor, the judge had pronounced with a bang of his gavel. Twenty years locked up. If they survived, they'd be old women by the time they got out—their lives done. She had to think of something. Ava would die in there as sure as she was born.

A scratching sound came from the wall, and a moment later a rodent scurried across their feet. Ava screeched and jerked her legs up.

Heavy footsteps sounded outside on the boardwalk. A key went in the lock. The door swung open. A dark figure moved to the lamp and struck a match. The soft glow revealed the frightening face.

Judge Ira McIlroy.

Melanie's blood went cold. She wished to pull the blanket over her head, but she refused to cower. She took in his head of thick, silver hair and the long, puckered scar running along one cheek.

The judge crossed the room and stood in front of their cell. "I have a deal for you."

It seemed too good to be true, and it probably was, but she'd hear him out. She got to her feet and moved to him. "I'm listening."

"I've gone through your belongings and see you've been

writing to that no-good outlaw Tait Trinity. Talking about being his mail order bride." He rubbed his cheek. "Marry him and gain his trust. Then deliver him and the money he's stolen to me."

"What money?" She knew Trinity had a price on his head but not what he was wanted for.

"The considerable amount he stole from the railroad. They want it back." McIlroy gave her a twisted grin that brought foreboding. "There's a sizeable reward in it for me."

The man's greed was only exceeded by his thirst for power. Unease told her to tread carefully. She narrowed her gaze. "In exchange for what?"

"I'll free your sister."

Melanie shook her head. "Not good enough. I'll be risking my life and still go to prison? I don't think so."

"Very well. I'll drop all charges against you both. But I keep Ava as insurance. She'll be safe here—and once you're done, you'll both walk free."

Melanie hesitated only briefly. Ava's life meant more to her than anything. "Shake on it?"

The judge stuck his arm through the steel bars and sealed the bargain. "It's a deal. I'll release you in the morning." He grabbed her arm and pulled her closer. "Cross me and I'll kill you and your sister both. Got that?"

At her nod, he dropped his hold, turned, and left the jail.

What would happen if she did go through with a marriage to Tait and he learned she'd betrayed him? He was a known killer. And there'd be no one to protect her.

Melanie shivered. She'd just made a deal with the devil. How it would end would be anyone's guess. But for Ava she'd do anything.

❧

There was an old cowboy saying: Never give the devil a ride or he'd always want the reins. Damn good advice, but even so sometimes the choice was out of a man's hands.

Especially the ill-tempered man challenging Tait to draw.

Nearby robins gossiped softly in the breeze, sounding like

many of the folk in this outlaw town. The rustle of footsteps behind him ceased. The birds stopped as though on command. His world froze.

Tait Trinity waited for death.

He didn't blink, didn't swallow, didn't move a muscle except in his flexing hand, inches from the smooth ram's-horn grip of his Smith & Wesson. He ignored the single bead of sweat that trickled into the lines of his left eye and stung like hell.

To lose focus for even a second could spell death.

A young man stood twenty paces in front of him, itching to kill him. He too seemed stuck in time. Anger reddened Ed Berringer's cheeks, and hate filled his deep-set eyes as his palm hovered above the butt of his gun. "I'm giving you a fair chance. That's more than you gave my brother."

The sun barely had risen on the new day, and Tait had yet to go bed. A crew of tiny workers inside his head sledgehammered thick iron spikes into his skull, and Berringer's yelling didn't help his headache one bit. Tait stood outside Hope's Crossing's only saloon and tried to steady the swaying boardwalk beneath his feet. It was far too early in the morning to make life-and-death decisions.

Tait shook his long hair back, wishing he had his hat. Where had he left it? His opponent's right eye twitched, the only sign of nerves. "Willie tried to shoot me in the back. He was yellow through and through."

"You lie." Ed shifted slightly. Except for the sneer, he wouldn't be bad looking.

"Where's your father, Ed? Kern's the one I want. You trying to prove how big you are by coming alone?"

"I don't need my father—or any of the rest of my brothers—to finish you off."

"This fight is between me and Kern. Go get him. I'm not going to shoot unless you force my hand." Damn his blurred vision. Tait blinked hard.

A few onlookers emerged from doorways, the town beginning to awaken. Tait hoped like hell no one else would get caught in the middle of this. Before he could blink, Clay Colby, the founder of the town and himself an ex-outlaw, stalked into Tait's line of sight and hustled everyone back.

Ed stared at Tait, hate settling in the deep creases around his mouth. His frustration was clear, and that made for a very dangerous situation.

A testy hiss exploded through Tait's teeth. "Either believe me about Willie or not. Frankly, I don't give two hoots. I'm tired, I'm grouchy, and I have no patience for bellyachers. Your brother got what he deserved. Now if you're in such a hurry to join him, let's get this over with."

The crowd grew, and Tait wondered who they rooted for. He hadn't been living in Hope's Crossing long and was no good at making friends to start with, so he hadn't bothered trying.

"After I kill you, I'm collecting the five-thousand-dollar reward for your hide!" Ed yelled.

That was a given. And it explained the true reason for this challenge. It wasn't about Ed's dead brother. It was all about the money. Just like it had been for Willie.

Sudden shouts and jangling rigging told Tait the early stagecoach was lumbering through the opening in the canyon wall and into town. Dogs barked furiously at the arrival, but Tait didn't swing to look. His gaze never left Berringer.

The man's right eye twitched again. He was getting ready to draw.

Maybe Ed would manage to get a lucky shot and Tait would make that final journey to Boot Hill.

Fate was fickle. Maybe Tait's gun would catch on the holster. Maybe it would misfire. Or maybe the sleep he yearned for would last for an eternity.

Dying would almost be a blessing. He'd messed up too much to straighten out in this lifetime. His road to perdition was already paved with wanted posters, posses, and too many bullet holes. Tait released a heavy sigh. What did a man like him really have to look forward to but a hangman's rope?

In her letters, Melanie had told him it was never too late

to change. Tell that to Ed Berringer and his .45. And if not Ed today, it would be another tomorrow, and another and another. They just kept coming, and the only thing that stood between Tait and certain death was his gun.

He just prayed he'd have the chance to make Kern Berringer pay for Lucy's death before he died. Anger rose up so thick inside it choked him.

"Did you go to sleep over there, Trinity?" Ed barked. "I think you're nothing but a coward."

"Just waiting for hell to freeze over so I can go ice-skating," Tait drawled lazily.

"Look, a gunfight!" yelled a kid. There was a flurry of movement off to the left and the sound of running feet.

"It sure is." The second new voice sounded equally as young.

"For God's sake, Colby, get those kids out of here," Tait ground out.

A crow's loud caws came from the roof of the saloon, and Tait heard Clay and his friend Jack Bowdre take the children in hand.

Tension mounted with each passing tick of the clock in Tait's head.

"Draw, you worthless, low-down son-of-a-sin-eater," he mumbled to himself.

Another bead of sweat rolled down his face and into his eye, stinging like holy hell. Even so, he didn't reach to wipe it away. Every muscle stretched to the breaking point, his breathing shallow.

Moments passed.

Ed Berringer whipped out his gun. Half-blinded by the salty sweat, Tait slapped leather with lightning reflexes honed from years of practice. He sent a bullet speeding into Berringer's heart before the man could squeeze the trigger.

Smoke curled around the barrel of Tait Trinity's gun and swirled up his nose, the acrid smell of gunpowder mixing with the scent of sweat and stale odor of alcohol. A bright light flashed from a camera that the town's newspaper reporter must've set up. Hell!

Tait stood silent for a long minute, trying to decide if he was alive or dead. He checked his body for holes and, finding none, finally slid his weapon into the holster.

Clay was the first to reach him. "You had no choice, Trinity. He was spoiling for a fight."

"Yeah." Tait turned and noticed the two boys and a little girl standing next to Jack Bowdre. "Berringer deserved what he got. But you know this is only the beginning. This'll bring the rest of the Berringer clan here." Still it was Papa Berringer that Tait hoped to finally come face-to-face with. They had unfinished business. Lucy business. He ground his back teeth. It'd be a blessing to finally get it over with and end this gnawing in his gut after three long years.

Still, at what cost to the town? People would die. Old man Kern would see to it.

Grim lines slashed Clay's face. "For sure."

"Damn!" The outlaw town of Hope's Crossing had survived so far by laying low and not drawing attention. Tait's stomach soured. He'd brought trouble.

"Whatever happens, we'll handle it. We always do." Clay stared off toward the hotel.

Jack, Clay's best friend and the local sheriff, brought the kids over. "We have a bit of a situation, Tait."

"It'll have to wait." Tait had more pressing matters. He narrowed his gaze at the newspaper man, Monty Roman, who was pushing his way through the crowd with paper and pencil in hand. Hell! Soon everyone in the Texas Panhandle would know where he was. Pictures and articles were the last thing he needed.

He had to get out of here. But leaving wouldn't fix the problem. Tait stepped in front of Roman. "I'll have to ask you not to print what occurred here—not the article or picture."

Roman blustered. "You can't silence the press. People have a right to know the happenings in this town."

Clay released a frustrated whoosh of air. "If you print this and send it out on the wire, it'll draw every bounty hunter and lawman in the country. Folks might die."

"Blood will be on your hands, Roman." Tait prayed that was enough of a reminder to keep the newspaper man quiet about this morning's set-to. "Do you want that for these women and children?"

"Of course not. But—"

Jack stepped between them, dragging the kids along with him. "When we let you set up your printer here, you agreed to never put any of us in jeopardy. Are you going back on your word?"

"No, but you have to give me something," Roman pleaded.

Tait released a weary sigh. "I'll make a deal. Kill the story and picture and I'll give you that God-blessed interview you've been pestering me about."

Monty Roman rested a finger on his chin. "I can ask any question I want?"

"No. You can ask anything except questions that might incriminate me. I'm not itching to get hanged. I'll tell you anything else." Tait held his breath and prayed that Roman would agree to the easy way. Otherwise, he'd be forced to break into the newspaper office and take the photograph back himself.

Roman scribbled something on his pad. "You'll tell me what brought you to Hope's Crossing all shot up and dying?"

"Yes."

"You'll tell me why you stayed?"

"As best I can explain it." It still wasn't that clear in Tait's mind.

"Deal."

Tait released a long breath, relieved to have arrived at a good trade-off. But hell! He didn't relish the notion of an interview. He tried to swing away only to have Jack lay a hand on his arm. "Not so fast. Did you and Ed fight during the night?"

"No." Tait shrugged and forced an even tone, stilling his trembling hand. "He rode into town late. Got a room at the hotel and this morning wanted to settle our differences. I'm tired and hungry."

"Did you shoot Berringer's brother, Mr. Trinity?" asked Monty Roman.

Irritation crawled up Tait's neck. "I have nothing further to say." As he pivoted, his attention wandered to the set of twins standing with Jack Bowdre. He took in the boys' rumpled clothes and the matched set of unruly cowlicks sticking from the crowns of their towheads. Obviously no one had given them much care of late. Both strained for a closer look at the dead man. Tait caught their attention and motioned them back with a jerk of his head. They sullenly returned to Jack's side.

Their parents needed to tend to them. They shouldn't be here.

The town only had a total of fourteen children, not counting the three babies, and these bore no resemblance to anyone. Neither did the little blond girl—couldn't be more than three years old—clinging to Jack's hand for all she was worth. Something in her face sparked a faint memory, but his head pounded too hard to try to call it up.

Jack stuck to him like a determined horse nettle. "We need to talk."

"Later." Tait inhaled some calming breaths. "You know where to find me."

"Dammit, Tait. I have something to tell you." Jack adjusted his hold on the little girl, now staring up at Tait with wide brown eyes.

Again, something familiar called to him. He shook it off. "After I get about ten years of shut-eye." Tait took three long strides toward his soddy.

"Nope, afraid this can't wait." Jack's grim voice made Tait stop and swing back around. Off to the side, Clay selected some men from the crowd to carry Ed's body away.

One of the boys stepped in front of Tait, his hard eyes flashing anger. "Our pa always said you were a no-account."

The other, his spitting image, glared. "And we don't wanna live here either."

Live here? What the hell did that mean? And who was their pa anyway?

"You'll get no argument from me on being a no-account, kid." Tait swung a hard gaze to Jack. "Talk."

"This is best done behind closed doors. My office." Jack transferred the little girl's hand to Tait's. "Might as well get used to this now."

The child puckered up to cry. Hell! Tait picked her up and marched toward the sheriff's small office in the hotel. She clung to his collarless shirt, gave him a shy smile, and quickly buried her face against his shoulder. Despite everything, his heart lurched and turned inside out. The girl was no bigger than a minute and couldn't weigh much more than his gun belt.

The sooner he found out what was going on, the sooner he could get some sleep. Jack had hinted that these three were his responsibility, but they didn't belong to him, and that was the end of the discussion. This was nothing but a misunderstanding. He'd always lived by one cardinal rule—no kids in his life. He and children mixed about as well as do-gooders and outlaws. Preachers and ladies of the night. Snow and hell.

Once in Jack's office, Tait sat the girl in a chair. The twins stood next to the scarred desk, both glaring at him like he'd stolen their lollipops. They couldn't be more than nine or ten and masquerading as mini-outlaws facing down an enemy.

And right there was the main reason for his no-children rule. You never knew what nonsense was going through their heads.

No-account, huh?

Tait straightened and glanced down at his rumpled, stained shirt, aware that he reeked of whiskey. He met their angry stares and raised an eyebrow. They probably would've stuck out their tongues at him if they'd thought they could get away with it.

"What's going on?" Tait asked.

"Better read this." Jack handed him a letter and settled into the chair behind his desk.

Tait moved to the window for better light and opened the envelope. Adjusting the paper at arm's length, he made out the flowing script of Flat Rock's sheriff, Hondo Rains. Hondo informed Tait that both his sister, Claire, and her husband had been gunned down by a group of murdering bastards on their remote ranch, leaving the children with no one to care for them.

Shock rippled through Tait. He blinked hard and read the words again to make sure.

"Rains sent the kids here to me, since he didn't know where to find you," Jack said.

Everything inside Tait turned to ice.

Of course, Hondo would've known Jack would care for the kids until Tait could be found. Tait, Jack, and Hondo had grown up together, hunting and fishing. With Tait and Claire's other brothers scattered across the West Coast and Alaska, finding them would've been much harder if not impossible.

Claire was gone. His only sister. It didn't make sense. Claire had been the one he talked to, the one who understood his troubles, the only one who'd ever given a damn about his sorry ass.

He inhaled sharply, folded the paper, and stood in stunned silence. What kind of sick joke was this?

No one was safe around him—especially these kids. He was an outlaw with a five-thousand-dollar bounty on his head. Bullets could fly at any given moment. Or he could wind up dangling at the end of a rope if the law caught him.

His legs tried to go out from under him. He needed to sit down. But first he needed a stiff drink. No, the whole damn bottle. What did he know about caring for children? He'd done a pitiful job raising himself, and he'd only taken over after he was half-grown.

"I know this came at you from the blue, but it seems you're all these kids have." Jack's chair squeaked as he leaned back and steepled his fingers under his chin. "You needed a reason to keep living, and here are three good ones."

"No, there's got to be some other way." Tait paced back and forth in front of the window. "Other family to take them in. What about their father's relatives? I don't know the first thing about raising kids."

Jack shook his head. "Hondo said he couldn't find any. I'm afraid you're it."

"I told you Uncle Tait wouldn't want us," one the twins sneered.

"We don't want *him* either," declared the other, folding his arms across his chest.

The little girl let out a piercing sob that grew into a regular dam burst. "Mama! Mama!"

The twins clapped their hands over their ears and looked at each other.

What the hell was Tait supposed to do now? He shot Jack a helpless plea.

His friend shook his head. "Nope. This is your bailiwick to handle, and I suggest you get to it before every guest in this hotel checks out. Oh, and the kids' luggage is waiting outside the stage office."

"What are their names—if you can tell me that much?"

"Rebecca is our sister," said the smirking twin, giving him the evil eye. "I'm Jesse."

The other half of their act spoke up, "And I'm Joe. You'd better not hurt us either."

Tait snorted. "Hurt you? Why in blue blazes did you say that? I've never hurt a child in my life."

"A warning, just in case you want to start," Jesse replied matter-of-factly.

"How old are you—thirty?"

Joe put his arm around Jesse's neck. "We're eleven, and Becky is three. And she ain't housebroke yet, for your information."

Housebroke? She wasn't a dog. Tait snorted again and strode to pick up the girl. That only made her cry harder. "Come along, boys." He didn't wait to see if they obeyed. His head had split plumb open, and little leprechauns were dancing a jig on what was left of his brains.

It didn't help that Jack was grinning, apparently thrilled by Tait's present predicament. If Tait hadn't been holding Becky, he'd have been sorely tempted to slug him.

"Some friendly advice." Jack chuckled as he held the door. "You might want to think about sending for that mail-order bride you've been writing. She might be your only hope."

Tait ran a hand across the bristles on his jaw and released a silent string of curses. He'd only been corresponding with Melanie Dunbar for the past month. The dressmaker was still as good as a stranger. If he did what Jack suggested, then not only would he have a niece and nephews to get acquainted with—but a bride too?

He suddenly lost his fear of hanging.

Two

His head spinning, Tait gathered the children's luggage in no time. Listening to the twins bellyache about having to help carry the small trunk, on the other hand, took a good half hour. Becky was still bawling no matter how much he jiggled her. By the time they reached his sod house, Tait was two seconds away from losing every bit of sanity he had.

Before following the twins inside, he held his wailing niece in one arm and a case under the other and shot a longing glance toward the saloon.

The boys dropped the trunk and gave the one-room shack a disgusted stare.

"Is this all there is?" Jesse—no, that was Joe—asked. "Looks like a pigsty if you ask me."

No one had asked the boy. Whichever one he was.

Hell, Tait was already entirely lost as to which was which. They were identical in looks—and in sour disposition. He sat Becky on the bed and dropped the bag on the floor.

"This is it. I'll have to do some rearranging." Tait threw the words over his shoulder while gathering up a couple of empty liquor bottles. He stuffed them in a burlap sack along with old newspapers and empty bean cans. "It's not like I had any kind of warning that you were going to show up today." A little advance notice would've been real nice.

Becky stopped crying, and the silence jolted him around. She stood on the floor, eyes wide, as pee ran down her legs and created a puddle around her.

"Damn it, Becky, you should've said something." He realized he'd uttered the curse word too late to take it back.

"Saw-wee." Tears filled the girl's brown eyes. She stuck out her bottom lip, and the waterworks started again. The twins snickered.

"We told you she ain't housebroke. And you ain't supposed to cuss around kids. Don'cha know anything?"

Which twin had said that? He was going to have to devise a way to tell them apart—and fast. "I'm sorry. I'm not used to having kids around." He motioned them toward Becky with a finger. "Change your sister."

"We ain't allowed."

Tait inhaled a deep breath and took a wild stab at guessing which of them had spoken. "Jesse, why aren't you allowed?"

"I'm Joe."

"Okay, Joe." Tait shifted his weight, narrowing his gaze at the boys. "Why can't you change Becky?"

"I'm just a kid. And besides, her parts are different from ours."

"Oh, for God's sake!"

"Are you fixing to cuss again?" asked Joe.

Tait was sure he had them right this time. "No, Joe, I am not." He was going to deal with the problem in a calm, logical manner. As soon as he could think of one.

"I'm Jesse." The boy grinned.

Tait wagged a finger. "I know what you're doing, and it's not going to work. We're not playing the confuse-the-stupid-uncle game. Once I get Becky cleaned up, we're having a talk."

The boys looked at each other then shrugged with wide-eyed innocence and snickered.

"Are you gonna shoot us?"

"Don't be ridiculous. Where did you get that idea?"

Another shrug, and Jesse—Tait was certain this time—answered, "'Cause you shoot people you're mad at. We saw you."

Regret that they had witnessed the gunfight wound through him. Not a good way to start off.

"I'm not shooting you, so get that out of your head." Tait directed his attention to Becky. "Would it be too much to ask that you find me some dry clothes for her? Or is that also not allowed?"

The boys opened the small trunk, and one of them yanked out a white dress and some underclothes.

Good Lord! White was the last color this little girl needed, but Tait took the garments, anxious to finish the unpleasant job.

He picked Becky up and laid her on his narrow bed. The child had stopped crying, but tears clung to her long lashes. She stared up at him with a quizzical expression. His headache had gotten considerably worse, and he could barely see. After working what seemed hours, he finally let Becky up, praying she wouldn't wet her clothes again. But where did he need to take her next time? The outhouse seemed too big for such a small little girl. And too far away.

Sweat had drenched his shirt, and his stomach rumbled, reminding him he needed to eat. There was only one thing to do. He picked Becky up. "Let's go, boys."

"Where?" asked one, never mind which one it was. He couldn't tell.

"To the café. Bet you're hungry."

"Daddy never took us to a café."

Probably because they acted like little heathens. But letting someone else handle the cooking right now was better than trying his luck. Besides, he needed time to consider how to enlarge their sleeping quarters. That, or find some large nails to hammer into the walls and hang each kid up on one. Somehow, he didn't think a nail would hold these twins or the little missy.

Before they went out the door, he rifled through a cigar box for a safety pin he knew he'd put in there. Finally spying it, he pinned it to Joe's shirt collar. He knew it was Joe because Becky had nodded when Tait asked her to confirm it.

"There."

The twins winked at each other. Tait wasn't sure what that meant, but it couldn't be good. He led the mini-gang across the wide-open space in the middle of town. In other villages, that might have been a green or a proper town square, but here drivers used it to turn the stage and wagons around so they could head out the way they came in. Hope's Crossing sat in a canyon, steep rock walls surrounding what had once been an outlaw hideout. This town had been Clay Colby's dream.

If the townsfolk's hard work was any indication, one day it would probably amount to something.

Becky stopped crying and clung to Tait's shirt, snot running from her nose. He paused and fetched a kerchief from his pocket. Probably wasn't clean, but the girl didn't mind. Ridge Steele, the town mayor, rode in through the pass and waved.

For once, the Blue Goose Café was only half-full. Usually the place was booming. Sid Truman had opened four months ago and never had more than two tables empty at a time, except at closing. Tait aimed the boys toward a table where they scuffled, trying to get the same seat.

He gave them a heavy scowl. "Do you want to take your meal outside with the dogs?"

"No, sir," Joe mumbled.

"Then straighten up. I know your mother didn't put up with ruckus, and I won't abide it either." Tait sat Becky in a chair. He nodded to Sid's wife, Martha, who came from the kitchen to see the commotion, her six-month-old daughter Noelle propped on her hip. She was the only girl out of ten boys. "Mrs. Truman, how are things going?"

The woman approached their table. "If my life was any better, I don't know what I'd do." She smiled at Noelle and ran a loving hand over the baby's red curls before swinging her attention back to Tait. "And who are these sweet children? I don't recall ever seeing you with youngsters before, but I can see the resemblance. The boys have your unusual gray eyes and mutinous profile."

Mutinous? He snorted. Hardly. "They're my nephews, Jesse and Joe, and this little girl is my niece Becky. They're staying with me for a…bit." Tait hated to hedge, but neither did he want anyone to think this was permanent.

"Well, she's a beautiful angel. You look like you could use some help." Martha sat her pride and joy on the scrubbed floor and whipped out some white cloths from her pocket. In short order she had tied one around each of the children's necks and brought a stack of seed catalogs for Becky to sit on that allowed her to reach the table. "There. Now they're set."

The eleven-year-old twins glared at Tait. He smiled back. They really were too old to be treated like babies, but a reminder of who was in charge didn't hurt.

"My sons will be happy to have your boys to play with, and so will Sawyer and Ely." Mrs. Truman smiled at the twins. "In fact, Sawyer is in the kitchen helping out now. He's twelve. I'll bring him out and introduce him." She collected Noelle and returned to the kitchen.

Tait leaned across the table. "Not one sour word or we'll do this at home. I know you don't want to be here, but we all have to make the best of it."

Becky patted Tait's arm. "Saw-wee." Her shy grin twisted something inside him.

"Not you, honey." Tait kissed her cheek.

Martha Truman returned with Sawyer and introduced him. Jesse and Joe wanted to know why he worked there and if someone forced him.

Sawyer shrugged. "I like it, and it's only an hour or two each day. Gives me a little spending money. You can sign up to work too, if you want."

"Not me," Jesse said. Joe sided—of course—with his brother.

"Suit yourself." Sawyer pointed to a small blackboard with the day's menu on it. "What would you like to order, Mr. Trinity?"

"What's good?" Tait squinted at the board, his head pounding harder.

Sawyer grinned. "Eggs, biscuits, and gravy is always my favorite, but you might like the pancakes."

Jesse bowed up, folding his arms across his chest. "We don't eat gravy."

"I'm allergic to eggs." Joe's strained half smile must be the kind he reserved for strangers and people he didn't like. Or when he felt like picking a fight.

Tait couldn't miss the challenge in the boy's eyes. He ignored the thrown gauntlet and smiled at Sawyer. "Pancakes and milk for the children, and I'll take the eggs over easy and some coffee. Hurry with the coffee and bring some extra gravy too."

"Coming right up." Sawyer headed for the kitchen.

Tait's gaze followed the orphan that Jack and his wife Nora had taken in. Why couldn't the twins be more like Sawyer— grateful for what they got?

Jesse put his elbows on the table. "What are you gonna do with us?"

"Well, I'm not shipping you out on the next stage." No matter how tempting. Tait glanced toward the kitchen, hoping to see Sawyer bringing that coffee.

"Milk." Becky patted Tait's arm. "Milk."

"Just a minute, sweetheart. It's coming." Tait aimed another look toward the kitchen. Where was his coffee? If it didn't come soon, he'd lose what was left of his mind. There was a flurry of movement behind him, but when he turned around, the boys were still seated in their places.

"Maybe you should think about what the sheriff said," Joe suggested.

"Which part?" Jack had been pretty free with advice and had seemed to delight in Tait's predicament.

"You're sorta ignorant about raising kids, and a woman knows about what kids hafta have. You need a wife." Joe leaned back, looking satisfied at speaking his mind.

"He's right." Jesse took up the cause, wagging his finger. "You need to get married. Why haven't you, anyway? You're old."

The last thing Tait needed was advice from kids, especially with Jack's grin still sticking in Tait's craw. "I haven't married because I've been busy. And I haven't found the right woman. Yes, I know I'm old. You don't have to tell me."

Thank God, his coffee. Sawyer plunked down a cup and filled it from a pot. "I thought you might be needing this, Mr. Trinity."

"You're a good man, Sawyer." Tait brought the cup to his mouth, and the first taste was worth every piece of gold in the Denver Mint. The coffee swept other distracting thoughts right out of his head and settled the jumpiness inside him.

Mrs. Truman brought a plate full of hot biscuits, and Tait thanked her.

Jesse stood and reached for a biscuit, handing one to Becky while Joe served himself. "What will happen to us when the lawmen come and arrest you?"

"Don't worry about that." Tait took a sip of coffee and let the hot brew take the jagged edge off his nerves. "I'll have things in place in the event they do find me." Who could he bribe to take the kids? Maybe Clay's wife, Tally. Or Bowdre's wife, Nora? But Nora was heavy with her third child, and Clay and Tally had two kids. Rebel and Travis's third was soon due.

Sawyer brought the glasses of milk, and Tait held Becky's to her mouth. She drained half and wore a milk mustache grin when he took it away.

"Did you rob banks and trains?" Joe asked.

Diners at the other tables stared.

"Joe, that subject is off-limits," Tait said quietly.

"I'm Jesse."

Tait leaned across the table and flipped the safety pin. "Nope. You have the safety pin on your collar. You're Joe."

"No, I'm Jesse." The boy was a little too smug. "I know who I am."

Tait finished his coffee in one gulp and motioned to Sawyer for a refill. Then he turned to the only one he could trust for the truth. "Becky, honey, who is this?" He pointed to Jesse.

She answered, "Joe."

Dammit! The boys had switched. "Thank you, honey." He grimly leaned across the table, using every bit of restraint he had. "Put the pin back where I had it. I'm not playing this game."

Jesse glared. "You don't want us. Just admit it."

"I loved my sister—your mother—very much, and I'll love you too if you'll give me half a chance." Tait's memory wandered to the only time he'd tried to see Claire after she'd married, all of four years ago, and he winced.

Claire's husband, John, had met him in the yard in mid-dismount. "Don't bother getting down," he'd said, his jaw set firm. "Your kind ain't welcome here, Tait."

His sister had stood at the screen door looking helpless.

Tait had never gone back. He was good at staying far away from the ones who didn't want him. If she'd written, her letters hadn't found him. But then, he'd kept on the move except for his time in Hope's Crossing. And now he'd never see his sister again.

He stared at the twins. "Will you give me a fighting chance to prove myself?"

"I guess," both mumbled at once.

"Good." And just when he thought he could relax, Becky knocked over her glass, and milk drenched Tait's trousers.

He couldn't wait for the meal to end. As soon as it did, he rushed to the telegraph office and left the children just inside by the door, telling them not to budge. He'd probably be able to keep an eye on them there, but where they were concerned, nothing was a sure thing.

Tait got in line behind the reverend.

Brother Paul concluded his business and turned. "Mr. Trinity, I'm glad I ran into you. I heard about your unexpected dilemma. I'll be happy to move out of the church and you can live there until you find more suitable lodging."

Yeah, and there'd be the biggest lightning strike anyone had ever seen if he stepped foot in a church. That was one place he couldn't go. He suppressed a shudder, remembering his father standing in the pulpit preaching fire and brimstone. Then another memory took its place—a dark barn, a razor strop, no one to save him.

Tait gave the reverend a wide smile. "Thank you for the offer. I really appreciate it, but I've decided to put me and the children up at the hotel."

"Well, if you change your mind, let me know." Brother Paul stopped to chat with the children for a moment while Tait turned his attention to more pressing concerns. "I need to send a message right away, Shaughnessy."

The young clerk, smartly dressed in a pinstripe suit and bow tie, glanced up at him and then looked again, seemingly taken aback by Tait's wretched appearance. "What happened, Mr. Trinity? Were you in a war?"

Tait jerked his head toward the children in the doorway. No words were needed.

"I understand." Shaughnessy handed him a pad and pencil.

Tait scribbled a plea.

Urgent. Come quick. I'll marry you the minute you step off the stage.

He thought a second longer then licked the lead of the pencil and added:

If you'll still have me.

Three

Tait handed the piece of paper to Shaughnessy. "Send this immediately—to Melanie Dunbar in care of Luke Legend at the Lone Star Ranch."

"Sure thing. That'll be two dollars, Mr. Trinity."

Once the telegram had been sent, Tait breathed a sigh of relief. He hated that all correspondence and messages had to go through Legend, but the man insisted on preserving the safety of both parties. His private matchmaking service was for men and women living in the shadows, folks who couldn't seek a mate through normal channels, and Legend had his rules. Tait didn't know Melanie's story, but her past couldn't be any worse than his own.

Truth was Tait had everyone from the East Coast to the West scouring the country for him, and the government had declared him an enemy.

A fine time for three kids to show up on his doorstep.

"Are you finished, Mr. Trinity?" Pretty Nora Bowdre smiled at him and rested a hand on her large stomach, a paper clutched in the other.

"Yes. Have a good day." He stepped aside. Even with food inside him his head was still splitting, and nothing short of sleep would relieve the pain. Best get checked into the hotel.

Outside the telegraph office, he grabbed the two oldest of the Truman ten and paid them to help move the kids' luggage to the Diamond Bessie Hotel where he took a two-bedroom suite on the top floor.

He was one step closer to much-needed sleep. Tait rustled the kids up the stairs. Only once he got to their floor, Tally Colby stood at the door to their room, blocking his path. "Mr. Trinity, I need a word."

"One moment." He unlocked the door and shooed the children inside. She looked angry, but maybe she was only concerned that he might snap and forget he was the only close kin the kids had left.

"Yes, Mrs. Colby?" He was proud of himself for managing a calm tone.

Tally lowered her voice and pulled the door shut. "What is your experience caring for youngsters?"

"None." Tait tried to reach for the doorknob, only to be thwarted by Tally wedging in between again.

"Then you need lessons. The welfare of these poor little darlings hangs in the balance."

He nearly choked. Poor little darlings? More like a gang of cutthroats—at least the twins.

"I'm afraid this will have to wait. Now if you'll excuse me." He reached for the doorknob again with the same result.

Tally scowled. "You don't look well at all. Have you been sleeping all right?"

"Not recently, no. It sounds like a great idea though."

"Then I want to suggest letting me keep the children until tomorrow and you can rest up. I'll see you for lessons tomorrow, say around noon." She was telling him, not asking.

He didn't know whether to kiss her or tell her this was none of her affair. But she was looking at the stairs, and fear set in she might leave. He grabbed her and gave her a big kiss on the cheek. In a matter of minutes, she left with the children in tow.

Tait locked the door and staggered toward the big, beautiful, fluffy bed, sprawling face-first into the clean softness.

⁂

Melanie's reply came the following day, and the week he awaited her arrival in Hope's Crossing was filled to the brim. He took lessons in child-rearing from the women in town—mostly about caring for Becky. He tried his best to learn how to read the girl's signs when she needed to visit the chamber pot, but it was very much a work in progress. He finally told her to yell out the word *pot*, and that seemed the solution. The women helped him with the laundry, for which he was accumulating a large number of owed favors.

The boys persisted in their shenanigans. Once when Tait's back was turned, they tied Becky onto a goat and slapped the animal's rear to send it running. The girl hung on for dear life and lasted almost five minutes. She was a tough little thing.

Then in response to his stern lecture, they'd put a snake in his boot.

Tait and snakes didn't mix. He didn't mind spiders, scorpions, or tarantulas. Just don't give him a snake.

Against his best efforts to control them, Jesse and Joe pretty much ran wild. Every day Tait was approached by someone lodging a new complaint. He hung on by a thread.

Clay caught up with him the morning following the goat and the snake incidents. "I need a word."

That seemed to be everyone's favorite phrase these days, and Tait was sick of hearing it. "Can't. I have to pick up Becky at the Bowdres', find the twins, and fix a gate the boys broke."

Clay's hand on his shoulder stopped him. "You'll be late. We have to talk."

"All right. Spit it out."

"You have to settle those boys down and make them mind."

"Or else what?" Irritation crawled up Tait's neck.

"Put the fear of God in them or we'll ask you to leave the hotel." Clay's voice held a firmness Tait had never heard before. "I mean it. We've already had several guests walk out, saying they couldn't get a wink of sleep for the boys running up and down the hallway. They've broken vases and knocked pictures off the walls while playing catch. The clerk has given notice that if they continue to act like heathens, he's quitting."

Tait let out a long sigh. "I'll lay down the law. Again."

"Make believers out of them. Keep them in their room for a day." A look of terror crossed Clay's face. "No, not their room. There won't be anything left. Take them to the church. Let Brother Paul preach them to death. I think they're bored. We need school to start, and soon." Todd Denver, the schoolmaster, probably wasn't that anxious. Not one bit.

"I'll see what I can do, Clay."

"When is your bride due to arrive?"

"Any day, and she can't come soon enough." He gave the saloon a longing glance. His life was so different now that he didn't recognize it. If he could just last until Melanie arrived. But that was starting to seem like one of those long shots he used to wager on.

An hour later, Tait sat the boys down for a talk.

"Me and Joe don't like rules," declared Jesse, crossing his arms.

As a last resort, Tait ended up seeking Brother Paul's help. However much that he and churches didn't mix, he marched the boys over to the house of worship. They were halfway to the church when Joe balked. "I ain't going there."

"Me either." Jesse jutted his jaw.

Tait wanted to balk as well. His mouth had gone dry and his chest heaved.

"Too bad. You have no choice in the matter." Tait kept herding them forward. On the steps, he almost relented. He glanced up at the blue sky, looking for bolts of lightning. When nothing happened, he opened the door and stepped into the domain he'd shunned for all his adult years. The cool interior seemed to reach for him with bony fingers. He shoved his memories aside and walked down the aisle, his bootheels resounding on the wooden floor.

❧

After Tait left the boys with the minister for several hours, Brother Paul was able to shed some light for Tait. "The boys are afraid you're going to give them to someone else to raise. They think if they act like holy terrors no one else will want them, and you'll be forced to keep them."

"But they as much as admitted that they don't want to live with me."

"That's far from the truth. They harbor quite a fascination with you." Brother Paul's eyes twinkled. "Their father wouldn't let them mention your name. He told them you stole pennies off dead men's eyes and would rob your own mother. And then they witnessed your shoot-out. They think you're the only one around tough enough to get justice for their parents."

Tait studied the floor. "I mean to try as soon as I get them settled."

"The boys have horrible nightmares about the men who killed their parents."

Why hadn't he heard them? Maybe because they slept in a room across from the sitting area. And another reason could be that they hadn't cried out.

Losing their parents the way they had would scar the bravest man, and for boys, the terror of such a traumatic event would be unimaginable. Tait shook Brother Paul's hand. "Thank you."

"I'm here if you need me."

The boys were quiet during the short walk back to the Diamond Bessie Hotel, and so was Tait. Once there, he sat them on the sofa. Their belligerence was gone. Becky crawled up beside them and put her hands over her eyes, peeking through her fingers. It was all Tait could do to keep a straight face at her antics.

"Is there anything you want to say?" he asked, his voice low.

Jesse squinted up. "Are you going to keep us?"

What the hell was he getting into? He didn't know one dadgum thing about how to be a parent and should have his head examined. He ran a trembling hand through his hair. Their expectant faces staring up at him with such hope punched him in the gut. They didn't have anyone else to care for them. To tuck them in at night or dry their tears.

"Of course I'm keeping you. We're family."

Joe scowled. "But we heard you say this is temporary."

Tait cringed as his words came back to slap him. "I was still trying to digest the news. I'm sorry for making you think that way. Come here." He pulled them up for a hug. "You're part of my life now. Okay?"

Joe squinted up at him. "You're not mad?"

"No." Tait sat down beside them on the sofa, silently vowing to do his duty instead of pawning them off on some- one else. "Tell me about those riders who killed your parents."

Jesse's face grew hard. "There were six of 'em. Daddy stepped out on the porch with a rifle, and they shot him dead."

Joe picked up the story. "We grabbed Becky, ran out the back to a little creek, and hid in the brush. They kept shooting and shooting and shooting. I was scared they'd find us."

"How long did the riders stay?" Tait's voice was low.

"Till dark." Joe shivered. "We found Mama dead. Lots of blood. Will you go find 'em?"

"Yeah, I'll find 'em." And then Tait would make them all very sorry they'd been born.

"Shoot every one of them!" Jesse got up and ran into the bedroom where they slept.

"Joe, did you see their faces?" Tait prayed the boys remem- bered enough to help him find them.

"One or two. They looked real mean. One had gray hair and hound-dog eyes."

"Describe them."

"Well, his eyes had bags hanging under them like a hound dog."

At least Tait had something to go on. "What else?"

Joe wrinkled his forehead in thought. "Real big ears."

"Bigger than mine?"

"Shoot, yeah. They stuck *way* out. And he was taller than a mountain."

"No one is that tall, Joe. How much taller was he than I am?"

Joe glanced around. "He was as tall as the blacksmith."

"Skeet Malloy?"

"Yeah. He was big."

That put the man about six foot six. "What did any of the others look like?"

The boy licked his lips. "There was this one with missing front teeth and bowlegs."

Sounded like most of the men in the Panhandle.

Becky crawled into Tait's lap and patted his chest. "Mama."

His heart melted. He was such an easy mark for a little girl's smile. Tait stood. "Let's eat lunch and I'll play catch with you. Let me get Jesse."

Tait found Jesse sitting on the floor in a corner. Tait sat next to him and put an arm around the boy. "I wish I could put everything back the way it was, but I can't."

"Why did those riders do it? Why kill our ma and pa? Why?"

"I don't know, but you can bet I'll find out." Tait handed Jesse a handkerchief.

That afternoon Tait headed over to Jack's office and told him what the boys had said. "I've got to go talk to Hondo and see what he knows. Will you ride with me?"

Seeing his old buddy would do Tait good. Neither time nor being on the opposite sides of the law had dimmed their friendship. Tait had often ridden by Flat Rock under cover of darkness to visit with Hondo, and being who he was, their old friend might have crucial information on Kern Berringer's whereabouts. If Tait could just find his hideout. But the area was vast, and his enemy could be anywhere.

"Yeah, I'll go with you. Want to leave tomorrow?"

"Sounds good." Tait itched to ride out, but first he had to find someone to keep the kids.

He was taking them into the café for supper when Shaughnessy raced from the telegraph office. "Have a message for you, Mr. Trinity."

Tait opened the folded slip of paper and held it at arm's length. Thank goodness. Melanie Dunbar said she'd arrive tomorrow on the evening stage.

Finally. Except that meant he'd have to delay his trip to Flat Rock.

∽

The following evening, he had the children lined up in front of the stage lines office. He gave each a stern eye and last-minute instructions. "Be polite, no tricks, and act like you have more than a lick of sense."

His glance then swept to the crowd gathering behind them. "Go home. I don't need gawkers."

Unperturbed, Tally smiled, not budging. "No offense, but we want to make sure she's suitable for the children."

Fine. He pulled a handkerchief from a pocket and wiped a streak of dirt from Becky's face just as the stagecoach raced through the gap in the canyon. This was it. God help him.

"Don't forget to smile, Uncle Tait." Jesse's sage advice came with a wink.

Joe added his two cents. "And don't say anything rude even if she's ugly. We need her."

Becky slipped her small hand inside Tait's and glanced up. "Mama?"

"No, honey, not your mama. Miss Melanie will be your aunt." Assuming she stayed. *Dear Lord, don't let her change her mind.*

Anguish bubbled in Becky's large eyes. "Mama."

Tait picked her up and wiped the silent tears rolling down the girl's cheeks. "I know, and I'm real sorry, honey. If I could bring your mama back, I'd do it in a heartbeat." And as soon as Melanie settled in, he'd hunt down the low-down scum who'd killed his sister.

The stage halted, enveloping them in a swirl of dust, and the driver pulled the hand brake. This was it. Tait lowered Becky to stand between her brothers, straightened his blue vest, and adjusted the gold watch chain. He'd brushed his boots, dusted his black Stetson, and shaved. This was the best he could do.

Why did it feel as though he was going to his hanging? What if he didn't like her? Or she him? So much hinged on this moment.

His chest tightening, he opened the stagecoach door. A woman in a becoming blue bonnet took his hand and stepped down. Long auburn hair tumbled over her shoulders, the loose curls begging for a touch.

Her dress, the same shade of blue as the bonnet, showed some wear around the hem and cuffs of her sleeves. Somewhere in the deep recesses of his mind came the thought that wearing frayed clothing seemed rather odd for a dressmaker. But maybe she'd fallen on hard times.

She raised her eyes to meet his, and his breath caught, startled by the mesmerizing color. They weren't quite blue and not quite green. Kind of turquoise—like an ancient stone revered by the Navajo.

Fierce determination, and maybe hope, shone in her gaze.

Tait's mouth dried. "Miss Melanie?"

Dimples formed in the lady's cheeks when she smiled. "I take it you're Mr. Trinity?"

The world became silent and still. Tait stared and tried to swallow but found it impossible. Melanie Dunbar possessed the kind of charm that warmed like summer rays and made him feel all man. A mere second had passed, and he already knew he'd bitten off more than he could chew.

Four

MELANIE TOOK IN THE SMALL TOWN, AWASH IN THE DYING, plum-colored light, and at first glance found it welcoming. Then she turned her attention to the man, this outlaw she'd corresponded with for the past month. Had manipulating Luke Legend been worth it? On the outside, Tait Trinity appeared every bit the lethal outlaw she'd once glimpsed aboard the train he was robbing. He'd had a bandana covering his face then, of course, but she'd never forget those eyes—hard and gray, like chips of ice.

What kind of a husband would he be? Only time would tell.

She took in his tall, lean figure, the long hair that touched his shoulders, and lingered a second longer than necessary on those gray eyes that now reminded her of quicksilver in the fading light.

He was a squinter, as evidenced by the crinkles around the corners of his eyes, and at the moment his eyes lacked the hardness she saw too often in men living on the lawless frontier. Yet, like quicksilver, she thought they might change very abruptly under certain situations.

Tait Trinity could buy her ticket to freedom. She took in the heavy gun he wore in the holster strapped around his lean hips.

Yes, she certainly had her work cut out. Suddenly her confidence slipped a notch. It had been one thing to talk about what she had to do. It was quite another coming face-to-face with the man whose life she meant to destroy. He wasn't some dumb hayseed—he was a killer.

Her pulse raced and her palms sweated under Tait's piercing gaze that seemed to notice every detail about her.

She nervously made a slight adjustment of her skirt to hide the mend, bemoaning the loss of her silk dresses. That was just one of many humiliating comedowns lately. One of the boys jostled Tait's elbow, and, shaking herself, she focused on the children. He hadn't mentioned having children to raise. This would complicate things.

She knew nothing about the care of children, and they were noisy and cried at the drop of a hat. Frankly, kids scared her, and she'd avoided any contact with youngsters as a grown woman.

Before she could open her mouth, Tait put a hand on each of the boys' shoulders, drew them forward, then lifted the small girl into his arms. "Miss Dunbar, meet my niece and nephews. The boys are Joe and Jesse, and this little one is Becky."

Only his kin. Melanie relaxed. They must live in Hope's Crossing with their parents.

She smiled. "Hello. It's really nice to meet you."

Tait captured her gaze and held it longer than was needed before he lifted the corner of his mouth in a sudden, crooked grin that almost vanished before she saw it. "I'm the children's guardian. Their parents were killed, leaving them with no one. I should've let you know before you came all this way, but frankly I've been a tad busy adjusting to this arrangement myself. I do apologize."

"I see. We need to talk, Mr. Trinity."

Tait scowled and glanced around, motioning to two women. He spoke in a low voice to them, after which the women collected the children and moved off toward a row of houses.

He picked up Melanie's heavy bags as though they weighed nothing. "Come with me to the hotel, Miss Dunbar."

She nodded and fell into step with him. They didn't stop until they reached a comfortable office in the Diamond Bessie Hotel.

"We can borrow this room." Tait removed his hat, laid it on a table, and closed the door. Streaks of blond shot through his caramel hair. No one had told her how handsome he was.

Painfully aware of his scrutiny, she swung to glance at

the room, admiring the blue velvet sofa, chairs, and pretty wallpaper. "It's nice."

"I didn't mean to mislead you, and I'm sorry if you feel that way." He paced in front of a large desk that had a painting of a snow-covered pasture behind it. "Have a seat."

Melanie removed her bonnet, but instead of sitting, she wandered to the window and pushed the thin curtain aside. "I wish I had known before I made the trip. I didn't sign up to be a nursemaid." "Wife" was about all she could handle. "This changes things."

Tait dropped into the chair behind the desk and let out a heavy breath. "What's the problem? Don't you like kids?"

"It's not that. I like them fine. Only I've never been around children and know nothing about their care." She let the curtain fall back into place and got comfortable on the sofa. She stared directly at him and gave him a warm smile as though they were discussing the weather. "I will not be a nanny, a maid, a cook, or a laundress, although I'll do my fair share."

Confusion crossed his face. "So, what are you saying exactly?"

"I came to be your wife, not to have you pawn your niece and nephews off on me and go your merry way. I've heard stories of widowers who advertised for brides with nothing more in mind than to dump a bunch of kids on them and take off for good." She removed her gloves. "If you intend that, then our business is concluded, and I'll leave on the next stage."

But could she truly accept the consequences of leaving? She could little afford to make demands. Only he didn't know that.

"Hold on a minute, missy. That was not my intention. I don't plan on dumping those kids." He paused, and the guilt in his expression told her that had been exactly why he'd sent for her. He straightened from his slouch. "Okay, I have to be honest. Maybe that might've been the reason I telegraphed you a week ago, but the situation has gotten better."

"Elaborate, please."

"I really need your help. I'm out of my element. What if the two of us work together as a team? We'd bear the load fifty-fifty."

Melanie narrowed her gaze at him. "You won't ride out at the first opportunity and stay gone for months at a time, leaving me stuck here with children I don't know?"

"I give my word." He rose and perched on the corner of the walnut desk, rolling his neck. There was something he still wasn't saying. She waited.

Tait cracked his knuckles. "What I have to tell you next may be the deal breaker."

"What's that?"

"The day I telegraphed asking you to come, the very day the kids arrived, I had a run-in with a dangerous man and killed him. He's buried in the cemetery outside the entrance to the town. Ed Berringer has a father, brothers, and uncles all meaner than the devil and twice as ready to settle the score. I don't know how this will play out." He gave her a smile that vanished before it finished forming. "I misplaced my crystal ball."

"I see." So even more trouble lurked. She'd already known how dangerous this would be from the first.

"Another thing you should know, Miss Dunbar. This high price on my head draws attention. Lawmen—or countless others—could ride in any day and haul me out of here, assuming they don't kill me outright. Are you a risk-taker?"

"From the day I was born." He had no idea exactly how true her answer was.

"Then I guess the choice is yours. Will you marry me or get back on the stage?"

Melanie liked his direct honesty. From his letters she'd learned that he was a man used to betting on long odds instead of the sure thing. They had much in common there.

"I'll marry you." She plunked all her cards on the table. "How about tomorrow?"

She might as well get started. The sooner she finished what she had come to do, the sooner her sister would be free.

Tait seemed taken aback by her rush but quickly recovered. "Sounds good. Do you mind living here at the hotel for now? My place is too small. And besides, it's a soddy. I didn't need anything much when it was just me." He stood. "I'll try to be a good husband, but I'm warning you, I'm not an easy man to like."

"As long as you don't abandon me, I'll stay by your side." She inhaled the first real breath she'd taken since arriving. "One more thing. Don't expect me to speak of love because I won't." She'd had quite enough of empty words and false promises. A man's actions were the things that defined him.

"Me either." A look of relief crossed his face. "I don't believe in such. I hope you can respect me when I earn it, and that'll be all I can ask for."

"Then we understand each other perfectly." No messy emotions to get in the way. That was better than she'd dared hope for.

Tait sauntered toward her, slow and easy like a wild animal stalking his prey, and when he stood a foot away, Melanie found the scent of his shaving soap pleasing. His height was imposing, and he appeared more than capable of protecting her from the dark storms about to engulf her.

But cross him? The magnitude of what she had planned suddenly hit her. She wouldn't get through this unscathed. An unexpected chunk of ice slid down Melanie's spine.

❧

They took supper with the children in the Blue Goose Café. Tait had never heard the three of them rattle on so much. Maybe their excitement stemmed from missing their mother but seeing Melanie as the next best thing. Melanie herself seemed a bit overwhelmed but handled it all with a smile and kind words. She even lifted Becky onto her lap.

Tait relaxed. She was gracious and kind to the children, and that was enough for him.

Jesse leaned over. "Did you kiss her? Girls like that."

"Where did you get that idea?" Tait asked.

The boy shrugged. "No place. My daddy was always kissing Mama."

"Well, don't expect everyone to be like them." He glanced

at Melanie and found himself studying her enticing mouth that tilted up at the corners with a defined cupid's-bow top lip. Very kissable. Her mouth's shape gave the impression she was holding back laughter. Thank goodness she didn't have the thin, puckered lips that he'd seen on spinsters that always suggested they'd eaten a persimmon. Maybe he would kiss Melanie tonight at her door. A peck.

Just to see what she tasted like, of course.

Tait pulled his mind away from her mouth, got everyone's attention, and announced the wedding plans for tomorrow. He pinned the twins with a sharp gaze. "And there'll be no tricks played on us. Got that?"

"Snake," Becky said, frowning.

"Especially not any snakes." Tait told Melanie about the reptile he'd discovered in his boot.

Melanie shivered. "Oh dear. I wouldn't like that at all."

"I don't think we'll have a problem. Will we, boys?"

"Nope." Except Joe's grin wasn't that reassuring.

It wouldn't hurt to keep checking his boots for a while. Melanie's shoes as well. Tait prayed Melanie was made of strong stuff because it was going to take real staying power to raise Joe and Jesse.

He puzzled over one of the things she'd said earlier: as long as he didn't abandon her, she'd stay by his side. What trouble had Melanie Dunbar faced in the past? Her eyes had seemed haunted. By what—or whom?

Now sitting across from her, he found no evidence of worry or distress. She certainly gave the appearance of being content, and she drew his gaze like water to the moon's force. But not just him. Everyone around couldn't seem to stop looking. She was a sight. Her auburn hair flamed in the light of the oil lamps hanging on the wall. Her blue dress, open at the neck, revealed a swath of golden skin, and her long, nimble fingers moved gracefully.

The woman who'd be his wife intrigued him.

She smiled at something Jesse said, and her dimples flashed once before they went into hiding again. Tait found himself leaning forward, hoping to catch those charming dimples again.

Melanie Dunbar would do just fine.

Both the meal and the company were excellent. The evening was over all too soon, and they strolled back to the hotel together, their heels resounding on the wooden boardwalk. Tait was more contented than he'd felt in a long time. He had help with the kids, Melanie shared his mindset regarding love, and he was still alive. That amounted to a very good day.

Scout and Bullet, the town's two dogs, ambled up, which halted the group's progress while the children introduced them to Melanie and petted the animals. It gave him a moment to quietly observe her, and he liked what he saw. Although his suspicious mind couldn't quite shake a feeling of something being off.

She'd seemed a bit too hasty to accept him. She'd gone from laying down the law to suggesting an almost immediate ceremony in no time at all. His skills of persuasion weren't that good.

Finally back at the hotel, he held the door for the group and turned to Melanie. "Will you wait for me? We need to iron out some details. I'll take the children up and come back."

She laid a hand on his arm. "Let me come. Maybe I can read them a story."

That she was making an effort to get acquainted with them warmed his heart.

A good hour later, children finally washed and in bed, Tait and Melanie sat down on the sofa together. He glanced at her tired eyes. "You're dead on your feet. We'll keep this short. What time would you like the wedding tomorrow?"

"Doesn't that depend on the preacher?"

"Right. What if we go over to talk to him right after breakfast and set everything up then?"

"I'd like that. It won't take me long to prepare. I'm a simple woman with quiet tastes."

He wanted to say that suited her, that she wouldn't look right in an elaborate dress with her hair piled high on her head like he'd seen with some highfalutin' brides. But he didn't.

When she smothered a yawn, he pulled her to her feet. "Let's get you to bed."

They made the short walk to her room, her hand tucked around Tait's elbow. He unlocked the door. "I'll see you around seven o'clock for breakfast?"

"I'll be ready. I had a lovely evening, Tait. The children seem so well behaved."

Thank God she hadn't come earlier that morning when they'd been running around like rabid coyotes.

He smiled. "They do have their moments." He went inside and lit the lamps then went to her and took her hand. "Thank you for taking a chance on me. I'll try to make sure you won't regret your decision."

"We have a lot to work out in our marriage, but I feel very confident that we'll manage."

Tait widened his stance. "Do you mind answering one question that's been on my mind?"

Melanie glanced down at the floor. "What would you like to know?"

He stared at her for several heartbeats, his focus on every facial expression. She seemed wary, too careful with her words. Maybe marrying a complete stranger would do that, but was that the only reason? "Out of all the men in the West, why did you choose me?"

She lifted her guarded gaze. "I liked what you said in your letters. Especially your honesty about your crimes. You didn't try to make excuses or sugarcoat anything. You admitted the truth straight out. I knew if you could do that, you'd be a man who wouldn't run from anything. That you were someone who'd stand and fight against all odds."

"No use trying to pretend something I'm not. Lying is overrated." Tait yearned to touch the curve of her cheek, smooth the wrinkle from her brow, but he kept his hands by his sides. It had been so long since he'd had anything but hardness in his life. "What do you want from this marriage, Miss Dunbar?"

⁂

The questions rattled Melanie, but she kept her voice steady and tried to face him openly. She'd anticipated this last question, but the intensity of his gaze when he asked it had caught her off guard. She raised her chin and dredged up a tear. "Call me Melanie, please. I want a home. A family. A space to grow a garden."

But even as she said the practiced words, she realized there was more truth to them than she liked to admit. She used to hide outside the big, fancy homes when she was a little girl going from town to town with her father and sister. The bright lights had shone through the windows like glistening diamonds. She'd huddle in the darkness and watch the mother setting food on the table, hugging her children, the family laughing together, and wish like hell she could trade the life she had for that one.

Of course, that dream hadn't come true. It was stupid to wish for something so far-fetched anyway.

A small voice in her head whispered that nothing was hopeless. Maybe that was true for some, but not if your name was Melanie Dunbar.

Five

Soft lamplight bathed her room, yet it seemed far too bright. He would see too much. Memories brought trembles to Melanie's hands, and she wished for a strong drink from the flask in her pocket. Anything to steady her nerves would have to come after Tait left.

"Are you all right?" His quicksilver eyes fixed on her, his gaze penetrating her thoughts.

"Couldn't be better." She tacked on a smile for extra measure.

"I can give you the home and the garden you yearn for." Tait's voice was soft as he took her hand. "I confess I was woefully unprepared for marriage this soon, so I have no place for us to live, but I can start work on one next week. You can design it however you wish. It'll be yours."

Melanie's breath caught. Her dream of having a real home and family peeked through the deluge of broken promises. All those nights spent huddling in the dark and the constant fear of being caught might soon be put to rest. Except now she really couldn't afford to believe in any of it. Despair, lies, and disappointment had left deep, permanent scars.

"How will we pay for it?" She lifted her brows, her eyes wide. Another practiced gesture. She might as well get started on her task. "Are you rich?"

"I have enough for our needs—honest money I've made." He fished a handsome gold timepiece from his pocket and flipped it open. "I should probably go and let you get some sleep."

She glanced down at her small hand in his, curled so contentedly, and pulled away, reminding herself that despite his pretty words, she couldn't trust him. He was no gallant knight in shining armor. Tait Trinity answered to no one and likely killed anyone who stood in his way.

"I have a question of my own." Melanie lifted her chin and boldly met his eyes. "What do *you* want, what do you expect, from this marriage? Be honest."

Tait ran his fingers through his hair. "When I first started writing you, I wanted an enjoyable way to pass the time. It seemed harmless. But when I sent for you with the marriage offer, I wanted your help with the children."

"And now?"

"I realize I want much more. I'm tired of the loneliness, tired of lying awake in the dead of night with only my heart-beat pounding in my ears. I want someone to share my life with—the sunshine, the storms, and the days when everything seems just about perfect." He moved close and lowered his head, his deep sigh ruffling the hair at her temple. Though she wanted to step back, she couldn't. "In all honesty, like you, I want a home and companionship."

"Do you plan to keep robbing trains?"

"I'm finished with that part of my life. I have nothing left to prove, and I have plenty of money, so you needn't worry."

She wanted to ask if he kept his money close by or buried or exactly where he'd put it, but she had to practice patience. She couldn't tip her hand too soon. "That's good to know. Maybe the lawmen and bounty hunters will stop looking for you."

"I can only hope." He tucked his watch back in his pocket. "I'll see you in the morning. Good night, Melanie."

She raised on tiptoe and kissed his cheek. "Sleep well."

He left, and the room seemed empty without his presence. Trembling, Melanie leaned against the closed door. Tait Trinity was far more complicated than she'd realized from his letters and that one glimpse of him she'd had on the train when he'd seemed to enjoy taking what wasn't his a little too much. But why? Had he been bored? Danger made some men feel alive. Was Tait one of those?

Yes, he appeared a whole lot more than she'd first thought.

Excitement curled inside her followed closely by guilt. Her own house built the way she wanted it. If only she was the woman he thought she was. One who could love being a homebody.

She'd spent too many years moving around for that. It would probably be boring to live in one spot day after day anyway. No smoke-filled saloons and back rooms where she could gamble all night and sleep the next day away. No more rushing to leave town before getting run out on a rail.

No fear of prison. Or worse.

She reached into the pocket hidden in the folds of her dress for the flask and unscrewed the lid. The long swallow burned a path to her stomach and calmed the million doubts burrowing deep inside. Thoughts of what would happen if she backed out ricocheted around inside her like a load of buckshot.

In addition to that, Tait Trinity was too smart, saw way too much. He probably knew every trick in the book and would discover her plan and stop her before she had a chance to finish.

Yet despite the enormous risks, she had to do this. The judge had given her no choice.

ক্ৰু

The next morning, Tait ushered the children down the hall and knocked on Melanie's door. She looked fresh and pretty in a yellow dress, reminding him of an April flower poking through a late snow. The boys pressed to her side, and Becky clamored to be picked up. And was.

Tait shook his head. "It appears you have some admirers."

Melanie laughed, those dimples flashing like beacons, and Tait added himself to the list of those admirers. Still, something didn't seem quite right. The warning sat in his gut, and he didn't like it. He'd be careful until he knew her better. To lose his edge would spell disaster.

Breakfast went off with nary a glass of spilled milk nor endless run of questions. The boys went to play with the others in town. He and Melanie left Becky with Nora Bowdre for a few hours and headed over to the church. Luckily for Tait's nerves, Brother Paul was outside watering the flowers around a small tree, and he didn't have to go inside the sanctuary.

"Nice day." Tait introduced Melanie to Brother Paul. "We want to discuss a wedding ceremony."

"When would you like to get married? Next week?"

"Today."

The lanky minister laughed, his eyes twinkling behind his spectacles. "You don't waste any time."

"We hope it won't be a problem," Melanie purred. She stared up at Tait, and he choked on his spit. "I can't wait to become part of this dear, sweet man's family."

"I think I can manage today." Brother Paul set down his watering can.

Tait took Melanie's hand. "Miss Dunbar and I haven't discussed where to have the service, but would it be possible to have it outdoors? Unless she has other plans in mind, that is."

"Outdoors is fine with me." Melanie squeezed his fingers. "In fact, I'd love that."

Tait pointed to the bluff overlooking the town. "How about up there at sunset?"

"Perfect." She sighed and let her shoulder brush against Tait's.

He liked having her next to him, feeling her warmth, but he wasn't sure why. He'd been alone for some time, not needing another's touch. Not needing someone to take care of, to be responsible for. A sudden fact hit him square between the eyes. He now had three children dependent on him and was about to add a wife. The thought was sobering.

"Then it's settled. My weddings are pretty standard," the pastor said.

Melanie lifted her face, and Tait saw panic in her eyes. "Pastor, leave out the obey and love part, and I think Miss Dunbar and I will be set."

"I agree." She gave Brother Paul an apologetic smile. "We don't know each other at all well yet, and it seems inappropriate to vow something that may or may not be true."

"I see." Though the pastor wore a puzzled expression, he didn't question them.

They thanked him and left.

"If that's everything, I really do need to prepare for tonight," Melanie said, glancing up at Tait, her voice barely louder than a whisper. "I think you look even more scared than I feel. Are we doing the right thing? This is what you want, isn't it?"

Her face had gone a little pale.

"Jitters are normal, I think. And yes, this is what I want."

"It didn't seem real until we spoke with the pastor. Now all of a sudden… What if we can't stand each other? What if I do something wrong and end up hurting one of the children? What if—"

"Would you like to sit down? The hotel lobby is close." He took her arm and hoped she wouldn't faint.

"Yes, that would be lovely." Her voice sounded far away.

He tried to hurry her along, but several ladies stopped them to introduce themselves. More color drained from Melanie's face the longer they stood there talking. Finally Tait had to apologize and break away, saying they'd have a reception after the wedding. Only he had no idea what a reception involved.

Seated on a sofa inside the lobby with a glass of water, Melanie's color began to return. "A fit of nerves," she explained. "I was fine until we talked to the preacher, and suddenly it became all too real. This is for the rest of our lives."

"It is sobering." For him as well. A step not to take lightly. "It's not too late to call it off."

"No. I came here to marry you, and marry you I will."

Tait leaned back on the green-velvet sofa and stretched out his long legs, crossing them at the ankles. In an effort to distract her, he asked, "What do I need to arrange for a reception? I trust you know about such things."

"It's customary to have a cake and some punch. Do you think that will be a problem?"

"When I leave here, I'll speak with Mrs. Worth, owner of the bakery. Would you like another glass of water?"

"No. I think I'll go lie down for a bit."

Tait saw her to her room then made a quick stop at the bakery before heading next door to the newspaper office.

Monty Roman glanced up from setting type, a green visor shielding his eyes. Black ink stained his fingers. "Mr. Trinity! It must finally be that cold day in hell. Have you come to give me that interview?"

Tait glanced around at the ink-stained contents of Roman's office. "Soon, I promise. You're the only photographer around, and I have a favor to ask."

"Shoot."

"I'm marrying today at sunset, and I'd like for the missus to have a picture as a memento. Can you—will you—do that for us?"

Roman stared at Tait, his mouth set in a thin line. "Be happy to, but only in exchange for that interview you promised."

Dammit. He might as well get it over with. "Fine. How about now?"

For the next hour, Tait sat and answered questions about his life as a boy, living on a farm in western Kansas, and why he'd arrived in Hope's Crossing shot up and near death. "Jack Bowdre and I have been friends a long time, and I didn't have anywhere else to go."

"Why did you stay?"

"I like it here." And the town was built like a fortress, which kept lawmen from snooping around.

"Tell me about your father," Roman probed.

"He was a hard-nosed, damn righteous Baptist preacher. Died eight years ago." Tait worked to control his voice as painful memories of the dark barn and that hated razor strop rose to choke him. "The railroad booted my mother off their farm after that, claiming eminent domain. The same thing also happened to friends of mine. The powers that be stole the property outright, never gave Mama or my friends one cent for their land."

Tait thought of his mother having to work in a laundry, the backbreaking days on her feet, too proud to accept help from him—or anyone else.

Roman scribbled on his pad. "Tell me more about your mother."

All this poking around in Tait's life was more than a little uncomfortable. "A saint if there ever was one. She raised four boys and a girl and put up with my father. She worked her fingers to the bone until she passed two years ago."

"Do you ever see your brothers?"

"Nope. They're in the gold fields of Alaska. Better to have distance between us." Out of the three, Blue was the only one who'd still give him the time of day. And all the while they'd been growing up, Tait had thought nothing would sever the brothers' close bond forged from common pain. He winced. "Are we finished?"

"A little more." Roman pursed his lips and asked about Tait's vendetta against the Missouri River Railroad.

Tait narrowed his eyes. "That's off-limits."

Roman scratched on his pad some more and then glanced up. "I'm sorry about your sister. Those kids got a rotten deal. Any idea who killed her and her husband?"

"Not yet, but I will find them."

His hard tone set Monty Roman back in his chair.

"Regardless of what you think of me, Trinity, I want you to make them pay." The newspaper man's black hair glistened with pomade under the sunlight that streamed through the window. "I don't wish you any ill will. I envy men who can live outside the law. You do the things we only dream of and get justice where there's none to be had. My little sister was abducted a few years ago, and it made me sick to my stomach when we found her. The things they did to her... They were animals. They didn't kill her, but she might as well be dead. She sits and stares out the window, barely alive. She won't speak, doesn't seem to know anyone."

"I'm sorry, Roman. Did they ever catch the culprits?"

"No," the man said quietly, a distant look in his eyes. After a long pause, he tapped the pencil on his desk. "Let's see, where were we? Oh yes. How long did you say you and Jack Bowdre have been friends?"

"Since we were kids. Jack lived on the next farm over, and we grew up together. His dad was as bad an outlaw as they come. Used to get drunk and wale on his mother and sisters. When Orin Bowdre got riled up, they'd come over to our place until he settled down."

"And Clay?"

"I knew him by reputation but didn't know him personally until I got shot up and found my way here. I admire Clay and his dream for this town." Tait rose. "I'm done."

"It's more than I'd anticipated getting. I'll take a wedding picture for you later on."

Tait nodded and left, anxious to be rid of the ghosts the questions had brought up. He was happy to have finally kept that old promise though. A man needed to keep his word. Sometimes, after everything was said and done, that's all he had left. Tait had let down far too many people.

It was good to be able to keep promises on his wedding day.

❧

Melanie put on her good dress that afternoon—a simple low-cut, peach muslin that hung off her shoulders, showing a lot of smooth skin. They'd let her keep this one to get married in.

But her silks and fancier dresses had all gone as payment.

Her auburn hair curled about her shoulders, glistening in the mirror. She took a lock between shaky fingers. Marriage was a drastic step to take, but it was the only way she could get close enough to gain Tait's trust. He wouldn't suspect her if she was right under his nose.

Or so she hoped.

Her stomach went off in a dizzying whirl. She clutched the mirrored dresser to steady herself and took deep breaths until her nerves passed.

Thank goodness Tait didn't expect her to love him. That saved telling more lies. No, this was a business agreement. She'd help him with the kids while she hunted for the evidence necessary to send him to jail. That would free her sister, and Melanie would get her pardon.

The betrayal was starting to gnaw at her though. Tait

deserved a fighting chance. But if he found out any of this, he'd just run, and both Melanie and her sister would go to prison instead of him.

She stayed in her room to avoid everyone until his soft tap came on the door. She opened it and swallowed hard at the picture he presented. A black cutaway coat accented his lean body to perfection, and added to that a white shirt and red brocade vest completed the image of a prosperous man. A gold watch chain gleamed smartly along with his polished boots. A low hum of anticipation of their first night together vibrated under her skin.

Melanie was no stranger to lovemaking, and the prospect of the attractive and dangerous Tait Trinity in her bed excited her.

He removed his black Stetson to reveal his sun-streaked caramel hair and whistled. "I'm a lucky man to have such a beautiful bride, Miss Melanie Dunbar."

"You look quite handsome yourself."

Tait took her wrap and slipped it around her. "The bluff is close enough to walk, but I thought we'd go in a borrowed surrey so the children can sit in the back. I wouldn't want you to get that dress dirty or turn an ankle. Unless you have other ideas."

"No, that's fine." She took his elbow and waited for him to shut the door. The scent of his shaving soap swirled around her as she hurtled toward what could be the biggest mistake of her life. She stood rooted in place even after Tait pulled the door closed. She yearned to bolt back inside.

"Are you all right?" Tait patted the hand curled around his arm.

She jolted out of her reverie and gave him a bright smile. "Perfectly."

Outside the hotel, the children waited next to a hired surrey. The boys looked fairly grown-up in suits, and Becky wore a pretty pink dress that Melanie learned Tait had bought from the mercantile.

"Mellie!" Becky cried, holding out her arms.

"No, honey, remember what we talked about," Tait said gently. "She rides in front with me. You sit back there with your brothers."

The girl pouted but hushed. Though children still made Melanie uncomfortable, Becky was such a sweet child and reminded her a little of her sister, Ava. With that thought, Melanie's resolve to rescue her sister settled in once again. Hell and be damned if she wouldn't!

A smile teased Tait's nicely shaped mouth. He shot her a sideways glance. "I like Becky's name for you. Mellie fits you much better."

"I've never been fond of nicknames." More truthfully, Melanie hated all the ones folks had bestowed on her—Mellie Nellie, Blue Eyes, Quick-Fingered Mel, cheat, and others far worse.

The children kept up a stream of conversation as they followed a faint trail outside the town's entrance that led up the bluff. The view was splendid, the gold-and-light-amethyst sky extending on forever. The sun sat low on the horizon, and Melanie hoped the sunset would be all the preview promised.

The surrey stopped, and Tait came around to her side. She took his hand and stepped down. It was odd how detached she felt. She seemed to be floating in a dream instead of being a part of her real life. Even so, she didn't harbor any doubts about the solidity of the moment.

Guests had already assembled, and it appeared most of the town had turned out for the occasion. Tait carried Becky in his arms as he greeted several of his friends in the crowd. Joe and Jesse ran off together, only to return a few minutes later.

Jesse thrust a single wild rose into her hand, a pretty ribbon tied around the stem. "For you, Miss Melanie. We took all the thorns off. But we might've forgotten one."

Joe handed her a second rose. "You're real pretty, Miss Melanie. I'm glad you came."

"Thank you, boys." Deeply touched, she kissed them each on the cheek.

At the moment the sky slipped down to meet the earth,

she took her place next to Tait and placed her hand in his. Ever-changing colors swirled above them—tangerine, copper, amethyst, and ruby. The kaleidoscope bled into one breathtaking spectacle after another.

Melanie shifted her gaze to Tait's profile. His face seemed set in stone, giving no indication of his thoughts. She repeated the preacher's words, vowed to stand by his side and be the wife he needed through good times and bad.

The sunset turned fiery red in an instant, and the weight of what she intended to do struck her. The ground whirled dizzily. Her chin quivered, and she bit down on her lip.

Just then came the flash of a camera from the side where the newspaper man had set up. Good grief! He'd undoubtedly caught her looking her worst. Still, a picture would be useful proof in case Judge McIlroy didn't believe that she'd gone through with her end of the bargain.

Tait bolstered her with an arm around her waist, his mouth at her ear. "I've got you. Take a deep breath and it'll be all right."

But would it ever be again? Dear God, she was now pledged for life to the man she'd committed to destroy.

Six

THE EVENING SHADOWS DEEPENED AROUND THE BRIDAL PARTY, and crickets chirped nearby. Melanie's lowered gaze gave Tait no clue as to what thoughts were spinning through her head. As for him, he just wanted to get the deed over with.

How bad could her life have been to marry a wanted man like him, practically sight unseen?

Before he knew it, Brother Paul asked for the ring. Tait pulled a silver one from his watch pocket and glanced at Melanie. She was as white as a cotton ball and appeared ready to collapse. Probably nerves again, but he should get her back to the hotel as soon as this was over.

It hit him that he was tying himself to another woman— something he vowed to never let happen again. Not after Lucy. Images of her grave still haunted him, the mound of dirt thrown on top of her.

He slipped the simple silver band on Melanie's finger. Then it was time to kiss her. He'd do his duty, and that would have to be enough. But the moment their lips met, he lost all sense of time and place. The sweet scent of the roses she clutched swirled around him as he held her, a hand bracing her back. Something unexpected and gratifying at the feel of a woman in his arms, her pliant softness, crept past the barricade he'd erected. She slid an arm around his neck, fingers winding through his hair.

Melanie gripped his vest and opened her mouth slightly as though begging for whatever bit of passion he could offer. He slipped his tongue inside, tasting her, savoring the sweetness.

Someone cleared their throat behind him. Tait ended the kiss and let her go, breathing hard. She seemed shaken as well, clutching his arm for support.

He met her shadowed gaze. "Lady, you sure know how to claim a man."

"Isn't that the only way?" she teased, brightening for a moment and showing her dimples.

Tait stood there lost in the moment, staring at his wife's dazzling smile, her bare shoulders shimmering in the low light of the sunset. What the hell had just hit him? He reasoned that it had to be the beautiful sunset and the fact it had been so long since he'd been with a woman.

❦

What was keeping Tait Trinity?

Melanie huddled in his bed at the hotel, alone, waiting for whatever came next. The Bowdres had kept the children for the night so she didn't even have their company to lift the loneliness and doubt from her heart and mind. Light from the bedside oil lamp cast a muted glow across the room, not quite reaching the shadows.

Nothing ever seemed to reach the dark corners.

Tait had disappeared after the reception—and to where she didn't know.

She swallowed hard to stop the tears, determined not to pity the forgotten bride. He'd told her to go to bed and that he'd be there soon.

That had been four hours ago. Where was her new husband? They hadn't discussed their wedding night, but she'd assumed they'd sleep together. Wasn't that the usual custom? But maybe she should be grateful for the respite and pretend to be asleep when he finally came.

But no, dammit. What she'd seen of his body had stirred that certain need to be touched, held, to be assured that she mattered. True, they didn't love each other, but she was a woman with womanly needs. She wanted to feel his hard body next to hers, to run her hands over his broad chest, shoulders, and muscular thighs—for him to melt some of this icy fear that gripped her.

The lifestyle of a gambler—among other things—had put her in contact with a lot of men, and she'd taken her pleasure with some. Horrified virgin she wasn't. She had expected Tait to show her the courtesy of sharing their wedding night.

Didn't he want her even the slightest bit?

Confusion swept through her. Desire had flared in his eyes when he'd kissed her. Melanie hadn't imagined that.

A noise sounded outside the room. Finally. She squinched her eyes shut, feigning sleep. But after several minutes of nothing, she rolled onto her back and stared at the ceiling instead.

Waiting. Wondering. Fearing he'd somehow discovered her true reason for coming.

Maybe that was it. He knew.

She thought of the reception, the beautiful wedding cake she'd shared with Tait after admitting that nerves had gotten the best of her. They'd toasted with several glasses of wine, and his friend Jack had offered a heartfelt speech. Everything had seemed fine.

But evidently it wasn't.

Maybe he'd gone off with his friends to drink. Entirely possible.

Well, let him. She threw back the covers. She'd have a drink of her own. She went to her bag and pulled out her flask, unscrewed the lid, and tipped the container up. But one good mouthful emptied it. Her search of the suite failed to turn up a bottle. Fine and dandy. She'd have to figure out how to buy more tomorrow without Tait knowing. She needed a nip now and then to settle her jumpiness.

Maybe he'd ridden out to dig up the train loot. If he planned to build a house, he'd need funds. But no, he'd said he'd pay for that with honest money, so he wouldn't need to dig up the loot. If it was even buried. Who knew where outlaws hid their money? She twisted the silver band on her finger. Darn it, she should've followed him.

Another thought gripped her, one far worse than the other two. Maybe he had another woman here in town and had gone to her bed instead. Her heart stopped. She blew back a lock of hair dangling onto her forehead. Had she misread him? Tait Trinity could be nothing but a low-down two-timer of the highest order.

But she didn't love him, so what did it matter? She frowned, confused.

Worn out and disgusted, she pulled a well-used deck of cards from deep in her bag and played a while, taking comfort in the familiar routine that never failed her. Anger built into fury the more the clock ticked. Just wait until she saw him. Piss on Judge McIlroy up in Canadian, and piss on his powerful friends. She'd find another way to help her sister. Something that didn't make her feel so dirty and cheap.

No man made a fool of her. Once the sun rose, she'd catch the first stage out of Hope's Crossing.

❧

Tait dismounted at the corral still in his wedding attire as the sun poked its head up on a new day. The town was just beginning to move about. Melanie would hopefully still be asleep. He unsaddled his roan and gave the mount some oats before heading to the hotel.

He'd spent the night thinking. He'd thought this was going to be an easy way to solve a problem. But nothing about this marriage was simple. For one thing, his gut told him Melanie wasn't being truthful. Her words and actions didn't match, and she seemed terrified of marriage. Or maybe it was commitment that scared her. At any rate, she wasn't a dressmaker. That much he knew. Though pretty, her wedding dress also was in need of mending. Plus he'd smelled whiskey on her breath.

Hell if he knew what she was hiding.

Who was the real Melanie Dunbar, and when would she show her true self? He didn't mind what anyone said or pass judgment as long as they were honest.

Another big concern was that kiss, one that had shaken him to his toes. This attraction he felt was wrong. His heart was cold—dead. He'd only loved one woman, and she was gone.

Staring up at the stars hadn't provided any answers.

He made his way to the hotel and up the stairs. Their suite was quiet. He turned the knob and opened the door. A well-timed shoe came near to plunking him in the head. Tait leaped back into the hallway, although not quickly enough to avoid the second shoe that came barreling after the first, striking his chest. Another followed, and then a heavy ashtray that crashed against the far wall.

"It's me, Melanie."

"I know." The words seemed to come through gritted teeth. Just then one of his old boots hurled past him.

He whipped out the white handkerchief he'd tucked in his pocket for his wedding and waved it around the door. "Cease fire. Let me explain."

When nothing else flew at him, he moved cautiously around the cover of the door. Melanie stood in the center of the room holding his other boot, wearing nothing but a thin white nightgown that revealed far too much. Her chest heaved, fire shooting from her eyes, her reddish-brown hair wild about her head. Tait had never seen a prettier sight.

Damn it, he didn't want to notice that, didn't want to be attracted to her.

"Give me one good reason not to let this boot fly." Her voice shook with anger.

"Sit down and we'll try to have a normal conversation." The corners of Tait's mouth twitched though he tried to keep a somber expression. He slowly moved toward her, ready to duck at any moment, and gently relieved her of the boot.

Melanie jerked back. "Don't think you can smile and I'll fall helpless in a puddle at your feet. I'm not that kind."

Of course, she wouldn't sit now for love or money. Dammit! Fine.

"I'm sorry." He removed his hat and laid it on a table. "I owe you a big apology."

Her glare burned with reproach. "You said you'd be right back. Well, guess what? You lied."

"Time got away from me."

"Where were you? Do you have another woman whose bed is softer than mine?"

"Don't be ridiculous." Where had she gotten that notion?

"What am I to think, Tait? On our wedding day, you

stayed out all the blessed night." She stared daggers. "Am I not woman enough for you? What about the vows you spoke? I don't feel one bit cherished. Or protected. Or wifely."

"I saddled up and took a ride. Spent the night up on a mesa, thinking." He ran a hand across his eyes. "I was trying to figure out some things."

"What things?" Her voice had lost some of the anger but was still tight and guarded.

"Like where we go from here. How to raise these kids together. How to keep you safe when bullets start flying. Before I knew it, the night was gone." His gaze went to a bulging bag sitting next to the door, and he swallowed hard. "Most importantly, I was thinking about how to make you happy. I've already failed at that, I see."

Theirs had to be the shortest marriage on record.

"I'm leaving." She refused to meet his eyes.

He went to the window and looked down at the thriving town that had once been an outlaw's hideout aptly named Devil's Crossing. A few early risers moved about in the street. "You could've given me half a chance," he said quietly.

"And you could've kept your word," she shot back. "You lied to me."

"Do you really want to leave?" He turned to study her. "If so, I won't stop you."

"I'll ask you again, and this time I'd like an answer. Can you assure me beyond a doubt you don't have another woman here in town? Someone you're keeping on the side?" Light from the window filtered through Melanie's thin nightgown, revealing a lush figure made for loving, her full breasts, the dark nipples at their peaks.

Tait's mouth went dry, and his body tightened.

When he could get his tongue unglued, he tried to explain. "I swear on a stack of Bibles that I have no other woman but you. Look. I know I messed up and shouldn't have gone out. But if you'll let me—us—start again, I think we can still make this marriage work. I'm willing to try. Are you?"

Melanie blew out a long breath. "Of course I want it to

succeed. You'll have to meet me in the middle though. And I expect you to sleep with me."

"That won't be a problem. What else?"

Her bare feet moved silently across the floor and she stopped in front of him. "Never lie to me again."

Tait lifted a curl from her shoulder, studying the depths of her eyes. His soft voice held a warning. "That works both ways, lady. I get the feeling you're keeping secrets and have been since you got here. Something isn't adding up."

A flash of panic crossed her face, then she gave him a sensual smile. "All ladies have secrets," she drawled. "Besides, you can't know everything about me in two days."

"Granted. But how about one great big juicy secret? I can see it in your beautiful eyes." He dropped the lock of hair. "We'll talk once about our pasts, then never speak of them again. It doesn't help to rehash what's over and done."

She took a step back. "You're right on all counts. I haven't been entirely honest."

Ah, here it came. Finally.

They sat down, and Melanie wet her lips. "I'm not a dressmaker like I told you. I'm a gambler, like my father and sister. We travel across the West, living in dingy hotels, making a living in smoky saloons. We've worn out our welcome more than once. I'm sorry I kept that from you."

Silence stretched while Tait mulled over her confession. While he didn't know the father's exact role in all this, Tait suspected Papa Dunbar had taught his girls the trade.

"I can see why you made up the story. We all want to appear better than we really are. What about your mother?" he asked.

"Died in childbirth having me and my sister Ava. We're twins."

"Interesting. You'll be a lot of help in figuring out Joe and Jesse. I'm sure you and your sister played a lot of tricks."

"We still do."

The smile that formed on Melanie's face told Tait there'd been at least one recent trick. He gave a silent groan. Another set of twins—just what he needed. Thank goodness Ava Dunbar wasn't in town.

Finally, Tait sat up straighter and steepled his hands in front of him. "I'm glad to know something about the real you at least. There's nothing shameful in doing what you must to survive. Everyone in this town is doing the same. You wanted better and got yourself free of that life. I dream of better as well and hope that one day I'll find absolution for my crimes." He swung around. "This gives us a common goal."

"Yes, we can help each other. This is the biggest gamble of my life."

"Mine too." She had no idea exactly how big. Thoughts of Lucy and all he'd lost swam in Tait's head before he forced himself back to Melanie. "Living that lifestyle, I'm sure you developed vices. I thought I caught a whiff of whiskey on your breath before. I assume you have a fondness for it."

"I do."

"I struggle with the same fondness, but haven't touched a drop since the kids arrived. I want to set a good example. What you do behind closed doors is your business, but I have to ask you to not drink in front of them. These children have lost everyone and everything they know and were thrust at a stranger for care." Another thought hit him, but he checked to see where the shoes were before he spoke. "Sorry for my bluntness, but I assume you've lost your innocence, having led the life you have."

Melanie winced. "I was going to confess last night, but you never came to bed. Disappointed?"

"Relieved actually." The graceful curve of her neck and dainty ears drew Tait's attention. How he'd enjoy trailing kisses along that skin. "I wasn't looking forward to introducing a virgin to the pleasures of the marriage bed. I've heard horror stories."

"Glad I could spare you that." She laid her hand over his. "We do need to discuss something else."

"What's that?"

"I've been lucky to have escaped having children thus far,

but I know it's only a matter of time. Do you want children of your own?"

Her question hit him hard. Pain pierced his chest. "No. A man like me lives from one day to the next, not thinking about the long term. Longevity doesn't exist for most outlaws. The odds are stacked against us from the minute we pick up a gun. From then on it's only a matter of time before our choices catch up with us. Sorry, I can't bring more children into my world."

For a moment, he thought she'd burst into tears. It seemed a strange reaction given how much she'd said she didn't want children herself, but maybe she was thinking about being left a widow with Joe, Jesse, and Becky to raise by herself. Although a beauty like her would have suitors flocking to her door.

"Tell me what led you to become an outlaw," she asked softly.

"Injustice. I saw too many folks suffering and dying at the hands of men who were supposed to be protecting them. I never was good at turning a blind eye." He flashed a crooked grin. "Jack and I once stood up against a gang of cutthroats that had taken over a town. We didn't care about the overwhelming odds, didn't even consider the cost. Especially once the evil bastards started lining up men, women, and children in the town square and shooting them."

He paused then told her about the corrupt railroad company that had stolen his mother's farm. "The government gives the companies free land on either side of the tracks. The officials of the Missouri River Railroad sold that clear land to other settlers and pocketed quite a hefty profit. They're swindlers. That's why I started robbing trains—to take back what they'd stolen."

The other, much more personal, part to that story would remain buried, too gut-wrenching to ever be spoken aloud.

"All the railroad money—what happened to that? Did you give it away?"

Tait frowned. Why the interest in that money specifically?

"Some has gone to help this town—to keep the mercantile replenished, pay the teacher's salary, buy books, hymnals—whatever's been needed. At least it's doing some good here and not just lining the pockets of crooked business-men and politicians."

"But you haven't used all of your ill-gotten gain?" Her shuttered eyes kept her thoughts hidden from him, but she leaned forward slightly as though hanging on his words.

"Some money I won't touch. It's too filthy. So yes, I still have most of it."

Melanie glanced down and smoothed the folds of her gown. "I once happened to be on a train you robbed. I watched you."

She'd said the statement like commenting on a pretty day. The impact stunned him. "When?"

"Six months ago or thereabouts, I believe."

Tait frowned, searching his memory for anyone of her description. If he'd seen her, he'd remember. Melanie was an unforgettable woman.

"It's okay to not recall it. I sometimes rode the trains and interested gentlemen in card games. You were a little busy, but I thought you were a most arresting man. Quite handsome actually. Dangerous."

He shook that thought aside for now, stood, and offered his hand. "We still have a while before we pick up the children. I could show you the town."

"I have a better idea." She let him pull her up and laid a palm on his chest. "You still owe me for last night."

"There is that, I suppose." His gaze dropped to her luscious mouth.

"I expect to be fully and properly cherished. I hope you're up to it, cowboy, having gone without sleep and all."

"Count on it, Mellie." Tait pulled her into the circle of his arms and kissed the tender flesh behind her ear.

Thick, dark lashes lay feathered on her cheeks. Eyes closed, she clutched him, apparently sharing his hunger to be touched, to feel something again, to matter to someone. Love wasn't involved in this. This was lust, plain and simple, the satisfaction of their bodies' cravings.

For one moment, he yearned to find purpose in the daily struggle for survival.

Tait slid his mouth to hers and gave her a tongue-thrusting kiss while his hands moved slowly downward, skimming the sides of her body. He explored the soft lines of her back, waist, and hips, letting his hands rest on her firm behind.

Her breath seemed to hitch in anticipation, matching the taste of yearning on her tongue. She slid an arm around his neck and clutched a handful of hair, her breasts tight against his chest.

Thank God for a passionate woman not afraid to show it!

"Tait!" Someone pounded on the door. "Tait, open up!"

He tensed and grabbed his pistol.

"Who is it?" she asked.

"Don't know, but sounds like trouble. No one hammers on a door like that when it's not important." He hurried to let in whoever it was.

"Tait, we have a problem!"

He yanked the door open to find Jack and the twins in the hall. "What's wrong?"

Jack stared at the footwear and glass laying everywhere and pushed past him followed by the boys. "Becky tumbled down the stairs this morning. She's over at Dr. Mary's office."

Jesse looked up. "We don't know if anything's broken or nothing. It wasn't our fault."

"Who said it was?" Tait raked his fingers through his hair. "No one's blaming you. Why don't you and Joe stay here with your Aunt Melanie and I'll see to Becky?" He glanced at his bride and her kissable lips, wishing he could've seen where their making up might have gone. She handed him his hat. His half smile held regret. "Sorry. Why don't you and the boys go to breakfast? Put it on my tab. I'll give you some spending money later."

"Don't worry about that now. Go! I hope she's not too hurt."

So did he, but sometimes the situation was out of anyone's hands. Lucy's and Claire's fates had proven that.

Seven

His thoughts in turmoil, Tait crossed the short distance between the hotel and Dr. Mary's clinic.

Jack stuck to him like an irritating thorn, matching his stride. "Anything you want to tell me?"

"Nope."

"Did it rain shoes outside your room last night?"

"Rather not talk about it." Tait opened the door to the small, two-bed hospital and stepped inside. He removed his hat and held it in his hands. Becky looked so small lying in a bed with the doctor bending over her. "How is she, Doc?"

Dr. Mary straightened her petite frame. "Nothing broken. The fall knocked the wind out of her, which scared everyone. I think she'll be fine."

Becky looked up at him, frowning. "Me fall."

"How do you feel, honey? Are you hurting?"

The three-year-old shook her head and reached for him. "Go."

"We will just as soon as the doctor finishes. Just lie there for a little bit longer."

"Eat."

Tait laughed, relieved that she felt hungry. "We will. Wait a minute." He turned to Dr. Mary. "What do you think?"

Sunlight through the door glinted off the necklace of bullet fragments around Dr. Mary's neck. Jack had once told him that she'd made it from slugs pulled from patients. "Becky seems fine, but any concussion worries. Watch her closely for a couple of days, and if she's sleepier than usual or starts having pain, I'll look at her again."

"Thank you, Doctor." Tait put his hat on, picked Becky up, and bid the doc a good day. He noticed Melanie and the boys almost to the Blue Goose's door.

They spied him, and Melanie waited while the boys raced on ahead to the café.

"How is she?" Melanie asked.

"Hungry. Doc says she should be fine." Tait put an arm around Melanie, wondering why he was so relieved she hadn't caught the first stagecoach out of town after all.

"Mellie." Becky reached for Melanie.

"Hey, sweet girl. I'm glad you're all right." Melanie kissed the girl's cheek and hugged her close, almost as a mother would do. Maybe she was warming to the kids.

"Me fall."

Despite what she'd said about not knowing anything about kids, Melanie seemed to have some kind of maternal instinct about her. The tender way she held the girl, one hand smoothing back Becky's wild curls, spoke of her capacity for deep affection.

Becky laid her head on Melanie's shoulder. "Eat."

Tait laughed. "I think she's starving. It was the first thing she said to me. Not *hello* or *I'm better.* Just *eat.*"

Their first official breakfast as a family went pretty well overall. Joe and Jesse picked on each other and rattled on and on about Sawyer Gray and the traps he built to catch small animals.

"I'm going to make me one when we get finished," Jesse announced, licking syrup off his fingers.

"What will you do with the animals after you catch them?" Tait asked Jesse. Or at least he thought he had the right boy this time. The safety pin was missing from his collar. But more than questions about his ability to tell the twins apart, he was concerned about the reason for the traps. What were they doing? "We don't kill for fun, boys. If that's it, you can forget it."

Anger crossed Jesse's eyes. "I wasn't gonna kill 'em! I don't ever want to be like *you.*"

Before Tait could process the outburst, his nephew jumped out of his chair so fast it tipped over and raced out the door. "Jesse, wait!"

His brother gave Tait a hard stare. "We were gonna train 'em. Joe and me don't like watching things die. And I'm Jesse.

You cain't even get our names straight!" He ran out to join his twin.

Tait glanced at Melanie. "I messed that up. He's right though. Not that they've made it easy—I can't tell them apart at all."

"I'll help you."

"Do you know which is which?"

"Of course. I noticed right off that Jesse has a freckle by his ear."

"A freckle. By his ear."

"His left ear."

"How did you even see that?"

"Because I was looking for something one had that the other didn't. It really upsets a person to be called the wrong name, especially twins. My sister Ava and I went through something similar. Our father still doesn't know us apart. I wanted to get it right for the boys."

Tait realized that in all the chaos he hadn't really sat down and looked at them. He sighed. "I have to go find them and try to fix things. I shouldn't have lectured them about the traps before I knew what they had in mind. Hell and be damned!"

"Don't beat yourself up. I think it must be hard stepping into a father role. Be patient with them—and yourself. It's just as difficult for them." Her voice was gentle and soft, not at all like it had been earlier when she was lobbing shoes and ashtrays at him.

"How did you get so smart?" he asked.

"I was a child once." She kissed his cheek. "I'll see you in a bit. I think me and Miss Becky are going to take a nap. You see, I didn't get much sleep last night."

A shaft of sunlight through the window fired the red in her hair, and her dimples peeked out, the combination stealing his breath. Her turquoise eyes held a teasing glint, and Tait grinned like he'd been handed a big pile of gold nuggets.

Becky patted his arm. "My Mellie."

"Hey, I'm not arguing, honey." He kissed the girl's forehead. "I'll see you back at the hotel, Mellie."

Her knowing smile sent memories of their interrupted interlude tumbling end over end.

Skin like silk.

Curves that made him weep.

Lips that could drive every sane thought from a man's mind.

They hadn't even been married a full day yet, and her body had already taken up residence in his thoughts.

Tait stepped from the café and adjusted his hat on his head, glancing around for the boys. He didn't know which direction they might've gone. Definitely away from people.

He stopped Ridge Steele, who'd been a preacher before he'd taken to the outlaw trail. Now he served as the town mayor. No one knew what had made him lose the way. Some things were best left private, and Tait respected that.

"Steele, have you seen the boys?"

A person rarely saw Ridge without his dark frock coat and twin Colts swinging from his hips. His angular jawline, quick smile, and an understanding gaze made him easy to confide in. A few streaks of gray marked his dark stubble, an indication he hadn't shaved in a few days.

Ridge motioned with his head. "They were hoofing it toward the valley. Trouble?"

"Nothing I can't handle."

"Good luck, then."

Tait took long strides straight east, thinking about what he was going to say to them. No matter what he came up with, he couldn't bring back their parents.

Soon he was at the mouth of the valley, tall cornstalks and wheat waving as far as he could see. If the twins had gone in there, he'd never find them. They could hide until the second coming of Christ. But to get back to town, they'd have to come his way.

He sat down, picked up a piece of wood, and started whittling. He didn't realize what he was making until it began to take shape under his knife—a train. The thing he hated most in the world next to churches. Hell!

Cussing a blue streak, he put the knife away and rested

back against a spindly tree, his gaze sweeping over the rustling green field.

His father's fury sounded in his head. *You're nothing but trouble, Tait. You're going to spend eternity in the fiery pits of hell if you don't stop your rebellious ways. You're my biggest disappointment, and you'll be my downfall yet. Leave and never come back. We don't want you.*

From the time Tait was ten on, he'd often been on the receiving end of verbal and physical whippings. The harder the Reverend Thomas Trinity had tried to beat the devil out of his son, the more vehemently Tait had vowed to leave. He'd finally done so the day he'd turned fourteen.

Now Jesse's angry words came back to him. *I don't ever want to be like you.*

Tait winced and swallowed. It was a blessing the kid didn't hold him in high esteem. He didn't want anyone to take after him, driven by revenge.

Just then he caught furtive movement, two figures weaving through the cornstalks. Tait maneuvered around and got into position where he'd be in front of them when they headed out.

He stood there, legs planted wide. Both boys jerked back in surprise when they saw him. "We're going to talk. Or I'm going to talk and you'll listen. Whichever you want."

"You can't force us to do either," Joe spat.

"That is true. I can't. But you will stay here," he said evenly. "Take a seat."

Though reluctant, the boys sat cross-legged on the ground.

Tait dropped down beside them. He apologized for jumping to the wrong conclusion before hearing them out. "I've made a whole lot of mistakes in my life and I don't want you to make them too. Your mother and I never had a patient father who took the time to really listen to us. I vowed to never be like him, but now I've done the same thing to you. The only difference is that I won't whip you. I never will."

He paused, searching for the right words. "We pay for our mistakes, and I've paid a tremendous price. I'll probably pay a lot more when the law catches me. Now, I'd like to hear what you plan to do with the animals you catch in your traps."

Jesse kept his eyes on his boot. "Well, Sawyer, us, and the Truman boys want to start our own circus."

"We'll train the animals to do tricks and put on a show for the town," Joe said. "We'll make people laugh. Sawyer says he heard about this man that puts on a circus. If P. T. Barnum can do it, we can too. Sawyer is real smart."

The crazy scheme made it hard for Tait to keep a straight face, but he had to look like he was taking them seriously, no matter what. He could see how important this was to his nephews, and it might keep them out of trouble. "You know, that's not a bad idea. What if I help you?"

"Sure. I guess." Jesse glanced at Joe. "But we sorta want to do it ourselves."

The answer surprised Tait a little and made him very proud. The boys needed to learn how to be independent, figure out things that would help them when no one was around.

"I understand. But if you change your mind, just let me know."

"Uncle Tait?"

He looked for the freckle by the boy's left ear that Melanie had mentioned but didn't find one. "Yes, Joe?"

"When are you gonna start looking for the killers of our mama and daddy? We want to know when you'll get even."

Guilt rushed through Tait that he hadn't done more to help them come to terms with the deaths of their parents. That he'd been busy wasn't much of an excuse. "I'm sorry this isn't happening fast enough. We've had the wedding to deal with and all, but I plan to ride out soon to see what I can find."

Claire's death weighed heavily on Tait. His sister deserved justice.

At least now Melanie could watch after the kids, but his pledge not to dump them on her and leave swept into mind—his pledge and her angry shoe-throwing. Maybe taking Jack with him would assure her he was coming back.

"I want you both to be on your best behavior for your Aunt Melanie when I do. Can I have your word?"

"We promise," both said simultaneously.

"I'm sorry, Uncle Tait," Jesse said in a low voice. "I shouldn't have said those things."

Joe lifted his eyes. "Me too. We'll try to do better."

"It's already forgotten." Tait got to his feet, brushed off his clothes, and then pulled the boys up. "I'm sure you're chomping at the bit to start making those traps, and I need to speak to Sheriff Bowdre. I'll see you later."

They parted ways, and Tait sought his old friend. "I'm riding out to see Hondo tomorrow. How do things look for you?"

Jack rubbed his jaw. "I think I can leave tomorrow. It'll take us three or four days to get there and back. What does your new wife say about you riding out so soon?"

"Haven't told her yet. Maybe she won't raise too big a fuss since you're coming along." Tait paused. "Jack, I can't stop thinking that someone might've killed Claire and John to get back at me."

"I haven't wanted to say anything, but the thought's crossed my mind too. It's too early to know for sure."

"It wouldn't be the first time. Lucy paid the ultimate price. Taking her life and making me live with the grief every single day was far worse than killing me."

"In that case, it's got to be Kern Berringer at the bottom of Claire's murder. He hates your guts, especially now that you killed his boys." Jack laid a hand on Tait's back. "If Hondo knows anything, we'll drag it out of him."

"I'll wring his fool neck. Hondo has this thing about protecting me."

"Yeah." They walked along for a few moments, then Jack asked, "Have you thought about seeking a pardon?"

"Yep. Now that I have a family, I have to find a way to clear my name—for their sakes."

"I'll help all I can. The governor gave Clay amnesty, and I traded information for my freedom. Luke Legend repaid all the money he stole." Jack pushed back his hat, allowing his light-brown hair to show. "Surely in all this time you've found some kind of information you can use in exchange for lifting the price on your head."

"Yeah, I've seen plenty. I'll think about this."

"Watch for an opportunity. I need to go help Nora. We'll talk later."

Tait watched his friend walk away, his thoughts turning. He still had a good bit of money stuck away from the train hold-ups. He could offer to give it back. And that led his thoughts in a different direction. Melanie's questions about that money had seemed oddly specific. Security? Maybe a wife needed to have a certain confidence about her new life. Especially one who was used to relying on a lucky cut of the cards.

She drank, she gambled, she had experience in lovemaking—a perfect wife for him.

But…

Tait released a long sigh and braced himself. He might as well go tell her he was leaving.

Eight

MELANIE WAS UNPACKING WHEN TAIT RETURNED FROM HIS talk with Joe and Jesse. She glanced at Becky, asleep on the bed, and went to greet him.

Looking every inch the dangerous outlaw with a stubbled jaw and brooding features, Tait somberly removed his hat and laid it on a table. Her thoughts went back to the air they'd cleared earlier that morning and his suspicions about her secrets. Thank goodness she'd covered up the truth. Confessing that small lie had kept her big secret safe, but she'd have to be more careful.

"How did it go with the twins?" she asked.

"Good." He crossed the space between them but didn't touch her. "You'll never guess why they want to trap critters. They're branching into the circus business. They're going to teach the animals to do tricks and put on a show for the town. Pretty smart thinking, but I didn't tell them how hard it'll be."

Melanie laughed. "Those boys are something. But you know it'll keep them occupied."

"That's why I'm all for it."

"Will we have to make room for cages here in our suite?"

"Nope. I'll make sure." He glanced toward the bedroom. "How's Becky?"

"Taking a nap. I thought I'd seize advantage of the quiet to unpack again." She wanted to lay her palm against his cheek, but she resisted. He seemed preoccupied, in a quandary about something. "Is anything wrong, Tait?"

"You might think so. I promised Joe and Jesse that I'd go see what I could find out about the men who murdered their parents. I know I promised not to dump the kids on you and ride out, but this can't be helped. Before you say anything…

Jack's going with me, so it won't be more than three, maybe four days at the most. We'll leave at daybreak."

The ends of Tait's sun-streaked hair nestled against his collar, and his gray eyes studied her. Slender strands of gold emerged from the dark pupils, cutting through the silver lightning of his eyes like the spokes of a wagon wheel. Such beautiful, expressive eyes that took in the room—and her. She wanted to look away, to hide from the things he saw, but found herself locked in place.

Melanie wet her lips, steadied her nerves, and smiled. Actually, this would work out nicely. She could search his soddy and send a letter to the judge reporting in without worrying that Tait would see her. "Some things you can't help. This is important, Tait. But I don't know how to care for kids. What if I mess up and hurt them?"

Real fear set in that she'd be alone with them.

Tait laughed. "They're not a lamp. They're pretty tough. You feed them, make sure they wash and sleep, and that's about it. The boys will keep occupied with the other kids, and Becky will be fine as long as you take her to the pot."

Melanie bit her lip. "I don't know. Other people find children easy, but they just scare me."

"You have the women in town to fall back on anytime you have a problem. They'll be glad to help. I'd stay if I could but I have to go do this. I promised."

She pulled her shoulders back and widened her smile. "Of course. I'm putting extra worry on your shoulders, and I'm sorry. I'll manage somehow."

"Thank you for understanding. I know my obligations toward you and these kids." He reached into a trouser pocket and pulled out some bills. He flipped off five and pressed them into her hand. "Here's the money I promised you."

She glanced down at the large bills. "This is too much."

"A wife should have her own money. You shouldn't have to ask me for things you need. Tell me when you run out." He put the wad away.

Melanie was touched. She hadn't expected an outlaw to

understand how important it was for a woman to have some independence. She slipped the bills into her pocket. "How long will you be gone?"

"Three or four days. Any longer and I'll telegraph to let you know." He smoothed her forehead with the thick pad of his thumb. "Maybe you can use the time to get acquainted with the children and make some friends among the ladies in town."

She laughed. "That and help Joe and Jesse train circus animals."

"You have experience at that. You trained drunks to give up their money at the card table."

"True."

Tait leaving was going to move her plans ahead faster than she'd expected. She wanted to get her task over with as soon as possible. Yet she compared poking around in Tait's things and trying to leave them looking untouched to swallowing a big dose of castor oil—except the aftereffects of this medicine would last a lifetime.

The risk was always present in her mind along with the question of what he'd do if he caught her. Oh God, she couldn't face his fury, his hurt.

On the other hand, watching everything she said and did around him was putting a strain on her. She could too easily mess up, and Tait seemed to have eyes in the back of his head. He noticed far too much. His absence would give her some breathing room.

Tait gave her a light kiss. "I was going to make up last night to you, but it won't be possible. Becky will have to sleep with us tonight so we can watch her. I'm sorry."

"There will be other nights." Despite her glib reply, she was disappointed. She'd been dying to see Tait naked, feel his body pressing to hers, feel him inside her, knowing she had what other women must desire.

Just once she'd like to lie in his arms, protected and safe where she didn't have to be the strong one. Her house with the gleaming windows and family inside began to slip away.

She had to stay focused on Ava and winning her release,

not a handsome outlaw with quicksilver eyes. She cursed Judge McIlroy and the deal she'd made with the devil.

✑

Darkness fell, and Melanie sat with Tait and the children in their suite discussing their day. Becky had crawled into her lap, and the boys worked on their traps on the floor with Tait. Warm lamplight bathed the handsome blue-and-tan sitting room, creating a cozy nest that was full of laughter.

Realization struck her from the blue. This was what a real family was like.

Tears burned behind her eyes. She'd never had this before, not even as a child. When she and Ava were small, her father had taken them to someone, usually a widow woman, until he'd finished gambling in the wee hours of the morning.

More than once she'd begged Mac Dunbar to stay with them and not go out. He'd laughed and said, "The sheep are ripe for the picking, little girl. I almost have enough to buy us a house." But he'd always come home broke.

On her and Ava's tenth birthday, he'd started teaching his girls to play cards, and it was then that she'd realized the truth. Her father would never want more than what he had. Inside him beat the heart of a swindler, and he loved the life of a vagabond. What's more, he expected her and Ava to be satisfied with it too. But they weren't. Not ever.

When Tait started building their house, she would design a room just like this.

Then a thought brought a stabbing pain in her chest. What if she found the train loot before he finished building? What if she never got to live a single day in the house she'd yearned for her whole life?

And worse, he'd know she'd betrayed him. How could she stand to see icy hatred in his beautiful eyes when she turned the money and him over to Judge McIlroy?

Becky patted her face. "Pwetty."

"So are you, sweetheart. You're beautiful. Are you getting sleepy?"

The girl rubbed her eyes, nodding.

"Then we should ready you for bed." She stood and lifted the child in her arms.

Tait looked up. "Do you need me to help?"

"I can do it. Go ahead and spend some time with the boys."

She'd just gotten Becky into a fresh nightgown when she heard a rap at the door followed by deep voices. Jack Bowdre? She listened but couldn't make out the words. Deciding she'd find out soon enough, Melanie finished readying for bed and brushed her hair. She was weaving the auburn strands into a braid when Tait came into the room. She met his gaze.

"Jack dropped by with news. He got a telegram from our friend Sheriff Hondo Rains, saying we'd better come. We'll still ride out at daybreak, same as we planned. But I wonder what Hondo found."

Melanie wanted to put her arms around him and smooth the worry from his forehead, but their relationship wasn't that kind yet. "I suppose you'll find out soon enough. I hope you catch the murdering bastards and, when you do, kill 'em. These kids are hurting."

"That's what makes me maddest. I'll be back before you can get settled in good. You can start drawing our house on paper, and I'll order all the lumber when I return." He looked at her funny. "You've changed. You're not the same woman who almost backed out of the wedding over the children. You've become a mama bear."

"I suppose I have." Melanie tied a ribbon around the end of her braid. "Tait, do you think we can have water piped into the kitchen and a bathing room? Jesse told me about Sawyer's, and it would be nice to be able to bathe Becky in a real bathtub like we have here at the hotel."

Tait kissed her cheek. "You can have anything your heart desires."

Except to both be able to tell Judge McIlroy to take a long walk off a short pier *and* have Ava free.

What would she do about her marriage once Ava was out of jail and Tait was in?

Divorce? Or stay married? A small sob escaped her.

Concern crossed Tait's tanned features. "What's wrong?"

"Nothing. I was blocking a sneeze, that's all." Struggling for composure, Melanie turned the covers aside and slipped between them, facing the wall.

What did it matter? He was a murderer, a criminal.

A small voice in her head whispered, *So are you. Admit how many you swindled, cheated, robbed. He robbed a railroad company, whereas you took men's savings, took food off their families' tables. Tell Tait how many times you left town in the dead of night to avoid an angry mob. Tell him about the men you slept with just to feel their touch, to banish the loneliness, men whose names you never knew.*

Memories pressed so close she could taste them. Memories she'd do anything to keep silent. Memories of things she'd done that would probably turn Tait Trinity's stomach.

The bedroom was quiet, and behind her came the quiet thud of boots hitting the floor, the rustle of clothing as Tait undressed. She fought desire to turn over, to see his lean body—just in case he didn't make it back. With a bounty on his head and men searching for him high and low, every time he rode out, the odds got slimmer that he would return.

Becky's breathing slowed, telling her the girl was asleep. Melanie tucked the covers around her.

The mattress shifted when Tait sat on the edge. "'Night, Mellie," he said softly and turned out the light.

"Good night, Tait," she mumbled. "I'll see you off in the morning."

She'd be a good wife and make sure his stomach was filled before he rode away. She could play the role even if she couldn't live it, and maybe he wouldn't hate her quite so much when it was all said and done.

❧

It was still dark outside when Tait awoke and dressed. He tiptoed to the window and glanced out at the lightening sky.

Melanie raised. "Is it time?"

"Yeah, go back to sleep."

"No, I want to see you off." She eased away from Becky's side and quickly dressed while he buckled his gun belt and pulled on his boots.

"You don't have to do this, Mellie."

"The children should sleep a bit longer. I want to see you off," she insisted.

Tait shook his head and eased the door of the suite shut. It seemed natural, in a way, to rest his hand against the small of her back. After all, they'd vowed to spend the rest of their lives together. What was one touch? The gray sky turned a pale pink as they made their way out to the café. Few people were up yet, so they had their pick of tables.

Sid Truman, the owner of the Blue Goose, brought coffee over. "You folks are up early."

"A little. Me and Jack're riding out. Thanks for the coffee." Tait accepted the full cup. "Sid, I'd appreciate it if you can bring my wife some hot tea."

"Sure thing, Trinity." Sid disappeared into the kitchen.

Melanie gave him a blinding smile that showed her dimples. "You remembered."

Tait nodded. "And that you take two lumps of sugar. I made a note of it the last two mornings."

He'd also noticed how quietly she'd sat with Becky last night, and the expressions on her face brought questions to his mind. She'd been smiling and content for a while, but then she'd been close to tears. And for God's sake, he wasn't dumb. He knew the difference between a sob and a sneeze. But if she wanted to pretend she hadn't been about to cry, who was he to stop her?

Maybe she'd just been missing her family.

Tait set down his cup and took her hand. "Why don't you invite your sister and father to come visit? I'd like to meet them."

The question seemed to jolt her into awareness. Her eyes became guarded again and she blinked hard. "My sister?"

"Yes, and your father too. I think we need to get acquainted. You do know where they are, don't you?"

"No. Yes. I mean, I'm not exactly sure." Then she appeared to recover her composure. "I think it's far too soon for them to come. Let's table this for now."

"I was just thinking of you. Sometimes you seem sad. You must miss them."

"Of course I do, although Mac Dunbar could try a saint. I love my father, but he exhausts me if I'm around him long. Instead of settling on one new avenue to make money, Ava and I had to try a dozen or more…and most times turn the profit over to him. You'll see what I'm talking about one day."

Sid brought Melanie's tea and took their order. Since Tait didn't know the next time he'd eat, he ordered a heavy breakfast while she settled on a biscuit and ham.

"You don't eat enough to keep a bird alive, Melanie."

"I get all I want. My stomach can't hold much. You shouldn't worry about me."

"I care about your well-being, and as your husband I feel I have the right." Tait motioned to young Henry Truman, who entered the room with a coffeepot.

"Mornin', Mr. Trinity. Fine day." Henry refilled his cup.

"Henry, how's the world treating you?"

"Well, I'm tired of sharing a bed with four of my brothers. Last night I finally just slept on the floor instead. It wasn't even that hard."

Tait laughed. "I remember those days myself."

Another customer waved for Henry to bring the pot, and he moved on. Their breakfast arrived, and they ate. All too soon, Tait and Jack were saddling their horses while Melanie talked quietly with Nora, who'd come to see her husband off. Tait hoped they'd strike up a friendship. Despite what she'd said, Melanie seemed lonely and homesick for company.

"I guess we're ready." Tait swung around to Melanie. "I'll try not to be gone long, but it depends on whether we find what we're looking for. I have to set this right for those kids. My sister too. I owe her that."

Melanie gripped her shawl, her sparkling gaze twisting

something inside Tait. He saw no sign of her dimples. "I wouldn't expect anything less. We'll be fine. I'll miss you."

Tait put his arm around her and kissed her lightly, then stuck his foot in the stirrup and swung into the saddle.

"Be careful, Tait." Melanie laid a hand on his leg. "Come back to us."

With a nod, he galloped from the town with Jack. He swiveled for a last look at the woman who'd tied her lot to his. He hadn't had anyone to say goodbye to in a long while. Certainly not someone who gave a damn about his welfare. Or anyone's curves to fill his arms. Come hell or high water, he had to make it back in one piece.

Nine

WHILE MELANIE WAITED FOR THE CHILDREN TO WAKE UP AFTER Tait left, she quietly searched the hotel suite for the stolen loot. Not that she expected to find it so near, but she wanted to leave no stone unturned. Once in the stillness, she thought she heard his slow, deliberate way of walking and whirled, expecting to see him standing there. First relief, then disappointment set in when he wasn't.

She sat down to think of where that railroad loot might be. In his soddy? She hadn't looked there. It seemed like a logical place.

After breakfast, she left the boys to their traps, took Becky's hand, and marched toward the sod house where Tait had been living. She glanced around to see if anyone was watching. She felt like a thief—which she would be if she found the stolen money. But was it really stealing to take from a robber?

If she did find it, what then? Borrow a horse and ride out? How heavy was fifty thousand dollars, the amount the judge claimed Tait had stolen? Maybe a wagon would better suit her needs. Even if he spent a couple of thousand, that still left almost all of it.

With one last glance around to make sure she wasn't being watched, she pushed through the door. The room was musty and rank. How could Tait stand to even sleep in such squalor? She was grateful he hadn't made her and the children live here.

Becky wrinkled her nose. "Stink."

"Yes, it does." Melanie sat her on the bed and pulled out a doll she'd bought at the mercantile on the way over. "Here you go, honey."

"Mine baby."

Melanie dropped a kiss on Becky's head and surveyed the room. Three crates stood stacked in the corner. She rolled up her sleeves and started there. The top box held things a typical man would stash like a few tools, a coil of rope, a few pieces of leather, old boots.

She let out an exasperated breath and glanced at Becky playing contentedly with her doll.

The second box contained a few ladies' hats, women's clothing, gloves, and shoes. She held up one of the dresses, a stylish Sunday outfit, and noted that the person it fit had been much smaller than she. Several other dresses were the everyday variety.

To whom did they belong? His sister? Why would he keep her things? Or maybe he had another sister he hadn't mentioned?

Her mind jumped to a second thought, and she could barely swallow. These could belong to a first wife, one he'd failed to mention when they'd spoken of their pasts. But he'd have no reason to hide the information. It didn't matter to her if he had been married before. The secret he kept was what concerned her. He was so big on telling the truth and then he'd hidden this.

Melanie moved to the last crate, this one nailed shut. She reached for a hammer from the first box and pried it open. A loud gasp flew from her mouth. Lying on the top was a shawl covered with dark stains—dried blood?

What the hell? She rocked back on her heels and gripped the crate with white knuckles. What had happened? What was she looking at?

What was Tait involved in besides robbery?

Her heart hammering, she picked up the shawl, blood-soaked and dried into stiffness. Had Tait killed a woman? No, there was no way she'd believe that. She was good at reading men, and Tait would never hurt a woman. No, these had to belong to another wife or sister. Had the woman who'd worn these met with a tragic accident? Or had she been murdered?

Sudden voices sounded outside the door, and Melanie gave a cry and almost leaped out of her skin. Some deep breaths let her settle somewhat, and she lifted out the blankets at the bottom of the crate.

The five blankets made of the softest lamb's wool brought even more questions. What? Why? What had happened to the baby? The woman must've been in the family way.

That really was the only logical explanation. Tears burned the backs of her eyes.

His flat refusal to have children drifted into her mind. His reply to her question had burst out with no thought whatsoever, and he'd been a little sharp about it. If his baby had died, that might explain his reaction.

This was all too much. She stuffed everything back into the crates and nailed the lid shut on the bottom one.

Though he'd told her the day after their wedding they'd only talk about their pasts that once, then never speak of them again, she was going to ask him about this. He'd probably refuse to say anything. Didn't matter. She'd ask anyway and not let on that she'd seen these things.

After she put everything back like it had been, she turned the place upside down yet didn't find a single bill or coin.

"Pot, Mellie. Pot," Becky insisted, crawling off the bed.

"Okay, honey. I'm through here anyway." She gave the sod house one last look. "Let's go."

Before leaving, she gathered up an armful of Tait's dirty clothes. In case anyone saw her leaving, she could say she'd come to collect them to wash. Then she took Becky's hand.

Tait and Jack rode into Flat Rock, Texas, under cover of the pitch-black night. Clouds obscured the moon, leaving nothing to guide them except for a dim light that shone in the window of the sheriff's office. They tied their horses in the alley behind the building and moved quietly around to the door.

A dog's bark drifted down the lonely street, but nothing moved. Businesses lined both sides of the street, with a bank on one corner. A lamp burned in that window too. If Tait was of a mind to rob it, this would be a perfect setup.

He shook himself, the noisy saloon further down the way drawing his attention. "A booming business tonight."

"Looks like." Jack turned the knob and opened the door to the sheriff's office.

Hondo glanced up from his desk. "What took you so long? Good to see you, Tait."

"Likewise. We came as soon as the wedding was over." Tait watched a grin curve Hondo's mouth and quickly set him straight. "Now, don't go thinking I fell in love or the other way either. I only got married because I needed help with the kids. It's nothing but business."

"It'd take a hell of a woman to penetrate that thick skin of yours. Would you like some coffee?" Hondo picked up the pot on the small stove.

"Thought you'd never ask." Tait warily eyed the two cells, recalling how it felt to be locked up. He forced himself to breathe easy. Both cages were empty, so they wouldn't have to worry about being overheard.

Jack dropped into a chair and propped his feet on a crate. "I'll take some too."

"Where's your deputy?" Tait took off his hat and hung it on a nail.

"Out of town. Won't be back until next week."

"That's good." Tait never knew who he could trust. He had to assume that everyone wanted the reward money.

Moments later they sat in a circle with cups of the strong, black brew. Hondo kicked off the conversation. "I'm glad you came, Tait. Have something for you." He pitched him a silver badge.

Tait caught it, the air whistling through his teeth at the shock when he realized what he held. It was a railroad badge, belonging to someone from the Missouri River Railroad. "Where did you get this?"

"At your sister's place." Hondo lifted his cup to his mouth. "This all but confirms what I originally thought—they killed your sister either to draw you out or because they couldn't get to you so killed her instead, knowing how much it would hurt you."

"Dammit to hell!" Tait jumped up out of the chair, needing

to move, needing to hit something, needing to put a bullet in the murdering devils.

His chest squeezed like a vise, blocking his ability to breathe. He gripped the odd-shaped piece of metal so tightly it cut into his palm. It burned in his hand like a hot poker. Now those kids really *would* have a reason to despise him.

They'd called him a no-account, and they'd pegged him to a tee.

"Whereabouts on their property did you find it, Hondo?" Jack took the badge from Tait.

"The bastards pinned it on Claire's dress. This was deliberate."

"What else?" Tait leaned over the desk, planting his arms wide. "I know there's more. Don't try to hide it."

"John went down from a clean shot that killed him instantly." Hondo paused a long moment as though wishing he didn't have to tell Tait the rest. "They tortured Claire before they put her out of her misery. Her face was battered to hell, and they shot both knees, sliced one arm deep to the bone. She fought them. Put up a hell of a fight, from the looks of things."

Bile rose in Tait's mouth. He closed his eyes, but the gruesome images forced them back open. He set his cup down and flung open the door, gulping the fresh night air into his lungs, struggling to hold down the contents of his stomach.

Behind him he heard Jack ask, "Do you have any idea who the low-down bastards were?"

"Suspicions are all. Nothing concrete."

Anger filled Tait. He whirled. "Why did you wait so God-blessed long to tell me this?"

Hondo gave him a level look. "The living are more important than the dead, Tait. You needed to take care of those kids and give them something solid to hold onto. Besides, I was trying to find out as much as possible about the killers' identities before I drew you in."

"You were right to hold it back, Hondo. Those kids were more important." Jack rose and walked to the bulletin board where the wanted posters hung. "Who do you suspect?"

"I hate to say."

"I'd hate to shoot you, but I will if you don't start talking." Tait knew threatening Hondo wasn't a good idea with the cells so close, but he couldn't help himself. "I want names."

"All right. The Berringers. The Vinson Gang. Then there's Walter Patrick and the sorry-assed men he's got working for him. The list goes on. Hell, pick any of those wanted posters over there. Are you happy now?"

"I get your point." Tait's anger cooled.

"Well, hallelujah!"

Jack refilled his cup. "As remote as their ranch was, it could've been someone passing through who saw it as easy pickings. But still, that railroad badge means it was someone who knows Tait and his history. It'd be one hell of a coincidence otherwise."

A knot formed in Tait's chest. "My gut says this was not random."

"Your gut and mine must be twins." Hondo locked his hands behind his head and leaned back in his chair. "How are the kids?"

Tait sat down, restlessness still itching up his legs. "Doing as well as they can. Gonna take time for the boys to get that chip off their shoulders, but they'll come around. Thanks for burying Claire and John and looking out for the kids. I owe you some money."

Pain filled Hondo's stare. "They were like my own flesh and blood. I gave them a good service with a preacher."

Tait swallowed hard. "After John stopped me from visiting, I felt better knowing you were close by."

"Those boys were a real mess at first while I was trying to find you and finally sent them to Jack. Didn't sleep, wouldn't eat for two days. Just stared into space. Kept asking why." Hondo sighed. "I can't wait to catch the bastards who did this. And I will sooner or later. You can bet your bottom dollar on that."

Something the twins had said clicked in Tait's brain. "One of the boys described the killers. Do you have any gray-haired men with protruding ears and deep bags under their eyes around here?"

"Not any that I can recall. The boys told me about that when they started talking again."

"Does the description fit any of the Berringers?" Jack asked.

"Nope, but with the passel of uncles, cousins, and kids, I doubt I've seen them all. Every last one of that bunch can get fighting mad at the drop of a hat." Hondo wagged his head. "I've never known anyone with a hair-trigger temper like they have. Took after Grandpa Berringer."

"Didn't Kern have some brothers?" Jack asked.

"It's possible, but if he does, they don't live around here." Hondo straightened and grabbed his hat. "I need to make rounds and check the horses at the hitching rail, see who's in town. I'll be back in a bit. Make yourself at home in the cells. They're unlocked."

Jack reached for his hat. "I'll come with you. I need to see to the horses. Tait, best if you stay inside. We don't need anyone to recognize you."

"I'll hold down the fort." Tait stretched. "Got some thinking to do."

The door closed behind them, and silence engulfed him. After a moment, Tait went to Hondo's desk drawer, pulled out a half-empty bottle, filled his cup midway, and wandered over to a cot in one of the cells. Even though he'd told Melanie he'd quit whiskey, he needed this right now to numb the sharp pain.

His thoughts tumbled inside his skull. Who besides Kern Berringer had such a vendetta against him?

Who had tortured his beautiful, sensitive Claire? The woman had never hurt a flea. She would've screamed at the top of her lungs. But the boys hadn't mentioned anything about that. Why? Unless someone had muffled the noise with either his hand or some cloth. Maybe.

Tait slid his Smith & Wesson from his holster and flipped the cylinder open. When he found the murdering bastards, he'd take his time. They'd pray to die, but he wouldn't let them until he was ready.

An eye for an eye.

Ten

OVER THE NEXT TWO DAYS, MELANIE DISCOVERED TAIT WAS right about caring for the kids. The boys pretty much stayed busy, and she and Becky spent a lot of time with Nora and Clay's red-haired wife, Tally.

They discussed the new house, the children, and their husbands. She liked the women in Hope's Crossing and shared a good deal with them, which was something of a revelation. They all either had been or were running from something, yet no one was shunned or talked about. No one was judged to be better than anyone else.

Also, after noticing Dr. Mary playing cards at a back table in the café, she'd introduced herself and played poker. The familiar feel of the cards brought Ava closer. The doctor turned out to be quite a worthy opponent, and Melanie enjoyed their games immensely. In addition, she'd learned more about this fascinating woman who wore a necklace made of bullets.

In all, everyone made Melanie feel welcome and accepted.

A group of them were having tea at Nora's one afternoon. Becky was playing with Nora's Willow and Tally's son, Dillon, both just beginning to toddle. Each time the babies would lose balance and fall, Becky's little voice would pipe up, "Saw-wee."

Nora waddled from the kitchen with a plate of cookies, her pretty blond hair curling about her shoulders. Melanie took in her tired eyes and relieved her of the plate. "When is your baby due?"

"About four weeks according to Dr. Mary, and it can't some soon enough. I didn't know how much chasing after a little one can exhaust a body."

Melanie selected a sugar cookie. "I noticed how much older Sawyer is than Willow, so it's no wonder you didn't have that problem with her."

"I didn't give birth to Willow." Nora explained that both the baby and Sawyer were orphans. "We found them, and they needed us. The child I'm carrying will be my firstborn."

"Oh, I didn't know." Melanie had thought that Willow's darker skin coloring was a bit odd, considering her parents' coloring, but hadn't wanted to pry.

Tally reached for a cookie. "My Violet is adopted as well. There are so many orphans in the world who need homes."

Joe had confided to Melanie that Violet was blind, and she'd watched the girl get around amazingly well with a long stick she held out in front of her to feel the ground. Sometimes she held onto Bullet and the dog guided her, seeming to sense she needed help that way.

"That is so true." Melanie sipped her tea. "I've traveled around a good bit, and I've seen many, all trying their best to survive."

"Death's shadow falls over us all." Tally wiped her son's nose. "The orphan trains have helped, but I often wonder how many kids are taken in by people just wanting to put them to work."

A knock sounded on the door, and Nora went to answer it. Melanie heard her say, "Come on in, Rebel. Join our tea party." Nora returned with an attractive woman whose hair was as black as midnight, also clearly in the family way. She seemed older than Nora, but then this land aged a person fast, so it was difficult to tell.

Melanie laughed. "I think you have something special in the water here." She stuck out her hand. "I'm Melanie, Tait's wife, and I'm very happy to meet you."

"Rebel." She shook Melanie's hand and untied her bonnet. "I'm married to Travis Lassiter. My Ely thinks the sun rises and sets on Jesse and Joe. What do you think about the kids' idea of putting on a little circus?"

"Anything that keeps them occupied gets my vote." Tally poured Rebel some tea. "They have little enough here to occupy them, and I think it'll be fun entertainment for all of us."

Nora nodded. "I'm for whatever makes our lives easier. Sawyer already has an assortment of raccoons and rabbits. We also have the goat herd to cull from and a donkey. Jack helped Sawyer catch a badger the other day, but the thing's so mean I doubt he can tame it. Those teeth scare me."

Memories swirled around Melanie. "I traveled a lot and once saw a real circus. The performers were exciting, flying through the air and doing stunts. In one of the tents, with all the curiosities, they had this one chicken that played a piano."

Unease fell over her at the rest of the memories that followed. One of the performers had fallen and broken a leg, and a woman in another tent had told her fortune…

Melanie stilled at the recollection. Her hand trembled, and she sloshed her tea.

"I'm sorry." She jumped up before Nora could move and went to the kitchen for a dish towel.

"Saw-wee," Becky said, following.

"It's fine, sweetheart. Just a little spill." Melanie picked Becky up and hurried to clean her mess.

"When do you expect Tait back?" Rebel reached for a cookie.

"I don't know, but I miss him."

"Watch out or he'll have you fat and rounded like Nora and me."

"He said he doesn't want children."

The women paused in the middle of eating and stared, as though she'd said Tait had shot his horse.

"Why?" Tally asked.

"He basically said an outlaw has no business bringing kids into the world because he won't live to raise them."

"Oh Melanie. I'm so sorry." Tally came around the table to hug her. Becky insisted on getting a hug in too. "Unfortunately, Tait is right. Some do have a short life span. But everyone has to have hope for brighter days. It's the only thing that keeps a person going."

"If a man lives every minute like he's dying, he won't grab hold of any good times." Nora lifted Willow into her lap.

"Jack was that same way when I first met him. He'd all but given up on life. He'd just been arrested and was on his way to jail, angry that he'd gotten caught. He invited me to come to his hanging. Then the stagecoach wrecked, and it changed everything. For both of us."

Rebel sipped her tea. "You may not know this, Melanie, but that husband of yours never killed anyone who wasn't trying to kill him and that's a fact. Just ask any of the men here. He only shoots in self-defense and only when his back is against the wall."

Then that meant he hadn't killed the woman whose clothes he'd kept.

Tally nodded. "And don't forget, he's kept this town from sinking into oblivion with part of that filthy railroad money."

He really does seem to be doing so much good, a small voice whispered. *He's not the money-hungry robber out for his own personal gain that you thought.*

"Few know he's opened his pocket to orphanages and other worthy causes," Nora added. "Jack tells me a lot about him, which is a good thing because you can't get two words out of Tait Trinity."

Very enlightening.

"Maybe one day Tait will come to see that his life isn't hopeless." Melanie handed a cookie to Becky. But when he found out she was working to betray him... A shiver sent ice careening through her veins. And her new friends around the table would despise her. The prophecy would come true.

The fortune-teller had peered closely into her outstretched palm. "Be true to a tall, handsome outlaw with silver eyes, or you'll see untold pain and despair."

Despite what she'd found in his sod house, Tait appeared to be such a good man, a decent man, and he loved his niece and nephews. No disputing that. Stinging tears pricked the back of her eyes. She couldn't bring him down and live with herself.

Dear God, a woman had to have some self-respect and honor or she'd be nothing.

But poor Ava. Her sister was depending on her. Dear God!

Melanie got to her feet, clutching Becky. "I have to go."

"Tomorrow again?" Nora asked.

"Yes." Melanie grabbed Becky and hurried from the house, away from the circle of new friends, before she said too much.

৵৹

Melanie was almost to the hotel, going slower than usual so Becky could keep up, when the clerk at the stage line office hollered that he had a box for her. Curious, she veered course and took it from him.

Who could've sent it? There were no markings, which was odd. Her father? Doubtful.

The rectangular box was about a foot long and twice as tall and made no noise when she shook it. She sat Becky in a chair on the hotel porch and unwrapped the brown paper from around it.

She opened the lid and made a strange gurgling sound. She couldn't move or speak—only stare in horror, her stomach roiling.

The cardboard box was full of long auburn hair. On top was a small container. Her hands shaking, she opened it, and inside was a tooth with dried blood around the roots.

God in heaven! She rocked back and forth, tears rolling down her face. Nausea stole over her in waves, and bile filled her mouth.

Even before she read the letter underneath the hair from Judge McIlroy, she knew the contents were Ava's.

This is only the beginning. Fulfill your end of the bargain, or I'll be forced into something more drastic. Unless you want your sweet Ava to suffer, you'd better hurry.

"Mellie sad?" Becky asked.

She'd even forgotten the child was there. Wiping her tears, she smiled. "Nothing to worry your little head over, sweetheart. Let's go inside."

A few minutes later up in their suite with Becky playing, Melanie hid the box under the bed and tried to calm her nerves. Every bone in her body screamed that Ava was in the hands of a dangerous madman. What could she do? The only recourse seemed to be to find the stolen money.

Melanie paced back and forth the length of the bedroom. She had to find the money before Tait returned. She couldn't afford to wait a second longer.

And the top of the bluff seemed the most likely place to start.

With Becky in tow, she went to knock on Rebel Lassiter's door. Rebel smiled wide and let them in. Her daughter Jenny peeked around her mother.

"I hate to impose, but can you please watch Becky for a bit? I have an urgent matter to attend to."

"Sure. Jenny was just saying how bored she was with no one to play with." Rebel laid a hand on Melanie's shoulder. "Is everything all right?"

Oh, how Melanie wished it was. "Yes. Thank you so much. I shouldn't be long."

"Take all the time you need."

"Bless you, Rebel. I'll return the favor." Melanie kissed Becky and hurried to find a shovel. A clock was ticking in her head, and she could hear Ava pleading for her life.

She found a shovel in the barn that everyone used. Grabbing it, she hurried to the path leading up the bluff. Once on top, she glanced around for the best spot to start. She decided to begin next to some large boulders.

With the first shovel of dirt, some of the angst began to settle. Then as she dug, the images of Ava's beautiful hair and her tooth filled her mind, spurring her on.

But the spot yielded nothing. She filled in the hole and dug another. Then four others. A glance at the low sun showed it sinking fast, and she had to accept defeat. Melanie sank down on a rock and put her head in her hands. This was impossible without Tait telling her where he'd buried the loot. Tears of frustration fell. Ava was depending on her. What would McIlroy do to her sister next?

Melanie held no cards to play.

~⁓~

The ladies' tea the next afternoon was mostly filled with more talk of babies and the bigger subject—the children's circus.

Tally and Rebel had brought their knitting and sat content-edly with their steadily moving needles. Rebel's pretty yellow, white, and green yarn created a striking snowflake design that sparked Melanie's interest. "I love the colors you're using, Rebel. What are you making?"

Rebel smiled. "A sweater for the baby. Do you knit?"

"No, I never learned. My mother died when my sister and I were born—twins, you understand. And my father scoffed at such things as knitting and sewing. He felt they were a pure waste of time." There had been one caregiver who'd tried to take her and Ava under her wing, the old lady she'd only known as Granny. Only her father yanked them out of bed one night and hurried out of town. She'd later learned her father had gotten caught cheating at the card table and the old woman really was her grandmother. Mac had left his own mother to bear his shame.

Then ten years later, he'd left her and Ava in jail to take his punishment. Disappeared into the night, leaving his girls to rot.

Melanie fought to swallow. Discovering how little he thought of her and Ava had shaken her to the depths of her soul. For all of half a minute at the beginning of her current troubles, she'd thought about trying to find him, beg for his help, but doing so would have been a waste of time. No, she and Ava were better off without him.

But each time she closed her eyes, she saw Ava's thin face and shorn hair.

"I'd be happy to teach you." Tally took a sip of tea and snipped her brown yarn, leaving a long tail.

"I might take you up on that." But what was the use when she wouldn't be in Hope's Crossing for much longer?

Besides, they were the wives of Tait's friends. Once she'd completed her mission to ruin Tait, they'd shun her like a leper. Immense regret swept through her. Damn it!

This town, these friendly people, the idea of friends of her own—they were sucking her in at every turn. She had to remind herself to step back and not fall into their open arms. But darn it, she wanted to finally become a part of something bigger instead of always an outsider looking in. How beautiful it would be to have true friends who would stick by her through thick and thin. And Tait. She didn't want to give up the man who'd shown her that dreams were possible. She wanted a home, a family of her own—a real life. Permanence was the siren that called to her in the dead of night and every waking moment.

To dig in the dirt, plant things, and be on hand to watch them grow.

To unpack and know she wouldn't have to leave in a rush.

To stretch, finally stretch her wings, and learn how to be a good person.

A knock came at the door. Nora went to answer it and returned with a newspaper. "Hot off the press, ladies."

"Oh good. I wonder what the *Frontier Gazette* has in this issue." Tally put her knitting away in her bag.

Rebel grinned. "Two pages this time. What juicy news did Monty Roman find to write about?"

Nora refilled all their cups and scanned the articles. "Here's one on the children's upcoming circus. Hmm, this is interesting. It mentions the performance date. Next month— September 3rd. I didn't know they'd set a date. I swear, we're the last to know anything."

Tally gasped. "That's only two weeks away!"

"Will they have the animals ready by then?" Melanie asked. Of all the things she was starting to like about Hope's Crossing, the children's circus was one she didn't want to miss. Joe and Jesse were having such fun training the animals. "Jesse worked for hours yesterday trying to teach a raccoon how to sit up on command. It was so cute. Joe had better success with getting a chicken to peck grain off the keys of a toy piano I bought the boys from the mercantile. They'd been determined to try it after I mentioned seeing that once at a circus."

"I, for one, can't wait to see what they come up with." Rebel sighed. "Ely and Jenny are so excited."

Still perusing the newspaper, Nora squealed. "Oh my goodness, here's an interview with Tait!"

Melanie mentally slapped herself to keep from ripping the newspaper out of Nora's hand. "Read it aloud to us, Nora."

As the woman did, Melanie learned a great deal more about Tait than he'd ever told her. He and Jack were childhood friends, which accounted for their strong bond. His father, a farmer and Methodist preacher, raised four sons and a daughter with his wife. Tait left home at fourteen. *Hmmm.* He'd not told her that. Where had he gone? Where had he lived? Melanie's heart ached for the boy he'd been, and she suspected a good portion of his experiences after that helped put the hardness in his eyes. In the interview, Tait called Thomas Trinity hard-nosed, strict, and judgmental. The situation must've been intolerable for Tait to have just up and left at such a young age and never returned.

But the most important information in that interview was Tait's vendetta against the railroad. Suddenly a great deal more about Tait Trinity began to make sense.

She listened to every word of the interview, but there was no mention of a previous wife at all. So whose clothes and things were packed away in his sod house? He'd probably have mentioned it to the children if they were his sister's. His mother?

Damn it, Tait! Why didn't you tell me more? Why don't you trust me?

Why should he? They were still practically strangers.

Melanie's brain whirled with the possible implications of what she'd discovered. It was possible Tait's woman, whoever she had been, had died in childbirth. It could explain why he couldn't bear to think of having children.

But why keep her bloody shawl?

A memory slammed into her. She was passing through St. Louis a while back and read a sad story in the newspaper. A man's wife had died, and he'd been so locked in grief he couldn't accept it. For a year or more, he'd ignored the smell and kept her propped up in a chair. The grief-stricken man had talked to her corpse like she was alive. Maybe that's the way it was with Tait—if he kept the woman's things close, he would never have to say goodbye.

Melanie wanted to cry for him. From the boxes of women's personals, he appeared to be locked in a situation similar to her own. He was held fast by the past as she was by the law.

If only she could ask her new friends. The ladies would probably know, but going behind Tait's back would sure get him riled. She would be upset if the situation were reversed. No, she'd face him directly but gently and ferret out the truth. But why the need to know? This had nothing to do with the reason she'd come to marry him.

Unless… Maybe that had something to do with where he'd hidden the money. Maybe he'd buried it with the mystery woman.

She had to go get her own newspaper and look over the article more carefully when she had time to think things through. Saying she didn't feel well, Melanie collected Becky and left the gathering. On the way to the newspaper office, she ran into Joe and Jesse, and they begged her to leave Becky with them. They seemed to have such a closeness with their little sister, and it melted Melanie's heart.

Monty Roman got up from his desk when she entered the newspaper office and hurried forward to greet her. "Mrs. Trinity, to what do I owe the pleasure?"

"I'd like to buy one of your papers." She took a penny from her pocket.

"Please, you don't need to pay since your husband gave me the interview."

"I insist." She pressed the penny into his hand, noting two missing fingers. She wondered what had happened. He was a fairly young man, no more than thirty at the most. His nut-brown eyes gazed at her so intently that she took a step back.

Roman gave her a smile. "Forgive me. But you look very familiar. Have we met?"

"No." If he knew how many faces she'd seen in her lifetime, he'd probably reach for a snort of something. "I'm positive we have not. My paper?"

"Of course." He pulled one from a stack. "I'm actually glad

you came in. I have something for you." He went to his desk and opened a drawer.

She followed him and took a tintype he handed her, a photograph of her wedding to Tait. She stared at the handsome couple, and her heart swelled. How odd the way a photograph made something look quite different than it actually was. The way he held her hand and stared into her eyes made it appear she and Tait were so much in love, yet they hadn't been. If anything, they had a remote interest in each other and maybe that had only been on her part at that.

"Mr. Trinity came by here that morning and asked me if I'd take a wedding picture for the missus."

"I didn't know he'd had it taken for me. I assumed he'd picked it up already."

"It's then that he let me interview him for the paper." Monty laughed. "I'd been after him for a while, and he'd always refused until that day. I guess I caught him just right."

He'd wanted it for her. She swallowed past the thick lump. She'd intended the tintype as proof to show Judge McIlroy, but now… Suddenly, she was confused about the impact it had on her and knew she'd never part with it.

First letting her have her own money, and now the picture that she'd always treasure.

She blinked hard and glanced up. "Thank you, Mr. Roman. I should go. I left Becky with the boys." She chuckled. "They'll probably have her strapped to one of those goats again and be teaching her to gallop by now."

"I hope not. Enjoy the tintype." He studied her. "I know I'll remember where I met you. Eventually."

Worry knotted in her stomach as she left the office. No doubt he would. She just prayed she wasn't doing anything shameful such as the way she'd dressed and teased men sometimes.

She stopped on the boardwalk two doors down and took the picture from her pocket, running the pad of a thumb across Tait's handsome features. Oh, to be the kind of woman in that picture for real. Able to be a devoted wife and spend a lifetime being loved.

But she wasn't and never would be unless she found a way out. She swiped at her eyes with an angry jerk of her wrist and put the memento away, torn between two equally difficult paths: save her sister or betray a man who had already suffered a lifetime of betrayals. She chewed her lip.

In the silence, she heard her conscience. She couldn't do this. Despite his hard outward appearance, Tait was gentle. He had a strong sense of justice, of responsibility to his kin…and she was beginning to care about him a lot more than she'd bargained for. One thing she understood now: he'd had a good reason for robbing those trains.

And it had never been about the money.

There had to be another way to satisfy the judge. She'd look until she found it.

She would fight to keep the life that she had begun in Hope's Crossing. A life that involved Tait Trinity.

Eleven

THE MORNING SUN SHONE DOWN ON TAIT AS HE DISMOUNTED at his sister's house. The land, the clapboard home, everything stunk of death.

Three black crows sat on the windmill, the blades spinning in the breeze. Their caws broke the silence, and a kitten streaked from the porch.

"I want to know every single detail. Don't leave anything out." Tait pinned Hondo with a sharp glance. "I want to know where the horses were tied, what you saw when you rode up, what you felt. I want to know the things you didn't see but your gut told you."

Hondo nodded. "I'll try. It was around twilight on a day pretty much like this one when the boys rode up to my office with little Becky. All of them were hysterical. It took them a while to calm down enough to tell us anything. By the time me and my deputy rode out here, it was dark. Couldn't see much in the blackness except John lying on the porch and the front door standing open." "Whereabouts was John?" Jack asked, beating Tait to the question.

"Right in front of the door." Hondo planted himself on the spot. "The hair stood on my neck. I struck a match and went inside and saw Claire on the floor. My deputy lit a lamp. Blood. So much blood. My boots slipped in it, and I nearly went down."

"Was it all Claire's?" Tait asked quietly, struggling for composure.

"Appeared that way. She was a mess, but I don't think they…violated her."

"That's a comfort," Tait murmured. A small one, but he'd take it.

Hondo ran a hand over his eyes. "Claire…Claire's dress was raised, and I saw they'd blown her knees out. I covered her up." Hondo's voice quivered.

"Thank you." Anger swirled and twisted inside Tait like a bunch of bees, trying to find something to sting.

"Her right arm cut deep. Lord, it was a mess in here. Blood on the walls, the floor, soaked one of Becky's dolls right through. And the smell—I'll never forget that smell if I live to be a hundred."

Hondo fell silent. Tait glanced around the room. Nothing appeared to have been taken since several items were left that a thief would've wanted. A brand-new Winchester hung over the fireplace, and an older one rested next to the door. Everything was as neat as a pin now.

"Who cleaned up the place?" Tait asked.

"The Harveys, who live on the next farm over. If the children came back, they didn't want them to see the house in that condition." Hondo stared out the door.

Tait scanned the room more slowly this time. What clues had the killers left behind? They always left something.

Every hair on his neck rose, and his gut writhed like a den of snakes. He struggled to keep his voice even. "Were drawers open and things strewn about?"

"No. The place looked just like this." Hondo inhaled a shaky breath. "After the blood, second thing I noticed was the badge pinned to Claire's dress. We got some blankets from the bedroom, wrapped the bodies, and hauled them to town. It was late at night when we got back."

The Trinity family Bible lay open on the table. Tait strode across the room to pick it up. He'd be the keeper of it now. The pages didn't lay flat, and that seemed odd unless…maybe there were dried flowers saved as a remembrance. He turned the book in his hands and flipped it open. Light from the window glinted on the pale metal. His breath hitched painfully when he picked up the ring.

"What is it?" Jack moved closer.

"A woman's wedding band."

Wait. It was too familiar. It looked like—

Oh hell!

His head swam when blood drained from it all at once.

Praying it wasn't what he thought, he held the ring to the light. Engraved on the inside was the word *Forever*—and the initials *TT*.

A loud, bloodcurdling cry sprang from his mouth, and he dropped to his knees. Three years he'd searched for that silver band, ever since finding it missing from Lucy's hand that horrible day. He gripped it so tight it left an impression in his palm. He could almost smell the rosewater she'd always worn.

Oh God! He shook from head to toe.

Jack knelt beside him. "Is that whose I think it is?"

Tait nodded, unable to speak.

Hondo stared openmouthed. "That Bible wasn't there the last time I came. The killers came back."

"Are you sure?" Jack got to his feet.

"Positive." Hondo squared his shoulders. "I would've seen something so obvious. I'm not some drunken bumbler who doesn't know shit from bootblack."

"You don't have to get so defensive. Just trying to figure out what's going on." Jack placed a hand under Tait's armpit and helped him into a chair. Then he and Hondo went out onto the porch to give Tait time to get his legs underneath him.

After a little while, Tait felt steady enough and wandered out to join them. "Why leave this here with Claire? What's going on?"

"Sick bastards!" Hondo spat. "Low-down sick bastards!"

"The killers had to have somehow gotten wind Tait was coming. Someone wanted you to find this. Maybe we were trailed from Hope's Crossing." Jack leaned against the post bracing the porch and stared off into the distance. "Are you all right, Tait?"

"Yeah." He lied. Tait stuck the ring into his pocket, still absorbing the shock waves, his heart and mind going numb. "What are they doing? Trying to mess with my mind?"

"Seems that way." Jack pushed away from the post. "Could Claire have had it?"

"No. She would've somehow gotten it to me. And how

would she have come by it? She wasn't around when Lucy was murdered. This is Kern Berringer's work—or one of his kin. A message to me that no one is safe." Tait scanned the brush. "Where the hell is Kern holed up? I've looked high and low for him for three solid years. Someone is protecting him."

Hondo spat into the dirt. "I'm betting it's Richard Markham, that damned railroad owner."

"Wish I knew." Jack squeezed Tait's shoulder. "It might not've occurred to you, but I think we need to get back to Hope's Crossing as quick as possible. They seem to be going after anyone close to you. Melanie and the kids might be next."

A hand seemed to reach into his chest and squeeze his heart. Tait nearly doubled over from the pain. The assumption wasn't nearly as far-fetched as he wished it was.

Hondo's voice was quiet. "Jack's right. There's not much more you can do here. I'll pack up everything and get someone to bring their things to you if I can't come myself. I'll also try to find a buyer for this place. When I do, I'll let you know."

"I want to see where the horses were tied," Tait insisted. "Need to look at the hoof marks, if any are still here."

"They're gone. We had rain not long ago. But I made sketches of the ones I saw. They're back at my office." Hondo moved off the porch. "The horses stood here, right along this railing. Five of them. I wish I could tell you the color and size, but I can't. The boys were too scared to pay close attention to that. They were running for their lives and dragging Becky with them."

Tait could picture the scene in his head and had to force air into his agonized lungs. If only he'd been here. He was the one the killers were after. Not his sister and not John. Or Melanie.

"I'd give every cent of the railroad money to find the godforsaken bastards." Tait ran a hand over the rough wooden porch railing. "What are your thoughts, given everything we know? Is this Kern Berringer?" He needed to know.

"The railroad badge and wedding ring seem to suggest that." Hondo scratched his head. "Who else would have the ring and know about your vendetta against the railroad? If nothing else, he knew this would draw you out in the open. You're too protected in Hope's Crossing. They couldn't get to you."

"Exactly. My bet's on Kern." Jack was silent a moment. "Your gunfight with Ed Berringer happened less than a week after this carnage. Maybe his father sent him to deliver a message, and Ed messed up."

"Do you think he forgot his mission?" Hondo asked.

"Hard to know with Ed. Here's a thought. Maybe he didn't tell Papa Berringer he was going to Hope's Crossing. He thought he could kill Tait, it would end the vendetta, and they'd all be safe to keep killing. He might've wanted to be the big man, someone important, prove his worth." Jack snorted. "No one ever said Ed was the smartest pup of the litter. Out of all those boys, Ed and Willie were the shortest on brains."

Tait mulled that over. It seemed to make sense. Only how did Ed know where to find him?

"I've always believed Kern didn't know where I'd holed up," Tait said slowly. "But I think he's always known. Ed showing up in Hope's Crossing proves that. Kern doesn't want me dead yet. He inflicts more pain on me when he kills those I love. Killing me is too quick. I have to end this. I can't let everyone I care about take what should be coming to me."

Hondo leaned against the railing and slapped at a mosquito on his arm. "Don't forget your brothers. Won't they be in Kern's crosshairs as well?"

"They're all out of reach. Alaska, last I heard. Hell, they could all be dead and I'd never know." And Tait hoped they stayed far away.

Hondo let out a low whistle. "Yep, that's a fair distance. I'd say they're safe."

Even so, there was no love lost between Tait and his brothers. Any one of them would turn him in for the reward if they ever learned about it.

"Something's still bothering me. The tall man with the killers—who is he?" Tait asked. "All the clan I've seen have been shorter than I am."

Jack sat down on the porch step. "I've never heard of the

Berringers letting strangers ride with them. For one thing, they have enough family."

"Not if he's a distant relative," Tait pointed out.

"Hell, all of this is making my brain tired!" Hondo released a string of curses. "Tait, I never heard what happened between you and Kern to cause such hatred."

"I crippled him." Vivid images of that day raced across Tait's memory. "I clubbed him across the knee with a rifle during a fight and shattered the bone. I was protecting a young widow he'd taken a shine to and holding her against her will."

Little had Tait known then how many deaths his actions would lead to.

"That would do it, all right." Hondo quietly got a box and started rounding up the kittens.

"If I'm not mistaken, the fight happened before Lucy." Jack wearily rubbed his eyes.

"Yep. I was a young pup, barely dry behind the ears. Kern was almost twice my age and itching to show me who was boss." Tait put the family Bible in his saddlebag. "He went to work for Richard Markham III, owner of the railroad, shortly after that. We went separate ways, and I lost touch until I married Lucy."

Then the devil had reared his ugly head and unleashed terror like he'd never seen.

Hondo caught the mama cat, set her into the box with her kittens, and closed the lid after making sure they could get air. The men mounted up without further conversation.

Tait spared a mournful glance back at the house as he galloped away. He prayed that Claire would forgive him for bringing death down on her. Then his thoughts turned to Melanie.

Kern was not getting to her or the children. Tait would make sure of it.

Twelve

THE NEXT MORNING, TAIT TELEGRAPHED CLAY BEFORE THEY left Flat Rock, warning him to keep an eye out for strangers. With Hondo's drawings of the horses' hooves safe in his pocket, he and Jack saddled up. After making a quick stop by the cemetery on their way out of town, they rode hell bent for Hope's Crossing. Darkness had settled in by the time they arrived, and Tait was relieved to see two men stationed at the town's entrance in the canyon.

"You boys look a mite tired," Skeet Malloy, the town blacksmith, said. "Everything's quiet here."

Tait rested his forearm on the pommel. "That's good. I guess Clay has replacements arranged."

Dallas Hawk grinned. "Yep. Just like old times. Say, what kind of trouble is coming?"

"Kern Berringer and his bunch."

Malloy let out a whistle. "Heard about them. We'll be on our toes."

Melanie and the kids must've been watching out the hotel window because Tait had barely begun to unsaddle his horse when Joe and Jesse ran up, skidding to a stop.

The twins talked his ears off, catching him up on their circus and their trap-making. Melanie held Becky and watched everything with a smile on her face. Tait didn't miss the hitch in her breath and recalled the kisses he'd pressed to her lips and how they'd molded to his.

All of a sudden he didn't know what to say to this woman he'd sent for sight unseen. He kept his focus on the children and getting his horse brushed and fed.

Finally, the twins slowed down and Joe's face turned solemn. "Did you see our old house?"

"Yes, I did. We'll talk about that in a minute." Tait finished his chore and followed Jack into the barn, leading his blue roan.

Nora and her children arrived out of breath to greet Jack. The women discussed their day while they waited for Tait and Jack, and the little ones played together. Tait caught part of the ladies' conversation and their worry that trouble was coming. Evidently Clay had told them enough to put them on guard.

Becky came running when Tait left the barn. He scooped her up and gave her a hug. "I've missed you, girl."

"Home." She pointed to the hotel and then patted his cheeks. "My wuncle."

He turned to Melanie. "You're a sight for sore eyes, Mrs. Trinity."

Her cheeks pinked. "I'm glad you're back. The children missed you." She took his elbow, and the twins fell into step with them. "Are you hungry?"

"Tired, dirty, and starving. We rode those horses hard trying to get here."

"What's happening, Tait? Clay only told me to not venture too far from the hotel."

"Wait until we're alone and I'll explain." He made a bee-line to the café, thankful it was still open even though only one other couple were there eating.

While he ate, he told the twins that he'd seen their kittens and the sheriff had taken them and their mother into town.

"I'm glad the bad men didn't kill them too." Joe frowned and took a drink of milk.

Jesse propped his elbow on the table. "I'll bet Tilda was hungry looking after her kittens all alone."

"I'm sure she caught some mice. She didn't look skinny. We'll find you another cat when we get our house built. Would you like that?" After what they'd been through, Tait would make sure the children were happy.

"Can we have a dog too?" Joe pressed.

"Goggy!" Becky clapped, her baby teeth shining.

Tait wiped off her milk mustache and kissed her forehead. Man, it was good to be home. "The sheriff is going to pack up your things and get them out here to us."

"I hope he remembers my yo-yo and marbles," Jesse said.

"I'm sure he will." Tait laid a hand on the boy's sandy hair.

"Sheriff Rains gave your mother and father a nice service, and I went by the cemetery before I headed out to pay respects. When Becky's a little older, I'll take you to see their graves."

Joe sat back in his chair, his face dark. "Do we hafta wait for Becky?"

Their sister crossed her arms and gave them a scowl.

"Yes, we have to wait for her." Tait wiped his mouth and rose, putting some money on the table. "Let's get you to bed."

He carried Becky, and they went over to the hotel. A hundred questions filled Melanie's eyes. Questions he didn't have any answers for.

Part of him was still out there in the vast rugged darkness, and he didn't know if he'd find his way back.

Melanie lay in bed, waiting for Tait to bathe. She hoped he wouldn't shave off the scruff along his jaw. That and his hair that was a little too long made him look even more dangerous, more handsome.

Part of her yearned to tell him about the box with Ava's hair and the tooth, but then her carefully orchestrated ball of wax would unwind. And Tait didn't appear in any condition to hear more bad news. The mess with McIlroy was hers to resolve.

He had yet to share the rest of his news with her. Clay had frightened her when he came with that dire warning to stay close to the hotel, but he hadn't told her anything else. And now Tait wore this haunted look in his silver-gray eyes.

At last he returned to the room, and she was happy to see water droplets clinging to the stubble that was still there. Without a word he turned out the lamp, undressed, and slid into bed. A shaft of moonlight came in through the window, giving her something to see by.

"I know you're tired, Tait, but you said you'd tell me what's going on. Am I in danger? Clay certainly seemed to think so."

"You could be." He lay on his back, staring up at the ceiling. He let out a heavy sigh, and when he spoke, his voice was low and raw. "The bastards tortured my sister."

The words shot fear through her. "Tortured her?"

He told her what they'd done to Claire. "They left behind certain items that only I would know the meaning of. I'm sure now that they killed her to shake me up. They wanted to hurt me, and going after the ones I love is a surefire way to do that. I don't care what they do to me. I can take it. But I can't take making the ones I love suffer."

"What things did they leave?"

"I'd rather not talk about it. I'm in a real bad place. Good night, Melanie."

Frustration wound through her. She hadn't had a chance to ask him any of her other questions—about whether he'd been married before, the bloody shawl, any of it. This new coldness in him scared her and put a chasm between them.

He lay there, a thousand miles away. Just staring up, not moving a muscle. Eyes unblinking.

Whoever had killed his sister had best run, far and fast. No one had to tell her what would happen to them otherwise. Hurt and filled with rage, Tait would be like a wounded animal that knew only one reaction—to strike back.

The results could be deadly.

When she thought her heart would break for him, he reached for her hand, and her fear settled.

Melanie awoke the next morning to an empty bed. Maybe Tait had waited until she'd drifted off and gone out again.

She drew his pillow to her face and inhaled his scent of wild sage, leather, and all man.

Her soul heavy, she dressed and left the bedroom. The sitting area was also empty. Sounds of the children stirring reached her, and she went to get them dressed.

"Where's Uncle Tait?" Jesse asked.

Not wanting to divulge that she didn't know, Melanie took a stab. "He had to go out early. I think Jack needed him."

"Will he eat breakfast with us?"

"Sure. He'll meet us over there." Melanie prayed he didn't

make a liar out of her, but she didn't see him anywhere as they made their way to the café.

They were halfway through their meal when he strode into the eatery, his bootheels striking the wooden floor, his heavy gun hanging from his side.

Bags under his eyes told the story. Melanie wanted to wrap her arms around him and tell him—what exactly? That she had a secret? That she knew more about what drove him than he knew? That she had to have the money he'd stolen before she could be a faithful wife?

Hellfire! Speak of any part of her treachery and she'd add more to the heavy burden he already carried.

"Sorry I'm late." After greeting the kids, he met her gaze. "I was figuring up how much lumber we'd need for that house I promised you, and I lost track of time. I need to get it ordered so we can begin building."

It shouldn't have made her so happy to hear that he was moving ahead with the house plans despite everything else weighing on him. Yet it showed he valued her, cared about her happiness. That meant more than he'd ever, ever know.

"Do you want to do this now with everything going on?" Melanie wiped Becky's mouth with a napkin.

"No, but it has to be done. You're probably wanting to have your own things around you and a kitchen where you can cook. Eating here will get old. I want to do the right thing by you."

Guilt rose and Melanie swallowed hard. Then the boys started telling Tait all about their circus and asking his advice about a dozen different problems they were trying to work out. After that, Becky had to have equal time, laughing and patting his arm.

Frustration bit into Melanie. Any further questions she had for him were going to have to wait.

❧

Over the next week, Melanie mostly slept alone. When Tait was in the bed, he did nothing but lie there, staring up at the ceiling, not saying a word. Not touching her. Was this cold distance going to define their marriage?

After one such night, she rose in the wee hours of morning before the children awoke, dressed, and went looking for him. She found him guarding the entrance to the town.

"What are you doing here? Is something wrong?" He stared at her with haunted eyes. "Are the children all right?"

"They're fine." Melanie drew her shawl tight around her shoulders. "We have to talk."

"About?"

"You and me. You've hardly said two words to me since you've been back, and when you do come to our bed, you don't speak or act like I'm there."

"I've got a lot on my mind."

"You came back from your sister's a different man. You don't touch me. Tait, we still haven't been together as husband and wife. Is it me? Don't you want me?"

Tait brushed her cheek with a knuckle. "No, it's not you. Like I said, I'm in a bad place and not fit company right now. Being at Claire and John's house made everything real. Each time I close my eyes, I see how Claire must've looked after they finished with her. I hear her pleading with them to stop or begging with them not to hurt her children. No one had more love than Claire. She was special."

"When are you leaving next?"

"Truth to tell, I'm not sure." Tait sighed and looked up at the stars. "If I knew where Kern Berringer was hiding out, I'd have left already. The man's like a phantom. Hondo—the sheriff of Flat Rock—is searching for him, and Jack sends out telegrams every day to different towns asking for information."

The moon ducked behind a cloud, and Tait's face was hidden in the darkness. She couldn't make out his expression, but it was probably stone cold, his eyes as hard as his words.

"What are you thinking? Why can't you find him?"

"He's protected by railroad officials. He could be anywhere up and down the line. It would be like looking for one sweet pea in a whole pot full of green beans."

"So, you're just waiting."

"My gut says he's coming here. He'll have to because I have no one else left for him to hurt me with."

No one but her and the kids. Melanie shivered. "Describe the despicable man so I can spot him."

Tait was silent so long she almost gave up on him answering. Finally, he spoke, his low voice bathed in loathing. "Easiest way to know him is that he's hairless. No eyebrows, no hair on his head, no facial hair. Not one speck. He shaves new growth off every morning. Forties and shorter than me." A smile curved his mouth. After a long pause, he added, "Walks with a limp."

"He'll sure stand out. Why am I sensing you know something about the limp?"

The smile vanished, and Tait's voice hardened. "I gave it to him."

A chill raced through Melanie and knotted her insides. Her husband had a dark side, to be sure, one that made people who crossed him very sorry indeed. Oh, God! Maybe it wouldn't be that bad if she confessed what she'd come for—before he found out.

Grasshoppers, cicadas, and frogs filled the air with racket. Melanie knew she had to go back to the hotel soon, but she loved being there with Tait. For some reason, it was easier to talk to him out in the open like this. He tended to close up when he was around people, and walls seemed to choke him.

A small voice in her head whispered, *Be honest. Tell him about the deal with Judge McIlroy and your sister's plight. Maybe he'll help instead of being angry.* It was worth a try.

"Tait, can we talk? I have a confession."

"Always feel free, Mellie." A smile was in his words, and she imagined he wore a crooked grin. "You know, I like Becky's way of saying your name."

"I confess that I've never cared for nicknames. Not just for me, but in general."

"That's not the confession that you wanted to make though. What do you want to talk about?"

Her stomach knotted. "Will you promise to try to understand?"

The moon emerged from the clouds, and the soft moonlight showed a wary expression lining what she could see of his face. His jutting jaw and rigid body said he was bracing himself. He pushed his hat back from his forehead, and her courage fled. His brooding expression coupled with his reputation did nothing to calm her nerves.

His quicksilver eyes narrowed. "What have you done, Melanie?"

Thirteen

MELANIE MOVED A STEP BACK, HER GAZE LOCKED ON TAIT'S ICY stare. She shivered in the moonlight that bathed the outlaw she'd married. Why had she thought she could escape his wrath?

This would end badly for her. For both of them.

"What have you done, Melanie?" he repeated. "I think you'd best tell me."

"Well, I don't know where to start." She licked her dry lips.

"At the beginning."

She gave him a weak smile and a false laugh. "You know, this can wait. We don't have to discuss it now. There will be a lot of better times."

How could she tell him when he was already getting upset? The best thing to do would be to keep quiet, keep looking for the money, and take it to Judge McIlroy as soon as she found it. She'd tell McIlroy that Tait rode out one dark night and she didn't know where he'd gone. Yes, that was a better plan.

Only Tait was looking at her with that piercing stare that made her want to crawl into a hole.

"Now is fine," he insisted.

Footsteps crunched on the ground behind her. A man spoke. "Trinity, Jack and Clay need a word right away. They're waiting for you at the corrals."

Melanie turned enough to see the speaker, the black-clad outlaw named Ridge Steele. They'd only met briefly, but she liked the man. He wore twin Colts that had apparently been well used. An ex-preacher, she'd been told, who'd long given up the pulpit.

"Be right there." Tait released a low curse. "We'll talk later, and I want the truth. Whatever you did isn't the end of the world, but I need to know. Don't keep secrets from me."

She raised her chin a trifle. "Or you from me."

"What's that supposed to mean?"

"Just what I said. I think you left something out when we spoke before about our pasts. Maybe I'm not the first Mrs. Trinity."

A threatening rumble rose from Tait's mouth, and she was glad for an audience.

Ridge Steele shifted uncomfortably. "They're waiting, Trinity. It's important."

Travis Lassiter emerged from the dark gloom. "I'll take over guard duty."

Without another word, Tait whirled and strode away with Ridge. Melanie released the breath she'd been holding. Her gaze followed her husband, admiring his figure. Lord, would he be mad when he learned she was after the money he'd stolen. Worse than mad. Enraged.

If she could ever find it. That had to come first.

She returned to the hotel, wracking her brain. Where had he hidden it? Her gaze scanned the dark landscape and the million hiding places it offered. Unless she followed him to his loot, she'd never find it. She blew out an exasperated sigh.

This called for a plan that would make him go after it. That, or else confide in him like she'd started to.

That thought again sent panic racing through her. Even though she knew he would never lay a hand on her, sometimes the ice in Tait Trinity's eyes struck fear in her heart.

Tait pondered Melanie's words all the way to the corrals. Her conscience was clearly bothering her, and she'd done something he probably wouldn't like. Had she made some decision about the children without consulting him?

Or maybe she'd decided to leave town.

His heart twisted. Hell, he wouldn't blame her. He hadn't paid her much attention, and as she'd pointed out, they still hadn't consummated their marriage.

How in God's name had she found out about Lucy?

No one in town except Jack knew about her, not even the other men's wives.

"Did you say something, Trinity?" Ridge asked, matching Tait's long stride.

"Nope." Hell! Had he been mumbling under his breath like some decrepit old man?

Jack and Clay had horses saddled at the corrals by the time Tait and Ridge got there. "What's up?"

Jack thrust the reins of Tait's blue roan at him. "Shaughnessy pounded on my door no more than thirty minutes ago and handed me a telegram from Hondo. He heard from a reliable source that Kern Berringer and his boys are camped at the Washita River and wants our help bringing them in."

Excitement buzzed along Tait's veins. "How sure is he about this?"

"Pretty darn sure." Clay stuck his foot in the stirrup. "Ridge, keep an eye on things around here. Especially the riffraff."

"I'll try my best," Ridge promised. "I don't know if getting a stage line out this way was a blessing or a curse. More bad seeds are coming in that way than by horse. Sure keeps a man busy."

"Gives us something to do." Tait swung into the saddle. "Will you tell Melanie I had to leave and keep an eye on her and the kids?"

Ridge scowled. "Yeah, I reckon, but I don't want her trying to pick a fight with me. It looked like she was about ready to slug you a minute ago. She's not what I call a meek woman."

Tait chuckled. "Hell, she scares the piss out of me too, Ridge."

She was a bit too direct, but she was the kind of woman Tait needed, one who would call him out on things, however uncomfortable. Like him keeping the story of his first wife hidden. He wished he knew how she'd found out.

"We should be back by sundown." Jack glanced at Clay and Tait. "Let's ride."

They galloped from the town and picked their way across the landscape. This area was riddled with gullies and ravines, and one misstep could land them at the bottom with a broken limb—or neck.

Tait thought about Melanie. He'd have to tell her about Lucy when he returned. Dammit, there was no way around it. It wasn't a secret as such. He just didn't want to pry the lid off that can of worms. The pain—his guilt for not protecting her—was all too raw to poke around in for long.

They rode at a steady pace and reached the Washita River a little after sunup. Hondo and two of his men joined up with them.

"We'll have to spread out and find their camp." Hondo pointed to Tait. "You, Jack, and Colby go west. Me and my men will head east. Don't spook them."

A muscle worked in Tait's jaw. "It'll take too long for you to get into place. If I see the murdering bastards, I'm going to open fire."

"Dammit!" Hondo spat in the dirt. "Jack, Tait's your responsibility. We'll come running if we hear shots."

They split up, and Tait rode downriver next to his partners, scanning the banks. The water was swift and muffled the sound of movements.

A splash quickly followed by three more alerted Tait.

"Someone's shooting at us!" He spurred his roan out of range, leapt off, and hurried back through the tall grass that grew on both sides of the river with Jack and Clay beside him.

More shots rang out as they neared the spot of the previous barrage. Tait got low to the ground, scouring the brush and trees. When orange flame burst into the darkness from a barrel, he fired.

Someone yelled, letting Tait know he'd gotten at least one hit.

"Good work, Tait." Jack rose and took off running in a zigzag line toward the ones in hiding, drawing fire.

Tait and Clay had their pick of targets and let loose. When Jack took cover behind a tree, Tait rose and raced his way, firing as he went. He reached Jack's tree without a scratch.

A lull followed. Had the enemy snuck off? Then someone yelled from across the river, "That you, Trinity?"

"Who are you?"

"The ones that killed sweet Claire. Lord, she was a fighter. I wish we could'a spared the time to get acquainted."

The voice sounded fairly young. Maybe one of Berringer's sons.

"Show your face, coward." The sound of riders came up behind him. Tait didn't turn, didn't take his eyes off the vegetation where the speaker was hiding. Logic said the riders were Hondo Rains and his men, or Jack and Clay would already be shooting.

A second later, Hondo spoke low at Tait's elbow. "How many are there?"

"Three at least, I'm guessing," Jack answered for him.

"They're probably holding us up to give Kern time to get away. Damn, I want them bad." Hondo dropped to his belly and crawled forward.

Another time swept into Tait's memory—a time when old man Berringer had forced him to crawl while he and his boys used Tait for target practice. He clenched his jaw so hard he thought he broke it. He was done with crawling. He removed his hat and dove from cover into the water.

Bullets landed around him. Holding his gun above the rippling current, he ducked beneath the surface and kept pushing toward the other bank, coming up to gasp for air several times before going back under. The men behind him would keep the shooters pinned down. But evidently not well enough.

A sudden, stinging pain along his ribs told him he'd been grazed, but he didn't stop. All he had to do was reach the shore. At last he met with the muddy riverbed and slipped into the thickness of nearby brush. A glance at his wound assured him it wasn't serious. Fine. He'd deal with it later. He made his breathing shallow and listened.

"Trinity's over here on this side," came a whisper. "I just know it."

"This is too hot for me," said a much younger man. "I'm getting out of here."

"Pa said to hold 'em off."

"I don't give a rat's ass. I've already got one bullet in me. Hurts bad."

Tait grinned and moved up a little higher on the bank to get a better angle.

The speaker gave a disgusted snort. "You ain't nothing but a whiny peckerwood, Earl."

Earl was ready to bolt, and when he did, Tait would get him. Rustling and whispers came from just ahead. A man rose and took off scrambling over dead trees and brush.

Tait gave chase, took aim, and fired, glad the water hadn't affected his weapon.

The bullet entered high on the man's shoulder, and Tait's target sprawled on the ground. Three other shooters raced toward some horses, leaped into the saddles, and galloped off. Tait kicked away the wounded man's gun and took off after them, firing until his Smith & Wesson ran out of bullets.

By the time he returned to the fallen man, the rest of Tait's group had crossed the Washita.

Hondo yanked the wounded man to his feet. "Well, well. Earl Berringer. What do you have to say for yourself?"

"I'm hurt. I need a doctor."

"You're a long way from one of those." Jack handed Tait his hat. "Nice shooting."

"Thanks." Tait adjusted his Stetson on his head, feeling better. Earl stared at him with sullen eyes. He didn't resemble hairless Kern in the least. On the contrary, Earl had an overabundance of hair that hung down to his shoulders and protruded from every exposed crevice of his body, giving him the appearance of some kind of mountain man.

Tait didn't recall ever seeing him before. He stood in front of Earl with fists clenched. "Who yelled that stuff about my sister?"

"Wasn't me. I think it was my brother Richard. Or it could'a been cousin Leo. Yeah, come to think of it, cousin Leo must'a been the one."

Tait grabbed Earl's shirt and yanked him forward until they

stood nose to nose. "I'm only going to ask once. Were you there when my sister was tortured? Did you take part?"

Earl's Adam's apple bobbed painfully. "No, I swear."

"Why should I believe you?"

"They left me at the turn in the road as a lookout. Said I didn't have the stomach for killing. I wasn't there."

"But you know who and why. Talk."

"A doctor first."

Tait closed his fists around Earl's throat and tightened his hold. Earl's eyes bulged, and his face took on a blue tint. He struggled but couldn't get free.

"Turn loose of him, Tait!" Jack tried to pull him off.

A second before Earl passed out, Tait released him. Earl gasped for air and fell to the ground.

Jack knelt down. "Tell him what he wants to know, or I'll stand by and let him kill you."

"I'll talk. I'll talk." Earl rubbed his neck. "John Abraham used to ride with us for a while. He was the best safecracker in the business. Pa went there to try to get him to come with us on a big job, but John turned him down flat, said he was a family man now. We left and the next day went back. John came out, and Pa shot him dead."

"Why did you kill Claire?" Tait snarled. "Why?"

"She ran out of the house with a rifle and shot Uncle Max. Pa took the gun away from her, and they decided to have a little fun. Some of the men carried her back into the house, but she wouldn't stop screaming and fighting them."

Tait could see Claire doing that. Even as a girl, she was like a wildcat and never gave up, even when the odds were against her. "What else did they do, Earl?"

"She pulled a knife from her pocket and stabbed my cousin in the arm." Earl blinked hard. "Everyone went kinda crazy trying to make her pay." He glanced up. "It wasn't our fault. If she'd been meeker, she'd be alive. She brought it on herself."

Jack grabbed Tait when he lunged at Earl again. "That's enough."

Tait breathed hard. "You sorry piece of shit, tell me why

someone pinned the railroad badge on Claire's dress and left Lucy's wedding ring."

"Because you killed my brothers and left Pa crippled." Earl sniffled and wiped his nose on his shirt. "He said it would be a reminder of what you took from him."

"I found their camp over here!" Clay yelled. "Coffee's still on. Want a cup?"

So they'd surprised them. Kern was getting sloppy. That put a smile on Tait's face. He flung Earl at Hondo. Next time he'd get Kern. Anticipation of seeing that hairless bastard beg for his life hummed inside him. He still burned to get proper justice for Lucy and Claire.

That day couldn't come soon enough.

⁂

The morning sun shone through the hotel windows, splashing bright rays inside. Thank goodness Becky had wanted to play with Willow Bowdre. It gave Melanie time to think.

She paced the floor of the bedroom, trying to calm herself. She was furious at Tait for not telling her he was riding out and sending Ridge to deliver the news instead. Like she was some mere acquaintance, unworthy of his time.

She didn't begrudge Tait the chance to catch his sister and brother-in-law's killer.

No, she wanted the murderers punished for what they'd done. What made her angry was his treatment of her. He'd ignored her for days and now this. Were they married or not? It sure didn't seem like it. His promise to not ride off and leave her with the kids hadn't meant anything. She felt more like a nanny than a wife.

Melanie stopped pacing. Why was she so all-fired mad? This marriage was only temporary. She shouldn't get so worked up over something that wouldn't last.

But, damn it, she wanted—what exactly?

Tears burned the backs of her eyes. She yearned for a real marriage. Real belonging. A real husband. She wanted to lay claim to the fake life she'd stepped into.

And now their last face-to-face talk had made her say things she hadn't intended. She dreaded his return. Dear God! He'd force her hand. She'd have to reveal that she'd snooped in his belongings. Then he'd ask why she'd done it, and that would lead to the big secret.

Air. She needed air.

Melanie smoothed her hair in the mirror, grabbed a shawl, and went out for a stroll. She made it halfway down the boardwalk to the mercantile when a well-dressed man with a gun strapped to his hip blocked her path. He was the kind that, even though wearing silk and fine wool, appeared dirty, cheap.

"I hear congratulations are in order, Mrs. Trinity." He gave her a cold smile and grabbed her upper arm. "We have things to discuss that require privacy. Unless you want these fine people to know why you're posing as a bride, you'd best talk to me right now."

Her heart raced. She tried to jerk away, but he held her fast. "Who are you?"

He took a step closer and placed his mouth to her ear. "Call me Spade. Judge McIlroy sent me."

Melanie glanced around to see if anyone was watching and noticed Ridge striding toward them, his features dangerous, his frock coat flapping against his thighs.

"If I were you, I'd take my hands off the lady, mister." Ridge's steely threat was the kind not easy to ignore.

Spade gave him an oily smirk and let her go. "We're having a friendly conversation."

Ridge's hand moved toward one of his twin Colts, resembling a coiled snake ready to strike. "I didn't see anything friendly about it. We don't treat our womenfolk like that around here."

Tension was thick in the air, and people had stopped to stare. Spade started to go for his gun.

She did the only thing she knew to defuse the situation—she laughed. "Oh good heavens, Ridge. This is a cousin—several times removed. A bit uncouth but no threat. My honor doesn't need defending."

Ridge relaxed his stance. "Then I apologize. I'll be around if he steps out of line."

"I do believe he's leaving on the afternoon stage, isn't that right, Spade?"

Anger flashed in the man's strange, birdlike eyes, and for a moment he appeared about to dispute her word. But he quickly tamped down his temper. "Yes, I regret that I can't stay. Such a nice town."

Once Ridge walked on, Melanie grated low, "You've got to be stupid. These outlaws will kill you and gut you like a fish in nothing flat if they get an inkling that you came to harm anyone. I'll give you five minutes. No more."

"I have the full weight of the law behind me."

"Do you think they care a fig about that? Good Lord, man, use your damn head."

They entered the hotel lobby and huddled in a secluded corner where no one could hear but where she'd have help should she need it. "Why have you come?" Melanie demanded.

"The judge is an impatient man. He wants results, and he wants them fast."

"For God's sake, I haven't been married to Tait more than a few days, not near long enough to gain his trust. I haven't found anything significant yet."

"Drag your feet and you'll regret it."

"If he doesn't like the way I'm doing things, then I suggest he come and find the money himself."

"I don't have to remind you that your sister is sitting in jail. She's gotten sick and isn't eating. Every day she asks about your progress. I fear she'll lose hope soon. I don't know what my report of 'nothing significant' will do to her sagging spirits." His voice dropped lower. "I assume you got the mementos the judge sent you. Next time I can assure you it'll be a finger or an ear."

Melanie's heart lurched, and pain pierced her chest until she could barely breathe. Ava had never been very strong, and now her situation had grown too desperate. She had to get

Ava out. Somehow. Some way. She couldn't let the judge start cutting off body parts.

Nausea brought bile into her mouth, and she struggled to swallow.

If Melanie trusted Spade, she'd write a note to Ava telling her it would be over soon. But Spade would never give it to her. That much she knew. Eyes told a lot about a person, and his spoke of treachery and evil.

Melanie glared. "I think you're lying. This is a ploy to put more pressure on me."

Spade moved his chair closer, his face dark and threatening. "Do you want to bank on that? You're a gambler, Melanie. Look at the hand you're holding and tell me if it's good enough to win. Tell me if I'm bluffing."

She raised her chin and scooted away from him. "I will get the job done, and I know what's at stake without you reminding me. There's no need for this ugly business. Now get the hell out of here and tell the judge he'll get his money in good time."

But if she had her way, he would never get Tait.

Fourteen

THE SKY APPEARED THE COLOR OF A DEEP-PURPLE BRUISE WHEN Tait rode home that evening. After the men had discussed the situation, Hondo decided to bring Earl Berringer to Hope's Crossing since its fortress walls offered better security than Flat Rock. Blocking the entrance would stave off any attack, and once inside, no one could touch them.

Papa Berringer would be itching to get his boy out of jail any way he could. Even risk death to do it. Tait prayed he'd try. Just once.

"Earl, you're a lucky man." Jack untied his hands from the pommel.

"Why's that?"

"You'll be the first to try out our brand-new jail."

They finished it six months ago but never had cause to use it—until now.

Earl glanced around, his gaze drawn to the outdoor cell made of strap iron. "I gotta have a doctor. You said I'd get one when we got here. I'm in terrible pain. You can't expect me to survive out in the open, exposed to the rain and hail and what all."

"You mean bullets?" Tait asked.

"Well, yeah. Ain't no walls to stop 'em."

Hondo handcuffed Earl. "Oh, I imagine you'll be fine, a tough man like yourself."

"I really have a weak constitution. I take after my poor old mama."

"Then we'll toughen you up." Jack winked at Tait. "And this way you'll have a front-row seat when we kill your daddy. I imagine he'll bust through the town's entrance with guns blazing."

Earl shook his head. "You're a cruel man, Jack Bowdre. Cruel. The whole lot of you."

Joe and Jesse raced up, both out of breath.

"Is he one of the murderers?" Jesse asked Tait.

Tait took in the boys' hard faces and put an arm around each. "He admits to being there but says he took no part in the killing. Did you see him at your house?"

The boys were silent. Joe stepped closer to Earl, eying the outlaw. "I cain't be sure."

"What'cha looking at, boy?" Earl snarled. "Go find your mama."

"She's dead, and you know it!" Joe launched himself at Earl, kicking and slapping.

Tait pulled him off. Joe just wanted someone to hit, and it didn't matter who. "Save your anger for the rightful ones."

"You're John's boys?" Earl looked confused. Maybe air wasn't reaching his brain.

Jack had been right when he'd said no one could accuse the whole bunch of Berringers of having an overabundance of smarts.

"We were his kids." Jesse joined his brother. "You ain't fit to wipe his boots, mister."

Earl smirked. "You didn't know him that well. Your daddy was one of us."

"You're a liar!" Joe screamed.

Before Tait could stop himself, he grabbed Earl's shirt and yanked the man so close the stench of his breath and body odor gagged him. "I'd watch what I say to kids fresh in grief."

Hondo yelled, "Let him go, Tait!"

"For now." Tait shoved the man into the sheriff. Then he put an arm around each twin and walked away.

The boys talked a mile a minute, asking one question after another. Tait unsaddled the horses while Jack and Hondo got their guest situated and his wound looked after. He glanced toward the hotel and thought he saw Melanie watching from the upstairs window. But maybe he was just beat down to the bone and seeing things.

He was back, but now what?

Had she left him? Neither Joe nor Jesse mentioned her, and

he didn't have the courage to ask. He realized he'd find a hole in his life if she had. Although they hadn't been married but a short time, he wanted her near. The lady gambler had started to grow on him. Plus she was good with the kids and kept their rooms neat and tidy.

But sometimes a strange sadness crossed behind her eyes and she looked ready to cry.

One thing for sure—if she stayed, he'd come clean about Lucy. He kicked himself for holding back.

Whatever *she'd* done and kept from him couldn't be that bad.

Hell! She didn't deserve a bastard like him. Either he was in this marriage all the way or he'd do the decent thing and send her back to her life. It was time to let the hide go with the tallow.

He finished with the horses and headed to the hotel. The air sparked with Earl's cursing, but Dr. Mary was the one tending to him, and she was giving back as good as she got. One tough woman there.

Tait and the twins entered the hotel and climbed the stairs. The door flew open before he could reach for the knob, and Becky threw herself at him.

He chuckled. "Hey, I wasn't gone that long."

"Wuncle! Hold."

Tait scooped her up and kissed her cheek. "I missed you, peanut! What's been going on around here?"

Jesse grinned. "We have a bunch to tell you."

"Yeah, Bandit got out of his cage and ran into Mrs. Truman's house." Joe laughed. "He ate her fresh-baked bread and broke stuff. She was real mad."

"Of that I'm sure. Refresh my memory...who exactly is Bandit?" Tait had never gotten a welcome like this, and he loved it. Mellie stood in the doorway watching it all, a smile on her face and dimples in her cheeks. This was family.

"He's one of the raccoons." Jesse huffed. "He likes to open all the animals' cages and let 'em out."

Tait could just picture the chaos.

Becky patted his arm, demanding her turn.

"What is it, honey?"

"Love you."

Tait swallowed hard, his heart swelling. "I love you too."

How had he managed the unbearable loneliness of his life before they came? He realized that was one of the reasons he'd turned to liquor—and why it had never been enough no matter how many bottles he'd emptied. Nothing could substitute for what he'd just now found with these kids and Melanie.

He went inside and set Becky down then turned to his wife. "I practiced what I'd say to you all the way home, only now that I'm here I can't remember any of it. I'm glad you didn't walk out on me as I feared you might. You had good reason."

"I considered it for all of a minute." A teasing glint lit up her eyes, and she wore a big smile. "But I didn't want to leave an opening for another woman."

"How about we start over?" He put an arm around her and pulled her in for a kiss.

The heat came to the surface in a flash, and he didn't know which end was up. All he knew was that he didn't want to stop. Melanie Dunbar had him in her clutches, and he didn't want to escape.

But Becky was clinging to his leg, and the twins were yelling for his attention. With regret, he released Melanie. "After we get these kids to bed, you and me are having a long talk."

"I'm all for that. But let me take a look at the source of that blood."

"It's nothing to fret about." He stilled, watching hurt cross her face, and he softened his voice. "I'm fine. Really."

She blinked and turned away. "Are we doomed to fight about everything?"

"No. You're welcome to look to your heart's content." He sat down and rolled up his sleeve, stiff with dried blood. "The bullet only grazed me. I think the water created a bit of a shield."

"What were you doing in the water?"

"Swimming. We were on one shore, and the Berringers on the other."

"Good heavens."

Becky leaned against his knee. "Hurt?"

"No, honey. It doesn't hurt."

Melanie mumbled something about Tait not feeling things like ordinary people, and she went for some water to wash the wound. He started to tell her that he was going to go bathe and would wash it then but knew his protests would do no good, so he held his tongue.

He suspected she needed someone to fuss over. Women tended to do that when they were nervous. As much as he hated it, he'd let her. Then they'd have to talk once the kids were in bed.

When she returned, he raised his shirt and sat patiently while she cleaned his wound. The bullet had taken a path along his lower ribs on the right side.

Melanie smelled of wild honeysuckle that grew in profusion across the prairie and down in ravines, and he wanted to pull her into his arms. Her gentle touch whispered over his skin like a summer breeze nudged by a river's rippling current.

"Thank you. This feels much better." He pulled his shirt down.

She gathered the pan of water and cloths. "You should get the doctor to look at it."

"For a scratch? Nope. She has more important things to do. She'd probably have a good laugh."

While the children took baths in the hotel, Tait gathered his things and went to the outdoor community bathing apparatus Jack had rigged up a few years ago. It consisted of poles in the ground, each set surrounded by walls of heavy burlap. Buckets of water sat on a high shelf, and when the bather needed to rinse, he pulled on a string and water gushed. They had to be the cleanest outlaws anywhere.

Tait stood in line with the other men, and when his turn came, he scrubbed every bit of dirt and blood from his body. Since everyone else had already eaten, he swung by the café for a quick bite. While he ate, he thought of what he'd tell Melanie about Lucy, praying he could get through the story without too much pain. He still found it hard to think about that gut-wrenching day. Even though three years had passed, he still woke up some nights dripping with sweat.

He didn't want to talk about it. To his way of thinking, the past was for the dead and the future for the living. But for Melanie, he'd do it.

Finally, he went back to the hotel and helped prod the kids toward bed. He listened while they said their prayers. All three asked God to tell their parents they loved them.

Joe ended his prayer with a deep sigh. "God, please tell Bandit he's not a kid and to quit opening all the cages or we'll never be able to have this circus."

For some reason, it struck Tait as funny that God would take an interest in one raccoon when there were so many serious things needing attention. But maybe Tait was wrong. Some things meant everything to a boy who'd lost it all.

At last, he and Melanie strolled toward their bedroom arm in arm. "You asked if I'd been married before. Let's go talk. I don't want the kids to hear this."

She nodded. They sat on the bed together, their backs against the headboard.

Tait took her small, delicate hand in his. "I didn't intend to mislead you. Jack is the only one who knows any of this, and the pain is as raw today as it was three years ago. I'm not at all sure I can talk about it." He turned to meet her gaze. "But I don't want anything to come between us. Yes, I was married before. Her name was Lucy. We lived on a piece of land up in western Kansas. I did a little farming, and we had a small herd of cattle—around a hundred head. It was nothing big, but we did okay, and we were well below the area where the Missouri River Railroad crossed."

Pictures swirled in Tait's head as he told the story. "One day railroad officials paid me and Lucy a call. Said they were dropping a spur line down to Dodge City and were going to run it straight across my land. I told them over my dead body."

Melanie shifted. "You said the railroad took your mother's land. Was this before or after?"

"After, so I already knew how they operated. I wasn't going

to just let them take what I had. Looking back, I wish I'd given them every last inch of my spread. Lucy was—" He swallowed the bitter taste in his mouth. "She was in the family way."

"Oh no!" Melanie clapped her hand over her mouth.

"I was proud. I insisted I would fight to the end if that's the way they wanted it. They kept threatening, each time bringing more and more men with them. Kern Berringer had been put in charge, and we tangled some. I shot two of his men, and that ratcheted things up to a fine level."

Tait took a deep breath to steady himself. "One day he and about a dozen riders galloped up with guns blazing—shooting cows, horses, dogs, anything that moved."

"The bastard!" Melanie spat.

"I opened a trapdoor to the cellar and put Lucy down there with a rifle. I held them off as long as I could, but there were too many. They shot me and dragged me out of the house. I heard screams, and saw them carrying Lucy, and I couldn't do one solitary thing to stop them.

"Kern Berringer told his railroad friends to have some fun. They formed two lines and made me crawl between them, kicking me mostly but one or two fired into me. I passed out, and they must've thought I was dead. When I came to, I saw—" Tait swallowed hard to control himself and finish what he had to say. But he couldn't stop the rushing memories and the tight panic in his chest.

Melanie squeezed his hand. "You don't have to do this. Please stop."

"No, you need to know exactly how deep this vendetta with Berringer goes." He jerked off the bed and went to the window, staring out at the blackness as dark as his mood.

"For God's sake, please stop," Melanie cried. "This is tearing you apart."

Tait's tongue worked in his dry mouth. "I saw Lucy… swinging…from the crossbar of our ranch." He broke down and sobbed. "She was dangling from the large wooden girder…our child…my beautiful Lucy. Hanging there like she was nothing—just a thing to discard." His shoulders shook.

Melanie's arms went around him, and she held him with tenderness he'd hadn't known for so many years. Tait clung to her and buried his face in her hair that carried the fragrant, life-affirming scent of the Texas land and wild honeysuckle.

"I'm so sorry," she whispered brokenly, her tears wetting his shirt.

He didn't know how long they held each other, but finally he regained the strength to speak. "Now you know the story." He led her back to the bed. "Thinking about that day rips the scab off a very large wound."

"How did you get to a doctor?"

"Jack found me barely alive. He hauled me into town, then buried Lucy for me."

"He's a good friend." She paused for a moment, thinking. "Why did they kill her? Their fight was against you."

"I heard she came out of the cellar and shot one of their men and killed him, but Kern Berringer never needed much of an excuse. He already hated me for crippling him."

"This is what drove you to rob trains. It wasn't so much your parents. It was Lucy."

"I wanted to break the money-grubbing railroad bastard. Still do, only I have the kids to consider now."

"I have a confession. I tried to tell you last night but couldn't." Melanie looked away. "I went to your sod house while you were gone to Flat Rock. I'm ashamed, but I did it." Her lip trembled. "I went through the boxes of women's things you had stacked in the corner." She glanced up. "I wanted to know the man I married. You tell me so little. I guessed you had a previous wife. I apologize."

After a long silence, he kissed her fingers. "I should've told you from the start. I'm not an easy person to get to know or live with."

Melanie laughed. "I don't think either of us are easy people."

The laughter died, and she kept her eyes on his. A wanting for something more darkened them. Maybe she wanted to be held. To be kissed. To be cherished. Most women wanted those things. But how much could he give for a man more dead than alive?

"I've sorely neglected my bride, it seems."

"You've been busy."

Tait trailed a finger along her arm and watched goosebumps rise. She shivered. "Are you cold?"

"No." She clutched his shirt and leaned in, barely breathing.

He swept her auburn hair aside and nibbled behind her ear, down her slender neck. Wild honeysuckle filled his senses.

"I've waited for this moment." She lowered her eyes, her lips parting.

Tait sucked her bottom lip into his mouth. Melanie released a gasp and slid her palms across his collarbones and down his chest. He trembled from her gentle touch. Releasing a growl, he pressed his mouth to hers.

He was burning alive with need, and he had to find a way to quench the hunger, praying she wouldn't change her mind and stop him. The kiss sent a strange quiver along his veins, and his heart beat faster. Despite their agreement that love wasn't a part of their marriage, there was a magnetism between them that he couldn't deny. It had been there on their wedding day, and it was here now.

He closed his eyes and felt the hurt and anger melt away.

It had been far too long since he'd listened to his needs. He slipped his tongue inside her parted mouth, and danced with hers in a mating ritual of sorts. He couldn't get enough of her. She was his every fantasy, every hope, every dream.

Melanie reached between them and closed her hand around his erection that jerked and turned painfully hard.

He broke the kiss then started on the row of buttons on her dress and removed it, caressing her warm flesh, kissing the swell of her breasts above the blue-satin tie of her chemise. One tug on the ribbon and it came loose. He pulled it off over her head.

Tait stared at her naked beauty, his breath hitching. Some men had a different woman every night, but Tait could count on one hand the women he'd taken his pleasure with. For him, the joining had to mean something. And this time definitely did.

He still needed to figure out whatever this was between him and Melanie, but something there was deep and real.

She worked to relieve him of his shirt then moved to his trousers. He laid her down and dropped next to her, shaking back the long hair that fell into his face. Every movement was slow and deliberate. He didn't want to hurry this.

At the beginning when Melanie first came, he'd thought making love to her would be a duty, not something to look forward to. But now, he almost burst with the need to kiss every inch of her luscious body.

His lips found hers again as his hands moved along her curves, exploring, savoring, molding each swell and dip.

A light caress across her flat stomach brought goosebumps to the surface.

He found a freedom with her. Melanie liked to be touched and wasn't afraid to admit it. Her response to him was openly enthusiastic, and that excited him.

Every movement slow, his fingertips brushed featherlike down her body, then he slid his palm across all that velvety skin. Every. Single. Inch. He explored her body, learning by her ragged breathing which areas were more sensitive than others.

And when he encountered the wispy curls that guarded the center of her being, she let out a soft cry. Tait weaved his fingers through the fine hair to touch flesh as soft as cottony down.

He traced her bow-like lips with his tongue and slid two fingers inside her.

Melanie gasped, pulling him closer. Her mouth closed around one of his nipples. Her tongue flicked over the hard nub, then her teeth grazed him. "Make love to me, Tait," she mumbled around his nipple. "Make me feel that I matter. I want you now."

Tait could hardly think for the strong suction of her mouth. He'd never been with a woman like this.

"Not yet," he rasped. He drew lazy circles on her flat stomach and down each shapely leg then kissed the underside of her arms, across the tender flesh covering her ribs. Her hard nipples strained for him, and he stroked them roughly with his tongue before drawing one then the other into his mouth.

"Please don't stop!" she cried in a fever pitch, arching her back.

He would have to stop soon, or he'd get carried away and end this too early, and he wanted to drag it out as long as possible. A man didn't get pleasured like this every day.

Melanie's touch was everywhere, searing his skin with her brand. Every stroke of her hand left a mass of sensation in its wake, twisting, swirling, settling through him.

Filled with insistent throbbing for her, Tait settled himself between her thighs and stared into her beautiful eyes. "Do you want this?"

"Yes. Please don't stop. I need you, Tait. I need to feel alive."

"You'll always matter to me sweetheart. After tonight you'll have no doubt." He lowered his mouth to hers and, locked in the kiss, pushed inside her wet warmth.

Her muscles clenched tight around him. Lord, she felt good, and it had been so long. She moved with him and they found a rhythm that would take them to the Promised Land.

Higher and higher he climbed.

Melanie arched her back, letting him go deeper. Touching. Pulling. Kissing him.

They were flesh against flesh, man against woman, heart against heart. Two people with a raw, aching need to feel alive.

Melanie gasped and cried out, shuddering beneath him.

Tait's being flooded with desire and longing. He too hurtled out of control, beyond a point of no return. Light burst around him, and for a little while, he found blessed peace.

For all he had once been, for all he now was and would ever be, this moment was branded forever on his memory.

Fifteen

Low light from the lamp beside the bed let Melanie see this beautiful man she'd married, his nicely formed body bare beside her. Skilled and caring, Tait Trinity had given her the happiest time of her life.

A sheen of sweat covered Melanie's skin, and her breath came fast and uneven, seeming to resist her efforts to calm it.

What the hell had just happened? She'd never been shaken like this. No one had ever made love to her with such gentleness. Tait's slow touch made her achy, and his kisses drugged her, heating her up inside like a glass of the finest bourbon.

Smooth. Slow. Hot.

Every bone in her body seemed to have turned to liquid.

Tait rested his head on her belly. Even through the haze of pleasure his confession about Lucy circled in her mind. She toyed with the soft strands of his freshly washed, sun-streaked hair and knew she was falling for him. Dammit! She couldn't afford to get emotionally invested. Common sense told her that.

She wasn't supposed to care. Dammit. Dammit. Dammit.

Melanie closed her eyes, soaking up the heat of his body. He'd seen so much heartache and despair. How in God's name could she tell him about her deceit now? She couldn't destroy him. She couldn't add to the losses he'd suffered, of Lucy and their child, his sister, and the hard work of raising these orphaned kids.

No, she'd wait and keep looking for the money. That was it.

Yet his words echoed in her head like a gong. *I don't want anything to come between us.*

Tait had exposed his raw, bleeding heart for her sake, and she still clung to her dark secret. Deep shame washed over her in waves.

She had to show him Ava's hair and tooth and tell him about the threat to chop off a finger. And soon.

Tait's knuckle brushed her cheek. "Thank you for your patience with me, Mellie. At least we'll be able to start on the house as soon as the lumber arrives. With as many men as we have, if it doesn't rain, it'll go up fast. Did you draw up some plans?"

She leaned on her elbow and pushed back his long hair that she loved so much. "I've made a few notes about certain things."

"Such as?"

"A big kitchen with water piped in and a cookstove. One with a warming oven above and a regular oven below."

Tait crooked an eyebrow. "Can you cook? I've never asked."

"I don't know. I've never had access to a kitchen. Once when I was young, we stayed with my grandmother. She let Ava and me help make cookies and pies. It was the best time of my life."

"What happened?"

"My father cheated at cards again, and barely escaped with his life. We had to leave half of our things behind." Including a locket Granny had given her for her birthday. Ava had been given the matching one, and it was only by luck that she'd been wearing it when they'd had to run.

"I know you must love your father, but he didn't seem to care much about you and Ava except when it was convenient."

"That's the crazy thing. I do love him. He could've dumped us with someone and taken off on his own at any time. But he didn't. He'd hold us and say that we were his good fortune. His lucky charms. He talked a lot about the importance of family and staying together through thick and thin."

"He's right." Tait released a deep sigh and moved up the bed to lie beside her. He took her in his arms. "That's why I have to do right by Jesse, Joe, and Becky. Sometimes family is all we have. When did you last see your father?"

The reminder that Mac Dunbar had done a vanishing act at the lowest point of their lives brought piercing pain. How could he have left them like that? Maybe she didn't know him very well anymore. "Two months ago."

She'd contacted Luke Legend shortly after and begun writing to Tait. Shoot, Mac could be in jail as well. Or dead. She'd always feared that someone would kill him over cards.

Tait placed a hand below her jaw and kissed her tenderly. She wanted to curl up beside him and stay forever. Forget about counting cards, keeping a low profile, winning enough to pay rent.

He ended the kiss and she wound her legs around his, laid a palm on his chest. "Back to the house plans. I want a bathing room like Jack and Nora's. Do you think we can have one?"

"You can have anything your little heart desires. That includes a bathing room. I only have one request."

"Oh? And what is it?" She drew circles on his chest.

"A large bed where my feet don't stick off the end. I hate small beds," he drawled.

"Good, because that was next on my list. A large bed requires a large room. We need plenty of space. I can't imagine how you lived in that tiny sod house of yours."

"It suited my needs at the time. I didn't require much."

"Me either." Just a bed and a place for her clothes. Going back to that empty life after Hope's Crossing would kill her.

"Who was the visitor in town? Ridge said he saw you with him and the man got rough."

Melanie jerked. Why had Ridge said anything? And to Tait of all people! What had she told Ridge? Sweat popped out on her forehead. Oh yes. "A very distant cousin I played cards with once. His last name is Spade. Never heard anything more than that."

"What did he want? Why did he put his hands on you?"

Think. Think. Think. What excuse could she give? "He claimed I owed him money." That wasn't a lie.

Tait lifted her hand off his chest and pressed a kiss to her palm. "I won't have anyone treating you with disrespect. Are you sure he left?"

She chewed on her bottom lip. No, she hadn't seen him

board the stage. She'd only assumed he'd keep his word. But what if he hadn't?

"I doubt he'll darken this town again. I think Ridge scared him good."

But if Spade had left and didn't return at some point, it'd be someone else. Judge McIlroy wouldn't let her forget their deal. And she couldn't forget Ava's hair and tooth under her bed.

⚬⚭⚬

Still glowing from making love to Tait, Melanie walked to the mercantile under a beautiful sky that afternoon, her thoughts on his skill at making her body hum.

When she was almost there, a man stepped out, blocking her path. Slade pulled her around the building. "I thought everything over and decided to stick around. Especially after I wired the judge and got his orders." His lips flattened in a thin smile.

Her heart jerked painfully against her ribs as initial panic swept through her.

Melanie looked around and noticed several of the men close by. They'd be there in an instant if she screamed. "I swear, you're the dumbest man walking on two legs."

"Watch it. Your sister's life is at stake. I can see that the judge kills her."

"No, you watch it." She glared and stood her ground, her chin raised. "I'll not be bullied. I can make sure you never leave here alive and be happy to do it." She stepped closer so he'd get the full force of her words. "All it'll take is one word from me, so back off."

Slade dropped his hold on her arm. She wouldn't say he was scared, but she could say with certainty she'd definitely gotten his attention.

Something she'd been pondering a lot over the past few hours swept to her mind. That hair and tooth might not belong to Ava. The judge could've gotten them from anyone. Just because the judge claimed they were Ava's didn't make it true. She felt better than she had in days.

"Now, excuse me. I have matters to attend to." She brushed past him then turned and smiled sweetly. "I'll give you until tomorrow morning to be gone. After that, I wouldn't give two cents for your life."

Slade quietly whirled and headed toward the hotel. Melanie let out the breath she'd been holding.

❦

In the days that followed, Tait seemed more relaxed and at peace than Melanie had ever seen him. Perhaps finally talking about Lucy had helped him come to terms with his wife's death. The darkness he'd lived with for so long seemed to have fled. He no longer shunned their bed, and that especially made her happy.

They almost seemed like a normal husband and wife.

He and the men tore down his old sod house and measured off the land for the one they were going to build. She even helped, and that made her feel useful. For a few moments she forgot her own dark cloud and the shadows that pressed close, at times strangling her. For a little while, she let a measure of happiness seep into her heart.

What she wouldn't give to be able to totally embrace this life with Tait.

But to do so meant she had to turn her back on Ava and throw her to the judge.

On a Thursday morning, she let Becky play with Violet Colby and Jenny Lassiter. Though Becky was quite a bit younger, she loved playing dolls with the older girls, and they were patient with her.

After making sure Becky was settled, Melanie headed toward the mercantile. Before she got there, Monty Roman burst from the newspaper office. "Mrs. Trinity! I remembered."

Her heart stopped. She forced herself to walk slowly toward him, and they met halfway. "You remembered what, Mr. Roman?"

"Where I saw you. It was outside the sheriff's office in Canadian."

Forcing herself to breathe and remain calm, Melanie put a finger on her chin and pretended ignorance. "I don't think so. Surely I would've recalled that. Did we speak?"

"I asked why you were crying and lent you my handkerchief."

Praying he didn't know about Ava's imprisonment, she smiled. "Oh dear, that must've been my twin sister. We look identical. Our father got into a scrape, and she needed money to get him out of jail." Please don't let him check out her story. It wouldn't take much for him to learn that Melanie's twin was locked up and for what.

Roman frowned. "I'm sorry I mistook you for her. You do look amazingly similar. I hope everything worked out with your father."

"Yes, it did, thank you."

The sunlight glistened on Roman's hair, the dark strands thick with pomade. "I have to say it's so refreshing to have you in the community. You add a certain class and charm that we didn't have before."

Melanie almost choked on her spit. If he only knew! "That's very kind of you to say, Mr. Roman. Now I must get to my shopping. Have a wonderful day."

He bade her farewell, and she hurried off. How many close calls would she have? Would it all end badly? The fortune-teller's prediction swept into mind. *Be true to a tall, handsome outlaw with silver eyes, or you'll find untold pain and despair.*

She wanted to come clean, but this wasn't the right time. Yet when would that time come?

How could she cause further pain to the man who continued to make such sweet love to her?

A loud commotion came from the strap-iron jail where Berringer was being held. She swung around to see Joe and Jesse standing in front of the cell. Berringer stretched his arm through one of the gaps trying to grab them. Though she stood some distance away, she could feel the man's hate.

A glance around the area failed to yield Tait, so she hurried to get the boys away from the despicable man. If the son was this bad, the father must be twenty times worse. And he hanged a pregnant woman. She shuddered, her heart breaking for Tait all over again.

Berringer railed as she got closer. "I took that mutt and snapped his neck just like this." He twisted his hands. "And I'll do it to you if you step closer, you little snot-nosed varmints."

Joe glared. "I ain't scared of you. I hope they hang you."

"Ain't anyone hanging me, boy." A string of cusswords flew from Berringer. "Did you know your daddy did some work for us? He was as sorry as the devil."

"Take that back!" Joe yelled.

Melanie reached the boys. "Come along. Leave him be."

Jesse dredged up a big spit wad and let it fly. It didn't make it inside the cage, but it got close.

"Stop that right this minute, young man!" Melanie grabbed his shoulder and pulled him back. "Find something else to do. If I catch you back over here, I'll…I'll keep you in your room for a week."

"My, my, what do we have here?" His hair wild about his head, Berringer closed a meaty fist around one of the flat bars of his cage. "Did you come to give me a kiss, missy? Come closer."

She tried to ignore the taunt and focus on the boys, who seemed drawn to the horrible man. "Let's go, boys."

"Cat got your tongue, missy?" Berringer called. "What's Mac Dunbar doing these days?"

She froze. How could her father have hung around people like the Berringers? Mac was a lot of things, but he was no killer. She took no more than three steps before Berringer called again.

"Mac 'n' me go back a long ways. Which daughter are you?"

Her head reeling and legs shaking, she kept walking.

"Hey, I'm talking to you!"

Suddenly Tait's arm closed around Melanie's waist. "I've got you." He swung to Berringer. "Shut your mouth or we'll gag you. Your choice."

Earl Berringer slunk down into a corner, sullen and quiet.

"Thank you, Tait," she whispered. "I went to get the boys away, and he started yelling horrible things."

"I know. I'll take care of it." He pressed a kiss to her temple.

They walked to the windmill, and Tait sat the boys down. His mouth formed a tight line. "I don't want to catch you near that cage again or you'll be in big trouble."

"But...but he said some bad stuff about Daddy," Joe spluttered.

"Just because he said it doesn't make it so. Earl Berringer wants to hurt you, and he'd rather tell a lie than the truth. He's nothing but bait to draw his father out."

Melanie's chest squeezed. Tait was so gentle with the boys even when he had a right to be upset.

She took Joe's hand. "Your uncle is right. Don't let that despicable man hurt you. They're only words. You know your father better than anyone. Keep believing in him."

But what about hers? Berringer had implied that he and Mac were close friends. The fact that he knew Mac's name proved they did have some kind of relationship...add to that the fact that Earl knew she was his daughter. How?

Jesse sighed. "We promise to stay away. Don't we, Joe?" His brother nodded.

Tait smiled and pulled them to their feet. "Okay, skedaddle. I'll see you at suppertime." The twins didn't waste a moment in running to join the other boys.

"Tait, do you think Earl Berringer was telling the truth about their father?"

"Sadly, yes. John Abraham was a safecracker and apparently rode with the Berringers. But he left them, straightened up, married, and tried to raise his kids right. That's what got him and Claire killed. They wanted his skills on a job, and he turned them down. His and Claire's deaths were retribution." He took her hand. "Don't give Earl a thought."

"I suppose you heard what he said about Mac. And he recognized me. But I don't recall ever seeing him before."

"Maybe your father played cards with him or something." His gaze was drawn to three wagons laden with lumber coming into the town. "If I'm not mistaken, there's our shipment."

"Oh good. We can start building our house." But would she ever get to live in it, to bustle around in the kitchen cooking something tasty for her family, to sleep next to Tait in a big bedroom of their own? Those were the questions that filled her *someday* dreams.

"We'll work on plans together tonight." He kissed her cheek.

"I'd love that." And maybe, just maybe, he'd need to get some money from wherever he'd hidden it and all this trouble could be over.

Tait hurried off to meet the wagons, and Melanie went to call on Rebel. Dr. Mary was just leaving, checking on Rebel in her last few weeks before the baby was due to come. The two children Rebel and Travis had adopted seemed overjoyed to welcome a new brother or sister.

Before Melanie went inside, she heard shrieks and a loud commotion behind her. She turned to see goats, raccoons, rabbits, and other animals coming at her followed by every child in town. Their circus animals! Bandit must've opened all the cages again.

"Stop them!"

"Don't let them get away!"

"Head them off!"

Melanie whipped off her shawl and waved it, stepping in front of the stampede. "Stop! Stop!"

The animals turned and started running back toward the kids. A chicken squawked and landed on top of the Truman three-year-old's head. The boy screamed and ran in a circle, fighting to get it off. One of the raccoons raced back through Ely's legs and tripped him. Two other Truman boys ran head-on trying to recapture the same raccoon.

As luck would have it, the stagecoach entered town at that moment. A goat tried to ram a horse, and the whole team took off at a gallop, clipping the corner of the saloon before the driver got them under control.

Melanie laughed so hard tears ran down her cheeks. When she was able, she used the shawl to help gather up the smaller runaways.

Once they were all corralled again, Jesse gave her a big grin. "Thanks, Aunt Mellie."

"You're welcome. How close are you to putting this circus on? I hope it's soon."

"It'll be Saturday, Aunt Mellie," Joe answered.

"Oh good." They'd better have it soon or they might not get to, the way things were going.

She and Rebel went inside and got out a deck of cards. Rebel loved playing poker and was quite adept at the game, forcing Melanie to use all her skill to best the woman. It was a pleasurable time spent. She'd learned that Rebel once worked in a saloon in Cimarron over in New Mexico Territory and her husband Travis was wanted for murder.

So many in this town had checkered pasts, and maybe that's why no one tried to be better than anyone else. They all had done things they regretted.

When Melanie emerged a bit later, she saw Tait striding out of town carrying a shovel. Curious, she followed.

Maybe this was the moment she'd prayed for.

Despite everything, her chest constricted with guilt over spying on him.

Sixteen

TAIT TOOK THE TRAIL THAT LED TO THE TOP OF THE BLUFF where he'd married Melanie. His mind was on the house and the work he would start the next day. He couldn't wait to get it built. He was incorporating some surprises into the design that would make Melanie's life easier. This was going to be special for her and make up for having gone without a decent place to live for so long.

A muscle in his jaw worked. He was going to have a long talk with Mac Dunbar whenever they met. The man hadn't done right by his girls, and Tait was going to tell him so.

A noise came from behind him, and rocks slid down the side of the bluff. He whirled but didn't see anyone. Maybe it was the boys and they were going to try to jump out and scare him. He grinned and hurried behind a boulder.

Footsteps came closer.

Tait frowned. It sounded like only one person. The boys were always together. Always.

Kern Berringer? He might've hidden near the town's entrance and followed him up the bluff. Tait eased his Smith & Wesson from the holster.

When the person came even with his hiding place, he stepped into the path and leveled the gun.

Melanie let out a strangled cry, her eyes wide. "Don't shoot," she squeaked, hands flying up.

He put the gun away. "What are you doing up here? I could've shot you."

"I came out of Rebel's house and saw you leaving town." She swallowed hard. "I sort of followed you. I thought we might take in the sunset. And maybe do what married folk do when they find themselves alone." She touched his arm.

"I see. This isn't a bad place to look at the sky. I sometimes come up here to think."

"Was that what you intended—to think?" Her gaze strayed to the shovel.

"No, not this time."

She wrinkled her forehead in thought. "Oh. Then I guess I'll go back down. All the animals the children caught got loose a little while ago, and it was chaos. Maybe they need my help. I'll leave you to whatever it is you came to do." Her voice caught on a strange hiccup.

For a moment he saw her insecurity and loneliness—the poor little girl with a father more interested in the next target to con than in his own flesh and blood.

"It's better if you don't know."

Her head jerked in a nod, and she turned.

Tait reached out to stop her. "On second thought, what I was doing isn't important. Stay and talk to me. We can catch that sunset."

Melanie brightened. "Are you sure?"

"Positive. That spot where we stood to say our vows is nice." With a hand on her back, he led her to the flat ground where his life had changed. In fact, he found it hard to recall the years between Lucy and Melanie. Everything had blurred, and most nights had seen him fall into a whiskey bottle.

"You can sit on my coat." He removed his frock coat.

"It'll get dirty," she protested. "My dress has seen better days. It won't matter."

"Who cares? I won't have my wife sitting on the ground," he said softly. "Which brings me to wonder about something. I would think a lady gambler would dress all fancy-like, in silks and satins. Yet you only have a couple of cotton dresses. Why is that?"

She lowered her eyes and picked at a loose thread. The silence grew loud until finally she spoke. "I hit a run of bad luck and fell on hard times. I traded my fancy clothes for things I needed more."

He spread his coat, and she lowered herself down without further protest. "Between Claire's and John's murders and the new house, I fear I've neglected you." He sat beside her and whispered in her ear. "When we go back to the hotel, you'll find a little surprise."

The satin dress he'd ordered from Mrs. Dunn's dressmaking shop in Tascosa had arrived by stage that afternoon, and he couldn't wait to see her wear it. And to see how closely the fabric resembled her eyes.

"You're spoiling me."

"Not near enough." He put an arm around her, and she rested her head on his shoulder. It fit perfectly in the hollow below his collarbone, a place that seemed made specifically for her. "You deserve a lot more for putting up with me and the kids."

"Oh hush! I love my life here."

The sun set low on the horizon, and they talked about their house and how they'd furnish it with all the latest styles.

"I already know the wallpaper for the parlor. I once saw a stunning light-blue swirl design in a hotel in San Antonio."

"Draw the design as best you can recall, and I'll send for it. Which reminds me, I should also order the cookstove you want so that it gets here on time."

They talked a little more about the house, then Tait switched subjects. "I heard some news that Sam Houston's son, Temple, was appointed district attorney in Mobeetie. That should clean out the riffraff over there, but it makes my situation more dangerous. From all accounts, Temple Houston is a tough man. The Panhandle is becoming too settled." Tait let out a worried sigh. "I feel a noose tightening around my neck."

Worry crossed her eyes, ancient eyes that seemed to hold secrets. "Then we have to find a way to get you a pardon like Clay and Jack. Tait, do you think if you offered to return the train loot, they'd forgive your crimes?"

Tait studied the stitching on his boots. "There's no forgiving what I've done."

"Please don't think that way."

"Markham wants me to pay dearly. He wants to take more than land and people from me. I have a bad feeling nothing will satisfy him. We may have to uproot and move farther west."

"If that will keep you safe, you should consider it."

"I'd hate to leave here, leave Jack and Clay."

"I know. I've also gotten close to the women in town. They've been my first real friends."

They lapsed into silence, watching the changeable sky start to darken. While the sky was clear where they sat, a summer storm built off to the west. Tait felt as though that storm was about to swallow him up. Melanie seemed just as unsettled.

"I want to stay up here and pretend that nothing bad can touch us. That we really can have whatever we want." Her words came no louder than a whisper.

He tightened his hold and kissed the top of her head. "I never was much good at pretending."

The swirling oranges and plums of the sunset took his breath away. He was glad she'd followed him and they could share the brilliant hues from up high like this.

But how many more sunsets would they have?

Dread clenched in his chest as he watched the storm grow closer.

❧

By the time Melanie and Tait picked up Becky from the Colbys, it had gotten dark. Melanie apologized. "I'm sorry for leaving her so long. We were taking a moment to watch the sunset."

Tally chuckled. "Not to worry. Violet and I enjoyed having her. She's such a dear child, and she loves playing with Dillon."

Tait lowered his mouth to Melanie's ear. "I told you so."

Her skin prickled with him so near. How she'd loved spending time with him.

He swung Becky up into his arms. "Are you ready to go, honey?"

"Me play." She puckered up and kissed his cheek. "Love you."

"I love you too."

The tenderness between Becky and Tait made Melanie's heart ache. He made a wonderful father. If only his child hadn't died.

If only life played fair and didn't force people to make horrible choices.

They said their goodbyes and collected the boys on the way to the hotel. The only bit of clean skin on Joe and Jesse was around their eyes; the rest was nothing but dirt. They looked like reverse versions of one of their blasted raccoons.

While Tait took them to bathe, Melanie went into the bedroom with Becky. A large box sat on the bed, a big red ribbon around it. Melanie sucked in a breath.

Becky made an O with her mouth. "Pwetty."

"Yes, it is, honey." Melanie fingered the bow, wondering what was inside. Though she burned with curiosity, she'd wait for Tait.

While she killed time, she wondered what Tait had been planning to dig up on top of the bluff. Logic told her it was the money. How could she sneak back up there to look around without the kids? A guilty conscience pricked. He'd given her so much. And yet she had to make a plan.

He soon returned with the boys. "Well? Did you like it?"

Melanie rose from the sofa. "I waited for you. Boys, bring me that box on the bed."

They sprang to their feet and returned with it. Joe held it out. "Here you go, Aunt Mellie."

She untied the bow and removed the lid. Nestled under a layer of thin paper lay a breathtaking satin dress. The deep turquoise would bring out the blue of her eyes. She let out a soft cry and held it up against herself.

Tait had leaned back on the sofa, his legs stretched out in front of him in a relaxed pose. "Do you like it?"

"Oh, Tait." His face was blurry through the tears that sprang to her eyes. "This is beautiful. Much too fine for around here. Wherever will I wear it?"

"Don't let on that you know, but the word is that we're having a town dance in a few weeks." He winked then rose and sauntered over to her, his eyes smoldering like embers ready to catch fire. "I wanted to give you something pretty to wear."

"You certainly did." She laid a hand against his jaw. "I can't wait."

"I'm going to enjoy showing you off. You'll be the prettiest lady there."

For a moment, they were the only ones in the room. She was caught in Tait's gray stare, and something strange and wonderful stirred inside her.

"Aww, shoot! Can we go eat now?" Joe whined.

"I'm starving!" Jesse exclaimed. "And it's thundering outside. Probably raining by now."

Becky hung onto Tait's leg. "Me eat."

Tait laughed and lunged for the twins. They screamed and ran. He chased Becky instead, and she let out a shrill scream too.

The suite turned into pure bedlam, but joy at being part of it spilled from Melanie's heart.

After a minute or two, she stuck two fingers in her mouth and gave a loud whistle. "Time out. We need to eat."

Joe gave her an envious stare. "How did you do that?"

"What? Whistle?" It was the only tomboyish thing she'd ever done. Hugh, a friend of her father's, had taught her behind Mac's back. He'd been like an uncle to her and to Ava, and she'd grown very fond of him. One dark, foggy night, someone took his life.

"How did you do it? Will you teach me and Jesse?"

"Sure, I guess." She beamed and went to lay the new dress on the bed.

After they ate supper, she spent until bedtime teaching the boys to whistle. Even little Becky tried her darnedest. The children fell into bed exhausted and seemingly happy. Funny how her feelings about children had changed from when she'd first arrived. They did cause a lot of extra work, but they made up for it in the sunshine they brought to each day.

That said, she still didn't want Tait to ride off and be gone for long periods, leaving their care solely to her. Nope. She wasn't having that.

She stood in the doorway of the children's room with Tait watching them sleep. "We're doing okay, aren't we?"

He pulled her close, and she thought she heard his heart beating steady and strong. "Yeah, better than okay."

They backed out of the room, and he kissed her long and deep. Her head spun, and she hung onto her outlaw for all she was worth. Maybe the best life was made up of a lot of little meaningful moments that brought so much happiness and satisfaction rather than large ones that came few and far between.

Seventeen

THE SUN ROSE AND PEEKED INTO THEIR BEDROOM WINDOW. Melanie woke, surprised to find Tait still in bed and staring at her with his quicksilver gaze. She became acutely aware that she wore nothing under the covers. "Good morning."

He lazily smiled and lifted a lock of her hair. "Why is it that you look so beautiful this early in the day?"

"I don't think you have your eyes open." She laughed. "I'm sure I look a mess. You didn't even give me time last night to braid my hair."

Memories of their lovemaking brought heat to her face. They'd done things she never had before. Whoever had taught Tait to use his mouth that way had done an excellent job. She'd never forget the breathtaking shudders that had left her feeling utterly boneless. The heat in his gaze right now was enough to send her back to that shattering light.

One touch here, a kiss there, a slow deliberate breath over her skin and she'd be spasming again.

"The complaint department isn't open yet," he murmured against her lips. He made her feel safe and cherished. For the first time in her life, she didn't have to pretend things she didn't feel.

She sighed and curled against his side, wondering how he managed to turn her topsy-turvy with a mere kiss. Her heart raced, and a low vibration beginning in her belly set every nerve ending humming, growing louder as it rose. She reached between their bodies and closed a hand around him. He gave a slight jerk, and his heartbeat pulsed against her fingers.

"My darling, I'm not complaining one bit," she purred. "I don't care what my hair looks like when you're next to me. You have something I need."

A quick move and he had her pinned beneath him, her breasts grazing his chest, his lips sealed to hers. Ragged breathing filled the silence in the bedroom.

The doorknob turned, thankfully stopped by the lock.

"Aren't y'all up yet?" one of the boys asked.

Tait groaned and rolled off. "Just about. We're getting dressed and will be out in a minute."

"Eat," Becky said.

Melanie threw back the covers. "Okay, honey, give us a second. What are you all doing up so early?"

"Sawyer knocked on the door. He said Miss Nora's having her baby."

"Oh good." She yanked on her petticoats, trying to pull her stare away from Tait's perfect backside as he reached for his trousers. It proved impossible, especially when he gave her a full frontal view.

What she wouldn't give for a few more minutes. But they had obligations. Her thoughts still on Tait's fine body—beautiful despite his many scars—she dragged her attention back to dressing.

She didn't know what she could do to help, since she wasn't at all versed in midwifery, but she could at least keep Willow for them.

Tait drew her against him at the door and gave her a sound kiss. "We'll finish this another time."

"Count on it." She just prayed that it wouldn't be too long. Her outlaw was finally getting the hang of marriage.

But what good was it when it wouldn't last?

❧

Tait and the men worked with the children and their circus, but his thoughts kept coming back to Mellie and her luscious body. She could make him sit up and beg. He'd never thought he could care for any woman, not after Lucy, but now he welcomed all the emotion that flooded over him. Mellie made him feel alive again and gave him a reason to wake up sober in the mornings.

Recollection of their previous night's passion and interrupted morning filled his head, making his blood hot in his veins. Tait grinned. She was a bold woman and wasn't afraid to try anything. He'd never had more satisfying lovemaking.

He caught sight of her walking across the compound with Becky and Willow, his gaze following the gentle sway of her hips.

"You've got it bad for your wife," Hondo commented with a laugh, shaking his head.

Tait shrugged. "It's called marriage. Maybe you ought to try it."

"Haven't found the right woman. I almost did—once—but she took off with the town undertaker."

The men jostled Hondo and kidded him unmercifully.

Earl Berringer called a taunt, trying to bait Melanie into responding, but she ignored him and kept walking. Smart lady.

His thoughts turned to the rotten Berringers. Earl seemed to know a lot about Melanie's father.

Selling information? Keeping an eye on someone for them?

Melanie admitted that Mac Dunbar was a swindler and con. Maybe Mac had seen a way to make some easy money? She'd claimed he wasn't afraid of the devil himself where a profit beckoned.

Shoot if Tait knew. His gaze swung to the town's entrance. Satisfied the guard was on duty, Tait turned his focus to helping Jesse and Joe make pairs of stilts. His nephews did seem to have quite a bit of natural ability for using their hands and training animals.

By noon more news came—Rebel had gone into labor. The women were running back and forth between her house and Nora's. Two babies born in one day was a first for Hope's Crossing.

"Care to make a wager as to who gives birth first?" Tait asked the men.

"Sure." Clay pulled out two bits. "My money's on Rebel, even though Nora started first. Rebel carved out a life by not messing around."

"I'll take Nora." Ridge added his money to the pot.

Jack grinned. "Nora will have my hide, but I have to bet on Rebel."

Each man joined in, even Brother Paul and the schoolmaster,

Todd Denver. When work was done for the morning, they took the kids to the café for lunch. The noise level there nearly deafened Tait. He yearned to saddle up and go riding, far away from crowds.

But he didn't. He wouldn't shirk his duty.

That afternoon, Travis Lassiter brought word to the men who'd gathered around the community fire that Rebel had given birth to a boy. The man was grinning from ear to ear. "I always wanted another son."

"Got a name picked out?" Tait asked.

"Rafe. After my brother."

"Rafe Lassiter—nice ring to it," Clay clapped him on the back. "We'll have to celebrate. I think I can dig up a cigar or two."

"Beat you to it." Travis held out a box of cigars and passed them around amid congratulations.

An hour later, the door to Jack's house opened, and the former outlaw strode out. The big smile that covered half his face said he had news. He walked straight for the group, never breaking stride.

Tait greeted him. "Let us have it. Rebel just had a boy. What's yours?"

"A girl. I guess we lost the bet." Jack didn't seem that heartbroken.

"You old dog!" Tait bumped his arm. "You name her yet?"

"Hope Marie Bowdre." Jack took a cigar from Travis's box and lit it. "Whew! I'm glad that's over. My nerves can settle now."

Sid Truman laughed. "Just wait until you have ten or twelve like me."

"No, thank you. Nora and I are probably done."

"You know, I said that same thing once." Sid's laughter faded. "Martha threatens me with the rolling pin now every time I get close to her."

Tait listened to the men joke, wondering if he and Melanie would one day have a child of their own. He'd sort of like having a boy to carry on his name.

But that couldn't come until Kern Berringer was dead and buried.

He thought about the drawings Hondo had made of the killers' horses' prints. Each time a new rider came into town, Tait checked their horse against the drawings, and they all stayed vigilant for any gray-haired men with big ears and hound-dog bags under their eyes who stood six foot six. He didn't know all the Berringers by sight. Some he'd never crossed paths with before, and it would be easy for them to slip into the town unchallenged.

Melanie and the children were his top priority. He'd protect them or die trying.

⁂

By the end of the following week, the new house's frame had almost all come together. Melanie loved to sit and watch them work, adding board by board. Excitement sizzled under her skin to think that the dream she'd long had would finally come true—a house, flowers, a garden. All her own. Permanence. Guilt washed over her at times about failing Ava, and there were days when she didn't think of her sister at all.

Tait climbed a ladder, and her breath caught. He'd shed his shirt in the warm afternoon sun. His body was nice and tanned, and muscles rippled across his back.

Melanie smiled to herself. She'd felt those muscles under her hand.

Although she'd climbed the bluff alone several times, she'd been unable to find the buried money or any sign that Tait had been digging. If she didn't find the stolen loot soon, the judge would send someone else to threaten her. A shudder raced through her at the thought.

Or he might come himself…and bring an army to get Tait.

And that fear that was like a steel band squeezing around her heart haunted her day and night.

They could kill him. The wanted poster said dead or alive, so no one would be too particular. She thought of Lucy, and tears burned her eyes. Her mind was doubly set. She'd never turn Tait over to them. They could rot in hell.

Becky squatted, playing in the dirt. Such a sweet child. She needed a mother, a real one. The child grinned up at her with brown teeth. "Eat."

"Oh, good Lord! Don't eat the dirt," Melanie scolded. "It might have poop in it." With all the horses, goats, and dogs roaming around, there was no telling what it contained. "How about I wash you up and we go visit one of the new babies?"

Just then, the sound of hooves reached her ears. A second later, one of the twins galloped by, hanging onto the pommel, his body against the side of the horse. Melanie gasped, afraid to breathe for fear he'd fall under the animal. The kids practiced for that blasted circus every spare minute. But this was dangerous, far more so than their other tricks, and one of them was going to get hurt—and that was assuming they didn't hurt someone else. What else did they have up their sleeves? She'd be glad once they gave their performance and it was all over.

Tait climbed down the ladder and walked over to give her a light kiss. "How are my girls?"

"Having a heart attack. Did you see that horse pass by with either Joe or Jesse hanging on the side?"

Tait laughed. "Pretty good, isn't he?"

"Tait Trinity, you need to put a stop to this, or we'll be dealing with broken bones."

"All kids do things like that. It's a rite of passage. That same trick saved me from getting shot full of holes riding away from a train." He brushed her cheek with a callused finger. "You worry too much. Didn't you and your sister ever try trick riding?"

"Nope. Father would've tanned our hide. Besides, he never let us get dirty." Melanie had always wanted to play in the dirt and make mud pies but had never been allowed to get close.

"More's the pity. He robbed you of a childhood." He glanced toward some riders who had just stopped by the guard at the town's entrance. Melanie noticed his sharp gaze that took in every new arrival. He never stopped being on watch. "I'll need to check those men out."

"You think it's Berringer or his sons?"

"Maybe. At any rate, I'll check their horses' hooves." He brought his attention back to her. "I'll speak to the boys about galloping through town like that. It's dangerous for the rest of us. I'll have to come up with a new place for them to practice though."

"Thank you, Tait." Melanie stretched to kiss his cheek, resting a palm on the warm skin of his bare chest. Tingles raced through her. This man made her knees weak and her blood heated. But it would all end soon enough. Her stomach twisted at the thought.

Why did life have to be so hard? Why did she have to destroy one to save the other?

Why couldn't she love him as she wanted without fear of her sister suffering?

Or dying.

Eighteen

IN THE DAYS THAT FOLLOWED, TAIT KEPT CHECKING EACH NEW set of horse hooves without finding a match. Work progressed on their house, and Tait spent many a pleasurable night with Melanie. He enjoyed making love and counted the days until they'd be able to do it in their own home.

He let Melanie pick out their furniture and ordered it. With luck it would arrive about the time the house itself was finished.

He was growing weary of hotel living, and the strain showed on Melanie's face as well. She needed her own things around her.

From what he'd seen, women were a lot like mama birds. They liked to build a nest and happily settle into it, and the feeling only got stronger once they found themselves in the family way.

He froze. She could be with child and not even know it.

An unexpected burst of happiness washed over him. He wanted to be a father one day. He hadn't felt good about that idea in a long time. The thought jarred him. Despite what he'd told Melanie about not wanting children, he might welcome a little son or daughter that he could mold into a responsible, caring person.

But not now. Not while they lived with so much uncertainty.

Before he could block the memory, Lucy's image hanging from the crossbar swam in his vision. The force of it knocked him backward. He grabbed onto the hitching rail in front of the saloon, inhaling great gulps of air until he could force the picture away.

However much strength it took, he couldn't let that happen again. He had to protect Melanie and the kids. To lose them would finish destroying him.

Tait stayed sharp and kept his hands occupied.

When he wasn't working on the house, he was helping the children practice their trick riding. He moved them outside the town and kept watch while they perfected their performances. Melanie was going to have a conniption when she saw the trick Jesse had planned. Tait grinned at the thought.

Kern Berringer was taking his sweet time showing up. But there were days when the hair rose on the back of Tait's neck and his gut told him the man was lurking nearby. Watching. Waiting. Plotting.

Yeah, he wasn't far away.

Experience told him Kern was waiting for the right opening. Once they relaxed and let their guard down, he'd strike. Hondo left Earl Berringer under Jack's watchful eye and returned to Flat Rock to take care of some business, saying he'd be back soon.

Finally, the calendar turned over to Saturday, September 3, 1881, and excitement rippled in the air. The boys were as jumpy as frog legs in a hot skillet and could hardly wait to perform their circus for the town.

"Do we hafta eat today?" Joe asked. "My stomach doesn't want food."

"Mine either," Jesse declared. "You don't want us puking all over everything, do you?"

"Can't say as I do." Tait buttoned Becky's shoes.

Melanie strolled into the room in another new dress that Tait had bought for her, and his heart stuttered. This one was a vibrant green fitted creation that emphasized her figure to perfection. Oh yes, he liked buying her new clothes.

Lured by her fetching dimples, Tait rose and wrapped her in his arms. "You look good enough to eat. I don't want food either, but I'll bet you can guess what I do want."

Her turquoise eyes sparkled. "I think I do. No hints needed, but it'll have to wait." She stepped from him. "Boys, you have to drink something regardless of not eating."

"No time," Joe protested. "We hafta get the horses and other animals ready and go over everything with the boys. Lots of work to do."

"It can wait." Tait sympathized with them, but he knew which side his bread was buttered on. "You heard your aunt. You'll drink something nourishing."

Becky patted his face. "Me eat."

He could always count on her. He scooped her up and tickled her. "Breakfast on the way for you, little lady."

The sullen boys went through the door when Tait opened it. "It'll only take a few minutes and then you can leave," he whispered. Then he winked at Melanie and put an arm around her, glad that the circus would soon be over and things could return to normal.

Tonight, he'd have fun removing that pretty dress and sate the hunger inside him.

❧

Melanie unexpectedly found herself with some free time that morning. She'd been watching Tait's movements and had twice seen him coming from the little valley where they grew their crops very late at night. It occurred to her that he might've hidden his loot somewhere in there.

It wouldn't take her long to do some digging. She'd be back in plenty of time.

With Tait riding herd on the kids, she sneaked into the barn for a shovel. Keeping her head low and walking fast, she crept behind the buildings. Every noise made her jump. If she got caught, she would have no excuse for carrying a shovel.

Halfway to the valley, she had to stop and rest. She hadn't realized it was so far, and the warm sun soaked her in sweat.

Melanie found a shady spot and sat down. Her heart thundered, and her mouth was like cotton. The danger of being discovered stretched her nerves thin. But time grew short. McIlroy wouldn't wait much longer.

Conscious of the time, she rose and reached the entrance to the valley where wheat, corn, and other crops filled the barren landscape with beauty.

After scanning the area, she decided the most promising spot was at the edge where someone had deliberately stacked three flat rocks. To her it signaled that they'd marked the spot for some reason. Renewed by hope, she plunged the shovel into the hard, rocky ground.

Twenty minutes later, she had nothing to show for her efforts except blisters on her palms and a small hole in the ground. Defeated, she sank down, dropping the shovel. Tears burned the backs of her eyes, and a thick lump blocked her air passage. This was impossible. Why had she agreed to this?

Ava, that's why. This was about freeing her sister. She had to remember that.

She heard voices and ducked into the field of corn, hiding among the tall stalks. And just in time. Travis and Ridge appeared. They stopped to inspect the small hole she'd dug.

"I wonder who's been digging. This is odd." Ridge picked up the shovel.

Travis laughed. "Probably some of those boys would be my guess. Not sure what they'd be looking for though."

"Pirate treasure?" Ridge chuckled. "An imagination is a powerful thing."

"Let's gather those stalks for the kids and get back. I don't want to miss this circus. Ely and Jenny would have my hide."

The two men reached for the stalks that were bare of corn and broke them off. Their arms full, they picked up the shovel and returned to the town. Melanie waited a little bit to make sure they weren't coming back and then crept from her hiding place.

This would be all of her digging. She was convinced that Tait had hidden the loot outside Hope's Crossing and she'd never find it. She bit back a sob and wiped her tears.

❧

After dressing Becky in a cute cowgirl outfit Tait had bought, he and Melanie dropped her off at the church where the contestants had assembled. At one o'clock sharp, everyone took their seats in the chairs that had been brought in from the saloon and all their houses. An arena had been set up and decorated in front of the church that doubled as the school.

Melanie took his hand. "I wish I knew what they had planned for Becky to do."

"Don't worry, sweetheart, I'm sure it's something safe." He was reasonably sure anyway. With the twins, you never knew.

He glanced at the town's entrance, satisfied the guards were on duty. Maybe Kern and his boys would try something today with everyone's focus on the children.

"I'll be back in a moment." Tait headed over to speak to Jack and Clay. "How's it looking?"

Jack crossed his arms. "Ridge volunteered for guard duty, and if Berringer comes, he'll handle it. No one's better with a gun."

Tait didn't know the man that well, but he trusted Jack's judgment.

"I'll keep an eye out after Violet gets finished with her part in the circus." Clay rubbed the back of his neck. "Frankly, I'm a nervous wreck, considering she can't see. Tally is too, even though she says she's not."

Jack glanced toward the church where all the children had assembled. "The girl will do fine, Clay. Violet's able to do things some people with good vision can't. You know that."

Mrs. Truman walked to a piano they'd hauled outside and began to play.

"Hell, I think we're all jittery about her performance." Tait scanned the crowd, glad to see the turnout. "Guess we'd better go sit down. It's starting."

Melanie gave him a bright smile when he returned to her side. "Is everything all right?"

"Seems to be."

Twelve-year-old Sawyer Gray strode into the center of the arena in chaps and spurs, wearing a black Stetson and flicking a horse whip attached to a rigid rod. "Welcome to the first-ever circus in Hope's Crossing. Get ready to be astounded, folks. We've got tricks and animals galore. Each contestant will get a chance to do something fun." He shrugged. "At least our idea of fun. I think you'll like it. Sit back and enjoy."

He pointed the whip at Mrs. Truman. "Music, please!"

A procession started. Becky meandered by in a small wagon pulled by Jack's bloodhound Scout. Dressed in her cowgirl outfit complete with a little hat, she waved like a regal queen, hollering hello every couple of seconds.

Melanie rested her cheek against Tait's arm. "Oh, Tait, she looks so cute."

Just then the wagon tipped over while trying to turn. Becky jumped up, all business, set it upright, and climbed back in. Tait's gaze followed her out of sight behind the church. If only her parents could be here. Pain tightened in his chest.

His nerves jumpy, he let his gaze sweep the bluff then the town entrance. If Kern was close, this would fit into his plans. Everyone other than Ridge was focused on the circus.

Two more wagons came behind Becky with toddlers Willow and Dillon inside. Willow was pulled by a goat and Dillon by his own dog Bullet.

Next came the twins with three other boys on stilts. One started wobbling, but he straightened himself out before he could fall. Tait whistled and called to Joe and Jesse.

He laughed. "I'm glad they didn't eat anything or they'd be puking."

"Heaven forbid that." Melanie joined in the laughter. "I love this."

Jenny strolled by wearing a cute, colorful costume and pulling a small wagon that contained raccoons. Halfway across, one of the raccoons hopped out and started pushing.

Two of the Truman Ten wore clown costumes. One tripped, and when he got back up, he stepped on his trousers and they fell to his ankles. Everyone chuckled.

Then came Violet riding a donkey, laughing and waving. The blind girl was having a great time and doing something safe.

A small herd of goats trotted past followed by rabbits in cages on a sled.

After the parade, Sawyer stepped into the center again. "Welcome the one, the only, the magnificent Kayden the Juggler!"

Fourteen-year-old Henry Truman strolled forward with purpose and removed three plates from inside a large coat he wore. "I am Kayden the Juggler. Feast your eyes on my skill. Next will come knives." He showed his teeth in a dramatic grin.

The boy flipped a plate in the air. Then he added a second and third, catching them all and throwing them back up. But the fourth one proved too much and crashed to the ground.

Henry shrugged. "Oh well. That was Billy's plate."

Tait cupped his mouth and called, "Looks like Billy will lose some weight. Don't try the knives."

Laughter swept the crowd. Tait again checked for movement on the bluff. He thought he saw something but after staring for what seemed a full moment decided it was his imagination.

Sawyer came out. "A big hand for Kayden the Juggler!" When the applause died down, he introduced the next act. "Now for the beautiful Princess Shiloh and her death-defying walk!"

Two of the bigger kids brought out a couple of sawhorses and stretched a two-by-four from one to another.

"Oh dear, please don't let it be Violet," Melanie moaned.

But out came the girl, feeling her way to the step that took her up and onto the board. The crowd gasped, and a murmur of dismay ran through the onlookers. Violet stood on the board, two feet above the ground, hands outstretched. One of the boys ran out with a parasol and put it in her hand.

Melanie hid her eyes and gripped Tait's arm. "Tell me when she's done. I can't watch."

"Chicken?"

"Yes, I am. I don't want to see her hurt."

Tait put his arm around her. "I think she'll be fine. The board is wide enough if she doesn't wobble."

A groan came from Melanie's hidden face. "That's what I'm afraid of."

Mrs. Truman launched into some dark music fitting for the trick.

Violet slowly felt her way along, sliding one foot in front of the other. Careful. Deliberate. Tait had to admit that even he held his breath. The girl was good at sensing the edges. Tait suspected she was counting the steps.

But if she miscounted and stepped off the end…

A hush descended over the crowd.

His glance found Clay and Tally together, clinging to each other, probably praying. He would be.

Suddenly, Earl Berringer bellowed from his iron cage. "Fall! Fall!"

Violet wobbled, and one foot missed the board. She gave a little cry and by God's grace managed to keep her balance. Clay jumped to his feet and stalked over to Earl one step ahead of Jack. One grabbed the man and the other hit him, knocking Earl unconscious. Good. That should keep him quiet.

One slow, careful step at a time, Princess Shiloh kept inching along until she reached the second sawhorse where she stopped. Sawyer helped her down amid thunderous applause.

The girl stood, arms raised in victory, a huge grin on her pretty face.

Tait touched Melanie. "You can look now."

"Was she good?"

"She showed no fear. I think that girl has ice water in her veins."

"Let's hear it for Princess Shiloh and her uncanny ability to see even though she can't!" Sawyer ran around the arena urging the crowd to their feet. The applause lasted for a full minute.

Violet bowed and made her way out of the arena. Up next was the funny menagerie of raccoons dressed as pirates. Jenny Lassiter pushed a baby carriage full of the ornery rascals. When one jumped out, she chased it down and put it back in. One raccoon held up her dress while another ran under it. Jenny let out a cry and went to whipping her skirt. She pulled the animal out by the tail and gave it a good scolding.

"I think that must be Bandit." Melanie squeezed Tait's hand. "These kids are very good."

"I'll say." Tait had never been prouder of the whole bunch.

While Jenny hurried her pirates out of the arena, two boys pushed out a little raised stage followed by Joe who carried a chicken and child's piano.

Melanie whispered. "I hope this turns out well. I bought him the piano."

"I think he'll work the trick just fine." Tait's nerves were jumping around worse than one of those Mexican jumping beans. He could barely keep his thoughts on the circus and kept expecting gunshots any second.

Sawyer raised his arms. "This next act will boggle the mind. Madam Henrietta will play a fine tune for your listening pleasure. She was trained by Mr. Joe Abraham."

Those seated in the front row leaned forward. One hollered, "Play *Oh, Susanna!*"

Joe scowled. "She don't know that one. Now hush!"

He set the hen in front of the piano and sneaked some feed on the keys. Henrietta began to peck until a large rooster hopped onto the stage and pushed the hen aside. The music was drowned out by all the squawking and fighting that ensued. Finally Joe had enough and snatched the hen up.

"Let's hear it for the magnificent Henrietta!" Sawyer hollered.

"Poor Joe," Melanie murmured. "That rooster ruined his trick."

"He'll be fine. His best trick is coming."

Ely the Magician came out next and, after several tries, managed to jerk a rabbit from his hat, then followed that with some simple card tricks.

"And now, folks, hold onto your seats." Sawyer turned to see if the next act was ready. "Don't breathe, don't make a sound. Most of all, don't leave. The lions are coming! Trained by the great lion tamer Jesse Abraham!"

Six goats trotted out, and everyone died laughing at the scruffy manes made of yarn tied below their mouths. Jesse carried a small whip that he tucked under one arm. He put two fingers in his mouth and released a shrill whistle that Melanie had taught him. The goats all raised on their back legs and began to turn in a circle. He whistled again, and they formed a singular line and put their hooves on the back of the goat in front until they were all standing on their hind legs.

The crowd burst into applause. The trick was pretty spectacular for a kid who was in the middle of rebuilding his life from the ground up. Pride swelled inside Tait.

Jesse put the make-believe lions through their paces and had the crowd on their feet. People nearby, many of whom had complained when the boys first came to town, nudged Tait to tell him how much they enjoyed the act.

While Jesse was getting the goats out of the arena, the clowns ran out and did somersaults and flips.

"Now for our world-famous trick riders all the way from Buffalo Bill's Wild West Show! Save your applause until the end," Sawyer urged.

Joe was the first one to charge into the arena on horseback. One lap around and he dropped to the side of the horse, clinging to the pommel. Then he pulled himself back into the saddle and, holding to the reins, stood straight up.

Melanie's nails dug into Tait's arm. "I can't look. I can't breathe. I can't stand this. Why did you let him do this, Tait?"

"The boy's fine, Mellie. I told you he was good."

"But it's so dangerous!"

Three other riders entered the arena, all making the difficult tricks look like child's play. Then came a fourth one, and Tait jumped to his feet, the spit dying in his mouth. "Dammit!"

Becky stood in the saddle, holding onto the reins. He raced down to stop the horse and only then did he see Jesse on the far side of the buckskin, holding onto his sister's feet. Becky was laughing and having the time of her life.

Just wait until he got his hands on Jesse! The horse jogged by a second time at a leisurely pace, and Tait could've stopped the animal, but he didn't dare for fear that Becky would fall. If she did, then probably Jesse would too. So he just watched, ready to run out and catch them if they fell.

An arm went around his waist, and Melanie stood with

him. She too seemed to hold her breath. He pulled her close, murmuring, "It'll be all right. It's going to be fine."

But his words seemed more to calm himself than her.

At last the horses left the arena, and he could finally release his grip on the nearby post.

Melanie pulled away and glared at him. "Did you tell them they could use Becky?"

"No. It was a surprise to me."

"What are you going to do about it? She could've been killed. She's so little." Her beautiful eyes flooded with unshed tears.

He reached for her. "I'll lay down the law to them—again. Everything you say is true. I won't have them putting her in danger."

But his thoughts were on Kern as well. If he hadn't struck now when everyone was preoccupied with the kids, when would he?

He barely heard Sawyer winding up the program and Clay announcing the fall dance the following Saturday. Folks around them began to leave, but Tait held Melanie tight, her heart thudding against his chest, breathing in her fragrance. He wished that time would stand still.

But change was coming. A knot clenched tight in his stomach.

Nineteen

THE HOUR WAS LATE BY THE TIME THEY HERDED THE KIDS FIRST to the café where Joe and Jesse ate like a pair of young horses, then back to the hotel. Melanie praised all three many times over. Let Tait play the bad guy.

Becky crawled onto the sofa. "Me ride horsey."

"Yes, you did." Melanie removed her hat and smoothed the girl's blond hair. She could hear Tait in the bedroom with the boys, and from the sound coming through the door, he was giving the twins a serious tongue-lashing. Seeing Becky on that horse had scared him into the middle of Christmas.

She undressed Becky and got her into a gown. The child could hardly hold her eyes open. Melanie held her in her lap and lightly rubbed her arms as her own grandmother had once done for her. Soon Becky was sound asleep.

Tait came out with the boys, and she saw no blood on any of the three. His bark was much worse than his bite, and the boys knew it. Despite the reprimand, they joked and laughed about all the circus mishaps.

"Next time it'll be bigger and better," Jesse told Melanie. "We have experience now."

The boy grinned at Tait, who snorted and dropped into a chair. "You got lucky is all."

Melanie was glad there wasn't any tension or hard feelings. "I thought you were all amazing. You did a great job with the goats. How did you train them to dance on their hind legs?"

"Well, I had a handful of oats and kept offering a little at a time."

"I didn't see you handing them anything. You hid that very well." Melanie kissed Jesse's cheek. "I'm very proud of both you boys."

"Me too." Tait pinned her with a gaze. "We have a date

a week from today, Mrs. Trinity. It was noisy when Clay announced the fall dance, and I don't know if you heard it."

"No, I didn't. People were starting to leave, and like you said, it was noisy." She had something else to plan for. If she stayed that long. Lately she'd started to consider leaving again. She could find her father, and maybe the two of them could think of some way to break Ava out of jail.

But the thought of leaving brought a searing pain to her chest.

It was a far better plan than hurting Tait and the kids. They'd never know what happened to her this way, never know what she'd originally tried to do. The trouble was she kept putting it off. There would never be a good time. That much she'd come to realize. She'd just have to get up one morning and do it fast before the hurt set in. Like ripping off a scab.

Tait stretched and rose. "Bedtime, boys."

They opened their mouths to argue, looked at Tait's expression, and quickly did as he'd said. Tait took Becky out of Melanie's arms, and his touch sent tingles rushing along her body.

His silver-gray eyes held wanting.

Melanie sucked in a breath. "I'll get ready for bed as well."

Anticipation danced through her veins. Leaving tonight was out of the question. Maybe a few more days.

She wasted no time in donning a nightgown and was brushing her hair when Tait entered the bedroom.

His unbuttoned shirt hung open. His lazy gaze slid over her body. "Leave it down. For me." He sauntered the few feet separating them and took the brush from her. The gentle strokes of her hair did nothing to cool the heat flowing through her veins.

"You have rich, vibrant hair. I think the color is what I first noticed when you stepped from the stage that day. It flared to life under the sun's rays."

"I was scared, you know."

"Of me?"

"You looked very stern and forbidding, with your long hair and piercing eyes. I could hardly breathe for fear of what you'd turn out to be like. I thought you might be mean."

But in the days since she discovered that although an outlaw, he had strength and scruples and a code he lived by.

Tait chuckled softly. "Silly woman. Maybe I should've growled or something."

"Then I might've stayed on the stagecoach." Her body tingled as he laid the brush down.

He was silent as he knelt, painstakingly pulled off her stockings and kissed each of her toes. "I wouldn't have let you. The moment I saw you I was sunk. You were like a piece of a puzzle that had been missing."

She closed her eyes to absorb every sensation so she could remember nights when she was wanted. No matter how old she got, she'd always remember them this way.

Even if he'd growled that first day and acted like he was going to carve her up, he wouldn't have scared her. Looking back, she'd seen what he'd tried desperately to hide standing there with three vagabonds—his heart. She'd seen the tender way he'd held Becky, heard the kindness in his voice.

Tait shrugged out of his shirt, unbuckled his gun belt, and removed his boots. Conscious of his attention on her, Melanie undid the buttons of her nightgown and let it puddle to the floor. He sucked in a breath, his heated gaze raking her body.

Every nerve ending alive, she turned back the covers and slid between the sheets as naked as a newborn.

❧

They spent that night, and each one of the next week, pleasuring each other and whispering in the dark, making plans for their future. Tait worked on their house and kept watching for Berringer during the day. But the nights—those he reserved for Melanie.

Now that the circus was over with, Joe and Jesse returned to their previous behavior, running wild and doing most everything they wanted. And what was worse was that they took Becky in tow this time, talking her into things she'd never have done on her own. Melanie was fit to be tied, and Tait wasn't far behind.

On one such particularly frustrating day, the boys disappeared with Becky and stayed gone until late afternoon. Her dress was torn when they finally returned, her face streaked with dirt, and she was so exhausted she could barely hold her eyes open.

Tait got Joe and Jesse each by the nape of the neck. "You oughta be ashamed. What if she got hurt or you ran into the men who killed your mother and father?"

Kern Berringer could easily have gotten them, and the realization made Tait's knees buckle.

Jesse's eyes grew round. "We didn't think of that."

"Well, you'd damn well better start. They're out there waiting for a chance to grab you. It's a miracle you're back alive. Don't you ever leave this town without me again."

"Okay," they both mumbled.

Tait shook his head and herded them toward the hotel for another come-to-Jesus talk.

But nothing did much good. A few days later, he found them in the hotel basement jumping from one huge pile of dirty linens to the other. He put them to work pulling out nails from the used boards at the building site, whitewashing the fence around the church where school would commence in a few days, working in the café, and building a dance floor for the harvest dance coming up. He kept them so busy they didn't have time to think about causing trouble. They collapsed at the end of each day and went fast asleep.

The boys had no time to be bored. They missed their old life and their toys. Thankfully, their belongings that Hondo promised to send arrived, which proved to be a tremendous help. They'd dived into the wagon like it was Christmas. All three kids seemed happy to have their treasures back and complete again.

Which made life pleasant for all concerned.

Work progressed on the house, and by the end of the week,

Tait gave their unfinished house an approving glance. The walls were up, and the dwelling was taking shape. He thanked the men for their long hours.

Clay stood beside him. "I appreciate you letting us use some of your lumber to make the floor for Saturday. I'll bring it back after the dance."

"The wood's just lying there. You're welcome to it."

Jack joined them, grinning. "Clay, we're getting pretty fancy these days. Used to be we had to dance on the ground. Now we get a real floor."

"It's called progress." Clay scanned all the buildings. "I never thought all this would be possible. When Tally arrived to marry me, the only two buildings we'd managed to erect had just been burned to the ground by Montana Black. There was nothing here except a few pitiful dugouts and soddies. I'd almost given up. Lord, that seems like a million years ago."

Tait followed his friend's gaze. "You created a fine town here. It's thriving."

"But one match can turn it all back to rubble," Clay answered. "I can't forget that, and we can't let down our guard."

Joe and Jesse fell to the ground and stretched out in dramatic fashion as only they knew how, completely done in.

"I've seen a small fire destroy whole towns before. Some never rebuilt." Tait remembered one that burned several times but the people there kept coming back. Losing heart was a terrible thing. "We'll have to stay vigilant for sure."

The faint sound of riders and bawling cattle reached Tait. He swung around to stare at the town's entrance. "What the hell is that?"

"A cattle drive? Why are they coming here?" Clay strode toward the sound.

Tait and Jack followed, joined by several other men. The twins jumped up, not a bit tired anymore, to go see what was happening. A bawling dust cloud came closer and closer. A rider broke away from the loud din and galloped toward them. As he neared, Tait could see a large man in the saddle, silver hair beneath his hat.

A grin spread across Clay's face. "Well, I'll be a suck-egg mule!"

Jack leaned forward to get a better look. "Stoker Legend?"

"Yep, that's exactly who it is," Clay replied.

Tait's interest soared. He'd long heard of the big rancher who owned the Lone Star Ranch and the power he still wielded, but Tait'd never had opportunity to cross paths with him.

Several minutes later, the rancher reined up in front of them on an appaloosa that stood every bit of sixteen hands high. Stoker leaned down and extended his hand to Clay. "Colby, it's always good to see you."

"Glad you paid us a visit, sir." Clay shook hands. "But what is all this? Are you moving your ranch to the Panhandle?"

Stoker laughed in a big booming voice. "It does look like that, I suppose. My sons have been speaking of this town and your work here in such glowing terms that I had to quit waiting for an invitation and come see Hope's Crossing for myself. And as long as I was coming, I thought I'd bring a few cows along for a gift."

Tait shot a glance at the herd. A quick estimate as the dust settled suggested they had to number at least two hundred. Nice gift. The town could sure use them, but where would they put them? The only place secure enough against rustlers would be a box canyon that lay within spitting distance.

"Hell, Stoker, if I'd known you were waiting for an invitation, I'd have sent one a long time ago." Clay seemed a little awestruck, and Tait could see why. Legend was a man who didn't stand on ceremony and seemed to live life as large as his stature.

But it was Stoker's sharp eyes that struck Tait the hardest. They took in every detail. He had to be somewhere in his sixties, yet no one with half sense would call him old.

Jack exchanged a few pleasantries, and Clay introduced Tait.

"I'm happy to meet you, sir." Tait offered his hand and found a firm grip.

"Trinity, huh? I've heard of you. You sure put a squeeze on the railroad, and I'm glad. The bastards deserve to sweat." Stoker's gaze shifted to the twins. "Are these young'uns yours, Trinity?"

"My sister's, sir. I took them in after she was killed. What do you say, boys?"

"Nice to know you, Mr. Legend," the boys said in unison. Jesse added, "You sure got a lot of cows."

Stoker laughed. "I'm giving these to the town, so I guess they're yours now."

"Oh boy!" Jesse rubbed his hands together.

It didn't take a genius to know the boy was already picturing himself on top of one. Tait gave him a stern glance and shook his head, to which Jesse shrugged his shoulders.

Three more riders approached and stopped—brothers Sam, Houston, and Luke Legend.

Introductions were made all around, and Luke addressed Tait. "I trust Miss Dunbar arrived and the wedding went off without a hitch."

"She did, and we're living in happy wedded bliss." Tait took Luke's measure. He'd never met the man who'd arranged the private bride service, but he instantly liked him. Luke had darker skin, unlike his brothers, which suggested Spanish blood. Tait had heard it said that Luke Legend, half-white, had once been an outlaw himself, and that was easy to believe. Luke hadn't quite broken himself of searching the nearby shadows.

Maybe men like them never did. The habit had become as much a part of them as breathing.

Tait was going to have to make big changes fast or he'd die an outlaw. Unlike Luke's story, there was no good end for him that he could see.

Twenty

TAIT STUDIED THE FOUR LEGEND MEN AND HAD NO TROUBLE seeing how they continued to cling to the huge Lone Star spread that covered six counties. Half a million acres, some said. It took a whole lot of guts, muscle, and brains to manage such a ranch.

"Come on inside. You're just in time for supper," Tait invited. "We'll put you up in the hotel."

"That's mighty generous," Stoker replied with a grin, sticking a cigar in his mouth and lighting it.

Clay folded his arms across his chest. "More than fair in return for all these cattle."

"Where are we going to put them?" Tait asked.

"I think that boxed canyon would be hardest to rustle from," Clay answered. "We can post two men at night, which might deter Kern Berringer if he's close."

"Oh, he's close all right." Tait scanned the brush. "He won't leave his son."

The saddle leather creaked when Stoker shifted his weight. "Who's Kern Berringer?"

Tait gave the rancher the short version while Clay appointed some of the men to take the herd to the canyon. Once they were off, Clay swung back to their guests. "How about we cook outdoors at the community fire again, like we used to do before we got too fat and civilized?"

Jack snorted. "Speak for yourself."

Tait shot Sam Legend—and the silver star pinned to his chest—a wary glance. He hoped he wouldn't have problems with the lawman, although Jack said Sam wasn't your normal sheriff. Sam had helped Jack gain his amnesty last year, after all. Still, he'd be committed to his job. He had a duty to uphold the law, so Tait had better keep a low profile.

At least Kern Berringer wouldn't force a showdown with such famous company in the town.

The Legends and their two drovers rode through the entrance straight to the Diamond Bessie, eyeing the saloon as they passed. Tait aimed the twins inside the hotel lobby and met Melanie and Becky on the boardwalk.

Tally shrieked when she saw the Legends and flew to greet their guests. Laughing, Luke scooped her up and swung her around. Clay told Tait that Tally had once saved Luke's life when he was on the run and then had helped his wife Josie through a difficult childbirth. They seemed to still be fast friends.

Melanie slid her arm around Tait, her fetching dimples deepening with a smile. "What's going on? Who are these men?"

"Stoker Legend and his sons. The dark-haired one is Luke, owner of the bride service." Tait drew her close, breathing in her scent.

"Oh my! I didn't know he was so handsome."

"Thinking of trading me in?"

"Not on your life. You're mine, Mr. Trinity."

"That's a relief." He let his hand slide to her firm bottom. "I think the plan is to eat outside tonight by the community fire. You'll get a chance to help cook."

"How fun." She gazed up at him, her blue-green eyes shimmering in the light spilling from the hotel.

Tait felt like he'd unearthed a diamond, and because he couldn't say what was truly on his mind, he blurted the first thing he thought of. "They brought a herd of cattle for the town."

"That's wonderful! They'll help feed us this winter and provide another source of income. The Legends must have big hearts."

Houston Legend strolled past, heading into the hotel. "We'll meet you men at the saloon."

The women huddled together, planning supper, then hurried off to collect supplies. Tait got the boys, and they went to use the outdoor bathing apparatus. Peace unlike any he'd known descended around him.

He was alive. He had friends and a family. And he had a wife who grounded him. On the surface, life was as near perfect as it could get. If he could only get rid of the five-thousand-dollar price on his head and Kern Berringer at his heels.

Later, after they'd eaten and were sitting around the fire, the night air brought the scent of sage and wildflowers. Becky was asleep in Melanie's lap, and Joe and Jesse were playing games with the other children, whooping and hollering like they'd known each other all their lives.

While Melanie talked with the women, she studied the faces of the Legend men and found them interesting. But her gaze lingered on Sam, the youngest of the brothers. A former Texas Ranger, he was now the sheriff of Lost Point. She longed to speak to him about Judge McIlroy and her situation, but she didn't dare. She couldn't let anyone know.

A boy a little older than the twins sat with the Legend men. He looked at Stoker with a good bit of hero worship in his eyes.

Melanie nudged Tally. "Is that boy over there with the Legends a grandson?"

"That's Noah Jordan. Stoker took him in to raise after his parents were killed. He's like another son. A sweet, sweet boy. I believe he's twelve, but Stoker is teaching him how to run the ranch. He loves that kid."

"Noah's a year older than Joe and Jesse, but he seems so much more mature. Lord, I'd hate to think of *them* running a ranch!"

"I wish the Legends had brought their wives. You'd love them. They're all women of iron."

"I have no doubt." Tait stood up at that moment and stole Melanie's attention. Thinking about bedtime brought a slew of tingles rushing over her.

The Legend men seemed larger than life, but they couldn't compare to Tait. She admired his lean figure and slightly too-long sun-streaked hair.

He turned, and his eyes met hers. He excused himself from the men and sauntered across the space. He leaned down and put his mouth next to her ear. "How about we call it a night and go to our room? I have a hankering to get you naked, Mrs. Trinity."

Heat rose to her face. He'd chosen time with her over their visitors. He wanted her more than whatever news the visitors had brought.

"I'd like that. You have the best ideas." Her heart raced as he took Becky, then Melanie's hand.

Seeming to pay no mind to the teasing hoots and calls, Tait put an arm around her, collected the twins, and moved them toward the hotel.

Over the next five days, the men worked on the new house every second they could spare. With Stoker and his sons helping, the work went more quickly, and they got the walls and clapboard on as well as the roof and set glass in the windows. All that remained was the inside work. Tait was happy with the burst of progress.

Often once they finished for the day, Tait would spend time talking to Luke. They had a lot in common. But sometimes Sam, Houston, and Stoker joined them.

It was on one such day that they all sat cooling off when Stoker asked about Earl Berringer. Tait told them about Kern, his job with the railroad—and Lucy.

Sam's eyes narrowed. "The bastard needs to be strung up. He's little better than an animal, and the law can only do so much. Out here, men have to find their own justice."

"I'd do that if I knew where to find him. He's like a ghost." Tait sighed and leaned back against a tree. "I don't understand how the law can favor rotten men like him and hang the ones trying to live right."

Houston stuck a stem of hay in his mouth. "One day the balance will shift and things will change."

"I hope so." Tait then told them about his sister and her husband. "Kern Berringer tortured her before ending her life."

The men were quiet, and then Sam said, "You can't do this

by yourself, Trinity. I'll wire the U.S. Marshal who oversees this territory. Also, the governor needs to know."

Tait had doubts that it would do any good. "Berringer's too slippery. He squirms out of everything."

"Not this time!" Stoker boomed. "I have a lot of connections with some powerful people. I'll bend a few ears."

"Thank you, sir."

Luke looked Tait square in the eye. "Trinity, how do you see your situation ending?"

"I've asked myself that same question over and over in the dead of night. I can't see a good way out of this."

Stoker rested a hand on Tait's knee. "You have to find one. Not only for your sake but for those kids and that pretty wife of yours. Do you still have the money you took?"

Tait nodded. "A good portion of it. If you have any ideas, I'm listening."

"You could make a deal. Return the money in exchange for dropping the charges, for instance. Depends on how badly they want it. You could arrange delivery through a third party so you wouldn't get in their sights. I need a few days to mull this over." Stoker sat back, and Tait could almost see the wheels turning in his mind.

For the first time in a long while, Tait had hope of ending this in a peaceful way.

No more hiding. Hard to imagine what it would be like not to worry.

Melanie came down from the hotel with Becky beside her. As soon as the child saw Stoker, she started hollering and made a mad dash for the Legend patriarch. "Gan'pa! Gan'pa!"

Stoker held out his arms and swung her up. "Hey, little lady, how's the world treating you?"

"Gan'pa ride horsey?"

"Not right now. I'm resting."

"Becky, stop bothering Mr. Legend," Tait scolded. Then he asked, "What is she talking about?"

Luke laughed. "Pa took her along on his morning ride today, and I think he's started something."

Melanie laughed and took a seat with them. "It all begins so innocently. She can charm the horns off the devil himself. But who taught her to say *grandpa*?"

Stoker kissed the little girl's cheek. "I did. I miss my grandchildren." She snuggled into the fold of his vest. "If anyone hurts this child, they'll answer to me."

Tait knew the man didn't say that lightly.

A familiar perfume drifted around Tait's head as Melanie scooted closer. He moved her hair aside and whispered, "Take a walk with me, pretty lady?"

"Are you sure you're not too tired after working all day?"

"I'm never too tired for you." He pulled her to her feet. He had just the place in mind.

Stoker and his sons stayed for the dance that Saturday, and the night turned out to be crisp and clear. Melanie felt beautiful in the pretty new dress Tait had bought her. The deep turquoise brought out her eyes and made her auburn hair glisten under the lights.

She took Tait's arm and strolled toward the musicians who were warming up, loving the swish of her satin dress against his trousers.

"I am a very lucky man," Tait murmured.

Melanie glanced up and saw desire in his gaze. "Why's that?"

"I think you know." His voice roughened. "I'm going to have to keep my gun handy. I can be a jealous man."

"Tait, you can't go around shooting everyone who asks me to dance."

"Who says?"

"I do. Now be nice and don't even think about fighting. These men are your friends. And we have honored guests who brought us a herd of cattle."

Tait released an oath under his breath. "I know."

They watched the musicians tuning their instruments. Tally had told her that at the first, they'd only had Dallas Hawk, who played the fiddle. Now, besides Dallas's fiddle, they had a guitar, a harmonica, and an accordion. One man had brought a pole sticking through an upside-down washtub with a long rubber band attached. The strange instrument gave a deep bass sound.

Folks were slowly gathering for the dance, excitement rippling through the crowd.

"Do you think Becky will be too much for Mrs. Franklin to manage?" Melanie asked. They'd been lucky to find the elderly woman who'd just arrived by stage to visit her sister. Mrs. Franklin had a room on the second floor of the hotel and had taken a liking to Becky right off.

"She'll be fine, sweetheart. Stop worrying." Tait's hand on her lower back filled her with warm tingles as he guided her over to Stoker Legend. "I'm glad you and the boys could stay for this, sir."

"Wouldn't have missed it." Stoker glanced around. "Where did you put Earl Berringer?"

"We moved him behind the mercantile for the night."

"Good place for him." Stoker kissed Melanie's cheek. "Save a dance for me, young lady. I'll be the envy of all these young bucks. That dress is stunning."

"Thank you. It's a gift from Tait."

Stoker winked. "He has good taste—in both clothes and gorgeous women."

"You do know I'm standing right here." Tait tightened his hold on her.

"Of course I know. Why else would I flirt with Melanie?"

Houston joined them and kissed Melanie's cheek as his father had done. "Pa, Trinity's frowning, and I have a feeling you're to blame."

"I'm only complimenting a pretty lady," Stoker shot back.

Sam wandered over. "Causing trouble, Pa? I swear, we can't take you anywhere."

"Watch it, son."

Melanie laughed. "It's such a joy having you all here with us."

"Would you like some punch?" Tait asked her. "I'm not much of a referee between a father and his sons."

"I'd like that."

Soon she was sipping punch and glancing up at the moon. It was a perfect night, and she couldn't imagine being anywhere else. Tait's attentiveness made her heart swell. No one had ever shown her such caring and devotion. Where most men would've joined their buddies to talk and drink the night away, Tait stayed with her. Tears blurred her vision.

Mayor Ridge Steele stepped up and got everyone's attention. "Tonight is a celebration of all our hard work to make this town everything it is. We're not perfect, but we're pleased with our progress. I'm happy to welcome our guests—Stoker Legend and his three—no, make it four—sons. Noah Jordan is as much a son as the rest. We're glad to have them and their ranch hands here with us. Let's give them a round of applause."

When the clapping died down, the band started playing a beautiful waltz.

Tait took Melanie's cup, set it down, and swept her onto the makeshift dance floor the twins had helped build. He drew her tight against him and placed his mouth at her ear. "Tonight we celebrate our marriage. I have something planned for later."

Her pulse raced, and she said low, "You're good at keeping secrets."

Good heavens, why did she say something like that? No one was keeping any except her.

"Only a few."

She glanced up into his face and found heated desire in his silver-gray eyes. "Are you glad you found me, Tait?"

"What do you think?" He pressed a kiss to her lips, and Melanie melted against him.

When she could talk, she warned. "I may still disappoint you. Will you still feel the same way? Will you try to understand my side?"

"What are you saying?"

Melanie wet her suddenly dry lips. "Don't make me better than what I am. It's only asking to be let down. Never put me on a pedestal."

Tait shook his head. "Not what I'm doing. We all have

faults. I just want to celebrate finding you." He paused for a moment. When he spoke, his voice was hoarse. "You have the most luscious body, darlin', and I can't wait to get you to bed."

Tingles cartwheeled through her. Maybe one more night wouldn't make any difference. She had to make love to him one more time before she told him the truth.

"Play nice, my darling husband. We have all night."

Just then the music ended, and Luke Legend was at her elbow. He was dashing, wearing black trousers with silver conchas up each leg and a short black jacket. "I believe it's my turn, *bonita.*"

"Oh good. This gives me a chance to talk to you."

A few minutes later, on the dance floor, Luke was the one to ask her a question first. "Are you happy with your choice of a husband, Miss Melanie?"

Her gaze found Tait dancing with one of the other young women. He was the most handsome man there. "Tait is everything I always yearned for. Tell me about your wife."

"Josie is headstrong, funny, and stubborn as a mule, and I love her with my heart and soul."

"Sounds like a perfect match." Melanie let Luke sweep her around the rough floor. "I'm curious about something."

"What's that?"

She glanced up into his dark eyes. "What led you to start a private bride service? You hardly seem the type for matters of the heart."

He laughed. "Clay, Jack, and Ridge paid me a visit at the Lone Star and told me about trying to start a town. I wanted to help. They needed brides, and Josie blurted out that we knew some womenfolk who could help with that. My wife is very persistent." Luke got serious. "Men like us live in the shadows and can't advertise like normal people. Women, as much as the men. So, I help match them up."

"It's very commendable."

They talked about the children and their circus until the waltz ended. Stoker was there to claim the next dance. Tait had wandered off to talk to Jack and Travis.

Stoker was an accomplished dancer and a perfect gentleman, not holding her too tight. "You look beautiful tonight, Miss Melanie. I hope Trinity knows what he's got."

She glanced up at the big man with thick silver hair that still had some dark running through it. His whole presence was comforting, almost father-like, and for some odd reason she wanted to confide in him. "Did you ever keep secrets from your wife?"

"Only once. I learned my lesson."

"What did she do, if I may ask?"

The Legend patriarch chuckled. "She locked me out of the house and said I wouldn't get back in until I set things straight. We were having one of the worst blue northers you've ever heard about, and I was freezing my tail off on the porch, so I didn't waste any time. You should've heard me."

Melanie laughed. "I think you could sweet-talk any woman you wanted and have her eating out of your hand."

"Not so, my dear. My Hannah was a tough woman even though she only stood five feet tall. She didn't mince her words, and she was a stickler for the truth. After that I never kept anything from her." Stoker grew silent, staring into her eyes. "I have a feeling you didn't ask that question lightly. If you're keeping a secret, Miss Melanie, you'd best get it out before it destroys you."

"I appreciate the advice." Melanie's gaze found Tait, and she knew she could not put this off. Not even if the price was that last night in his arms.

Twenty-one

AFTER STOKER LEGEND, MELANIE DANCED WITH EACH OF THE sons a second time before Tait lost patience and claimed her. "My turn. And if anyone tries to cut in, I'm shooting them."

"My heavens, Tait! You've gotten to be quite a grouch."

"I've just had it. I'm tired of sharing my wife." At the first strains of music, he drew her into his arms.

Melanie sighed and rested her head on his shoulder. She was home. But for how long? "Tait, when this dance ends, let's take a walk. I want somewhere private."

"We can do that." He put his cheek to hers, and they weaved in and out of the other couples, swirling around and around.

Sweat lined Melanie's palms, and her nerves grew ragged. When the music stopped, Tait led her out into the night. They silently climbed the bluff that overlooked the town.

She pulled away, putting some distance between them. Feathery night air brushed across Melanie's bare shoulders. Her satin dress whispered around her ankles as though unaware they'd left the dance. She glanced at Tait's shadowed profile, struck by how much she truly and utterly loved him. Despite her resistance, without knowing it, love had somehow snuck past the high wall she'd built.

And one thing was clear.

No matter how difficult or how painful it would be or how afraid she was, she had to come clean, tell this beautiful man exactly why she'd married him, and beg his forgiveness. And if he couldn't give it, that would be the end of their happy marriage.

Her insides felt alive with nervous jitters. She knew he wouldn't forgive her. No man could.

The sting of her betrayal would go straight to his gut and twist like a knife. Melanie closed her tear-filled eyes, trying to find the courage. If she didn't tell him now, her soul wouldn't be worth saving.

She snuggled against his side, breathing him in, knowing this would be the last time. "I enjoyed tonight. You surprised me. I didn't know outlaws could dance."

Her words came softly, beginning what would be the end of all her dreams.

Tait brushed a tender kiss across her forehead. "We're pretty much like regular people. We all want the same things." He lifted a tendril of hair. "You're quiet tonight, and you're hiding those cute dimples."

"Thinking of my sister. Tait, I haven't been honest about a few things." She moved away from his embrace and perched on a large rock, needing something solid under her.

"You don't talk about her much. What is it you want to say? You're troubled." Deep shadows hid Tait's face, cloaked his eyes that saw everything. "Can I help?"

"There's the thing. You can. But—" She wet her dry lips. "First I need to get something off my chest."

"I'm listening. Tell me. Whatever it is, we can work this out together."

If only they could. Her chin quivered, and she clutched her hands. "Ava is in jail in Canadian. They…they had me too, until a judge there hatched a vile plan and used my sister as a bargaining chip." She stared out into the darkness, afraid to glance at Tait, afraid to see him change from a tender husband to an enemy full of disdain and loathing. "We… we got scooped up in a raid and caught with fraudulent bank notes. My father escaped, *vanished*, and left us to face the consequences of the scheme *he'd* cooked up."

"I'm sorry, but if I ever lay eyes on your father, there'll be hell to pay. I can promise you that."

"Hear me out, please. I had just started writing you when this all happened. The sheriff found one of the letters, which he took to Judge McIlroy. The judge said that if I came and married you…if I found the stolen money you took from the train robberies and brought it to him, he'd let Ava out. But if

I failed, he'd send both of us to prison for a very long time. I made a bargain with the devil, Tait, and I wish every day that I could go back."

Silence dragged between them, and she finally glanced up at him. His jaw was clenched, his face made of stone, his quicksilver eyes flashing with hurt.

"Please say something," she whispered, gripping her hands.

"You were going to give me up. You made me think you truly cared. For me. For the kids. But you were only after my money. No wonder you kept asking about it." His spat the words like hard projectiles. Melanie winced, recoiling as though he'd struck her. His voice raised several octaves. "How could you? We made love. You *acted* like a wife." He took a step back, his face a dark mask of pain. "Do you even have a conscience?"

Melanie winced at his yells. "That's what makes this so difficult. My plan had been to come here, get the money right away, and leave. Only—" She paused. Tears rolled down her face, and she couldn't stop them.

"Only I had it hidden too well?" He stalked to the rim of the bluff and stared down at the town below.

"No." Melanie bit down on her bottom lip to stop it from quivering, her voice dropping to an anguished whisper. "Only I came to care deeply about you and the children. I opened my heart for the first time." A cry sprang from her. She wanted to tell him that she loved him and that she wanted to spend the rest of her life by his side. That she didn't want his money, only to free her sister any way she could. But he wouldn't believe any of those things. Not now.

Once trust was lost, everything else was gone. She'd ruined the best thing she'd ever found.

He suddenly whirled, his eyes dark, frightening, hurt oozing from their depths. "What else?" he barked. "I know there's more. This judge doesn't just want the stolen money, does he?"

Melanie squeezed her eyes tight against his blinding fury. Another flood of tears broke free. "He…he wants you too.

But I decided weeks ago that the money will have to be enough for McIlroy."

"Why?" He snorted and threw his arms up in the air. "Why not make this complete? Why not put the damn noose on me yourself? Christ, I told you my darkest secrets!"

Yes, he had, at great cost to himself. A part of her wanted to shrivel up and die.

"Please!" She jerked to her feet. "Understand that I didn't want to do this. But Ava sobbed, begging me to save her. She's terrified. McIlroy sentenced her, me too, to twenty years of hard labor. Ava was always weak. She'll die. She may already be laying cold. McIlroy sent me a box filled with her hair and a tooth while you were gone to Flat Rock. He threatened to send a finger or an ear next. I've been searching for the money, and that's what I was doing in your soddy too. Hoping to find it."

Melanie twisted her hands, her stomach in knots. "Please try to understand. I didn't have a choice."

But if possible, his anger grew hotter. Flames shot from his eyes. "If you'd found the money, then what? Trick me into taking you to Canadian so they could grab me? How many tricks *do* you have up your sleeve, Melanie? How could you have made love to me all these nights while you were busy plotting?" Hurt and devastation dug craters in his face. "My God, how? You told me you cared for me."

"I do care. This is tearing me up inside." She reached for him, but he stepped back.

Tait snorted. "If you'd told me from the first, maybe we would've had a chance."

Yes, if only. She wished she could smooth the lines from his face, offer some bit of comfort. She let her hand drop. "I felt like your wife. I wanted to be your wife. I still do." Her voice broke. "As soon as I got to know you, I realized I couldn't go through with the scheme. I've been trying to find a way out of the deal I made ever since."

"I *trusted* you! I thought you were everything I'd been waiting for. I was a blind fool."

She opened her mouth to apologize, but he never gave her a chance to speak.

Tait's eyes blazed. He held up a finger. "Don't. Just don't. I'm leaving before I say the words that are blistering my tongue. Find your own way down. You're a resourceful gambler. Lady, this is one hand you've lost. I'm done."

His bootheels crunched on the rocky ground, then deafening silence enveloped her. She put her head in her hands. If a heart could truly break, hers did.

Her world had ended. Everything she'd wanted was gone. A few words had changed her life forever.

And there was no way to get it back.

The moonlight shone on her wedding band. Memories of the day Tait had slipped it on her finger flooded back. He'd been so handsome in that red vest and black coat. After a while spent getting to know his heart and what drove him, she'd thought she hit the jackpot.

But it had only been a bit of fool's gold sparkling from the chips on the table.

The minutes ticked by until she finally dried her eyes with the hem of her dress. She'd pack tonight and leave on the morning stage. But what about tonight? Where would she sleep? She still had a little of the money Tait had given her. Maybe she'd take another room.

Then another thought hit her. The children. What would she tell them? Or would Tait even let her say goodbye?

She keened in the dark, picked up the hem of her satin dress, and began to feel her way down the pitch-black path. A few steps from the bottom, a rider galloped from the town.

Tait.

Where was he going? What about the children? In his immense hurt, he must've forgotten them. She hurried. If she could just hold Becky one more time and tell the twins she had to go away for a while, that would be enough.

She slipped and had to grab the low brush to keep from falling. The tears blurred her vision. This was what dying probably felt like, but she wasn't that lucky. She had to keep living and face what she'd done. No matter what else happened to her in life, she'd never care for anyone else like she did for Tait.

"I love him," she sobbed into the night. "Oh God, I love him so much."

When she hurried into the town, the twins came running, tears streaming down their faces. Joe was carrying poor Becky by a leg and arm, and the little girl was wailing.

"What's wrong?" Melanie rescued Becky from her brother.

Jesse wiped his tears. "Uncle Tait left us, and we thought you had too."

"We thought nobody wanted us." Joe dragged an arm across his nose.

Melanie's heart broke all over again. It must be the kind of night to make everyone feel unwanted. "Oh honey, that's not true. Your uncle and I had some things to discuss, that's all."

"Where did he go?" Joe asked. "It's too dark, and we're scared."

"Me scared," Becky cried.

"I don't know where he went, honey. But I'm here and I'm not leaving you. We're going to make our beds in the sitting room and all sleep together tonight. How's that?"

"Can we have a light on?" Jesse moved close, touching her dress, to reassure himself she was there.

"Of course. I think that's a wonderful idea." She didn't know how she could tell them that their uncle might not return—and that she was to blame.

But where did that leave her?

She refused to think about riding out like she'd planned. Yet she couldn't stay. McIlroy would send men after her again, and more dangerous ones this time. Taking the children with her was also out of the question. Anger rose. Tait shouldn't have left the kids. He could do whatever he chose to her, but not to these orphans whose world remained so terribly shaky.

On the way to the hotel, she thought over her options. She'd stay a few more days. Maybe Tait would return once he'd cooled off. Her heart broke for him as she stared into the darkness, wishing he had a friend to talk to—someone to put an arm around him.

The mournful cry of a lone coyote sounded from beyond the town entrance. Melanie shivered, the new dress Tait had bought her no protection against the sudden chill.

Twenty-two

TAIT GALLOPED ACROSS THE HARD-PACKED GROUND, HIS HEART raw and aching. He'd allowed himself to believe that Melanie was one of the forever kind, the woman who would help him learn to love again.

Yet she'd betrayed him, taken his trust and threw it back in his face. He winced.

All for thirty pieces of silver.

Well, there was quite a bit more than that, but the idea was the same. Money had been the motivator for a betrayal of the worst kind.

"Fool!" he yelled into the night. "You're a stupid fool."

Maybe the story about her sister was true. Or maybe not. He really couldn't let himself believe her. Although, to her credit, she'd seemed in genuine pain and no one had forced her to come clean about the deal with the judge. She could've kept quiet, kept looking for his stash, and he'd never have known. That sudden realization jarred him.

So why *had* Melanie told him?

Could her claim that she had come to care for him be true? What if her twin sister *was* in jail? Their worthless father sure wouldn't lift a finger to help if she were, that much he knew. Something like that would've pushed Melanie into a corner. And when someone's back was against the wall, it made them willing to do most anything. He knew what that was like. He'd been there far too often.

Still, if she'd come to him at the first, he might've helped her.

Who was he kidding? No, he'd have reacted as he just had and sent her on her way.

Tait slowed his roan to a walk. As he rode through the night, he pondered the whole situation, and his burning, righteous anger began to deflate like a pricked balloon. He climbed to the rim of the box canyon and stared down at the dark shapes milling around below, listened to the lowing of the cattle.

The animals were peaceful and content. He envied them.

Kern Berringer was somewhere nearby, but Tait didn't care. A bullet might be a godsend right now. Dying almost seemed better than living with this misery gnawing at him.

After letting the cattle's gentle sounds soothe his soul, he rode on and dismounted at a little stream, sat down beside it to think.

There in the thin light of a fingernail moon, he mulled everything over. He'd go back, of course—for the kids. But Melanie? Despite seeing her struggle, could he truly salvage anything from their mockery of a marriage? With the night air whispering around him, the home he was building for her seemed like a bad joke.

Secrets had a way of stealing faith. He wouldn't be able to trust her again. How could a marriage survive that?

At an impasse, Tait lay down on a patch of wild buffalo grass, too weary and heartsick to think.

❧

Melanie pulled the covers off the beds, and she and the kids all slept together on the sitting-room floor. The children seemed less scared once they'd settled in, but the twins woke up several times in the night, checking to see if she was still there. Her heart broke for them.

Poor darlings. They'd lost everyone they knew. Tait should've known what leaving would do to them.

She lay wide awake, staring at the ceiling, her heart an aching wound. She'd gambled and lost the biggest hand of her life. Even if Tait was able to tamp down his anger long enough to listen, what could she say that would really change anything?

Slowly there in the dark, her heartbeat loud in her ears, a vague plan took shape. With luck, and maybe some help from the Legends, she might somehow be able to broker Ava's release and get Tait a pardon for his crimes. Then she'd disappear.

Hope of redemption soared, and she pulled Becky's small form against her, covering the restless young sleepers with the warm quilts.

They dozed until rays of soft sunlight peeked through the windows. Becky stirred and rubbed her eyes. "Mellie?"

"Yes, honey."

"I sleep."

"Yes, you did." Melanie kissed her soft cheek. How had she ever thought children too much trouble and something to avoid at all costs? She'd certainly changed her opinion.

Joe rolled over and tickled his sister until peals of laughter filled the suite. Jesse still wore that frightened stare.

"It's going to be okay. Let's fold these quilts and go eat some breakfast," she suggested.

"Yeah, maybe Uncle Tait is at the café." Hope filled Jesse's voice.

She didn't have the heart to burst his bubble, so she kept silent. Sometimes a person had to cling to hope no matter how slender the thread.

In no time they were dressed and headed to the Blue Goose for breakfast. The children talked nonstop all the way, but when they saw that Tait wasn't inside, they lapsed into silence and remained quiet until midafternoon.

Melanie saw him first. She steeled herself for a scene, praying she could talk some sense into him before anything worse could happen.

Tait rode in, looking like death warmed over. He pulled a travois behind him made from two long poles. Whatever was strapped onto it was covered with pieces of burlap. He stopped in front of the hotel, dismounting slowly.

Joe yelled, "Uncle Tait! You're back!" He and Jesse ran to meet him.

Melanie slowed her steps, unsure what to do. She and Becky had been on their way to visit Nora, needing someone to talk to, even though she couldn't have told her friend the truth about her rift with Tait.

"Wuncle!" Becky clapped. "Down. Down."

The child squirmed out of Melanie's arms and ran as fast as her little legs would carry her. Melanie stood on the shaded hotel porch and waited. Tait never spared her a glance, not one, his focus riveted on his niece and nephews.

He looked like a man headed to the gallows. His eyes were nothing but hollows in his face, and the lines around his mouth had deepened overnight.

She wanted to go to him but didn't dare.

If she could get a do-over for her marriage, she'd grab it in an instant. But he might not want a do-over. The first time appeared to have been all he could take.

Finally, he pulled his hat low on his forehead and stepped onto the porch. "Boys, take your sister inside. I'll follow in a minute."

Only when the door closed behind them did he swing around to even acknowledge her presence. The barely restrained anger emanating from him struck her full force. She took a step back.

His voice turned as hard as granite. "You wanted the money. There it is. Take it. Take it all. Then leave." He whirled to walk away.

"Wait. Please, just give me a moment. I have a plan to get us out of this mess."

But he never blinked an eye, never acknowledged that she'd spoken. A turn of the doorknob, and he walked out of her life.

❦

Tears streaming down her face, Melanie pulled back the burlap and stared at the sacks of stolen money. This was what she'd come for. Only now she wished to send the sacks back to their hiding place forever.

In getting them, she'd lost everything.

She wiped her eyes with an impatient hand and glanced around. Where could she put the money until she could find a wagon?

A man's shadow fell across her. "Can I help, my dear?"

She glanced up to see Stoker Legend. He opened his arms, and she walked into them without a word. In that moment, he was the grandfather that she'd never had but needed all her life—a safe haven, warm and comforting. Eventually, she was able to tell him that she had to find a place to take the sacks.

Stoker nodded. "Let's take the money to the sheriff. Then I'm here if you want to talk. I have a feeling you need help."

Melanie smiled. "I think you must be an angel."

The rancher chuckled. "I've been called a lot of things, but never once an angel. Devil would be more like it, according to most."

"Well, not me. I stick to my original assessment."

After finding Jack and locking the sacks of money in his office, she and Stoker went to the café and sat at a back table. Soon she was sipping hot tea and spilling out the whole sordid story—ending with how she couldn't possibly go through with the original plan now.

Stoker lifted his coffee cup. "Ira McIlroy is a cheat and a fraud himself. I know the man well and have not one iota of respect for him. I had heard from a reliable source that he recently bought the judgeship in Canadian."

She traced a design on the checkered tablecloth with her finger. "A thought came to me during the night—of how maybe I could help Tait get a pardon. I can give back the railroad money now. All I need is some leverage to force McIlroy to drop the charges against Ava and me. I have a feeling he was never going to honor our agreement even if I did deliver Tait."

"You're absolutely right there. You can't trust that snake to keep his word. You can expect more boxes to arrive containing pieces of your sister if you don't meet him head on."

"Oh God!" Melanie's shoulders slumped. "I have to help her. And Tait, even if I do go to prison. I'll face being locked up gladly if that will get him his freedom." She paused a moment to still her trembling lips. "You see, Stoker—I love him."

"That much is plain. Don't worry." He patted her hand. "I

know a lot of powerful people, and McIlroy is not going to get away with this. Give me a day to see what I can do. And I'll go with you to Canadian to deliver that money. You're not alone."

Relief flooded over her. "I don't know what to say. Thank you."

"Now about fixing your marriage…give Tait time to cool off. But only you can straighten that out."

"I know." Melanie sighed. "I'm willing to do anything I have to."

"Love is a strong motivator. If he cares for you, he'll meet you halfway."

Except—he didn't believe in love. He'd stated that up front. And now she understood why. Lucy still had his heart and probably always would. There was no room in it for her.

Melanie thought over their conversation as she left the café. Her first step was to get a separate room at the hotel, hoping desperately that she wouldn't run into Tait. Or the children. What reason would he give them for her absence? She prayed he would consider their feelings.

She entered the hotel and went straight to the clerk's desk. "I'd like a room of my own please. Somewhere on a lower floor in a far corner."

Curtis Winfield shot her a strange look but asked no questions. "I have such a vacancy on the second floor. It's very small, but it's only half price."

"I'll take it." Her hand trembled, making her name illegible in the register. She'd signed with her maiden name, which brought further scowls from Curtis. But she didn't feel married anymore.

"That'll be fifty cents, ma'am."

She paid it, and he handed her the key. She made it to her room without running into anyone she knew. As she sat on the narrow, one-person bed, she wished for her belongings. How would she get them?

The more she thought, the angrier she became. If he was ending their marriage, throwing her away, he'd have to tell her to her face. She gathered her tattered pride and marched from the room.

Tait answered her knock by jerking the door open. He stared at her with those cold, quicksilver eyes.

Melanie inhaled a sharp breath. "I want to talk. And I want my belongings if this is what we've come to."

The children's voices drifted from the room behind him. He slipped out the door and closed it, leaning against the frame. "I have nothing more to say. I'll pack your things. I've told the kids that you received an urgent message and had to leave."

"Fine. But if you want a pardon for your crimes, you'll listen to me." She told him about what Stoker had said and the help he'd offered. "He's trying to gather information against the judge right now. Once they free you of all charges, I don't care what happens to me." He glanced away, making it difficult to read his expression. She lowered her voice to a whisper. "I deserve punishment for what I've done and what I originally intended to do. After this ugly business is over, I'll disappear from your life for good."

She lifted her quivering chin. "But know this, Tait Trinity—I love you."

Twenty-three

THE HOTEL HALLWAY WAS EMPTY EXCEPT FOR THEM, AND Melanie knew if she didn't bare her soul now, she'd never have another chance. She clasped her hands together, her words soft. "I never expected to fall in love. I never believed love like this existed. Maybe it didn't until I met you. I've never felt this way about any man before. I can't breathe or think or imagine a life without you. I've found out that love is like the flow of a river— constant, something that fills up all the aching, empty places. But maybe you don't believe in that, and I wouldn't blame you."

She dropped her hand and took a step back to leave.

"Wait." The rigid lines of Tait's face relaxed, but he still didn't smile. "You did what you had to for yourself and your sister. McIlroy had you caught in a snare. I see that." He lowered his voice. "You'd go to prison for me?"

"I'd go to the ends of the earth and beyond if it would make you whole. Will you help me in this fight? Together we can get exactly what we both want."

He was silent for a long moment. "I'll help. I want to clear my name and get rid of this black cloud hanging over me." He took a shaky breath and ran his fingers through his hair. "As for us...once trust is gone, it's hard to get back. I want to think you'll change. But you've told me nothing but lies since we started corresponding."

"Necessary ones. I understand though. I accept your decision, whatever it is."

"I have all these doubts and uncertainty twisting and turning inside me." He paused as though trying to find the words to say what he wanted. "As the old timers used to say, 'We'll see what's left after the dust settles.' I don't have an objection to you moving back in. I'll sleep on the sofa. The children need you, and your presence will calm them. They're terrified we'll abandon them."

"I noticed that last night. They wouldn't let me out of their sight."

"My fault. I rode out without giving them a thought." He wearily wiped his eyes.

Heavy sadness sank over her and she could barely nod.

Tait opened the door to let her into the suite, and the rambunctious gang she thought she might never see again besieged her. Only Tait's guarded expression reminded her that the problems between them were far from settled.

That night they took supper in the café as a family. On the walk over, they passed passengers getting off the stagecoach. Tait watched as Melanie paused to speak to one gentleman who appeared down on his luck. His clothes were shabby, and he hadn't shaved in a while. She welcomed him to Hope's Crossing with a smile and pressed the key to the room she'd rented into his palm.

Melanie did have a big heart. Tait suspected it came from times when she and her sister had struggled through too many fearful nights. He was hard-pressed to separate the woman he'd come to know so intimately from the woman who'd kept such a destructive secret.

God help him, he still cared for her in spite of everything.

She'd shocked him with her declarations of love. Did she really love him? In time, could he feel more than betrayal and this gnawing in his gut?

He pondered that and held the door of the café. What he'd felt for her before her confession had come close to the way he had felt for Lucy. The realization shook him. Without consciously deciding to, he'd accepted Melanie as his wife in every way.

They sat near the front of the café, and it wasn't long before Stoker Legend and his sons entered and took the table next table to them.

"Evening, folks. Nice night." Stoker gave Melanie a wink before he sat down.

In no time, they pulled the two tables together. The children—especially Becky—loved the big rancher, and Tait admitted he'd developed a certain fondness for the Legend family himself. They didn't pretend to be anything except what they were: honest men who were happy to make the world a better place when and as they could.

After they finished the meal, Stoker wiped his mouth and put down his napkin. "Trinity, my sons and I would like a word. There have been new developments."

The request didn't come as any surprise. Melanie had already filled Tait in on her discussion with the rancher. "Tell me where and when."

"My room at the hotel in an hour. Bring your lovely wife." Stoker kissed Melanie's cheek and said good night to the children.

Tait got his gang back to the hotel, and he and Melanie put them to bed. Jesse hugged them both extra hard then bit his quivering lip. "You won't ride out and leave us?"

The question had cost the boy a lot. Tait realized how his actions the previous night had shaken the foundations of their already-shaky world. "No, I don't plan to ever leave like that again. Your aunt and I are going to meet Mr. Legend in his room, but we'll be back. Okay?"

Joe and Jesse nodded and snuggled beneath the covers. Becky was already asleep.

Melanie kissed them. "If you need anything, come get us. Room 207."

"We will," Jesse assured them.

A minute later, they knocked on Stoker's door. Luke let them in. The sitting area was spacious enough for two people, but once they got five large men, the boy Noah Jordan, and Melanie in there, Tait felt smothered. He opted to stand, as did Sam.

Noah sat cross-legged on the floor.

Sam took the lead and apologized to Melanie. "I hope you don't mind that Pa told us about Judge McIlroy's shady dealings. Let me assure you, he far exceeds his authority. Judges don't act this way, and I suspect he's in the Missouri River Railroad owner's pocket."

"I'm relieved to hear you say that, Sam." Melanie gave him a sad smile.

Tait nodded. "I figured as much. Richard Markham wants me bad, and he has Kern Berringer and McIlroy willing to do his dirty work."

Stoker's eyes hardened. "Men who threaten women ought to be horsewhipped. We're going to do something about that when we're able, but unfortunately our current plans have changed."

Houston turned his straight-backed chair around and rested his forearms on the smooth wood. "Miss Melanie, we had decided to take the money for you if that's what you wanted, only now we can't. We just received an urgent telegram saying there was a wildfire on the ranch, and we have to leave at first light."

"How horrible!" she exclaimed.

"How much did you lose?" Tait knew how devastating a wildfire could be. And losing a lot of cattle could wipe a rancher out.

Worry rode in Houston's eyes as well as those of all the Legends. "The message from our foreman said we suffered considerable losses, both cattle and buildings. Miss Melanie, you'll have to take the money to Judge McIlroy yourself and demand your sister's freedom."

Melanie released a strangled cry. "But what if he doesn't comply? I have no leverage. He'll have the money *and* will send both me and Ava straight to prison."

"Not if I'm there," Tait said, hating the thickness of his voice. "Going alone is not an option."

"Here's the thing, Miss Melanie." Sam spoke softly and reached for her hand. "I know how McIlroy works. He's a snake, and his word as worthless as a two-dollar greenback. Wherever he goes, trouble follows because he can't keep his hands clean. I'll write a letter to take with you. If he refuses to let your sister out, show him the letter and telegraph me.

I'll be there before he can bat an eye, and I'll bring the Texas Rangers with me. I don't think he'll want anyone coming and snooping around."

"My poor Ava. Do we know if she's alive?" Melanie's lip quivered.

"No," Sam replied quietly. "The sheriff wasn't very forthcoming."

Tait widened his stance. "I'm going with you, Melanie, and don't even argue about it."

Anger tightened the lines around her mouth as she stood to face him. "They'll get you. Maybe both of us. And then what? Who'll raise these kids? They're already terrified that they'll be all alone to fend for themselves. You can't destroy their last shred of security and hope."

Stoker drew his broad eyebrows together until they were silver slashes against his tanned face. "She's right, Trinity. Let her try this first. If it doesn't work, then me and the boys will ride to Canadian. I'd love just one excuse to knock McIlroy's brains out."

A muscle worked in Tait's jaw as he faced down the big rancher. "There's only one thing wrong with that, Legend. This is not your fight. What kind of man would I be if I let you solve problems I created? McIlroy wants *me*."

"No, it's not my fight." Stoker slowly took a cigar from his pocket and snipped off the end with a cutter from the stand beside his chair. "But I can make it mine real fast. This country is worth fighting for. I fought for Texas independence, fought outlaws, drought, and everything else to make this a place for decent people. By God I'll fight anything to make this land safe for all of us."

The room lapsed into silence. Stoker lit his cigar and leaned back. Tait's admiration for the man grew. They wanted the same things. Only Stoker stood a better shot at making it happen.

Luke rose after a moment and sauntered to the window. "We've got to talk to the governor when we get some time. This calls for going straight to the top and exposing all the corruption, including possibly charging Markham with Lucy's murder."

Cigar smoke filled the room as Stoker mulled something over. "That still leaves Trinity without a pardon. Once the money is gone, he won't have anything to bargain with. We have to make this all work together at once—Melanie's sister, returning the money, and a pardon."

Tait brushed a hand over his eyes. He was tired of running around the same cactus bed.

"It's best to apply for a pardon *after* you return the money," Sam told Tait. "Tell the governor about taking in your niece and nephews and all your contributions to this town. Also, the fact that you're married and settled with a house under way and have stopped robbing trains." He paused and gave Tait a piercing stare. "You have stopped, haven't you, Trinity?"

"Yes, on my honor." Melanie and the kids had taken the need for revenge from him.

"And you haven't broken any more laws?" Sam pressed.

"No." Tait had wanted to kill Earl Berringer but in his own opinion had shown remarkable restraint. "Look, I appreciate what you're doing, but this is getting too complicated." Tait sighed. "It's best if I just turn myself in along with the money. That way it'll protect Melanie."

"No!" Shock froze the lines of Melanie's face. "There's got to be another way."

"I'll take my chances." He wouldn't let her go to jail. "For you."

Tears filled her eyes. "You can't trust McIlroy. He'll take you and still not give my sister back. Besides, once he has the money, you're as good as dead. Tait, all of this is crazy."

"I'd listen, Trinity. McIlroy doesn't plan to release her sister." Houston got to his feet.

"I have a question for you, Stoker." Tait swung his attention to the seasoned cattleman. "Would you let your wife walk into that mess alone?"

Stoker let out a snort. "Hell no! I wouldn't let her get close to them."

"There's your answer."

Sam rubbed the back of his neck. "I suppose the question is—what are you willing to risk? You strike me as an all-or-nothing kind of man."

Tait mulled that over. Despite what Melanie had done, he still cared for her. "I'm willing to risk everything to save her sister."

Melanie gasped, and the room grew quiet for several heartbeats.

In the stillness, Stoker went to a side table and held up a bottle. "Would anyone care to join me?"

Tait was tempted to down the entire bottle, but he had to stay sober for the kids. Nevertheless, both he and Melanie each took a small glass with the men whose name seemed synonymous with the lives they'd led.

Noah had been silent until now. The kid rose. "I want to do something to help. I could take a note to that judge if you want me to."

Stoker draped an arm across the kid's shoulders. "We'll use you somehow."

"Thanks, Papa Stoker." Noah yawned. "I'm going to bed."

"Good night, son."

Tait watched the exchange, wishing for the power to change his wretched childhood.

Melanie stood. "We should probably go, Tait."

He reached for his hat. "Not much more can be decided tonight, and the children are jumpy anyway. Sam, let us know the minute you find out anything about Ava."

"You got it."

They said good night, and Tait and Melanie returned to their suite one floor up. Everything was quiet, and the children were asleep. Melanie started toward the bedroom, but stopped when Tait didn't follow.

"I'll sleep out here," he said, grabbing a blanket.

Sad lines deepened her face. "For what it's worth, I keep wishing I could turn back time. But then if I did, I'd never have met you. And I don't think I could live with that."

The tears bubbling in her eyes were almost his undoing.

She'd had a good reason for keeping her secret. Hell, he'd have done the same thing to save someone he loved.

Tait dropped the blanket onto the sofa. "Give me some time. I have a lot to think about."

"Can you ever forgive me?"

He crossed the space and kissed her forehead. "I already have." But trusting again? She'd have to earn it.

"Thank you. I'll never keep another secret from you." She squeezed his hand, then turned and went into the bedroom.

Tait laid down on the sofa, but the thoughts whirling in his head made sleep impossible. What would having his freedom feel like? To not worry about arrest, a trial, hanging. He could barely remember a time when he didn't have to start at every movement.

He tried to pull up Lucy's face, but as hard as he concentrated, he couldn't. Melanie, her blue-green eyes shining bright, was the lady he saw in his heart.

∽

Melanie lay awake. She couldn't sleep without Tait's breathing next to her. He'd forgiven her and had let go of his anger. But how long would it be before he slept in their bed once more?

Would he ever want to feel her beside him again or make love until dawn? Maybe he'd turn to another woman for comfort. One who hadn't hurt him. The thought brought a low cry of pain. She clapped a hand over her mouth to stifle the sound.

She'd messed things up good. But as long as he let her stay, she had hope for things to go back as they once were. Yet she knew nothing would ever be the same. Things could eventually be good again, but everything had to change. She and Tait weren't the same people.

Melanie's thoughts turned to her sister. If Ava were dead, wouldn't she feel it? They'd always had a close, almost eerie, connection. But Melanie didn't sense the cold emptiness that accompanied death.

No, Ava had to be alive. If only there was some way to let her twin know she would soon be on her way.

Melanie closed her eyes and envisioned her sister's face. Using all her energy, she projected two words into the dark. *I'm coming.* And then all she could do was pray that the message got through.

She'd take the money to McIlroy and let the cards fall where they may. At least the Legends would be her ace in the hole if she needed them. Her hardest task would be keeping Tait far away from Canadian. They couldn't have him. Not now. Not ever. She'd take his place if she had to.

"I'll never stop loving that man as long as I draw breath." Her soft whisper bolstered her low spirits and eased the heartache that seemed to crowd out every one of her hopes and dreams.

Twenty-four

THE FIRST RAYS OF DAWN SPREAD FALSE CHEER AS THEY GOT THE children up and went outside to see off the Legend men and their drovers. Stoker and his sons strode from the Diamond Bessie, their spurs jingling. Melanie was again struck by their large figures and the easy way they moved inside their own skins. Tait shared that self-confidence with them, and it had been one of the things that had captivated her about him.

Becky clamored to get down from her arms. The minute Melanie set her down, she ran to Stoker, who scooped her up. "Hey, pretty girl."

The child kissed his cheek and put her arms around his neck.

"Good morning," Melanie greeted the men.

"My gan'pa." Becky grinned and snuggled against the rancher's large chest.

"You are getting way too spoiled, little girl," Melanie scolded before addressing Stoker. "Do you have more information about Ava?"

"Sam heard back late last night. She's still in jail in Canadian but very ill." Stoker reached to steady Melanie when her legs buckled.

Melanie sucked in a breath. "What's wrong with her?"

"Something she contracted in there. Not sure what."

Fear clenched every muscle inside her. They had to hurry and get Ava out. "I can't bear the thought of her sick and locked up in that cell. But as long as she still lives, I'll cling to hope."

"Details are sketchy." Sam slapped his gloves against his trousers. "The sheriff is mighty stingy with information."

Melanie had disliked the sheriff of Canadian on sight. His shifty eyes, the way he'd looked at her had made her feel like a common whore. "Are they letting a doctor treat Ava?"

"That's anyone's guess."

Tait came from the direction of the corral and stopped next to her. "Now what? Where do we go from here?"

Houston Legend shifted a toothpick to the other side of his mouth and leaned against a post. "We'll contact an old friend, U.S. Marshal Tyrell Renick, just over in Indian Territory. He may be able to help on his end. At least McIlroy and the sheriff won't do anything obvious with Renick watching."

"Change is coming to this part of Texas." Stoker grinned when Becky patted his cheek. "The governor has set up the 35th judicial district in Mobeetie, and they're going to clean up this lawlessness."

Tait met Melanie's gaze, and she could almost feel the heavy weight sitting on his shoulders. If he had no choice but run, she'd be by his side—if he wanted her there, that is.

Luke's hat shaded his eyes and hid his expression, but Melanie suspected he'd done that on purpose. The half-Spanish former outlaw enjoyed taking people's measure in private. She liked and admired him more than just about anyone. She'd never have met Tait without his help. Was Luke angry at what she'd tried to do? She hoped not.

"Renick can put pressure on McIlroy and Markham." Luke's Spanish accent was smooth and mellow. "I think he can also be a big help to you, Miss Melanie."

"What happens to Judge McIlroy? Will he get off scot-free?" Tait demanded. "I can name a dozen crimes he committed that we know about, and I'm not even a lawyer."

Sam put his hat on and adjusted it. "I wired the governor and apprised him of the situation. He'll likely strip McIlroy of his judgeship and send a temporary replacement in a few days, but I won't know until I get the governor's reply."

Stoker squeezed Tait's shoulder. "As far as your pardon, you'll have to throw yourself on the governor's mercy and be prepared to explain in detail why you feel you deserve clemency."

Pain filled Tait's eyes, and Melanie could see both how scared he was and how carefully he tried not to let it show. To fail meant he'd have to remain in hiding the rest of his life, and it was the long odds that had him by the short hairs.

"I'll help, Tait." Melanie threaded her fingers through his. "Together we can do this."

Tait gave her hand a slight squeeze, which heartened her, then released his hold. "What happens with Kern Berringer?"

The lines of Stoker's face relaxed. "He'll be arrested if he shows his face near Mobeetie or Canadian. Renick will throw him in jail before he knows what's happening."

"But with so few lawmen to cover that area, they can't spend weeks and months searching for him." Luke's voice was low. "Trinity, it might be best to go after him yourself. Get your justice as men like us have had to do our whole lives."

Luke was right, and tears welled in Melanie's eyes. Outlaws like them wanted to do right, many really tried, but when things went sour and the law was far away, they had no choice but to fix the problems themselves.

She stood beside Tait, not touching but close enough so he would know she supported him.

"Understood." His face set in hard lines. "I have the will, and I have a good gun."

"One more thing." Stoker lowered his voice. "I don't know if you can use this or not, but Ira McIlroy almost beat a working girl to death last year over in Indian Territory. He thought he'd covered it up." Stoker grinned. "Thankfully, people didn't turn a blind eye. Some of them are talking. You might mention that and see what happens."

"That's very interesting." Melanie filed the information away just in case.

"We hate to say goodbye, but we've got to ride." Stoker shook Tait's hand then hers.

"I'm forever in your debt." She stood on tiptoe and kissed Stoker's cheek. "I hope you live a long time. Texas needs you."

Houston grinned. "Hey, don't swell the old man's head any more than it is or we won't be able to live with him." He drew Melanie into a hug and passed her on to Sam and Luke.

Noah arrived with the horses. "I have them saddled, Papa Stoker."

"You know, I'm going to have to keep you around. I can't remember how I managed before you came, son." Stoker affectionately ruffled the boy's hair.

It seemed like the whole town had come to see them off. Jack and Clay thanked them for the cattle. Tally had tears in her eyes, and Melanie put her arm around her.

Tait reached for Becky, but she clung to Stoker's shirt. "Gan'pa! Gan'pa!" The rancher gave her a kiss. "You be a good girl and mind your aunt and uncle." His voice broke as he pulled free of her hands and handed her to Tait. He stuck his foot in the stirrup and swung over.

Melanie sniffled and waved until the riders disappeared through the opening. Becky was bawling her eyes out, and Melanie didn't blame her.

Why couldn't Stoker Legend have been *her* father? Her life would've been so different with someone who had cared.

❧

The early-morning rays shone bright and cheery through the windows of the Blue Goose, and Melanie embraced the new beginning as a good sign. Becky had settled down and sipped on her milk. Tait actually made an effort to talk over breakfast.

He didn't look as haggard as he had the day before, so she thought he must've slept some. Sweet Becky seemed to sense her uncle's need for extra love the way she kept patting and kissing on him. The girl chattered up a storm, making up words for some she didn't know how to say. And the boys asked Tait's advice about school and various other subjects.

Joe propped his elbow on the table and put a hand under his chin. "We turned loose all those animals that we'd captured, but Bandit won't leave. He hangs around the café, and Mr. Truman is real mad, says we have to get rid of him or else."

"We've tried everything," Jesse added. "What can we do, Uncle Tait?"

"I have to take a ride out to the cattle in a bit. I'll take him with me and release him far from here. We'll see if that does the trick. But I think you tamed him a little too good. He seems to think this is his new home." Tait wiped the milk from Becky's mouth.

"I guess so," Joe replied. "I wish a real circus would come along and take him."

"Poor Bandit," Melanie murmured. "He gave a great performance, and now you want to get rid of him."

"He's making everyone mad, and we need him to leave." Jesse huffed.

Mr. Denver, the schoolmaster, entered the café. "Good morning, Mr. and Mrs. Trinity."

Joe and Jesse ducked low in their chairs.

"Morning," Tait answered before reaching over and pulling the twins up by their collars. "What do you say, boys?"

"Good morning, Mr. Denver," they replied in unison.

Tait took a sip of coffee. "I'm sending Joe and Jesse over after breakfast to help you get the school ready for Monday. They're excited, aren't you, boys?"

One thing Tait loved to do—tease. He was quite good at doing that, and Melanie almost felt sorry for the twins.

Becky grinned and clapped. "School."

"Afraid not, honey." Melanie handed her a biscuit and looked up. "Mr. Denver, the only one excited about school is too young to go."

Denver laughed. "Isn't that always the way? I look forward to teaching Joe and Jesse. The trick is finding the one thing a child is passionate about."

Tait snorted. "Good luck there."

The teacher moved on, and Melanie's attention returned to her husband. How was she going to convince him that she had to take the money to Judge McIlroy alone? Each time she brought it up, all he'd say was that it wasn't an option.

Still, her way was best for all of them.

❧

Once they'd finished eating, they left the boys at the church that doubled as a school and took Becky over to Nora's. Tait rode out with Bandit and came back alone an hour later. Melanie was walking through their new home when he strode in. "Tait, I love the roominess."

"Glad you approve."

The house seemed to close welcoming arms around her. *Please don't let it be too late for me to live here.*

Tait disappeared for a minute and returned with a hammer and a board. "Would you like to put your stamp on our house?"

"Absolutely." Happiness filled her that he'd said *ours*—and that he'd obviously seen her need to be a part of the building process.

"I thought you might." He handed her the hammer and nails, holding the board beneath the window. "When you're lying there in bed, you can see your handiwork."

"I'll remember this day. Both these nails and the precious gift of a second chance."

He studied her. "We all need one now and again. You did the only thing you could to try to help your sister. Can we get back what we had?" He blew out a deep breath. "I don't know. I guess time will tell."

"I'm sorry, Tait. But you probably want more than words. Give me time and I'll show you that I'm still the same woman you came to care about."

He gave her a curt nod and positioned the board. "Pound away. Just watch out for my fingers. And yours."

A nervous laugh rose as Melanie took a nail, held it in place, and struck it until it was embedded. Over and over she hammered until the board was secured. The more strikes of the hammer, the lighter she felt. Hitting things seemed to have a calming effect on her aching heart.

Her gaze followed Tait's lean form as he moved through the house in that loose, meandering gait that filled her dreams. His dark-blond hair brushed his shoulders, and stubble clung to his jaw, but he made her knees as weak as jelly when he turned those silvery-gray eyes on her.

At least he hadn't made her leave, even though she still saw hurt in his eyes. She wished she knew how to fix things.

Especially the ache in her heart. Hopefully time would heal them both.

~❦~

Tait spent the day with the men at the new house. He figured another week until they finished. A few of them were out tending the cattle, and Tait had warned them to watch for Berringer. Now that the Legends had left, Kern would be bolder. He was one who liked the odds in his favor.

When they stopped to rest and cool off with water, Jack laid a hand on Tait's shoulder. "Are you all right, brother?"

"I'm fine. Why are you asking?"

"Don't want to pry, but I have eyes. Something happened between you and Melanie the night of the dance. And the next thing I knew, you'd dragged that railroad loot into town."

"You might as well know. I'm giving it back." He kept his voice low and told Jack about Melanie's confession and her explanations. "I have to get her sister out. Prison is no place for a woman. What kind of man would I be if I didn't?"

Jack released a low whistle. "No wonder you looked all hollowed-out inside. Damn, Tait. I think helping her sister is right. I'd do the same thing if I were in your shoes. And who knows, maybe returning the money will get you a pardon to boot. It certainly can't hurt."

Tait stared at his hands, thinking of how many times they'd curled around his gun and the lives he'd taken. "I just want to get out from under this darkness that eats and eats and eats at me."

"I can vouch that nothing can compare to the feeling of freedom." Jack poured a dipper of water over his head. "Back to your marriage—you're a good man to give Melanie another chance. She didn't want to hurt you."

"Yeah." Tait took off his hat and wiped his forehead. "She said she loves me."

"There you go. Marriages tend to start off rocky in the getting-acquainted stage. Mine and Nora's was the same way, but we kept working at it, and now our relationship is solid."

Tait was considering Jack's words when four shots rang out and the guard at the entrance toppled to the ground. "Come on, Jack!" Tait pulled his weapon and ran.

Bullet and Scout barked madly and raced toward the danger.

Others beat him to the downed man, so Tait kept going through the entrance, pausing at the opening in the canyon. His heart pounded as he glanced out, gripping his Smith & Wesson.

The dogs didn't stop. They kept running even as the shooter tried to kill them too. He only missed them both by some miracle.

Jack and Clay pressed to the other side of the entrance, peeking around their cover to get a sense of the situation.

Nothing moved in Tait's line of vision except the dogs. Bullet and Scout dove into the dense brush, still raising hell. One of them gave a loud yelp. Tait picked up a rock and threw it in the opposite direction, away from the dogs. A burst of rifle fire erupted. Using his hands, Tait signaled to Jack and Clay to ask if they could see anything. Both shook their heads.

Tait motioned for them to cover him. As shots burst from his friends' position, he rushed out and dove into some tall bushes. He kept a close eye out to see where the return fire came from. There! The shooter ducked down in a clump of mesquites.

Wishing he had a rifle instead, Tait raised his gun, took aim, and squeezed the trigger.

The gunman yelled profanities, letting Tait know that his shot had hit the mark. Jack and Clay ran from their cover, creating a wall of fire as they went. Tait rose and joined them, and they reached the wounded man at the same time. Bullet and Scout were sniffing him over and snarling.

Tait grabbed the attacker's rifle, tossed it aside, then checked for other weapons, finding none.

Clay stuck the barrel of his gun against the gunman's forehead. "Who are you?" Blood oozed from between the man's fingers as he clutched his chest and dribbled from the corner of his mouth. His eyes were glazing over as they watched, and Tait knew he wouldn't be telling them one blessed thing. A second later he went limp, life leaving his body.

Tait scanned the landscape for any other movement—any sign that he'd come with friends. Nothing moved.

The dead man looked to be older than Tait. "Do either of you recognize him?"

Both said no. Jack closed the man's open eyes. "I'd put his age at about thirty-five or so."

Tait put his gun away. "Could be another of Kern's sons. I never saw very many of his boys, only the old man."

"We'll see if Earl recognizes him." Jack slid his gun into his holster.

"I'm betting he's a brother or cousin." Tait hoisted the dead man up and over his shoulder while Clay kept a lookout.

They were almost to safety when a rider burst around some boulders, thundering toward them and shooting as he rode. He galloped past, raising a dust cloud.

Clay returned fire rapidly, emptying his gun at the fleeing figure. "Hurry inside before he doubles back."

Tait and Jack wasted no time. They moved quickly back into town, and men were waiting to roll wagons across the opening behind them. Melanie ran to them, her eyes large in her ashen face. She stopped five feet away as though afraid to come closer.

Tait laid the dead man into the back of a wagon and straightened. "I'm fine, Melanie."

"I was afraid." A strangled sob rose, and she twisted her hands.

"It's okay." He covered the space between them and pulled her close.

Tait held her for a long moment, glad she cared for his sorry hide. A rock in the wall between them fell, leaving a small chink for sunlight to come through.

Twenty-five

THE NEXT TWO DAYS PASSED IN NERVOUS WHISPERS, WHICH kept Melanie on edge. The guard who'd been shot was recovering in the small hospital, thank goodness. Barricading the entrance had cut them off from the two men guarding the herd, however, and the town didn't know their fate.

With snipers outside taking potshots at anyone who dared to try to leave, they had to assume the worst for the men.

She'd stood by with the other women while the men kept trying to sneak out under cover of darkness only to be driven back. Finally, Tait and the men had hatched a plan to see how many shooters there were. Tait climbed to the top of the bluff by rope, and when Clay showed himself at the opening, drawing fire, Tait was able to see what they'd feared.

It wasn't just one sniper out there—there were a dozen or more. Probably every single member of Kern's gang.

Earl Berringer identified the dead man as an older brother and delivered a dire prediction. "My old man will ride in here any day and kill every stinking one of you. This town will run thick with blood. Just wait and see."

The men set to work on trying to clear enough debris from the back entrance that they'd sealed with dynamite several years previously. But snipers there also made that impossible.

They were totally surrounded. Melanie tried to remain calm, but growing panic rippled just under the surface.

She worried about Tait and what he'd try next. Except for that one embrace, he hadn't come near her again. After Earl's identification of the dead man, Tait had become a man obsessed. He didn't sleep and rarely ate. Melanie didn't know how long he could continue like this, but she kept quiet. A nagging wife was the last thing he needed.

She sometimes saw him talking with the men but didn't

approach. It was best to keep her distance. The strain on their tenuous relationship frayed her nerves, and she shifted her entire focus to the children. Keeping them calm, however, was no easy task.

"They're gonna sneak in here and kill us," Jesse predicted, edging closer to Melanie on the sofa.

"Stop thinking that way," Melanie scolded. "We have plenty of men and guns to keep that from happening, and they have no way inside. Don't frighten your sister."

Becky put her hands over her eyes. "Me scared."

"See there?" Melanie said, picking up the girl. "Honey, we're all going to be just fine. Your uncle will shoot anyone who tries to get inside. He's not afraid of killers."

"No, he ain't." Jesse seemed positive of that at least. "Uncle Tait will stop 'em."

Since the siege, the stagecoach had ceased to run. And if they made it by the snipers outside, no one got past the barricade inside without proving their identities and stating their business. Melanie knew the men worried about the two guards with the cattle, and she feared they were probably dead. Earl had loudly proclaimed as much.

Melanie was pulling Becky along the road in a little wagon when the evening sun shone on a man carrying a bag at the entrance to town. Why would anyone brave the danger to visit a town under siege that had to be kept locked down?

Maybe he was delivering a letter or something from Sam about her sister.

The dogs ran toward him, barking their lungs out. The man wore a jaunty bowler and a two-dollar pinstripe suit. When he got closer, her mouth dried.

Mac Dunbar.

Melanie stared, neither moving nor speaking. Why had he come now, except to start trouble?

Mac opened his arms. "Come here, girl. Give your old papa a hug."

"What are you doing here?" She didn't try to hide the ice in her words, her stiff lips, or the hard glint in her eyes. "Leave.

Disappear from our lives. You're good at that, and we don't want you."

"Don't be that way, Melanie." When she didn't make a move toward him, he let his arms fall to his sides. "I've had hell finding you and come all this way from St. Louis. I had to walk a mile from where a freighter I hitched a ride with let me off, and I'm tired and dirty. I don't appreciate this reception."

Everything was *still* all about him. He hadn't even asked how she was, what she was doing in Hope's Crossing, or anything at all about Ava.

"You know what? I don't care how far you've traveled." She felt a large presence move in behind her and heard Tait's voice.

"You heard her. You're not welcome here. You're a self-centered cheat and a scoundrel, and I have half a mind to shoot you on the spot."

Mac scowled. "Who are you? This is a private conversation."

"I'm Melanie's husband. Name's Tait Trinity."

Shock rippled across Mac's face, and the color drained from his cheeks. "I see. Well, sir, perhaps you're right about some things, but you can't separate me from my daughter. Melanie, I've been worried sick about you and Ava. You're my girls. Don't treat me this way." Mac spoke the words with false feeling behind them, just like an actor saying his lines. "I remembered your name. Doesn't that count for something?"

She snorted. "You only know because Ava sits in jail all alone."

Mac glanced down and dug at a tuft of grass with the toe of his boot. "I had to pay Judge McIlroy a tidy sum to tell me where you were."

Revulsion swept over her that her father would have dealings with the judge who was trying to put her and Ava in prison. Hot anger surged. "Did you offer to pay a *tidy sum* to get her released?"

When he didn't reply, she asked again through clenched teeth. "Did you offer to pay to get your daughter out?"

"No. How much money do you think I have?" His eyes blazed.

"I don't know, Mac. It depends on which day of the week it is," she snapped. "I'm guessing you have to be pretty close to broke to look me up." She took a calming breath. "Did the judge tell you Ava is very sick?" She found his white face immensely satisfying.

He appeared even more shaken—or was she imagining it? "No."

"Did you visit her? Did you do that much?"

Mac's nostrils flared, and a vein pulsed in his neck. "I asked to see her, and McIlroy refused. I do have a heart."

"That's debatable," Tait replied dryly. "From what I hear, you don't have a caring bone in your body for anyone other than yourself."

Melanie glared at the man who'd fathered her and raised her chin a notch. "I'd be in jail with her if not for a deal I made with McIlroy. If you'd cared about us a single iota, you'd have stuck around when they arrested us for *your* crime."

"They go easier on women, or so I thought. How was I to know they'd throw you in jail?"

She wouldn't dignify that with a response. Another thought hit. She narrowed her eyes. "Why did the snipers let you by? Did you pay them too? Or was it because you've had dealings with the Berringers before?"

The remaining color left Mac's face, and he swallowed hard, unable to find a reply.

"I have my answer." Melanie picked Becky up and turned to Tait. "Let's go. There's nothing here of interest."

"Dunbar, find your way back to where that freighter let you off or you and me will have problems." Tait put an arm around her and drew her away, leaving Mac Dunbar standing alone in the middle of the town.

"You're shaking," Tait said quietly once they were out of earshot.

"I'm so furious. I finally see him as he really is. I mean, I knew, but I had blinders on. Well, no more. Thank you for backing me up."

"I didn't know who he was at first, but from the cold way you treated him, I thought it must be your father. If he doesn't leave, I'll hurry him on his way. Go ahead and get Becky into the hotel."

"Will you please take a meal with us tonight? The children need to see you." And so did she. To sit across from him, the flickering light catching the streaks of blond between chunks of warm caramel hair, his eyes full of desire the way he used to look at her—that would be worth a small fortune.

The dark hat shaded his face, but even bathed in shadows she could sense no anger in his expression—only terrible weariness.

"I know I haven't been doing right by the kids these days. Tell them I'll take supper with them tonight." He stopped and held her face between his hands. "And you. We'll be a family."

Something about the word *family* sent warmth through the layer of ice around her heart. "Tait, I'm sorry for the extra annoyance Mac added. Now you know what I was talking about."

"I've seen plenty of men like him. I can manage Dunbar just fine. I'll make sure he doesn't bother you."

"Thank you. How long is this siege going to last? I wish Berringer would give himself up."

"Not going to happen. I know him. He's out to make me pay for crippling him, and nothing but death will stop him."

"Everyone is jittery. We can't keep this up. The town will run out of food."

"It'll end soon. I'll make sure of it one way or another." He released his hold and stalked toward the blockade that stretched across the town's entrance.

"My wuncle," Becky said.

"Yes, he is, honey. And he loves you very much." Maybe one day after his memory of all this started to fade, he'd be able to have feelings for her again too.

She had a mountain to climb, but climb it she would because a big reward awaited her at the top.

❦

She didn't see Mac the rest of the evening but found out from the desk clerk that he'd checked into the hotel. At six o'clock she took the children to the café. There was no sign of Tait at first, but just as they got seated at a table near the back, he walked in. Removing his hat, he wound his way over to them.

All three children started talking at once. Tait raised a hand. "One at a time."

"We start school tomorrow," Joe said glumly. "I don't know why we hafta go to school when we can't even open the town."

"Because you need something to do to take your mind off the danger." Tait straightened Joe's shirt, his buttons in the wrong holes. "Tell me, what would you do if you didn't have school?"

"Well, Jesse and me would play with the other kids."

"I like school," Jesse announced, stunning everyone. "I get to help Violet with her books and things. She smells real good."

Tait's laugh lifted some of the heaviness from his face. His gaze met Melanie's, and she grew warm. "It only gets better from here, son. I think you're growing up."

Melanie grew warm under his attention. Was he starting to thaw?

Jesse propped his head on his arm. "Well, it's not like we're going to get married or anything. I'm scared of Mr. Colby. He don't like me much."

"Why do you think that?" Melanie asked.

"'Cause he growls at me and looks all serious."

"I'm not ever liking girls. They're too bossy," Joe declared. "I'm just gonna live by myself."

"I can't wait to see this." Tait stopped a waiter. "I think we're ready to order."

After the waiter left their table, Tait leaned back in the chair. "I don't have much time. I'm on guard tonight."

The thought of the danger that waited in the darkness stilled Melanie's blood. She prayed for his safety. Kern Berringer wanted Tait dead and meant to see it happen.

A memory floated into Melanie's mind. She had been ten years old and had gone to play with another little girl. The girl's father, killed by a robber, had been laid out on the table. The mother had gathered water and cloths to bathe the body. She'd shooed them out and locked the door, and Melanie had later learned that it was the custom to ready someone for burial.

If Berringer's bullet found Tait, it would be her duty to bathe him. She'd lovingly wash every inch of his body even as her heart broke.

She shook herself. *Don't think of such things.*

Becky stole Tait's attention, patting and loving on him. "I go with you."

"Hey, you're talking in a sentence, peanut." Tait beamed like a proud parent. "But you'll have to stay with Aunt Mellie. It's too dangerous where I'll be."

"A bad ghost will come and get you." Joe snarled and raised his curled arms at her.

"No!" Becky tried to climb into Tait's lap to get away.

"Stop that, Joe. Don't scare her that way," Tait scolded. "Honey, stay in your chair. I won't let anything get you."

Becky pouted. "Joe mean."

The kids settled down, and soon their food came. Melanie sat watching their faces, scoffing at her previous notion that they were too messy, too difficult to raise, too intimidating. She couldn't imagine not ever having them in her life. They added layers of satisfaction, joy, and richness. To ride away and leave them would kill her.

Tait laid down his fork. "A penny for your thoughts, Melanie."

"I think they'd be way overpriced." She took a bite of mashed potatoes.

He smiled. "I told your father he'd have to leave tomorrow. He said he has to talk to you before he goes. What are your feelings?"

"Whatever gets him gone fastest is what I'll do. I'll let him have his say. He can't hurt me anymore. It's strange. I don't hate him—I don't feel anything one way or another. It's how I'd feel about a stump. It's there, but I have no fondness for it. I just know I can't have him around." Melanie took a sip of hot tea. "I'll never forgive him for leaving Ava and me to take the fall."

He laid his hand on top of hers. "I can't imagine how it is for a woman in jail. It's bad enough for men used to such treatment. As soon as I deal with Kern, I'll work on Ava's release, even if I have to break her out."

Melanie knew he meant it. Just as she was certain he'd be hanged if caught.

Twenty-six

THEY CAME AS DAWN LIT THE WALLS OF THE CANYON—TWO hundred bawling, snot-dripping cattle busting through the opening. Tait leaped out of the way from his guard post to avoid being trampled as the animals flowed inside, like floodwaters rushing over the riverbanks.

"Watch out, Jack! Get to safety!" Tait yelled, pressing flat against the rock wall next to the entrance.

He was out of the reach of most of the trampling hooves and had a good view of the horsemen driving the herd. Taking the lead, firing his gun into the air, and yelling obscenities was none other than the man Tait sought—Kern Berringer.

Hell! Tait tried to get to him, but the steers between them blocked his path.

Kern managed to ride clear of the animals and made his way to the outdoor cell where his son Earl was imprisoned. Tait darted out into the herd, dodging and weaving his way toward the two. He was almost there.

Aiming his gun, Kern shot the lock holding Earl. Clay stepped out of the darkness, gun drawn. "Raise your hands, you hairless bastard!"

The hated killer whirled and fired, forcing Clay to dive behind some barrels that held pitch for their roofs.

"Hurry up, Daddy!" Earl screamed. "Let me out of here!"

They hadn't seen Tait yet. He was hidden by the swirling mass of cattle. He raised his gun and fired, striking Kern's arm and spinning him around.

Jack and Dallas Hawk appeared, blocking Kern's path. Kern saw the futility of trying to free Earl and leaped into his saddle instead.

"Don't leave me, Daddy!" Earl screamed. "Come back! I need you."

But Kern spurred the animal forward and galloped in the

direction of the hotel. Tait emptied his gun without hitting the man a second time. A crowd milled around on the boardwalk in front of the hotel, and he could make out Melanie and the children among the astonished onlookers.

Onward Kern galloped, scattering the herd as he came. The spit dried in Tait's mouth. Kern was going to shoot them!

"Get back inside!" Tait screamed, running as fast as he could. In all the chaos and noise, Melanie couldn't hear him.

Kern drew closer, any opposition stopped by the gunfire of the men with him. There must've been about a dozen riding among the cattle, and they shot at anything that moved. Tait pressed to the side of the newspaper office and waited for a chance.

He peeked around the corner as Kern rode his horse onto the boardwalk. His breath froze as Kern reached out and ripped Becky from Melanie's arms.

"No!" Tait raced out only to have a bullet pierce his side. Instant icy-hot pain zigzagged through him, rushing along his body. He fought for breath and to slow his thundering heartbeat even as he knew he had to move. He shook his head and blocked the agony.

He had to get to them!

Kern rode toward Tait with Becky under his arm, screaming at the top of her voice. "You took my boys. This one belongs to me now."

"No!" Becky yelled. "Help! Help!"

"You bastard! Harm one hair on that little girl and I'll kill you."

The early morning rays of the sun glinted off Kern's face, making his slick head and no eyebrows look like the face of the devil's own scarecrow. Tait wished for just one bullet in his gun. Just one.

Clay and Jack ran toward them, firing, until Kern lifted Becky up in the air. "Shoot me and this child dies."

Melanie raced down the steps. "Stop!"

Kern's eerie laugh tore through Tait's soul. Sobbing, Melanie stumbled to Kern's horse and grabbed his leg. "Release her. She's just a baby."

"Mellie!" Becky cried.

He spurred the animal, and Melanie clung fast. The horse dragged her several yards before her hold broke and she fell to the dirt. Becky's screams ripped through Tait until horse and rider disappeared through the town's mangled opening. Tait clutched his side, blood running through his fingers, and hobbled to Melanie.

"I'm all right, Tait." She sat up, sobbing, tears rolling down her cheeks. "I couldn't save her. I couldn't hold on. I couldn't…"

Tait sat down with her and pulled her to him. "We'll get her back. Hold that thought."

The twins plopped down with them, crying.

"He got her," Joe said. "He was there when our mama died. I saw him."

Tait must've groaned in pain because Melanie pulled away and looked down at his side. "You're shot."

"Just a bee sting. I'll be fine." He took in her torn dress, hair stringing down, and bloody arms. "You're hurt."

"A few scrapes—nothing serious. I thought I could stop him."

"When a stone-cold killer enters your town, no one can stop him."

"You shot him, Tait, but will that only drive him to kill Becky?" She grabbed his arm, her fingernails digging into the flesh. "Oh God, we may have sealed her fate!"

"Try not to worry." But a nagging feeling whispered the same fear. "This is not over."

The townsfolk hurried to their aid, helped them up and moved them to Dr. Mary's. The commanding lady directed them the whole way, refusing to listen to Tait's insistence that he needed to ride out.

"Listen here, Trinity." Dr. Mary put her hands on her hips. "Let me get that bullet out and put a stitch or two in or I'll have the men tie you down so I can do it without your say-so. You won't do that little girl any good if you lose half your blood and fall from your horse. Do we understand each other? You're her best hope, and I'm going to see that you're able to go get her."

"Then get it done." He could hear Clay barking orders outside, rounding up the cattle, and he could do nothing to help. Not one blessed thing. "Melanie? Where's Melanie?"

Her voice came from nearby. "I'm here, Tait. Please do what the doctor says."

"Get your injuries tended."

"I am. Tally's taking care of me."

"Good."

A few minutes later, bedsprings creaked and Melanie bent over him, smoothing his hair from his eyes. "I'll never leave you. I'll stay right here while the doc fixes you up."

"I should've done more to stop Kern." He worked to swallow the thickness that sat on his tongue. "If I'd just saved one bullet. He has our child, and I couldn't do anything. It's just like it was with Lucy." The piercing pain in his side took his breath. "Dammit! What good am I? What good?"

"You'll get her back. You said so. You're all I've got, so don't give up." Melanie brushed her lips across his. "I love you, Tait. Yesterday, today, and all our tomorrows."

"I'm sorry for the things I said. It was hurt talking." Jagged pain tore through him as the doctor probed in his side, and he released a sharp cry.

"It's already forgotten."

"Be still, Trinity, I almost have the fragment." Dr. Mary's bullet necklace clinked together with her movements. "Once I get it out, I'll sew you up, and you can ride after that little girl."

"Melanie, can you get Jack?"

"Sure." She left his side for a moment and came back with his friend.

"What is it, Tait?" Jack asked.

"Saddle me a horse. I'm riding out the second the doc's finished."

"Your roan's already saddled. We'll ride the moment you get through here."

"Good. I've cost us too much time as it is."

Doc Mary dropped the bullet fragment into a bowl. "I'm ready to stitch you up."

Jack left, and Melanie sat on his bed. "Tait, I'm going with you."

"Over my dead body! It's too dangerous. And besides, the boys need you."

"It's my fault that Berringer took Becky. I should've hurried back inside the hotel when he started toward us, but I wanted to see what had happened to you. I have to get her back. If they hurt her, it'll be my fault. Don't you see?"

The sob underlying her words struck a chord in him. He fumbled for her hand and gripped it. His voice was thick. "Given the chance, Kern will kill you just like he did Lucy. Human life means nothing to him. I can't let him have you too."

"He won't get me." Melanie's brow knitted. "Becky will need someone to mother her once you get her back. I want to be there." Her voice broke. "Who knows what horrors she'll endure."

"Hopefully, it'll be short-lived. If Kern hadn't driven the cattle inside, we could've stopped him." He turned toward the wall, wishing for impossible things.

Melanie was probably right in that Becky would want a mother once they found her, and Melanie was closer to that than anyone. Still, he couldn't stand the thought of what Kern would do if he got his hands on Melanie.

"You make a good argument, but I simply can't let you come. The boys need you, and to do what I need to, I have to know you're all safe."

"Fine." Her tone was short and terse, but he couldn't help it.

"You done, Doc?" He gave his hair an impatient shove and tried to get up but was stopped by a firm hand.

"You'll lay there until I say," Dr. Mary barked, laying down her needle and catgut. "I'll bandage it, and you'll be out of here. I want you to kill every one of those bastards."

Five minutes later Tait strode out into the early-morning light. Jack and Clay were waiting with the horses. Jack handed Tait the reins to his roan.

Tait turned to Melanie. "I'll be back when this is done."

"Be safe." She stood on tiptoe and kissed his cheek. "Godspeed."

With a nod, he climbed into the saddle, gritting his teeth against the searing pain that swelled up with every step. "Let's ride."

⁂

Still in their nightshirts, Joe and Jesse rose from benches on the boardwalk in front of the hotel and put their arms around Melanie.

Jesse sniffled and glanced up. "Do you think Uncle Tait will find Becky?"

"Yes." She didn't hesitate. She knew one thing about Tait—he would never give up. "He's going to end this and give your parents some justice."

"What if they hurt her? We won't be there to stop 'em." Joe's face had drained of color, leaving his freckles as dark spots on the white background. "What if they kill her, Aunt Melanie?"

The boy echoed her thoughts. She pulled the twins tightly to her, and they walked toward the door of the hotel. "They won't, and you know why?"

They shook their heads.

"Because your uncle will go berserk, and they won't want to face wrath like that. When a man gets in those kinds of rages, he's very scary." Melanie kissed the tops of their heads. "Now, let's get you dressed and something to eat so you can go to school."

"Aw, shoot." Jesse reached for the doorknob.

"Look at it this way…you have a story to tell, and everyone will clamor to hear it. You'll be very popular."

Joe followed them into the hotel. "Yeah, but Becky will still be with those killers."

Yes, she would, and Melanie had no uplifting words to offer on that.

The best thing to do in a situation like this was to keep busy. She changed clothes and put the boys to work straightening up the suite—making their beds and putting their things away. The only problem was Becky's empty bed, staring at them. Melanie finally took them to the café.

Everyone, including Martha Truman, stopped at their table to offer condolences and to help in some way.

"Thank you, Mrs. Truman. I'll let you know if there's anything you can do. Right now, I'd love to have some more hot tea."

"Coming right up." Martha rushed off to get it and came back with an invitation for afternoon tea at Nora's.

"Thank you. I have to keep occupied while Tait's gone or I'll go crazy."

Just then her father entered the café. Mac caught her eye, nodded in her direction, and took a seat at another table. Good. She'd keep the children away from him. It hit her again that Becky was gone, and for a long moment she worked to tamp down the urge to scream at the cruelty of it. Instead, she uttered a prayer that God would be merciful and let Tait find her.

And send Kern Berringer to the hottest part of hell.

❧

After dropping the boys at school, Melanie went to meet Mac Dunbar in the hotel lobby. She wanted to get the whole thing over with as fast as possible.

He stood when she entered. "Thank you for coming. I wasn't sure you would."

"I didn't know if I would either, but here I am. Say your piece."

"Melanie, I'm sorry I left you girls. I panicked. All right? I wanted to do the right thing, but that sheriff already had you and…" Mac glanced down. "He'd caught me once before and said the next time would mean prison. So I ran."

"You did that, all right." Her dry tone was sarcastic, but she didn't apologize for it. "We needed help, Mac."

"I didn't think he'd put you and Ava in jail. I thought you'd pay a fine or something and you'd be out in no time. Did you ever think what it was like for me, knowing my only girls were in danger?"

She stared at him, dumbfounded. "Stop. I'm not going to listen to 'poor pitiful me.' A little girl is out there with one of the meanest, baddest killers in Texas, and you want an audience so you can play the victim. I don't have time to waste on you. I have to try to figure out how to get Ava out of jail, keep my husband alive, and focus on getting Becky back. I have no room for pathetic whiners." She turned to walk away.

"Wait. Tell me what I can do. I'll make this right."

For the first time in her life, she imagined she heard sincerity in her father's voice. But would it still be there when the chips were down?

"Would you be willing to accompany me to Canadian?"

He hesitated for a beat too long.

"That's what I figured." She took another step and felt his hand on her arm.

"Yes, I'll go with you. I want to set things right between us. When?"

"When Tait returns." She didn't know how far she could trust him to keep his word, but based on the past, it was about as far as she could sling a buffalo. "I have to go now. I'll let you know more later."

"Absolutely. Yes, I'll be ready."

"One more thing, Mac." She leaned closer. "Try to run your con games and schemes here, and these outlaws will string you up. I won't lift one finger to stop them. Understand?"

He nodded. "Got it."

Melanie strode from the hotel, shaking inside. The heart-to-heart with her father had taken a toll on her nerves, but she was satisfied with the outcome.

With luck, maybe Mac could help her get the stolen money to the judge. If not?

Then he'd have used up his last chance, and she'd cut ties and go alone. She was already used to that.

Twenty-seven

TAIT RODE SLOWLY, SCOURING THE DIRT FOR THE BROKEN horseshoe print, and found satisfaction when he spied the signs on the hard-packed ground. He dismounted and followed the tracks, leading his horse. "I think Kern and his bunch might be heading north toward Mobeetie."

"Or Canadian." Clay stared across the barren expanse, a muscle in his jaw twitching.

Jack reached for his canteen and took a drink. "That little girl had best be unharmed when we find her, or I wouldn't want to be any of these Berringers."

"I'll take pleasure in stripping every inch of hide from them." Tait mounted back up and spurred his roan, glad to have company. There was no one better than Clay and Jack in a scrape, and his gut told him he'd need every gun. "I won't go back without Becky," he said into the wind.

And if he didn't get to her in time...

Tait recalled how desperately Melanie had clung to Kern's stirrup, trying to stop him. She loved Becky like a daughter, had risked her life to get her back, and that much Tait knew to be true. No one could fake love like that.

The silence of the land surrounded him, and with each mile covered, he prayed they'd catch up with Kern. They had to. If only they hadn't lost so much time while Dr. Mary removed the bullet. He glanced down at his side at blood that had soaked his shirt. His wound must've broken open.

Dammit to hell!

Why couldn't he catch a break?

Tait galloped up the side of a barren hill and reined to a stop, Jack and Clay beside him. He had a good view for miles in all directions. If luck was on their side, maybe Becky had held them up. Traveling with a young child would pose difficulties. He took a pair of binoculars from his saddlebag and adjusted them on his eyes.

"See anything?" Jack asked.

Tait stared intently toward the north. "No."

"They got a pretty good head start, but I hoped Becky would slow them down." Jack cussed a blue streak. "Doesn't seem to be the case."

"Here, see what you can find." Tait handed Clay the binoculars.

~~❧~~

After several moments, Clay asked, "Did you look toward that watering hole, Tait?"

"Yep, didn't see anything. You?"

"Maybe, unless my eyes are playing tricks on me." Clay handed the binoculars to Jack.

After a long moment, Jack raised his head. "Someone's down there. Not much more than a dot. Too far away to tell anything for sure."

Hope surged through Tait. "Let's ride."

He touched his heels to the roan's flank, not even waiting to get the binoculars back. He galloped down the hill and had the roan stretching out in no time. His every breath, every thought, every heartbeat was focused on reaching Becky. Over the uneven ground he flew.

They neared a place called Heaven's Gate, where the road split two mesas. A place well known for ambushes.

Maybe it was instinct, or maybe it was a glint of the morning sun on something, or maybe the fact his horse was giving out from the hard pace. Whatever the reason, Tait began to slow his roan.

Several strides later, shots sounded, and bullets flew around them.

There was no brush in which to take cover. Then he spied a dry creek bed and dove into it. Jack and Clay followed. They landed in the shallow part of the creek, barely three feet deep. They ducked, returning fire at the men shooting from some large rocks halfway up the side of one of the mesas.

It was clear to Tait that these men had fallen back to hold up anyone who came after Becky. The tactic usually worked, and frustration bit into Tait. Every second Becky was in Kern's hands lessened her chances of survival. If she cried too much, he'd silence her. If she proved too much trouble, he'd silence her. If he lost patience for any reason, he'd silence her.

The wound in his side burned like someone had stuck a hot poker to it. He blinked hard and labored to breathe.

Pinned down like this they couldn't go forward—or back. They were stuck.

❧

Melanie helped clean up the shambles the cattle had left of the town, but her thoughts were on Becky and Tait. If the church wasn't being used as a school at the moment, she'd have gone in to sit and pray. Not having ever attended services, she would feel foreign, but she'd do anything that might add the slightest chance of helping the ones she loved.

She shuddered to imagine what losing Becky would do to Tait. He'd lost too many loved ones already. He couldn't stand any more sorrow without breaking.

A possibility froze her. She went into their unfinished house, closed her eyes, and bowed her head. "Dear God, please. I beg you to spare Becky's little life. But if she has to die, let Kern kill her suddenly, without suffering. Let Tait get to her and wrench her away from the evil man. She hasn't gotten to really live yet. Amen."

She felt a little better as she went back to help put the fledgling town in order once again.

Mac came out of the hotel, and Ridge put him to work. Her father didn't look very happy, but she didn't care. So far he seemed to be staying away from the saloon, and that was good. She didn't need trouble between him and the men in this town, which was like a powder keg anyway.

The door to the telegraph office opened, and Shaughnessy

hurried toward her. Each step that brought him closer made her heart pound against her ribs. She gripped the rake handle tighter.

"Got a message for you, Mrs. Trinity." He handed her a rumpled piece of paper.

Melanie gave him a tired smile. "Thank you, Shaughnessy. I hope it's good news. I can use some about now."

The sadness in his eyes told her much more than any words could, and her heart froze. She opened it.

No more stalling. Bring the money and Trinity in two days or you'll never see your sister again.

                                        —*McIlroy*

Melanie stifled a cry and worked to keep her composure. "Can you please send a reply that I'm on my way?"

"Absolutely. For what it's worth, ma'am, I pray everything works out for you and Mr. Trinity."

Unable to trust her voice, she nodded. Her thoughts were on everything she had to do before she could leave. She glanced up at the sky. It had to be nearing noontime. Come hell or high water, she'd ride out that afternoon. Even then, she couldn't make it to Canadian inside two days, and the judge knew it. Anger rose. He wasn't giving her a real chance, but that had been his intention all along.

She found Mac with Ridge picking up what was left of their outdoor bathing room, although Ridge was doing the bulk of the work. Figured. "I need a word, Mac."

"Sure thing." He put down broken pieces of two poles.

Ridge shot her a look. "Is everything all right, Miss Melanie?"

She handed him the telegram and turned to Mac. "Can you be ready to ride in two hours? The judge is threatening to do something to Ava if I'm not there with the money and Tait in two days. Even if we left right now, we couldn't make it in time."

"The bastard!" Ridge folded up the paper. "I'd go with

you, but with the town left crippled, I have to stay here. I can look after the twins though. Would that help?"

"You're a godsend. I hesitated asking Nora or Tally. They have so much extra work with their own broods."

Ridge shifted. "What will you do when you get there without Tait?"

"I don't know yet, but I never intended to turn him over anyway. I'll think of something between here and there."

"How will we cart the money?" Mac ran a hand across his stubble. "It'll be heavy."

Mac didn't inspire trust when it came to money. The old greed was starting to creep into his eyes.

Ridge spoke, "A packhorse. It's the only solution. You have to move fast."

"Will you help me load the money?" As scattered as Melanie's thoughts were, she'd not get the sacks strapped on right and they'd lose them. And Mac didn't know about anything other than cards.

"You don't even have to ask." Ridge rested a hand on her shoulder. "I'll pick out a sturdy horse and get started."

"Thanks, Ridge. You don't know how much this means."

"I'll pack my things, girl." Mac headed off toward the hotel.

With Ridge taking care of the packhorse, she turned toward the church, dreading to tell Joe and Jesse goodbye. They needed the stability she brought right now more than ever, but this couldn't be helped.

All eyes turned to her when she opened the door of the makeshift school. "Mr. Denver, may I have a word with Joe and Jesse please?"

"Take all the time you need."

She led the boys out the door and stood on the steps. Their eyes were large, scared. Tears welled up in Jesse's eyes. They seemed to sense bad news. "Boys, I have to ride out in an hour or so, and I wanted to come and tell you myself."

"Is it Becky?" Joe asked quietly.

"No. I got an urgent telegram about my sister. She's in a bad way." Melanie smoothed back Joe's hair. He was the quiet one who felt everything deepest, the one who kept his feelings the most locked up on the inside. "I hate that I have to leave you right now, but Mr. Steele is going to look after you until your uncle or I can get back."

"No. We can't stay with him," Jesse blurted. "Please don't leave us."

"Honey, I have no choice. Mr. Steele's a very nice man."

"He never laughs. Heck, he doesn't even talk—or crack a smile. I don't think he can." Joe sat on the top step and put his head in his hands. "He only takes care of horses. He'll put us to bed in a horse stall and feed us hay."

"We'll probably start whinnying," Jesse predicted.

"Stop. He will not." Melanie added a firmness to her words. "I can't change what's happened. I have to leave, so you have to stiffen your upper lip and make the best of this." She pulled the wedding tintype from her pocket. "I dearly treasure this picture of your uncle and me, and it pains me to part with it even for a little while. You boys keep it as proof to remind yourselves that both Tait and I will be back."

"We'll look at it all the time," Jesse promised, sticking it inside his shirt.

She pulled Joe up and gave both boys a hug. "Please don't make this harder than it is. I love you so much. Now, go back inside and mind Mr. Denver."

"Please don't do this." Joe sobbed. "Don't leave us. You'll never come back."

"Yes, I will, and that picture of me and your uncle is a promise." She couldn't bear the tears running down the boy's cheeks. Any longer and she'd be a blubbering mess too.

She kissed them then opened the door. "Now go."

They trudged inside as though moving toward the gallows. Tears stung her eyes, and she felt as though someone had stomped on her heart with a pair of hobnail boots.

A few minutes later, she went up the hotel stairs to their rooms and changed into a riding skirt, soft shirt, and jacket. In quick order she threw some clothes and necessities into a bag and grabbed a brown felt hat on the way out. Ridge had almost finished strapping everything to the packhorse by the time she joined him outside the barn.

"I threw in a skillet, a coffeepot, and some food." He pulled the last rope tight and tied it.

"You think of everything. I went to the school and told the boys they're to stay with you." She touched the former preacher's arm. "I told them to be nice to you, but that's not saying they will. They tend to do whatever they take a notion. Don't hesitate in making them mind."

Ridge chuckled. "We'll be just fine. Contrary to public opinion, I was once a boy myself."

"True. Have you seen my father?"

"No." Worry crossed Ridge's angular face and sat in his amber eyes. His dark frock coat seemed to have been left from his church days, though now he never darkened the door of the place. "Are you certain he'll get you there? I guess what I'm asking is—can you trust him?"

Good question. And the answer was no. Especially not around money. But she pasted on a smile and fibbed. "Mac looks soft, but he can get the job done." And if he failed her, she'd leave him and go on alone. "I'll be fine."

Just then Mac Dunbar strolled up, carrying his suitcase and whistling like he was going on a Sunday stroll. "Got a horse for me?"

Irritation crossed Ridge's face. "Not yet. I've been getting the packhorse ready. You can ride that docile gray one over there. It's about your speed."

The gray mare seemed to be dozing. Melanie hoped the old horse wouldn't have to run, or they'd be in trouble.

Ridge saddled a fine-looking black horse with a star on his forehead for her. "This is Cherokee. He'll take care of you, Miss Melanie."

She rubbed the gelding's face and sleek neck. "Hey, Cherokee. I'm glad to know you." The horse nuzzled her palm.

At last it was time to say goodbye. She stood on tiptoe to kiss Ridge's cheek. "Thank you for everything."

"Be careful." He slipped a gun into the saddlebag. "For

security." He gave her a hand up and handed her the reins to the packhorse.

Melanie gave the outlaw town one last look before tucking her chin, squaring her shoulders, and riding out.

Twenty-eight

THE SUN CLIMBED HIGHER, AND STILL THE MEN IN THE ROCKS kept them pinned down. The longer Tait waited, the farther away Becky got. He had to end this. Somehow. Or they'd soon be out of ammunition.

He glanced at the dry creek bed, noticing it got deeper farther down to where a man could stand up and still be protected. Maybe….

"Keep drawing their fire." Tait stayed low and crept along the bed, eventually able to straighten and look around. The creek bed seemed to curve around the mesas.

He hurried back. "I have an idea."

"I'm all ears." Jack squatted down and wiped his forehead with his sleeve.

"I'm tired of being a sitting duck." Clay raised his head. He'd already removed his hat, and it rested beside him. "If we only had some help, dammit. I'm ready to give those bastards up there a dose of their own medicine."

A projectile landed much too close, spraying dirt, and all three cussed a blue streak.

"This may not work, but it's worth a try." Tait pointed to their Stetsons sitting on the ground nearby. "We'll use our hats to make them think we have reinforcements."

Jack grinned. "Like put our hats on sticks up and down here?"

"Exactly." Tait felt hope rise. "And this creek bed appears to go around these mesas. What if two of us follow it to the back side of the shooters? We'll leave one man here to keep firing. What do you think?"

"It's a good plan. We've got to flush them out before dark, or we'll be in a hell of a mess." Clay leaned back on his heels. "At least we'll be doing something."

"The longer this takes, the greater the chance of running

out of daylight." Tait wiped his forehead with his sleeve. "It's not foolproof though. Lots could go wrong."

Jack chuckled. "Hell, I've lived a lot longer than I ever thought I would."

Clay let out an oath. "We're going to die anyway if we stay here. I'd rather go out fighting. I'll volunteer to stay behind with the hats."

More rounds landed around them.

"I think this'll work." Tait lowered his voice. "There's no other way out of this."

"Then let's do it." Jack raised his gun and fired off two shots.

"I'll go along with your plan." Clay peered over the rim of the creek, took aim, and pulled the trigger. "It's better than mine."

"What was yours?" Sweat soaked Tait's underarms, thinking of the danger.

"Let the horses go and pretend to be dead. After not returning fire, they'd eventually come down to check on us. When they did, we could blast them into hell." Clay chuckled. "Of course, they could fill us with lead before they even got close enough for us to shoot. Make sure we're good and dead before they come down. That's why I said my idea has holes."

Tait clenched a fist. "I want to climb those rocks and make them eat some hot lead. For Becky." He glanced up at the sky, the sun drawing closer to the noon position.

"For Becky," Jack answered.

They propped their hats on sticks, and Tait nodded. "See you on the other side of hell. If I don't make it, take care of Melanie and the kids."

Clay murmured, "Same goes for us." He reloaded his rifle. "Go."

As he let loose, Tait and Jack clutched their rifles, stayed low, and hurried down the bed to the deep section where they could stand up and run. When they rounded the mesas and reached the backside, they paused before climbing out to make sure those above them were still firing in Clay's direction. Three horses tied up off to one side must belong to the gunmen.

Tait pitched a rock against a large boulder to see if anyone would fire at it, but nothing happened. "Clear."

The echo of blasts from Clay's rifle filled the air as he and Jack left the creek. They raced for cover at the foot of the mesa and began to scale the side while trying to be as silent as they could. Five feet from the top, Tait made a right turn around the land formation. If his estimation was correct, they'd come out on the hill above the shooters.

Every nerve stood on alert. They had to hurry before the men realized they'd been tricked and Clay got more than he'd bargained for. Traversing the rocks wasn't easy, and Tait's boots slipped several times. The sharp pain in his wounded side took his breath.

Becky's face swam before his vision and kept him going. She needed him.

They were getting closer to the report of the rifles. Tait slowed in order to quiet his approach. Clay kept up a steady firing pace down below, but he had to be getting low on ammunition. The shooters had already blown the Stetsons all to hell, so they had to suspect a trick by now. Dammit.

He inched over a few more feet and peered down.

At last he finally got eyes on the bastards. Three of them.

Using sign language, Tait relayed the information to Jack, then, raising his rifle, he squeezed the trigger.

A round knocked the closest gunman against the rocks, blood spreading across his shirt. Another of them turned and glanced up, firing. The projectile grazed Jack's arm, but he ignored it and sent a round careening down into the second shooter.

Tait leaped from his perch onto the third man before he could take aim, losing his rifle on the way down. Tait delivered a hard blow to the man's jaw that left Tait's knuckles raw and bleeding. The man's hat flew off, showing an abundance of gray hair beneath.

The beefy older man went for Tait's throat, squeezing, tightening, swearing he'd kill him.

"Not today." Thrusting his arms upward in a sudden move, Tait broke the hold. He gulped in air and jabbed an elbow into the man's stomach. "Where is she? Where's the girl?"

"You'll never find her." The gray-haired man gasped and bent over, breathing hard.

When he straightened, Tait noticed his large ears and tremendous height. That plus the deep bags under his eyes matched the twins' description. Rage shot through Tait. "You killed my sister." Tait swung a fist and connected with the bastard's nose. Blood streamed down his face and mouth.

The older man grinned, showing his bloody teeth. "Kern will make you beg just like we did your sweet Claire." He spat a tooth onto the dirt between his feet. "This ain't over yet."

Tait pulled his Smith & Wesson and jammed it against the man's cheek. "Where are they? Where is Kern taking the girl?"

"Go to hell." Another bloody grin broke free.

"I'm already there." Tait's finger tightened on the trigger.

Jack leaped onto him. "What are you doing? We need him alive if we hope to find Becky."

Tait bit out a curse and rammed his pistol back in the holster. "I want him dead."

"You'll get your chance. But for now he can give us information."

"I ain't gonna tell you one damn thing!" the man yelled.

"We'll see." Tait shoved him against the rocks. "Move a muscle and I'll blow your kneecap off." Then he turned his attention to the two he and Jack had shot. "How are they?"

Jack picked up the rifles. "One's dead. The other's got a wound to the shoulder."

Clay arrived from his climb up. "Looks like you did okay." Then he noticed Jack's arm. "On second thought, I see a bullet found you."

"Only grazed me. I'm fine." Jack grinned. "At least you got here in time to help us get these bastards down to the ground."

"They say anything?" Clay glanced at the groaning men.

"Not yet." Jack yanked the older man forward. "What's your name? Are you a Berringer?"

"Wouldn't you like to know?"

Tait pulled a piggin' rope from his back pocket, turned the sullen shooter around, and tied his hands behind him. "He's not going to talk, Jack, and Becky's getting farther away. We'll take him and these others to town and turn them over to Marshal Renick if he's there."

"And if he isn't?" Clay threw the dead man over his shoulder.

"Good question. I can't afford to waste time looking for Renick." Tait put an arm around the second wounded man and started down the hillside. "I guess I'll figure it out as I go."

Jack helped the sullen, tall man Tait had fought around the first boulder. "Maybe Kern will be there."

"Maybe." But Tait would bet on a stack of Bibles that Kern would keep riding to Canadian. He'd be safe there with crooked Judge McIlroy and Richard Markham.

Or so he thought. As long as Kern had Becky, there was no place on earth where he'd be out of Tait's reach.

It would take even more time to round up their horses, and Tait prayed they hadn't wandered far. He was desperate to catch a break after losing hours here. And he'd give everything he owned to know Becky's condition. Imagining the worst was driving him insane.

With the wounded and dead, it took a good hour to reach solid ground. Tait was breathing hard and soaked in sweat and blood. Pain tore through his side, and white light exploded in his head. He swayed, dizziness making him unsteady as he fought to stay on his feet.

When he could focus, he cast his gaze to the north and prayed for his little niece. She didn't stand a chance against Kern—and had not one person to help her.

His hands turned clammy as images of what could be happening flashed in his head.

Would he find her lifeless body at the end of the trek?

～

Melanie focused on the path ahead of her and on keeping a firm hand on the reins of the packhorse. She wouldn't lose that valuable cargo.

Mac had been silent except for the occasional question about why she'd made her home in such a desolate outlaw town. Now he grunted and added more commentary. "You were born to greater things, wearing satins and silks and raking in the money like I taught you." He snorted. "You look like a dowdy housewife with not a penny to your name."

"Stop." She glanced over at him riding next to her. "I'm far happier now with Tait than I ever was in that life. Besides, remember where that led me? Straight to jail."

"We'll get your sister out, and she'll probably be happy to pick up where we left off."

"Don't bet on it." Melanie's tone was as dry as week-old toast. Ava wouldn't put herself in this situation again. That much Melanie knew. This experience must have scared her sister out of her mind. Once Ava was free, Melanie would try to get her to come live in Hope's Crossing where she could make a whole new life. One where she would matter to someone.

"I can manage the packhorse if you're getting tired."

"No, thanks. I'm fine." She'd caught Mac eyeing those sacks of money. He wasn't above stealing from her. She knew where she stood with him, and he loved himself far more than anyone.

They lapsed into silence, and when the daylight faded, she looked for a place to camp. She found a tiny stream off the trail—barely a trickle, hidden in a stand of mesquites and scrub oak. It bubbled when it came to the surface which told her it sprang from an underground well.

"We'll camp here." Melanie dismounted and stretched.

"It ain't much in the way of comfort. We need grass and more water than that."

She gave him a look of disbelief. "Were you expecting the Cattleman's Club in Fort Worth?"

"That would be nice, daughter." Mac sighed, his arms folded.

"You've gotten too soft. But then I think you always might've been, and I just didn't notice." Meeting and marrying Tait had shown her how strong a man could be. Melanie pulled the saddlebags and bedroll down from Cherokee.

"Watch it, girl. I did the best I could. I can't help it that I was better suited to sitting at a card table." Mac lay down on a patch of buffalo grass.

Melanie nudged him with her toe. "Get up and unsaddle your gray. I'm not going to do all the work." She should've left him behind and come by herself, but at the time it had seemed that having the company was better than traveling alone.

A memory came to her unbidden, and tears burned her eyes. She must've been eight or so and had gotten very sick. Mac had held her in his lap all night, bathing her with cold water to keep her fever down. In that moment, at least, she'd felt protected and loved and known he would fight to get her well.

She shook her head to rid herself of the picture. Did any tiny portion of that man still exist inside Mac now? The caring had certainly vanished somewhere along the way.

Although Mac grumbled at her orders, he got up and removed the saddle from the gray. Melanie left the packhorse as it was with the other two, close to a patch of grass and able to get to water. She longed for a small fire but didn't make one for fear of drawing trouble. Thank goodness the nights weren't too chilly yet. Releasing a sigh, she sat down on the ground and reached into the saddlebags.

"Here." She removed her hat and shared the ham and bread Ridge had packed. Mac grunted and selected what he wanted. She was thankful he didn't complain.

"I hardly know you anymore, daughter. What happened to the beautiful gambler?"

"That woman doesn't exist anymore. She was shallow and very bored." Melanie pinched off a portion of bread and threw it to a blue jay that hopped over to take it. "My life is much more satisfying now." Even with Tait offering a lukewarm shoulder these days, she'd rather have him that way than not at all. She twisted the wedding band on her finger, trying to stop her lip from quivering.

"I have a purpose for the first time in my life, Mac. But I don't expect you to understand."

"You had lots of purpose. You and Ava were helping

me make my fortune." Mac cut his eyes at her in a sideways glance. "I was saving up for that house you girls wanted. Almost had enough too."

Melanie raised her hand. "Stop. No more lies. I'm not a little girl anymore. There was never going to be a house, and you know it." She got up and spread out her bedroll, putting herself between Mac and the horses.

Trust was not a word she'd ever use with Mac Dunbar in the vicinity.

"I don't know why you want to settle down in one place. That would bore me stiff."

"I have a question for you, and I want the truth. How well do you know Kern Berringer and his sons?"

"Who said I know them?"

"Earl Berringer. In fact, he bragged about it. Don't try to lie."

"I know 'em. Played cards with 'em and helped 'em out a time or two."

"Doing what?"

"They pay well for information, and my funds had sort of… well, dried up."

"In other words, you sold…what? The location of people they were looking for?"

Mac winced. "Something like that."

She studied his face, sick that he was her father. "Why did you risk coming to Hope's Crossing with Kern keeping the town locked down? But then seeing as how you were buddies—"

"I don't aim to ever share a fire with that crazy, slick-skinned bastard. Gives me the heebie-jeebies the way he keeps his hair shaved off." Mac shivered. "Not natural."

She agreed. She could still feel Kern ripping Becky from her arms. Those eyes were the coldest and deadest she'd ever seen.

"What did you have to give his men in order for them to let you pass safely into Hope's Crossing? I want the truth."

Mac sat silently, chewing his meat and bread.

Clearly he didn't intend to answer, and that frightened her. "What did you promise Berringer's men, Mac? You don't have any money to pay your way in, so it had to be information. I'll keep on until you answer me."

Her father whirled. "I said I'd report back on the situation inside and where everything was located, especially Earl. All right? Are you happy? I had to get in somehow, and they were about to carve me up."

Melanie's blood froze. He'd provided Kern with what he'd needed. He'd as well as have put Becky in Kern's arms himself. "And did you?" she asked through stiff lips.

"I slipped out late my first night there."

Fury crawled up her neck. Melanie didn't trust herself to look at him. She removed the gun from her saddlebags that Ridge had put there, slipped it under her blanket. Once she'd gotten situated, she lay on her side away from him. "We leave before dawn," she snapped.

It must've been near midnight when a snapping twig woke her. She opened her eyes, searching the darkness.

Mac's bedroll was empty.

Melanie reached for the gun, closed her palm around the handle, and slowly rose to her feet. She caught furtive movement from the corner of her eye. Swiveling, she noticed a man untying the packhorse. Quiet and sure, she crept toward him.

Pain and disappointment shot through her heart. He was doing it again. She raised the gun and barked, "Hold it right there or I'll blow your damn head off."

Mac whirled, his eyes wide. "This ain't what it looks like."

"You mean you're not trying to steal the bags of money that will free Ava and give Tait back his future?"

He snorted. "The horse had gotten loose, and I was retying it. You know me."

Yeah, she did. That was the problem. "Lies roll off your tongue like sweet molasses. Get back over there and lie down."

"I'm no child." Mac's voice held a challenge. "What will you do? Shoot me?"

"You're damned right I will. I won't hesitate one second." When he stalled, she pulled back the hammer. "I will fire if you don't step away."

Twenty-nine

MAC SLOWLY RAISED HIS HANDS AND SAUNTERED TOWARD HER. "We've come to a sad state of affairs when a girl threatens to shoot her own father."

"It's no idle threat." She tucked the gun in her waist and flew at him, raining blows on his face and chest. "I'll beat you into the middle of next week. You disgust me. Think about someone other than yourself for a change." She jerked off his hat and started whipping him with it.

Mac threw up his arms in self-defense. "Stop! Do you know what that money could buy?"

"Don't even think about it. That will save Ava's and Tait's lives."

"Hell, I wasn't going to take it all. Just enough to give me seed money. They never would've missed it."

"You're pathetic. Don't you know those railroad people have every cent Tait took written down somewhere? And if they don't get it *all* back, Ava will suffer for it." It was true Tait had given some to the town, but she wouldn't tell Mac that. The less he knew, the better. "What's happened to you? Don't you even care about your own daughter anymore?"

"Of course I care." Mac sat down and glared. "I'm her father."

"Then act like it!" Melanie dropped onto her bedroll and pulled the blanket over her. Weariness seeped into her bones. This was hard enough without Mac pulling his stunts. "Try that one more time and you'll find a bullet in you. Do you understand what I'm saying?"

"Understood." He lay back on his bedroll, turning his back to her.

Thoughts tumbled end over end in Melanie's mind long after he began to snore. She had so much riding on her shoulders, and failure could mean all their lives.

And Becky. Where was she? What was the sweet girl doing right now? Did she have anyone who gave a damn about her shielding her from the night? Taking her to the pot. Wiping her tears. Feeding her.

Melanie drew the blanket closer, smothering her sobs. She'd never felt so alone.

∽

Midnight tolled on a clock somewhere when Tait and the others rode into the raucous town of Mobeetie. Even though the hour was late, the town was lit up like Fourth of July fireworks. Music burst from the various saloons, dogs barked in the street, drunks hollered and carried on, gunshots rang out. They'd entered the bowels of hell.

Tait's wary gaze swept both sides of the street, but he didn't see Kern or anyone he recognized from the attack. He reined up in front of a building he'd never seen before, and the smell of fresh sawdust hanging in the air explained why. The words on the building proclaimed it the Wheeler County Courthouse.

"Hell and be damned! Look at that, Jack."

Jack released a whistle. "The law has come to the Panhandle. About time."

Clay scowled. "I don't know what it'll mean for half the men in Hope's Crossing. Those who are wanted might have to up and leave, head farther west."

Tait felt a noose tightening around his neck. He undid the top button of his collarless shirt to escape the feeling. The country was changing too fast, and if he didn't adapt, he'd get caught up in all this progress. A tall man strode toward them from a side door of the building. He stood well over six feet and made an imposing figure in his black frock coat, twin pistols in his holster.

"You look in need of some help there. I'm Temple Houston, the district attorney of the newly formed 35th judicial district." He glanced at the dead body draped belly-down across one horse, the wounded man barely able to stay in the saddle on another, and the restrained gray-haired outlaw.

Temple Houston's fame preceded him. He looked the spitting image of old Sam Houston himself.

Tait ducked his head and pulled up the collar of his coat to shield his face. "We'd be obliged if someone would take these men off our hands so we can ride on."

Thankfully, Clay moved around him and introduced himself and Jack. "A child was abducted this morning from Hope's Crossing, and we're on the trail of the bastards who took her. These three tried to stop us."

"I need a doctor," moaned the wounded outlaw. "I'm dying here."

"We don't have a doctor anymore. I'll see what I can do for you in a minute." The son of a Texas hero moved to the man's horse. "What's your name?"

"Roy Berringer. The old man is my uncle Leo Berringer, my father's brother." They finally had a name to pin on the old bastard, and he was Kern's brother. Tait should've known. The mean streak ran a mile wide in both of them.

"How many damn Berringers are there?" Temple Houston snapped.

"Only eleven now. We started with twenty-five."

Three of them Tait could take personal credit for killing. He took Temple's measure and liked what he saw. Houston had sharp eyes, but a smile curved his mouth. His shoulder-length hair added a rebellious edge to his look that would probably help win court cases. He was intimidating as hell.

"Maybe you've seen a strange-looking hairless man riding through here?" Jack leaned forward in the saddle.

Temple chuckled. "Hairless?"

Clay pulled out cigarette papers and tobacco from his pocket. "I know it sounds crazy, but he has this weird obsession. Shaves off every sprig of hair each morning. Even his eyebrows."

"That's crazy all right," Temple admitted. "But if he wore a hat and didn't cause trouble, I wouldn't notice him."

"His name is Kern Berringer. He'd have the little girl with him."

"How big is this girl he took?"

"Three years old." The words slipped out before Tait could let Clay answer.

Temple swung his piercing gaze to Tait. "Three, huh? I didn't catch your name, mister."

"She's my niece. Name's Tait." Maybe that wouldn't be as memorable as Trinity. He hoped so anyway.

"I'd ride with you men if I could. Anyone who kidnaps a three-year-old deserves to be strung up from the nearest tree. But at least I can take these sorry bastards off your hands and lock 'em up so you can go on."

"Much obliged." Clay handed him the reins of the dead man's horse. "By the way, Leo was riding with Kern and his bunch when they killed Tait's sister and brother-in-law a month ago. Maybe Roy was there too."

"You got no proof of anything!" Leo hollered. "I demand to be set free."

"We'll be happy to testify at his trial." Jack transferred the surly man over to Temple. "He was seen at the sister's murder site, and witnesses can identify him."

"Tait's a wanted man! His name is Trinity!" Leo yelled. "What'cha gonna do with his ass?"

Temple swung around. "That true?"

A hard swallow nearly choked Tait. "You'll find my name on posters, sure, but I'm trying to change."

"Half the men in Mobeetie are on wanted posters." Temple's dark eyes raked over Tait. "I won't stop you from going after your niece. I have a feeling her life isn't worth much to these men."

Relief flooded over Tait. "Thank you, sir."

"This country is changing though. You'd best clear your name," Temple warned. "And soon."

"I intend to try. Thanks again."

Leo made a desperate attempt to spur his horse to move, but the district attorney grabbed the reins. "You're coming with me. We're going to clean up this last section of Texas and rid it of the stench of men like you."

Once Temple Houston had moved down the street with his prisoners and their dead friend, Tait turned to Jack and Clay. "We have to check this town before we ride out. Just because Houston didn't see Kern doesn't mean he isn't here."

"I agree." Jack glanced at the row of saloons. "If anyone knows anything, they'll be in there. If we spread out, it won't take long to finish."

Clay nodded. "And we'll also check the horses tied in front."

They split up, and Tait moved through the Bucket of Blood and Rose of San Antone. No one had seen a hairless man or a child, and none of the horses wore a broken shoe. Jack and Clay had no better luck.

"Not here." Tait was dead on his feet, and his side burned like a red-hot ember, but he had to keep riding. "Let's go."

The weary men saddled up, but five miles out of town Jack pulled to a stop. "I can't go any farther, and I don't think either of you are any better. Tait's about to fall off his horse. We'll stop here and sleep a few hours."

"I'm going on without you then. I have to." Tait jerked on the reins.

Jack reached out and grabbed the headstall. "No. You'll sleep a bit. Riding on in our condition is foolish, and you know it. Kern could be lying in wait, and we're not alert enough to see him."

"He's right," Clay said firmly. "Two or three hours of sleep will make a lot of difference."

"Fine." Tait knew they were right, but the guilt ate away at his insides. Becky needed him.

He dismounted and led his horse into a bunch of scrub oak where they wouldn't be seen. He pulled a bedroll from his roan and stumbled toward a flat piece of ground. He thought he'd be asleep the moment he laid down, only his brain wouldn't shut off.

Becky's little face swam before his eyes. She was crying, saying, "Saw-wee."

And he couldn't help her one damn bit. He clenched a fist until his nails dug into his palm.

Melanie rose before daylight and tied her bedroll onto the black gelding. The packhorse was still there along with all the bags. Her father gave her black looks but didn't have to be prodded too much. He seemed to somehow sense that she'd leave him afoot in a heartbeat. And she would. She had no time to waste on coddling him. The words on the telegram raced through her head.

Bring the money and Trinity in two days or you'll never see your sister again.

Her hands trembled, and she wished like hell that Tait was with her. His strength would give her courage for what lay ahead.

"Come here," Mac said gruffly and put his arms around her. "I may not be the best option, but I think you need someone, daughter."

"I'm scared, real scared." She laid her head on his shoulder and for a moment took what scraps of comfort he was willing to offer. A night spent with little sleep had laid her spirits lower than they'd ever been. She was second-guessing herself, and worry had taken hold. Plus she couldn't seem to stop shaking. "What if I fail? What if the judge still sends Ava to prison and me with her? What if Kern kills Becky?"

Tait might as well be dead if that happened. That sweet girl meant everything to him.

"You can 'what if' things to death, and it won't change anything one bit." He patted her back awkwardly. "I haven't been the father you and your sister deserved, but I'm not going to let you go through this alone. We'll figure everything out together."

He was silent for several long heartbeats. When he spoke, his voice broke. "I'm sorry for trying to steal the money. You're right. Everything you said hit me upside the head. Greed came over me, and I'm ashamed."

Melanie leaned back to look at him. Real, genuine emotion filled his eyes. To hear him admit his shortcomings softened her heart a bit; however, it would take more than mere words to believe this was a long-term change.

"I'm glad you recognize your failings, Mac. None of us are perfect. Let's ride. Time is against us, and Ava needs her family."

No one needed them more than Becky though. Tears burned the backs of Melanie's eyes. She prayed Tait had caught up to Kern and rescued the child. But...a chilling thought hit her. What if Tait was dead and she'd never see him again?

Sharp pain shot through her, and she stumbled toward her black gelding. She needed good news, and soon, or she'd lose her sanity altogether.

Thirty

Tait jerked awake in the darkness, listening, every nerve standing on end. Becky had called out to him. He'd heard her crying out for him as plain as day. "Me hurt. Me want you."

He got up and glanced around but saw nothing.

Jack raised from his bedroll. "What is it?"

Tait struggled to speak and finally got some words out. "Heard something—Becky."

"Are you sure you weren't dreaming?"

"Not sure of one damn thing. It sure sounded real though." Tait let out a long breath. "I think I might be going crazy."

Clay rolled over and stood. "With good reason. You're dealing with some heavy stuff." He scratched his belly. "As long as we're all up, we'd best ride. Maybe we'll catch the bastards."

Tait pulled out his pocket watch. "It's four o'clock. Still three hours to daylight. We could be in Canadian by then and possibly get a jump on Kern—if he's there."

"My thoughts exactly." Clay rolled up his bed. "Let me take a look at that wound before we head out."

"Hell! You might as well give me a sugar teat too, Mother!" Though Tait complained, he was glad they cared about him, so he sat patiently while Jack wet his bandana and washed some of the blood away.

"I don't think you're going to die." Clay went to his saddlebags and pulled out a jar of ointment, smearing the separated, angry wound well.

In a few minutes, they saddled their horses and galloped down the trail. They kept up the pace and made Canadian as a red dawn broke over the town, casting it in eerie shadow. Tait slowed his roan, scanning both sides of the street. It was possible that Kern hadn't come here, that he'd gone to a ranch or his home. In all the years since Lucy's death, Tait had still never learned where the man lived. He realized how little he knew about Kern.

And riding in the dark, they hadn't even been able to track the strange hoofprint.

Tait avoided some chickens scratching for food in the street, and they squawked loudly back at being disturbed. A cat streaked in front of them followed by a large barking dog. Few people stirred in the early morning.

Tait's breath fogged in the cool air as he desperately searched for some clue that would tell him where Becky was. They pulled up in front of the Wild Jacks Saloon, the location offering a good view of the jail sitting opposite. All was quiet in the limestone building. He wondered if Ava Dunbar was shivering inside in the dim light, praying for her sister to come. After he got Becky back, Ava was next.

"What do you think?" he asked his companions.

Clay took tobacco and papers from his pocket. "We need to scout around and talk to a few people, but it's too early." He rolled a cigarette and licked the paper to seal it.

"Since me and Clay aren't wanted, we can go speak to the sheriff. Maybe that judge too." Jack nodded at a rider coming toward them. "I think that might be the sheriff now. I see a tin star."

"Just what the hell would you say to him? He's crooked. They're all crooked and lining their pockets with Markham's money. All you'll do is tip them off." Tait eyed the weasel with distaste as he stopped in front of the sheriff's office and dismounted.

The short man stared back. Then, instead of going inside, he crossed the street. He seemed less like a weasel as he got closer—more young and anxious to prove himself. "You boys look like you lost your way. State your names and the reason you're here."

"We're not bothering anyone." Clay took a drag from his cigarette, the smoke curling around his head. "Name's Colby, and we're just passing through, Sheriff—"

"Quitman." The lawman patted the head of a mutt that had wandered up.

Tait glanced around for some establishment to disappear into. His name would give them away immediately. Jack introduced himself and launched into a long story of how the Great Western Cattle Trail originated, and right then Tait decided Jack had a real talent for spreading hogwash. Several times Sheriff Quitman tried to talk, but each time Jack cut him off. The young man, probably not a day over twenty, had certainly never run up against anyone like Jack.

The door of the saloon rattled behind Tait as someone opened it. Not taking any chances that Quitman would some-how manage to get the best of Jack, Tait slipped into the dim interior of the Wild Jacks.

A man with a broom in his hand jerked around at the noise. "We're not open yet. You'll have to come back."

Tait thought fast. Almost every place had a Mary, and he'd bet one worked upstairs. "I'm just here to give Mary a message."

"All right. Go on up." The man motioned with his head and resumed sweeping.

Before Tait did, he asked, "Hey, did you see a man with a little girl come through here yesterday? Name's Berringer. Tall, walks with a limp, shaves his head."

"Yep, I saw him. He brought that child in here, and I ran him out. She wouldn't hush bellering. Last I saw, he went to the mercantile. I got no use for him."

Seemed few people did. "Much obliged." Tait climbed the stairs and paused on the landing. Anger boiled inside him. Becky must be terror stricken. He had to find her fast.

Light at the end of the hall indicated a door to the balcony. He hurried toward it and down the outside stairs. Keeping close to the side of the building, he stole around to the front and carefully peeked around the corner. Jack was still talking. Tait got Clay's attention and drew his hand across his throat, motioning to cut the conversation. A few moments later, Jack and Clay joined him.

"Are you hoarse?" He grinned at Jack.

"No. By the way, you're welcome for saving your rear."

"I got some information from a man inside this saloon." Tait relayed the conversation.

Jack glanced toward the C. R. Ussary and Sons Mercantile down the street. "We need to talk to the owner. Besides, I need to buy me a new hat."

"We all need new ones." Clay laughed. "That's the second I've lost this year."

"I vote for eating first. That looks like a good café over there." Tait motioned toward the Hot Biscuit Café, its doors just being propped open. "I'm starving."

A full stomach and hot coffee would do wonders and give him the strength to find Becky. He wondered how well they were caring for the sweet girl. Maybe Kern had a woman who'd see to her. But knowing Kern—Tait couldn't complete the thought that sent pain spiraling into his chest. The fact was he did know the depths of that bastard's ruthless evil.

The little café was still wiping sleep from its eyes, but they grabbed a table near the door and ordered coffee and a full breakfast.

Thirty minutes later, they emerged. Tait definitely felt much better. He kept an eye out for Sheriff Quitman and turned toward the mercantile with Jack and Clay flanking him.

A one-armed clerk came toward them. "Morning, gentlemen. I'm Charles Ussary. May I help you?"

Tait glanced around. "We need hats."

"All of you?"

"It's a long story." Tait spied hats hanging on a wall and headed toward them. Ussary followed. "Say, have you seen an older man and a three-year-old? They would've come in yesterday. His name is Kern Berringer."

A wary expression crossed Ussary's eyes. "Are you kin?"

"No. He took the child, and I've come to bring her home." Tait reached for a black hat, checked the size, and tried it on. "I'll pay for any information."

The lines of Ussary's face relaxed. "He came in late yesterday with the child wailing. She was dirty and terrified. Kern was none too gentle, in both voice and the way he jerked her around. She kept trying to get down and actually bit him once. Made him real mad. If I had been able, I would've tried to take her from him." He glanced at his empty sleeve. "Couldn't do much of anything."

Tait's heart squeezed. Kern would pay for hurting the girl. But if she didn't stop biting, the man would kill her. By the looks on Jack's and Clay's faces, they worried as well.

Jack adjusted a hat on his head. "I'll take this one. We heard Berringer has a place outside town."

The owner nodded. "It's well hidden. You'll never find it on your own, but I have to deliver his order in a bit. You can follow me. I want to help that little girl."

Hope soared in Tait. Somehow, someway, before dark, he'd have Becky out of there or die trying.

∽

After first stopping to bury half the loot outside of town, Melanie rode into Canadian about ten o'clock on the morning of the third day. The Hot Biscuit Café was still doing a booming business as was the mercantile across from the Wild Jacks Saloon. A few folks stared as she, Mac, and the laden packhorse slowly made their way to the sheriff's office and went around back. It was best that they keep out of sight as much as possible.

Her sweaty palms stuck to the inside of her soft leather gloves, and droplets of sweat inched between breasts. This had to work. Still, when the judge found out she'd only brought half of the loot, he'd be furious. Holding back part of the money gave her bargaining power.

"Mac, wait here with the money." She swung her leg over the saddle.

"I hope you know what you're doing, daughter." Mac released a wad of spit onto the dirt. "If you're not out in ten minutes, I'm riding off with this packhorse as we agreed."

"Wish me luck." She gave him a smile and strode around the stone building to the door.

Sheriff Quitman looked up with a cruel smirk when she entered. "About time, girlie. Got the money with you?"

"Half."

He stood, anger glittering in his eyes. "What was that you said?"

The man's long, skinny neck resembled a chicken's, and it seemed to stick out even further now. She could see his Adam's apple bobbing up and down as he came close to shouting.

Melanie glared. "I said I have half of it. The other half is in safekeeping. Give me my sister, and you'll get it."

Quitman stalked around his desk, fury turning his face red. He drew back a hand to slap her.

The door behind him opened, and Judge McIlroy barked, "Not yet, you fool."

For several heartbeats, Melanie stared at the silver-haired judge. If it wasn't for the long, puckered scar on his cheek and the way his lip curled up in a sneer, he'd be a handsome man. But she couldn't see anything except his greed and spite.

Though she trembled inside, she wouldn't show him anything but cold disdain. She slowly tugged off her gloves and planted her feet. "Give me my sister."

"My dear, you're hardly in any position to make demands. You only brought half the money, *and* you didn't bring me Trinity." McIlroy strode into the room, gripping an ivory-handled black cane. "Cuff her, Quitman. See how she likes a cell."

The young sheriff jerked her hands behind her and leaned close. "You thought you were better than me. I'll show you."

She refused to cry out, her gaze never leaving the judge's face. "No matter what you do to me, you'll never get Tait Trinity. He's off the table."

She took a deep breath and continued. "You might not think twice about loading me and Ava up and carting us off to prison, but you might care that Stoker Legend and his sons are involved now. They know all about you and that poor young woman you almost beat to death over in Indian Territory." She tsked him. "According to Stoker, people are ready to talk. You're the one who's about to go to jail."

The color drained from McIlroy's face, and he glanced around the room as though the Legend men were hiding in the corners. "What are you talking about?"

"I have a letter in my pocket from Stoker and Sam Legend. I would also be remiss if I didn't share that you should expect a visit any day now. The governor is sending someone to investigate you and all your shady dealings and criminal enterprises."

"Let her go, Quitman."

"But Judge—"

"Hand over this letter—if you truly have it."

"Gladly." Melanie pulled the paper from her pocket and handed it to McIlroy.

His face turned gray as he read, then he crumpled the paper and tossed it in the trash. "I don't plan on being here when they arrive. Until then, you still have an obligation to turn over every cent of the money Trinity stole." He jabbed a finger in her chest. "Every red cent."

"Not before I get Ava." She glanced at the clock on the wall. "You have five minutes to release her to me, or you won't even get half of the loot."

"You're threatening me?" McIlroy went to the window and glanced out, probably looking to see if she had any accomplices lurking. Or if Stoker Legend and his boys were waiting for him to step outside. He was clearly shaken. But what if he disappeared before anyone could get here to strip him of his judgeship?

Melanie shrugged more casually than she felt. "Just stating a fact. The clock is ticking. My sister, please."

"You can't expect me to trust you," McIlroy answered.

Quitman's thin lips curved in a sneer. "We don't trust nobody."

Crooks were awfully full of mistrust, in her opinion.

"That's fine, have it your way—if you'd rather deal with Stoker Legend." Her heels struck the wooden floor as she moved to the door. "And when Richard Markham comes into town to collect the money, what do you think he'll say?"

"Wait."

She turned, a look of innocence on her face. "Yes, Judge?"

"Give me the first half now and bring the rest to the bridge crossing outside town tomorrow at daybreak."

Yeah, and he'd have a nice ambush set up.

Why was he stalling? Was Ava even here? Maybe they'd moved her.

"No, I'll have her today."

McIlroy's face became a stone mask. "I'm afraid that's impossible."

Fear swept over her in waves, and she grabbed the back of the nearest chair. She was too late. Ava had to be dead.

Thirty-one

THICK GRIME COATED THE WINDOW OF THE SHERIFF'S OFFICE and blocked a good portion of the sunlight, just as the judge was blocking Melanie at every turn.

Melanie glared at Judge McIlroy, her voice as sharp as honed flint. "Then our deal is off, and you get none of the money." She swung toward the door, hoping to make it outside before she collapsed.

"Wait, it's not what you think. We had to move your sister at the doctor's orders. She's very ill but alive. You'll see her tomorrow." McIlroy took out his pocket watch. "I'm late for a meeting. Be at the bridge crossing tomorrow at daybreak. I'll have your sister then."

"I'd think long and hard about double-crossing me." Melanie had one last question. "What's wrong with my sister? If you hurt her in any way, I'd say my prayers."

"The doctor says she has weak lungs. He called it pleurisy. He's treating her." McIlroy gave her a grin that chilled her blood. Her breath hung painfully in her chest. He was hiding something.

"I don't care what shape she's in, I want her released. Today." She pulled on her gloves. "I want her within the hour."

"I can't do that."

"Then you'll never see one cent of Markham's money."

Silence filled the office. Finally, the judge nodded.

"One more thing. Where has Kern Berringer taken Trinity's little niece? Since you and Markham employ him, you'd know where he hides out. Help me get her back and the governor might be lenient."

"I don't know what you're talking about or who Kern Berringer is."

Melanie again made a tsking sound with her tongue.

"Denial will get you a cell in Huntsville—how about the same one where you were going to send me and Ava? I hear it's hard on an old man."

"Where's the first half of the money? Give it to me."

"Tell me where Ava is or take me to her."

"Can't do that."

"Then I'm afraid the half I was prepared to give you just shrank. You get a quarter." She stepped onto the boardwalk and whistled. A few moments later, Mac appeared with the horses. "He wants his money, Mac. Let's give it to him—a fourth only."

She moved to the pack animal and removed the canvas covering the sacks. One by one, she and Mac launched them at McIlroy, who leaped back to avoid being struck. One of the bags came open, and money spilled everywhere. The judge scrambled on his hands and knees to pick it all up, looking anything but dignified.

When they'd finished, she climbed onto the black gelding named Cherokee. A backward glance showed the judge still scrambling for the money. She and Mac galloped to the edge of town where she pulled to a stop.

"Ava wasn't at the jail. We have to find her. The judge said she has pleurisy and the doctor is treating her. She's somewhere in town."

Mac grunted and scratched his head. "Pleurisy is real bad. It's put plenty in their graves. Any idea where they took her?"

"No, but the judge agreed to bring her in an hour. He's mad that I outfoxed him and kept back most of the money so I don't trust him. He's also furious that Stoker Legend knows what he's doing. I suspect he's plenty scared too."

"What exactly did the judge say?"

"He first promised to deliver Ava to the bridge crossing tomorrow at dawn, but I'm betting he'd have set up an ambush. I don't think he intends to bring her to us in an hour or even today. He can't afford to give her back and lose his ace in the hole. That's what my gut is saying." She met Mac's stare. "Ever get those hunches?"

"Sure." He grinned and ran a hand over his stiff stubble. "Right before I draw an inside straight."

"That's what we're going to do. We'll draw us an inside straight. We'll ride back and try to talk to the doctor, ask him where he's keeping Ava."

Mac shook his head. "No, he might be in cahoots with the judge and warn him."

"All right. If Ava is really sick, the doctor will have to check on her, and when he does, we'll follow." Melanie glanced at her father. Lord knew he wasn't perfect by any means, but she was glad to have him along.

Sometimes a person had to settle for what she could get.

They turned the horses around and snuck into town the back way, keeping to the alleys and shadows. She located the doctor's office, and they got comfortable across the street where they could watch.

Her thoughts turned to Tait. She prayed he had Becky now and that the fight hadn't cost him, Jack, and Clay their lives. The enormous pain made it hard to breathe.

To never be able to touch Tait or kiss him again would be worse than death.

❧

A little past noon, Tait and his friends followed Ussary's wagon until the mercantile proprietor neared Berringer's hideout. They hid in the thick brush and watched a well-armed guard check the wagon before letting it through.

The house was just over the rise, but unless you knew it was there, you'd never see it. No wonder Tait had never been able to find Berringer's place.

"We've got to get closer," Tait murmured to Jack and Clay.

"He could have the whole area booby-trapped. Wouldn't put it past him." Jack raised the binoculars and peered through them. "The brush is too damn thick. I can't see anything."

Tait tugged his hat low on his forehead. "You both wait here and catch Charles Ussary on his way out. Then we'll know if Becky is even on the premises."

"And where will you be?" Jack put the binoculars away.

"I'm going to scout around, something best done alone. I'll be back in a bit." Maybe sooner, depending on how thickly the guards were placed.

"Take these." Jack handed him the binoculars.

"Thanks."

Clay laid a hand on Tait's back. "Don't try to be a hero. If you fail, it'll put Becky in more danger."

Tait gave him a nod and moved slowly and steadily through the brush. Each step drove home his determination not to make any noise.

He kept an eye out for booby traps but still almost stepped right into a piece of thin wire stretched between two small trees before he noticed. If he'd have tripped it, a net would've dropped on him. Another one a little farther was harder to see, but he managed to spot and avoid the leaves and brush covering a thin piece of wood—over a large hole, if he had to guess.

Slowly and carefully, he crept forward until a house came into view about three hundred yards away. Cottonwood and elm trees ringed the property around it.

The house was small and built from stone, which ruled out setting it afire. He couldn't anyway, not if there was even a sliver of a chance that Becky was inside. The windows were covered hide or oiled paper—some type of material so no one could see in. A half-dozen armed men milled about in the early-afternoon sun. Tait lifted the binoculars to see where they kept the horses and where they drew water. He needed all the information he could get.

Finally satisfied, he started to turn away when a bloody scream shot chills through him. Not an adult's voice. No, this was a young child—*Becky*.

It took all his willpower not to run to her. He closed his eyes and sat there with clenched fists, tears running down his face.

At last the screams died, and the silence was more frightening than the noise. Had Kern killed her? Lucy's face swam in front of his vision, and he knew it was possible.

Tait wiped his eyes and returned to Jack and Clay as quickly as he could. "I heard her screaming. I have to do something, and I won't wait."

"We heard her too. On his way out, Ussary told us he saw her and said we better get her fast." Jack's voice lowered. "Kern hasn't hurt her yet, but he put her in a dog cage."

A string of cusswords left Tait's mouth. He'd never wanted to kill anyone so bad. Kern was nothing but an animal—no man with a conscience could make war on children. "I'm riding up to that house and taking Becky's place. It's me he wants—he can have me."

"He'll kill you, Tait, you know that." The look in Clay's eyes said he'd do the same as Tait.

"Doesn't matter. I'll gladly give my life for that innocent child." He unbuckled his gun belt and slung it over his shoulder. "So would you."

"If you think we're going to let you ride into the lion's den by yourself, you're crazy." Jack stuck his foot in the stirrup and waited out his gelding's nervous dance before he swung his leg over.

"I was hoping you'd come. I'll need someone to take Becky back to Hope's Crossing." Tait took his knife out of his boot along with another gun. "One of you needs to stay behind."

"I will," Clay volunteered.

"Then take care of these." Tait handed him his hardware.

"Mine too." Jack added his to the pile.

Tait glanced up at the sky, the sun past the midway mark. It was a pretty enough day to die, he supposed. That Kern would torture him first was a given. There was no way to steel himself against that kind of pain, so he turned his thoughts to something else.

Damn, he wished he'd have made love to Melanie once more, told her the things in his heart. He thought he'd have plenty of nights ahead.

He swallowed hard to get past the lump. "I have a favor to ask. Tell Melanie that I lied and I hope she'll forgive me. I love her more than I ever thought I'd be capable of loving again." His voice broke, and it took several heartbeats before he could inhale a shaky breath and finish. "I wish I had time to prove it. Maybe she'll finish raising the kids. If not—"

Jack's voice came out thick and raspy. "If she can't, Nora and I will take them. Don't worry about that."

"The same goes for the new house," Tait said as he and Jack climbed into the saddle.

Clay glanced up. "Tait, you don't have to do this. We could ride in tonight with guns blazing and do some damage."

"And Kern will put a bullet in Becky's head if he hasn't already. No, this is the only way." Tait touched his bootheels to his roan's flanks and moved out toward the guard post.

When they rode up, the hefty man on duty jerked to his feet, his weapon pointed at them. From the dull glaze in his eyes, it appeared he'd been half-asleep. "Stop! You ain't allowed in here."

"I'm Tait Trinity, and I'll have a word with Kern. You do know who I am, don't you?"

"Yep, I reckon there ain't too many in Texas that don't know about you."

"Good. Then take us to him."

"Who's that with you?" The guard stared at Jack from beneath his hat, a worn-out thing that had seen far better days. His front teeth protruded over his thick lips.

"A friend. He's coming along for insurance. A problem?"

"Not as long as he lets me check for guns."

"We're both unarmed. You know, I came here in good faith, and I wouldn't want to be you when Kern finds out you turned us away." Tait slouched in the saddle and sighed. "I'm sure I don't have to tell you about his temper."

Kern had been known to gun down his own men when he was angry.

Finally, after patting them down and checking their saddlebags, the guard let them through. "The house is half a mile down this road. Stray from it and you won't need them boots you're wearing."

As Tait and Jack moved out, the guard shot into the air to signal the ones ahead.

Tait's gaze shifted from side to side, taking in every detail. He knew Jack was doing the same and committing everything to memory in case he had to leave in a hurry—or in the dark. They didn't talk, and Tait didn't guess they had anything left to say. His thoughts were on getting to Becky. He knew what lay in store for him, but he couldn't think of that. His little niece had to be saved. He owed that to Claire.

If he had to sacrifice himself, so be it. He'd do it willingly.

Melanie's face filled his vision. She deserved a better husband than she'd gotten. His biggest regret now was that he would never see her again, fall into the depths of her turquoise eyes, run his fingers up a silky thigh. He lifted a shaky hand to his jaw. Lord knew, she was everything he wanted.

He could've been more understanding, bridled his tongue, opened his heart more. Damn.

When he and Jack rode into the compound, a group of armed men instantly swarmed them and jerked them from their saddles.

"I think we're going to have a little fun, boys." One of Kern's men snickered, his mouth curling back over yellow teeth. "We've waited a long time for you, Trinity."

A fist slammed into Tait's face, knocking him sideways. He wiped his mouth on his sleeve and snarled, "Release the girl and we'll finish this."

Kern Berringer limped from the house, his shiny head glistening in the sun. "I thought that would bring you running. All this time and we finally, finally get to settle up."

"Me for Becky—do we have a deal? Otherwise, I'm signaling my men and riding out." It wasn't a total lie. He did have two men with him, and he'd put them up against an army.

Jack wrenched free of the arms holding him. "We want the girl. Trinity's agreed to take her place. What more do you want?"

Kern's amber eyes swept over Jack. "Bowdre, right?"

"That's correct. Jack Bowdre. Maybe you've heard of me."

"I know you've put a lot of men in early graves. Some were my friends." Kern spat on the ground. "But I got no quarrel with you. It's Trinity I want. He'll pay for crippling me and killing my boys."

Kern was silent for a long moment. Finally, he nodded and gave the order to bring Becky out. Several moments later, the door opened, and Becky slowly climbed down the steps.

Tait's heart twisted at the sight. Dirt covered her from head to toe, and tears created muddy rivers down her cheeks. She ran toward him, tripped, and sprawled headfirst. Tait tried to go to her but was held fast.

Becky picked herself up and stumbled the rest of the way, wrapping her arms around his legs. Even from there, he could smell the urine where she'd gone in her clothes. Rage went through him that they'd had no decency to let her use a pot.

"Go home. Me go home," Becky cried.

Tait gave the men holding him an icy glare, his voice hard. "Turn me loose. Now."

When they did, he picked Becky up and held her tightly. He struggled for a bit of composure before speaking. "Honey, you're going to go home with Uncle Jack. He's going to take you to Mellie and the boys."

"No, you go too."

"I can't. There's something—" His voice broke. "Something I have to do here." He tried to hand her to Jack, but she clung to his neck, sobbing. "Take her, Jack. Ride out and don't try to save me. I've given my word."

"Come on, honey." Jack took Becky and sat her on his horse. He swung around to Berringer. "I'm coming back after his body and killing anyone in my way." He clasped Tait's hand. "I'll see you on the other side, brother."

"It's been a good ride," Tait managed, his tongue thick. "No regrets." No one had been a better friend or a better trail partner.

Jack put his foot in the stirrup, settled behind Becky, and galloped out, the child's sobs thick in the air. Tait's roan followed.

A sudden gust of wind blew the stovepipe hat off the head of the yellow-toothed man, and a large group of grackles flew into a nearby tree, settling on every branch and creating a noisy din.

Becky's wails lingered on the breeze, cutting into Tait's heart.

But she was safe, and that was all that mattered.

A whip cracked, the metal on the tip biting through his shirt into the tender flesh of his back.

Thirty-two

THE DAY STILL YOUNG, MELANIE AND HER FATHER HUNCHED IN the shadows, watching the doctor's office. It sat four doors down from the jail, and a simple shingle swinging above the door read *Dr. Levi McIlroy*. Shock jolted her. Kin to the judge? If so, he'd probably be like-minded as well. She reached into her pocket and found the weight of the gun reassuring. Her mind slid back to the people she loved.

Please, God, don't let Becky die. Or Tait. Or Ava.

She couldn't bear to lose any one of them. She bit down on a knuckle to silence the cry that rose up from her aching heart. She lived for the moment when they'd all be reunited. She'd changed, grown wiser in the time she'd been Tait's wife. He'd helped her see what was truly important—that it was a person's deeds, not money or power, that counted most.

Just then Quitman stalked away from the sheriff's office. He shoved some things in his saddlebags then swung up on his horse and raced from town in a cloud of dust.

What was that about? Getting out while the coast was clear? Probably, given that the good sheriff was a low-down little weasel. Or maybe he was taking something to the railroad owner Richard Markham, wherever it was he stayed when he wasn't causing trouble. At least they wouldn't have to worry about Quitman for a while.

The door to the doctor's office opened, and an elderly man emerged, a black bag in his hand. Melanie punched her father's shoulder to wake him up. "He's leaving. Come on."

They collected their horses and set out a fair distance behind the doctor. He moved slowly, shuffling his feet and checking a gold watch. The man of medicine shared no similarities with the judge. He was of short stature and had a nicely trimmed white goatee—almost fatherly. Dr. Levi glanced around several times, perhaps worrying about being followed, and at each instance, she and Mac ducked behind their mounts.

Dr. Levi McIlroy walked across town to a two-story clapboard house and knocked. A woman who appeared by her dress to be a housekeeper let him in.

Melanie tied their horses out of sight and moved closer, Mac following behind. A large crepe myrtle bush laden with pink blooms beckoned as a hiding place, and Melanie pulled her father deep into the fragrant branches.

Mac nudged her. "Wonder who lives here."

Before she could reply, Judge McIlroy rode up on a handsome palomino and paused for a second, his gaze scanning the area, before heading around to the back.

"I think that answers the question. If Ava's in there, we have to get her out. He's not above putting a bullet in her head."

Minutes passed in silence as she studied the windows for movement. Finally, she could stand it no longer. "I'm going to go peek inside. You stay here and be quiet."

"Be careful."

She nodded and slipped from the large, colorful bush and ran to the house, crouching low against the side. Methodically, she began a slow turn about the house, rising up on her toes just enough to look into each window. At the back of the house, Melanie came to what appeared to be a study. The judge was inside, and she crouched low so as not to be seen. Popping up again a moment later, she saw him open a safe, grab some papers out, and shove them into a briefcase. A half-empty glass of amber liquid sat on his desk. The neat, composed high-ranking official had vanished. In his place was a disheveled, frantic rat about to be caught.

He tossed back what was left of the contents of the glass and ran his hands through his hair.

McIlroy appeared to be getting ready to carry out his threat to leave town before the governor's man arrived. Her heart sank. He might get away with what he'd done, but there was nothing she could do about that. First and foremost she had to keep Ava alive.

When she moved on to the kitchen, an idea came to her. Two men sat at a small table playing cards. Guards, she assumed. The despicable rat needed them.

A distraction would come in handy. If Mac could somehow get in there and keep them busy, she'd find a way to search the upstairs rooms.

After seeing nothing else of interest, she hurried back. "Mac, you have to find a way to play cards with those guards."

"Leave it to me." He removed his jacket, rolled up his sleeves, and rumpled his hair. "I'm a hobo asking for a hand-out, willing to play cards for food. I'll ante up with the bottle of gin in my pocket."

"Perfect." She kissed his cheek. "Hopefully the judge won't remember you if he spots you. I'll give you a few minutes to get inside, then I'll climb that lattice over there to the second story."

The danger dried the spit in her mouth. Anything could go wrong. One thing about it, she was not leaving Ava behind again.

"Here I go." Mac stood up and hobbled around back like he was in pain. Melanie had to admit his acting was good. He looked exactly like an old bum.

She counted to one hundred, and he wasn't back, which likely meant they'd let him in. In no time, she scaled the side of the house and leaned over to peek into the upstairs window. The doctor stood in a bedroom doorway, putting something in his black bag.

When he moved away a few minutes later in the direction of the stairs and didn't return, she climbed silently through the window and took the gun from her pocket. Still not seeing anyone, she tiptoed across the hall and eased the door open just a crack. Other than a form lying in the bed, the room was empty. Melanie slipped inside and quickly closed the door.

The dim light of the room kept her from seeing the figure clearly, but she made out an ashen face. The person appeared dead.

Oh God, was she too late?

A searing ache in her heart, Melanie stole to the bedside and drank in the sight of the mirror side of herself—same delicate features, same auburn hair. She smothered a cry and touched Ava's blunt, chopped hair, no more than three inches long. Their identical looks could have been useful for their escape, except now it was out of the question.

"Ava, wake up." Her sister didn't move. Melanie touched Ava's forehead and found it feverish. She shook her. "Ava."

This didn't seem right for pleurisy. Her breathing was shallow but she wasn't struggling enough for her lungs to be bad. No, this was something else.

"Ava, wake up." Melanie shook her. "Wake up, we need to go."

"Who—?" Ava's eyes fluttered then flew open, and she brushed Melanie's face with weak fingertips. "Is it really you? I waited and waited."

"It's me. Let's get you out of here. Can you walk?"

"So tired." Ava sat up slowly, her legs hanging off the bed. She only wore a nightgown and couldn't leave in that.

Melanie glanced around and snatched up a wrapper off a chair. "Put this on. We have to hurry."

"He'll be mad. Don't want him…to get you." Ava thrust her arms into the wrapper and tied it while Melanie put some shoes on her.

"Ready?" Melanie pulled Ava to her feet and put an arm around her waist. She held the gun in the other hand. "Lean on me. Do you know a way out where we won't be seen?"

"Sorry."

"Doesn't matter. I'll find something." Now that they were together again, Melanie wasn't leaving without Ava.

They moved out into the hallway, each step seeming to take an hour. Her nerves screamed at her to hurry, but Ava was doing the best she could. At one end of the hall lay the front stairs with McIlroy's study just off of it. At the other end was what appeared to be the back stairs, and that's where Melanie turned.

Two more steps and they'd be there. Her heart pounded.

"Hey, what are you doing?"

Melanie swung around to see the doctor. She pointed the gun at him. "I'm taking my sister out of here. Try to stop me and I will shoot you."

"There's no need for gunfire." The doctor came closer, squinting. "I'd know you anywhere, Melanie. You're the spitting image of Ava. Get your sister out of here. Mr. Markham and the judge plan to use her to kill you, and no one will be able to stop them."

"They might try." Melanie let a smile form. She wasn't the woman they'd sent off to lure Tait to Canadian. She was lots tougher now and much wiser.

"I'm glad you came. She needs you."

Melanie relaxed and lowered the gun. He seemed warm and genuine, but she kept her guard up. Looks could often deceive.

Dr. Levi reached into his black bag and handed Melanie two brown bottles. "Take these. Give a dose of each to Ava twice a day. Also, when you get to the bottom of these stairs, take a door to the left and it'll let you into the yard. It's the fastest way out."

"Thank you." Melanie put the two bottles of medicine into her pocket. "What will the judge do to you once he finds her gone?"

"He's my cousin, worse luck, and I think I can handle him. He may be up here any minute, so hurry," the doctor urged. "Also, you should know that the judge has been giving Ava something to keep her knocked out. I suspect morphine."

So, that's what was wrong. "Thank you for telling me, Doctor."

The doctor laid a hand on her shoulder. "There's a large dog tied up out there. Stay clear."

"Appreciate the warning." Melanie tightened her grip on her sister, preparing to go down the stairs.

Ava turned around. "Thank you."

"My pleasure, dear," the doctor answered.

"Where do you think you're going?" Judge McIlroy thundered.

Melanie swung. Her nemesis stood on the landing at the other end of the hall. She sat Ava on the floor and raised her weapon. "I don't want to kill you, but I will if you force my hand."

The doctor took a step toward them. She couldn't trust him. She couldn't trust anyone. "Get back, Doc!"

The man of medicine obeyed, standing by Ava's bedroom.

The judge slowly came closer. "You're just a two-bit gambler with a pretty face and no brains. You'll never be worth a hill of beans. You can't even complete one simple task. You couldn't even do that much."

His arrogance was no shock. This whole thing had been about profiting him.

"Levi, take that gun away from her," McIlroy ordered his cousin.

"No. You're on your own, Ira," Doc answered.

McIlroy huffed loudly, taking three more steps.

"Stop where you are, McIlroy, or I will blow your head off. Everything is over. The governor's man will be here soon. All that power you craved is gone."

"They'll have to snatch it from my hands." McIlroy's crazed eyes glittered. "I worked hard to get this job and made people respect me."

The man was looney. "You can't make people give you your due. You have to earn it."

His steps lagged, but he kept coming, his hands hanging by his side, his face a gruesome mask.

Filled with terror, Melanie tightened her finger on the trigger. She didn't want to kill him. She didn't know what it was like to take a life, but by all that was holy, she would put a bullet in him. "I'll warn you again. Stop."

"You don't have the guts," he snarled and jerked a gun from inside his coat.

She watched in horror as he aimed and pulled the trigger. Oh God!

Her eyes closed, she kept expecting a loud explosion, waited to feel the fiery path of a bullet entering her body. She stiffened, her heart racing. Her life couldn't end here. Not this way.

But the shot sped past her head and into the wall.

Frozen in horror, her eyes flew open. She put McIlroy dead center and squeezed the trigger of her weapon. The bullet entered his chest and ripped through muscle and bone. Surprise flitted across his face as he went down.

Was he dead? She shook violently from head to toe. Oh God, so much blood!

"Get your sister out of here," the doctor ordered. "That shot'll bring people running. I'll take care of Ira and keep the guards up here until you get away. Take her to the mercantile and ask for Virginia. She'll help."

Heavy boots pounded on the stairs at the far end. They had to hurry.

"Thank you." Melanie helped Ava down each step. The process was agonizingly slow, and by the time they reached the bottom, sweat lined Ava's forehead. Melanie let her rest a minute while she listened to the noises in the house. While there were sounds and voices above, no one seemed to be moving in their direction. So far so good.

Drawing in a deep breath Ava nodded that she was ready, and Melanie opened the door on the left. They found themselves in a secluded garden. A large furry dog sprang up, baring his sharp teeth.

Melanie stilled her shaking and stared into the animal's eyes. "We're going past you now, and you're going to be a nice dog. We won't hurt you, but if you decide to be mean, I'll have no choice but to shoot you. Do you understand me?"

The dog looked confused, turning his head from side to side, but he quit growling and let his lip fall over his teeth in a less threatening pose. Melanie and Ava took one step and then another. The dog laid down, his eyes following their progress.

"Good dog." Melanie kept her voice gentle but watched for aggression. "That's good."

They reached the gate leading from the garden where they were stopped by a man who resembled a tree in both height and breadth. He smelled like the inside of a whiskey bottle. He glanced at her and then Ava and scratched his head. "What are you doin'?"

Taking a deep breath, Melanie hid the gun in the folds of her dress. Fire it and she'd bring everyone. She drew herself up straight and put a good dose of authority in her voice. "Getting some fresh air. What does it look like?"

"Does the judge know about this? He didn't tell me anything about you taking walks." He leaned closer to peer into her face. "How come there's two of you?"

Movement behind him caught Melanie's eye. Mac was stealing up behind the guard with a raised club. Just a little closer.

"Maybe because you're drunk, you louse. I could smell you a mile away."

The guard put out a hand and first touched her and then Ava. "You both feel real. I don't know what you're trying to pull, but I'm taking all four of you back inside."

Mac raised the club with both hands and gave a mighty blow to the guard's head. He went down with a thud.

"Thanks, Mac. We've got to get out of here, but we'll be exposed going down the drive. Plus the other guard is going to miss this one and come looking." Her hold on Ava began to slip. Melanie got a better grip.

Ava struggled to breathe and sagged heavily against her. "I can't…make it."

"It's just a little way to the horses."

"I can't. My legs won't work."

Mac got on the other side and helped hold her up. "Keeping close to the trimmed shrubbery is our best bet."

Melanie's heart pounded, and she kept expecting to be stopped.

With no one emerging from the house, they reached the horses without problem. "The doctor said Virginia at the mercantile will help us," she told Mac. They put Ava on Melanie's horse. Melanie walked and led her black mount, following Mac into the alley behind the mercantile.

"Help me with Ava, then I'll go find Virginia." Melanie went to the right side of the animal.

Mac lifted Ava down and sat her on a barrel. Her sister's head sagged. Seeing her shorn hair in the bright light made Melanie's chest ache. She hurried inside the establishment, praying desperately that this wouldn't turn out to be a trap.

❧

Jack rode out with Becky crying in his arms, clawing at him to get off the horse. "I'm sorry. I'm sorry. I wish I could change things."

His insides were raw and aching. His heart too seemed to release its own wail. He was leaving his best friend to face a torturous death alone.

Back when they were kids, Tait had always been uncommonly stoic, even after beatings by his father. He'd always headed for Jack's place after. On more than one occasion, he'd been in serious pain but refused to shed a tear or do much more than grimace.

Even when Tait had stumbled into Hope's Crossing six months ago all shot up, he'd held all his agony inside. Like an old dog, he'd curled up and licked his wounds.

Jack prayed that death would be quick. Maybe Tait would lunge for one of their guns and they'd just shoot him. Although the chances of that were slim.

He rode past the frowning guard. A little further on, when he was out of sight, he cut into the brush to find Clay. Thankfully Becky had hushed her wailing, but she was still snuffling and clinging to Jack with both hands. He wanted to tell her she'd be all right, but he knew nothing would ever be all right again—not for anyone.

Oh God, how was he going to tell Melanie? She loved Tait so much.

Clay stepped out from their hiding place. Jack dismounted and filled him in on what had happened. Clay's face turned deadly, and the look in his eyes was frightening, even to Jack. He swung a hard fist into a tree trunk and bloodied his knuckles, not seeming to feel it.

"He told me not to try to save him, but I'm going back and

I'm killing that bastard and everyone who gets in my way," Jack declared.

Clay cursed and took Becky, rocking her. "We have to be smart about this or they'll outthink us. We need more guns, and we have to do something with Becky. Maybe you can ride into town and try to find a woman who'll look after her until we finish. The doctor's wife or maybe they have a reverend."

"As I rode out, I heard one of Kern's men say that they would take their time torturing Tait. They're not planning to kill him until tomorrow."

"That buys us a little time, but I'd hate to be in Tait's boots right now." Clay had a far-off stare. "It's the beforehand trials that test us the hardest."

Yeah. And Kern Berringer was an expert at making a man, or woman, want to die.

Jack thought of Lucy. He hadn't told Tait everything. Some things a man was better off not knowing. Especially that.

He chambered the secret he'd carry to his grave before it could take root. "It occurs to me that people like Ussary at the mercantile or the owner of the Wild Jacks Saloon might lend us a hand with Berringer. No one we've met seemed fond of the bastard."

Becky stared silently at him from Clay's arms, her eyes huge—accusing. He had to see to her care first. A bath, clean clothes, and food. Tait would want that.

But damn, he hated leaving!

"Anything is worth a try." Clay handed Becky to him. "See to her welfare. I'll stay here and keep watch."

"I know it's not in you to sit still. Just watch out for booby traps." Jack rose, took his guns from Clay, and saddled up with Becky. Her eerie silence was downright spooky. Maybe she'd lost her voice from all that crying.

"Good luck. I hope you find a nice woman to keep her. After what Becky's been through, she needs the kind of comfort that only a woman can offer." His face grim, Clay started to turn away and stopped, his voice hard. "Buy more ammunition. Lots of it. The moment you get back, we're going in for Tait."

Thirty-three

PAIN SLICED THROUGH TAIT, STINGING, BLINDING. HIS TEST OF endurance had begun. He faced the man with the whip and grabbed the thin leather as it cracked the air again. It sliced into his palm, but he held fast. He would not go down without a fight.

With one mighty jerk, he ripped the whip from the bastard's hand. The men standing in the circle around him lunged, piling on top, forcing him to the ground.

Tait kicked, hit, and pushed, but he couldn't escape their fists. A gun blast ceased the fight.

"Stop!" Kern yelled. "I get him first, and I've got something special planned for Trinity. You can have what's left when I finish."

The men rose, and Tait got to his feet, wiping his bloody mouth. "It seems to me you've done more than get even already. You killed my wife, sister, and brother-in-law."

"I haven't begun to settle the score, Trinity," Kern cursed, rubbing his crippled leg. "You put me in agony for the rest of my life."

"Couldn't let you hurt that young widow. She never did anything to you." Tait had helped her onto a stagecoach that carried her back east, far away from Kern. He'd been young back then—hell, Kern had too. He hadn't yet seen the depths of Kern's hatred or known that revenge would take Lucy and Claire from him. Still, given the chance, he'd probably do the same thing again. Only he'd protect his loved ones better.

"Wasn't your business."

Tait spat blood on the ground and stepped closer to Kern. "Let's you and me settle this. Right here. Right now. Your choice of weapon."

"Now why would I do that?" Kern laughed, and the rest of his band joined in. "I got you right where I want you, and you won't escape me this time. Boys, hang him from that large cottonwood over there—by his ankles."

Doom clawed its way from Tait's belly. He lunged to the right, evading one man's grasp only to find another waiting to drive a fist into his jaw. Stars twinkled in his vision.

He was done for. His torments would end here, on this desolate spot in Texas. He didn't even mind going to hell. Because one day Kern would join him, and they'd have a level playing field.

⮞⮜

Melanie hurried into the store and spoke to Virginia, telling her what the doc had said.

"Let's get her inside. Thank you for trusting me."

"I had no choice, ma'am."

They emerged into the alley where Mac was holding Ava up. Melanie smoothed back Ava's jagged hair and felt her forehead. Still hot.

"Sorry." Ava gave her a sad smile. "Tried to be brave." She wet her lips. "Like you. Not as strong. Did you get…outlaw's money?"

"Don't apologize. You did just fine. I only gave McIlroy a little of the money. I told him he wouldn't get any more until I had you back."

"Didn't strike a very good bargain. I'm half-dead." Ava leaned her head against the wall. "If I die, bury me…pretty stream."

The weak words struck Melanie like a hammer. She knelt and squeezed Ava's hands. "I'm not going to let you die, so don't even think that. You're going to get well and come live in Hope's Crossing with Tait and me and three of the best kids God ever set on this earth. You'll love it there."

She thought of Becky and Tait and prayed she wasn't being overly optimistic. She and Mac lifted Ava up and half-dragged her into the establishment while Virginia held the door and directed them.

Virginia was a slight woman, and her high cheekbones,

olive skin, and black hair indicated some Comanche or Apache blood. "I have a small bed set up in the storeroom. She'll be safer there should anyone start snooping around."

A lamp lit the dark space, revealing a small bed hidden amid the stored merchandise.

They got Ava under the covers, and Virginia spread a warm quilt over her. Ava gave a deep sigh, snuggled into the folds, and closed her eyes.

Melanie and Mac went out into the store to talk to Virginia. "Thank you for everything. I don't know what we would've done without your help."

"It's my pleasure. She'll feel much better when the drugs Doc Levi mentioned clear her system." Virginia gave them a sorrowful smile. "We don't hold with what McIlroy, Markham, and Sheriff Quitman are doing. But the worst is Kern Berringer and his rowdy boys. They ride into town and take whatever they want, sometimes shooting the place up. If anyone says a word, they kill them. It's terrifying. And now Kern has taken a poor little girl."

A jolt of excitement went through Melanie. "Did you see her?"

Virginia nodded. "He came in here yesterday. Such a sweet thing. She was screaming, then Kern got rough with her, and she bit his arm. Chomped right down on it and drew blood."

Melanie inhaled sharply. "What did he do?"

"He slapped her, jerked her around. The judge was in the store and stopped him, or it would've been worse." Virginia poked a strand of hair into the low bun she wore on the back of her head. "Charles told me three men rode in here this morning asking about Kern and the child."

Tait, Jack, and Clay were here? Help was so close. Excitement rushed through Melanie. She described them, and Virginia confirmed their identities. The woman explained how her husband had showed them Kern's place. Were they still there? Melanie had to find them. "Will you draw me a map?"

"Oh no, dear, you can't go out there. It's far too dangerous. You don't know what those Berringers are like."

"I'm sorry, but I do, ma'am. That child is a niece of my husband's, and he's hell-bent on getting her back any way he can. I have to go."

Mac put an arm around her. "You'd just be in the way, daughter. Let them do what they came for and get little Becky. It's best if you wait here."

Anger flared. "I'm going, and that's that. I'd like to speak to Mr. Ussary please." And if he refused to show her where Kern lived, she'd find someone who would. She had to get to Tait. He loved that little girl and would do anything for her—even swap himself.

Ice coated her insides, and she could barely breathe as thoughts circled in her head.

If he fell into Kern's clutches, his life wouldn't be worth two cents. Kern would kill him sure as the sun shone bright outside.

"Charles isn't here right now, but I'll tell him you want to talk to him."

Melanie sat with Ava until she fell asleep, then wandered into the front area of the mercantile. What was keeping Charles? She needed to find Kern's place before dark.

A rider had stopped in front of the mercantile, and there was something about him that drew her gaze. Or maybe it was the fact that he held a child in his arms. She pressed her face to the window glass.

Jack Bowdre! And the child had to be…Becky?

She raced out the door. "You saved her!"

Jack glanced up. Becky was asleep in his arms. "Where did you come from?"

One look at his haggard face and red-rimmed eyes and she sucked in a sharp, shocked breath. "Where's Tait?"

"Kern's got him. He traded himself for Becky. I've got to get back and save him."

"Oh no! Oh no!" Melanie let out a wounded cry, wrapping her arms tightly around her middle. She rocked back and forth, moaning.

The noise woke Becky, who raised her head and looked around, eyes wide. "Mellie! Mellie."

"Yes, darling. You're safe now." She took the child from Jack and gasped at her condition. She'd have to be cleaned up at once. But where? "It's all right, honey. I've got you."

"Me hurt."

"I know, sweetheart, and I'm sorry." Melanie smoothed the matted hair from her face.

"Wuncle." Tears rolled down Becky's face as she pointed to the way they'd just come.

"There, sweet girl. We're going to get him away from that mean man." And she meant to go help but first had to find someone to watch Becky for a while.

Jack dismounted and looped the reins over the hitching post. "Now, explain how you ended up here."

She quickly told him about McIlroy's threatening telegram and how she'd brought him the money. She smiled at the memory of the judge's frustration at getting only a small portion. "I shot him. I think he's dead, but I'm not certain. I have my sister back and have hidden her inside the mercantile. McIlroy kept her drugged with something, and she's terribly weak. And Jack, he chopped off her hair and pulled a tooth. I hate that man. What are your plans now? Please tell me you'll get Tait out."

"Sorry your sister suffered at the judge's hands. He deserves death. Saves us the bother." Jack pinched the bridge of his nose, his gaze sweeping the dirty street. "I have to try to recruit some men here to go back with me. We need every gun we can rustle up. But first, I need to buy a lot more ammunition. Kern has an army with him."

Ammunition meant lots of shooting. Men dying.

Mac came up behind her. "I don't know if I'll be much use, but I'll ride along."

Jack's brows drew together in thought. "Thanks, but I'm not sure that's wise. The women need someone to protect them. Would you be willing?"

"Sure. I'll keep anything from happening to them, and I should probably stay with my daughters anyway."

"Exactly what I was thinking." Jack shook his hand. "Thanks, Mr. Dunbar."

Melanie liked the respect Jack showed her father, although she wasn't sure Mac deserved it. "Come inside. Maybe Virginia can point me toward a place where I can clean this child up." She turned to her father and caught him staring at the Wild Jacks Saloon. "Mac, don't even think it. If I catch you in a saloon again, I'll shoot you. Ava needs you."

Mac ran a hand across his coarse gray stubble. "Cain't a man even look?"

"Not in your case." She watched him sulk away, but Mac's mood didn't concern her at the moment. "Jack, I need to talk to you about something."

The afternoon had begun to wane, and night would fall in two more hours. If they meant to rescue Tait, their best chance was after dark, and she didn't know how far it was to Berringer's place.

Jack angled his unshaven jaw in her direction. "I reckon I know what you want, and the answer is no."

"Come inside before anyone sees me. I have lots to tell you."

He held the door, and inside she introduced him to Virginia. "This lady is an angel and helped with my sister."

"Thank you, Mrs. Ussary." Jack clutched his hat, searching for the man he needed. "Is Charles around?"

Virginia repeated that he'd be back any minute. While she got the boxes of ammunition Jack requested, Melanie rocked Becky, who continued to whimper and cry. "Poor baby. Once we get home, I'm not letting you out of my sight."

Jack met her gaze. "She's been through hell."

"I can tell. I despise Kern Berringer!" Melanie turned to Virginia. "I hate to keep asking for favors, but I'd be obliged if you can point me to some water where I can bathe this child."

She nodded. "Upstairs. The poor dear. While you wash her, I'll find some fresh clothes for her."

"I'm truly indebted to you." Melanie turned to head up the stairs but stopped before taking a step. "Jack, I'm going back with you. Tait is my husband, and he belongs to me—not Berringer. I have to go get him."

Jack let out an exasperated breath. "I let you come and Tait will kill me."

Melanie grabbed his arm. "You need me. I can go in with a gun hidden underneath my clothes, and Tait will have a way to fight from the inside. Just think…Tait with a weapon can inflict a lot of damage. You *know* that."

Jack was silent, pondering her words. Finally, he nodded. "If he's in any shape. But that *would* give us an edge. What about Kern though? He's already killed too many women. What makes you think he won't kill you too?" He walked around her and grabbed some medical supplies off the shelf.

Her heart stopped, seeing the bandages, bottles of antiseptic, and needles and thread. Oh God, how badly hurt would Tait be?

"A chance I'll gladly take. I can carry an extra gun for myself." She stepped in front of him and brought him to a stop. "What do you think is going to happen the moment you and a posse ride in with guns blazing?"

"Kern will shoot Tait." He released a low oath. "All right. I see your point. I'll get you an extra gun, and you'll be our inside man." He mumbled something under his breath. "I just pray I'm doing the right thing."

That made two of them. She knew the horrors Kern liked to inflict on women, and if he made Tait watch… Ice filled her veins at the very thought.

Becky frowned and patted her cheek. "Mellie scared?"

"Just thinking, honey. I'm so happy to have you back. You were a brave, brave girl."

The child teared up and stuck out her bottom lip. "Man mean."

"Yes, he was, but he won't ever get you again."

"No." Becky sniffled, and a tear fell down her cheek. It would be a long time before her memory faded.

"Jack, how soon will you leave?"

He stood at the counter while Virginia rang up his purchases. "Half an hour at most." He paid his bill. "Will you be ready?"

It didn't give her much time to settle Becky, and she hated to ride out leaving her with strangers so soon, but it couldn't be helped. She had to go to Tait, had to be there to hold him.

"Yes." She gave him a hard stare. "Go without me and you'll regret it."

A man entered, one Jack called Charles. Melanie rushed up the stairs at the back of the store with Mrs. Ussary and soon had Becky sitting in a tub of warm, soapy water. Only then did the tense muscles in Becky's thin body relax.

And then too Melanie saw the bruises beneath the dirt.

Sympathy filled Virginia's eyes. She clucked over Becky but was unable to get a smile from the little girl, so she excused herself and came back with fresh clothes. "These belong to our granddaughter. She wears them when she visits, but she has more than enough, and these probably won't fit any longer anyway."

The sunny yellow dress and underclothes were well made and soft to the touch. "You're a godsend." Melanie finished washing Becky's hair then lifted her out of the water and wrapped a towel around her small frame.

"Just getting rid of Kern Berringer is thanks enough. That man makes my blood boil."

"Mine too. I've never known an eviler man. The things he's done terrify me to the bone." Melanie listened for Jack's voice downstairs as she dried Becky and dressed her.

"Yet you'll still put yourself in danger going out there?"

"For Tait I'll do anything." Even die. A moment's silence filled the room. "Virginia, I hate to ask because you've already done so much but—would you know of anyone who'd keep Becky until I return? There's my father, but she doesn't know him." Then there was an issue with trust. Knowing him, he might leave the girl alone to follow the smell of money—or whiskey.

"This darling child can stay right here. I know my Charles, and he'll ride out with the men. Your sister and Becky will be safe with me and keep me company to boot."

A big load lifted from Melanie's shoulders. She reached for the woman's hand and squeezed it. "Thank you."

After that, she went to check on Ava and found her awake. She smiled at Becky. "Who's this?"

"My husband's little niece." Melanie sat on the side of the bed and told her about the kidnapping and that Tait had traded himself for the child.

"Takes a strong man to do that. She's so sweet." Ava took Becky's hand and said hello.

Then Becky did an unbelievable thing. She lay down next to Ava and sighed like she was with family.

Maybe she was.

"Ava, I'm really sorry about your hair. I almost died when McIlroy sent it to me." Melanie lightly touched the short bob, her heart breaking, recalling how long and beautiful her hair had been. "There was also a tooth in the box. Did the judge pull any?"

Her sister nodded, anguish lining her face. She opened her mouth and showed her a gap on the bottom. Thank goodness it wasn't right in front.

"I'll never forgive myself for what you went through. I should've been the one to stay behind."

"No." Ava weakly touched Melanie's cheek. "My choice."

That did little to ease her guilt. Not long after, Ava fell back asleep, and Melanie took Becky out. She felt much better about leaving her behind at the mercantile. Once she got Tait out of Kern's clutches, things would be almost perfect.

But she knew better than to count on too much. Situations like this had a way of turning on a dime.

❧

Tait hung by his ankles from a tall cottonwood. Blood trickled into his mouth, choking him. He tried to spit but found it impossible in his position. All he could do was hang there and wait for what would come next. Whatever it was, he knew it would be excruciating.

At least Becky was free and could grow up into a fine young woman. Nothing else mattered. He didn't matter. He'd ruined his life long before this. Maybe doing one noble thing could change where he'd spend eternity.

He heard his father's voice in his ear. "You're worthless, an evil seed. Better to cast you out than try to save your sorry ass."

Yeah. He thought of other things he'd been called—scum, killer, bastard, and worse. His eyes filled with tears. This was a fitting way for him to die. Maybe he could do better in the next life.

His vision blurred, but not enough to block out the sight of Kern approaching, a thick piece of wood in his hands. Dread crawled from Tait's stomach, and he gritted his teeth.

"Before I'm finished with you, Trinity, you'll wish I'd just killed you." Kern knelt down and grabbed a handful of hair, yanking Tait's head up. "And look who else is here—your friend Markham."

Markham bent down, careful not to wrinkle his expensive suit. "How's it going, Trinity?"

"I'd like to chat, but I'm kinda tied up at the moment, you sonofabitch."

The thin mustache above Markham's top lip didn't move when he gave Tait an arrogant smile. "I intend to let Kern take every cent of the money you stole from me out of your miserable hide."

"That won't put it back in your hands, now will it, Markey?"

"Maybe not, but I'll get immense satisfaction from the process." Markham smoothed back his hair even though every greased strand was glued in place.

Tait's skin turned clammy. The only reason Markham was there was to see him die. He had one last barb to throw. "I noticed business has fallen off. Could it be folks are afraid to ride the Missouri River Railroad? Not that I blame them. They probably don't trust you."

The man's face flushed as he straightened. He nodded to Kern and stepped away.

Tait looked up at the sky, thinking it had never been prettier. The blue was giving way to darker colors and gave the appearance of a swirling kaleidoscope. He tightened his jaw as the first blow struck mid-back, sending him spinning away from the tree. Burning, piercing pain shot through him.

A second blow came and a third before blessed darkness closed around him and the world went quiet and still.

Melanie's face floated in front of him. She reached for his hand and led him to a beautiful garden filled with every kind of flower. He lay down on the carpet of grass and put his head in her lap.

No one could touch him here.

She lowered her head and placed her lips on his. God, how he loved this woman. Why hadn't he told her when he'd had the chance? Now she'd never know what was in his heart.

Thirty-four

MELANIE SAT IN A CHAIR IN THE MERCANTILE HOLDING BECKY. Partially hidden by a pile of leather goods, she stared out the window, waiting for Jack, praying he hadn't gone back on his word.

Virginia finished waiting on a customer and came over to check on them. Melanie knew she had to break the news to Becky, and this seemed as good a time as any.

"Honey, I'm going to have to leave you here with Miss Virginia for a bit. I don't want you to be scared. All right?"

Becky glanced up, her blue eyes bright amid the bruises that marred her skin. "Go get wuncle."

"Yes, honey, I will. You won't be afraid, will you?"

"Me scared."

"But not of me, are you?" Virginia asked gently.

Becky shook her head. "Like you."

Virginia patted the girl's leg. "I'll keep you safe, and we'll have a good time. You can help me take care of your aunt Ava."

One short nod sent Becky's blond curls dancing, and she stared at her hands.

Melanie hugged her close. "Do you know how much I love you?"

Again, a nod. It seemed the girl didn't want to voice the things that frightened her. Melanie didn't blame her. The more danger she herself was in, the quieter she became.

Becky raised her head, tears bubbling in her blue eyes. "Wuncle hurt."

"I don't know, honey. But I have to go help him."

"Me stay with other Mellie." Becky pointed toward the room where Ava was sleeping and made her announcement as though it settled everything. And truly it did. Becky felt close to Ava because she looked like Melanie. Now Melanie could go without feeling guilty for leaving.

Her gaze landed on a knife case. Who knew what she'd run into out there? She should prepare for any situation. She carried Becky over to look at them. A small knife would be easy to hide in the straps securing the guns.

Footsteps sounded, and Mac nudged her arm. "Here, take mine. It might come in handy."

"Thanks." She took his pocketknife and, ducking into the storeroom where Ava lay, secured it under her riding skirt next to the gun on her right leg. Becky grinned.

When she came out, movement through the window caught her attention. She leaned forward and stared at three men striding through the mercantile door. She recognized Jack and Charles Ussary, but the other…

Could it be?

The three men entered the building, their bootheels striking the wood floor. Melanie's breath stilled. She propped Becky on her hip and rushed over. "Sam Legend!"

The man's wide grin showed his teeth. "In the flesh, Miss Melanie." He kissed her cheek. "Jack filled me in on everything. I'm sorry about Tait. His situation is grave."

"I keep thinking I hear his voice or the sound of his bootheels on the floor." She struggled to find a smile. "I thought you were headed home to the Lone Star." She watched Ussary go to his wife, how he pulled her against him, the tender way he held her. Tears burned her eyes as cherished memories crowded new thoughts from her mind. Melanie blinked hard and swallowed.

"I was." Sam thumbed back his hat to expose trail-weary lines around his mouth and eyes. "On the way through Saint's Roost, the telegraph operator flagged us down with a message from the governor. He ordered me to come take care of McIlroy, so Pa and the others went on, and here I am."

"I shot McIlroy. He tried to stop me when I went for Ava."

"He earned what he got, so don't waste time on regrets." Becky grunted and reached for Sam. He took her, and she looked at home in the big lawman's arms. His mouth tightened at Becky's bruises. "I'm glad this little girl is safe. Berringer better hide because we're coming."

"We can sure use you if you can spare the time. I take it Jack didn't mention that I'm coming along."

Sam's startled gaze shot to Jack.

Jack gave him a nod. "I was against it at first, but she can out-argue my wife. Melanie will be a big help."

"I trust your judgment, Bowdre." Sam's gray eyes shifted to Melanie, and he gave her a slight nod as though to say everything would be all right. "Tell me your plan."

Sam's quickness to jump in warmed Melanie's heart. She grew fonder of this Legend man each time she saw him. He had the kind of spirit that never backed away from a fight.

While Jack explained, men on horseback began congregating in front of the store. Jack appeared to have found a few good citizens to ride with them after all.

When Jack finished, Melanie asked, "How many extra men signed on?"

"Five. Given more time, I probably could've gotten more. Still, that's a fair amount to add to Clay, Sam, and me. If you're ready to ride, we should get going." Jack took Becky, kissed her, and handed her to Melanie.

Melanie struggled with her composure as she hugged Becky and told her how much she loved her.

The child blew her a kiss. "Love you."

"I love you too, sweetheart." She let Virginia take her and hurried outside before she could start blubbering. She adjusted her hat on her head and looked around for her father.

When she glanced up, Mac came toward her leading Cherokee. She gave her father a grateful smile and climbed into the saddle, vowing to be more understanding. Maybe she'd misjudged him a little. Time would tell—as it usually did.

"Take good care of Ava and Becky, Mac."

"Will do." He rested a hand on the black gelding's neck. "Be careful. Kern's a mean one."

She gave him a nod, and the group left town. They galloped for about half an hour before cutting down a narrow trail for about a mile where they crossed a creek, then rode through a tangle of brush and undergrowth.

Fear gripped her heart tighter with each thundering hoof. Would Tait be alive by the time they arrived? It had been hours since he'd ridden into Berringer's place. From what she'd heard, Kern didn't seem a man given to patience.

"Hold on, Tait. We're coming." She clung to the reins, urging her horse faster, praying they'd get there in time. If they didn't, she wouldn't be able to go on. Tait gave her courage and made her believe in herself. Without him, she'd be lost and afraid all the rest of her days.

Full dark covered them by the time they rode into the small, cheerless camp. Clay came to meet them, and she sensed thick displeasure at her presence.

He shot her a black look and jabbed a finger in Jack's chest. "Why did you bring her? She has no business here."

Melanie dismounted and marched to him. If he intended to send her packing, he'd have a fight on his hands. "Tait is my husband, and I have more right to be here than anyone. Regardless of how you feel, I think I can be of real help. Now would you like to hear our plan or not?"

Jack and Sam swung from their saddles, and the rest of the men gathered around.

"Calm down, Clay." Jack handed him a box of ammunition. "Melanie is the only one of us who can get inside and close enough to Tait to give him a gun. We have to get a gun in his hand before we launch an assault, or Berringer will put a bullet in his head before we get within firing range."

"I was thinking about trying to slip in around midnight. I'd like to spare her the risks." Clay's dark gaze pierced her. "You know what Kern is capable of."

Anger sparked inside her. Melanie straightened her back and raised her chin. "Stop it. I know what Kern's done. I heard it in gory detail and I've accepted what he might do to me. Does it scare me? Shoot, yeah. But I have to help Tait, and like it or not, I'm the best hope we have."

Sam spoke in the moment of silence. "She's right. From what I've heard about Berringer's hideout, they have it locked down tight with guards. There's no way to sneak a man inside and get to Tait. Whereas Melanie can demand to see her husband."

Clay snorted. "Fine. We'll do it this way. I pray to God you're right."

They checked their guns, gave Melanie an extra and waited while she secured it under her skirt. Clay led four of the volunteers on foot across the dark landscape toward Kern Berringer's house. They'd attack from there while the others mounted a frontal assault.

Melanie and the rest of the men climbed into their saddles in silence.

Terror gripped her like bands of steel until she could barely hold on. Tait's voice was in her head, describing how his wife and sister had suffered before they met their end. If this mission to save him went wrong—was she truly ready to die at Kern's hand?

She wound through the mesquite and scrub oak, every second taking her closer to the villain who held her beloved in his grasp.

"Yes, I am," she whispered into the night. "Tait took a chance on me, and I'll give my life for him."

Berringer couldn't take away her memories of the hours spent lying in Tait's arms, his body next to hers. The kisses. The caresses. Talk of the future. The children.

Jack reached for her gelding's bridle and held it. "After the guard lets you pass, we'll take care of him and the next one too so we can get closer. You still sure you want to do this? There's no shame in backing out."

"I'm going." She steadied the quaking inside. "I'll sacrifice anything for my husband."

"Okay. Keep riding on this road and lock your eyes ahead."

"You're not alone. At the first shot, we're riding in," Sam reminded her. "Berringer won't have time to blink."

Yes, but it only took half a second to kill a person. She immediately put the thought from her head. This was going to work, and they'd all live long and happy lives. She had to believe.

"Thanks, Sam." Melanie gripped the reins tighter to hide her trembles and the magnitude of what she was about to do twisted in her stomach. "I'm glad you're here."

A glance up at the stars and the reminder of what Tait had probably already endured settled her nerves. She nudged her gelding forward until she came to the road that led to Tait.

The guard stepped out. "Halt! What in the hell are you doing here, lady?"

"I'm Mrs. Trinity, and I demand to see my husband."

"This ain't no palace, ma'am, and you ain't no queen. Turn around and go home."

"I'm staying. I'll sit right here with you until I'm allowed to see Tait. I'm a talker when I'm nervous, and I wonder what shape you'll be in after listening to me all night." When the man still wavered, she added. "I can be a real pain in the rear end, mister. You won't get any rest."

"Hellfire!" The man removed his hat and stared up at her, his thick mustache and beard almost completely hiding his mouth. "I'm in trouble no matter what I decide. I reckon you can go on." His sour tone matched his expression.

"Thank you so much," she said sweetly as he fired his gun in the air to alert those farther up the trail.

About a half mile onward, another guard jumped down from a tree branch into the road in front of her, a gun pointed at her heart. "Who the hell are you, and what are you doing here?"

Melanie lifted her chin a trifle. "I'm Mrs. Trinity, and I've come to see my husband."

"Turn around and go back the way you came. I can't let you pass."

She released a sob that didn't have to be the pretend kind. "I've come so far and ridden for days. I can't go home until I at least see him one last time." Tears rolled down Melanie's face. "I have to say goodbye if he's going to die. It's barbaric to keep me from doing so. Every condemned man gets one last request."

A man on a horse materialized from the thick gloom. "It's

fine, Dan." He took the reins of her horse and began to move toward a house rising from the landscape. The guard didn't protest.

Melanie tried to see his face, but it was too dark, and his hat created even darker shadows. Kern Berringer? Quite possibly. He definitely held some kind of authority. She didn't speak, determined to wait him out. She didn't have a long wait.

A house emerged from the darkness, and they reined to a stop. Melanie glanced around, hoping to see Tait, and was disappointed that she didn't.

"Off your horse," the rider barked.

A group of well-armed men gathered around them as she obeyed, her knees trembling. The rider jerked a lantern from one of his followers and held it up. The terrifying sight of him drove her back. The hair lifted on the back of her neck and along her arms as she stared into the face of evil.

She couldn't tell the color of his eyes, but the glittering, feverish glow from them struck fear into her very soul. She gasped and stepped back. Chills rose on her arms. His stark features, totally devoid of hair, appeared like something from hell.

The man took a slow turn around her. He pinched her bottom, a breast, a shoulder. It was as though he tested her will. She didn't cry out or flinch, just glared.

Inwardly, though, her knees shook and mouth went dry. She'd entered the lair of a certified born killer.

Had he already snuffed out Tait's life? If so, her chances had sunk to zero.

"What're we gonna do with her, Pa?" one man asked.

Kern didn't answer him right away. "You're the spitting image of your sister. You oughtn't have come, Miz Trinity."

"I want to see my husband." She cleared her voice and put some starch in her request. "To say goodbye. Surely you won't prevent me from doing so."

"What makes you believe he's here?"

So he was still alive at least. Hope filled her.

"I saw Jack Bowdre, and he told me. Thank you for releasing little Becky." A little praise didn't hurt anything.

"Can't stand bawling kids. The brat bit me too." Kern spoke to the young man on his right. "Check her for weapons, son."

The nice-looking underling moved forward, a little hesitant at first then with more surety as he must've realized his father was testing him. "Hold out your arms, ma'am."

She sucked in a breath and obeyed, a rivulet of sweat trickling down her back. "I have no weapon, but you're welcome to see for yourself."

The man had lost the last traces of boyhood and appeared about nineteen or twenty. He placed his hands on each of her sides under her arms and proceeded to pat his way down her body. His palms lingered a moment too long on the sides of her breasts, then he felt around her waist. "Nothin' here, Pa."

Kern nodded to another, an older man who bore facial features to Earl back in the cell in Hope's Crossing. He appeared older than her by five years at least. "Frank, take her into the house, check her again. Women like to hide things. Then tie her real good. You know what to do."

Panic swept over her. "I demand to see Tait. Just let me talk to him one more time. Please."

"Miz Trinity, you should know your chances of leaving here alive are pretty slim." Kern stuck his face into hers, his rank breath gagging her. "I want to make Trinity lose his mind, and I can think of nothing that'll do the trick faster than having to watch another wife die a horrible death. Maybe I'll use fire this time." His twisted grin triggered waves of fear that strangled her and stole her voice. "Yes, that'll drive Trinity over the edge."

What if she couldn't find Tait in time? What if Kern burned her alive before Jack, Clay, and the others could get here? So much was at stake.

And if they found the guns...dear Lord! She swallowed her panic and focused on putting one foot in front of the other.

"Come on!" Frank jerked her arm and half-dragged her into the house. She lost her footing several times, and at one point, Frank grabbed a fistful of her hair.

Inside, he slung her against a wall where she collapsed on the floor. Her gaze went to a dark form on the other side of the room. He lay in a shadowy corner where low flickers from a lamp on the table didn't quite reach. Tait? She couldn't tell.

Frank yanked her up. "Brought you something, Trinity." He reached for the lamp, raised the wick, and held the light close to her face. "You get to watch me search her."

"Touch her and I'll kill you," Tait snarled.

Relief flooded over her. She'd found him, and he could speak. Now to get one of the guns to him. That would test every skill she had.

Frank laughed. "You ain't in no shape to kill anyone, Trinity. Haven't you realized that yet, you sorry bastard?"

More snarling and cursing came from the shapeless lump across from her. How bad was he? Would he even be able to walk?

Now that she had light, she took in Frank's handsome features. It couldn't be easy to live with such a bloodthirsty family.

"Are you married, Frank?" she asked. "Have children?"

"Shut up." He set the lamp down. "You and me ain't friends."

"You don't have to do this. I can scream and carry on, and your father will think you've carried out his order."

"I got a job to do." Frank held her tightly against him, running his hands over her.

Keep him talking. "Do you have any sisters? I have one."

"Four that I know of. Shut up talking." He stuck his hand down the front of her dress.

Melanie tried to block the feel of his probing touch. She glanced around the room—empty of furniture save for a few chairs and the table. "I can tell you're not like the rest. You don't take joy in being cruel like they do." Two doors led to other parts of the house. Possibly some of Kern's people were asleep in there, but she had no way of knowing.

"You don't know nothin' about nothin'." Frank shoved her against the wall, a hand around her throat.

Melanie held her arms straight out to the side and ground out the words. "Then do it and get it over with!"

Tait cursed and muttered threats. She still couldn't see anything but a shadow where he lay, could only feel enormous rage. In his mind, he was probably seeing his beloved Lucy hanging from the crossbar all over again. Pray to God he didn't do anything foolish.

"My, my! You're in a hurry." Frank grabbed the front of her bodice and ripped it open. He leaned forward, his breath hot on her skin. He stuck out his slobbery tongue and licked up her neck while one hand closed around her breast like a vise. It was all she could do not to cry out.

She stiffened, praying for the moment when she could end his miserable life. But if he stripped her now, he'd find the guns. She had to get rid of him somehow. But how? An idea came to mind. She made her voice go low and silky. "Enough. Frank, I'll cooperate if you don't hurt me."

"You'll be good?" Frank loosened his hand.

"Yes, and we can have some fun. Isn't it better when the woman is willing?"

"Ain't never had one that didn't fight."

"Then this is your chance to find out. I wonder if I could have some water to wash the dirt off. I want this to be perfect for you."

Frank's mouth went slack. "I don't mind dirt."

"But water makes my skin so slick and supple." She placed a fingertip on his chest and let it slide down ever so slowly to his belt. He swallowed hard. "Just a little water works wonders. And then I'll show you a real nice time."

Hopefully one involving a hail of bullets.

"Well, I reckon." He dropped his hand, a flush on his face. "I'll hurry."

He snatched a bucket next to one of the doors and left out the back way. She lifted the lamp and hurried to Tait, shocked to find he wore no shirt or shoes. Her hands shook as she gently brushed long strands of hair away from his face.

Tait lifted his head, and she inhaled sharply. God in heaven! His face was bruised and battered, and the weak light revealed a large purple injury covering one whole side of his chest. His hands were behind him, probably tied.

"Sweetheart, we don't have much time." She tenderly smoothed back his hair and kissed his cheek.

Tait licked his lips, all caked with blood. He worked to move his tongue. "I dreamed you came and led me to a cool stream. Are you a vision?"

"No. I'm very real." She helped him sit up, reached under her skirt for Mac's knife, and went to work on the rope binding his wrists. "Becky's safe in town. She's all right."

"Good."

At best she would only have a couple of minutes.

His quicksilver eyes blazed with fury, taking her aback. "Why are you here, Melanie? I told Jack no one was to save me. You've just given Kern more ammunition to try to break me, and I don't know——" His voice broke. "I don't know… if he tortures you, I won't be able to bear it. I'm not strong enough." His voice dropped to a whisper. "I want this hell to end and no one else to die. Especially you."

Her heart broke. He'd already endured so much. He coughed and winced.

The thick rope was knotted and difficult to cut through. Hurry!

The creak of a pump outside reached her. Frank would be back any minute.

She'd expected his horrifying condition but not this anger. She raised her gaze and stared into his beautiful gray eyes. "Sweetheart, listen. I brought you a gun. Our men are waiting and when we start firing, they'll ride in. We can fuss and fight later once we're out of here and safe. Can you walk?"

"I'll manage."

Melanie gently kissed his cheek again and worked feverishly to free his hands, only managing to fray the knotted rope. Why wasn't she stronger and able to just slice through it?

Hurry! Hurry! Frank was coming.

Almost through. Keep sawing the rough hemp. Just a little more. Be careful of getting his skin.

Cuts and bruises covered his face; in fact, they covered what she could see of the rest of him as well. Kern had hurt

Tait bad. She blinked hard to clear her vision. "You asked why I'm here. I love you, and where you are, that's where I always want to be. We belong together for all time, and we'll share this test. If it's death we face, then I will die by your side. Whatever happens, we'll be together—in this life or the next."

And that much she promised.

Tears clouded his eyes, and his voice grew hoarse with emotion. "I thought I'd lost the chance to finally tell you."

"Tell me what?"

"I'll love you…" He struggled to finish. "Till I die."

Thirty-five

Tait loved her. After everything she'd done, he loved her.

Tears blurred Melanie's vision. She'd never expected to hear those words, and that they came in the middle of so much danger made them even more precious.

"You don't know much I treasure those words." A sob escaped.

At last the rope around his wrists gave way—and just in time. A door banged, telling her that Frank was back.

"Here's the knife. Cut the rope at your feet." Melanie grabbed the lamp and scurried across the room just as Frank entered.

"Here." He set the bucket down and pitched her a dirty rag. "Now wash."

"Thank you." She gave him what she prayed was a hopeful smile. "A lady needs a bit of privacy."

"This is all you get. I ain't leaving no more."

"Fine." She turned her back on him and dipped the rag into the water, her mind working. She needed to send him on another errand, something he couldn't refuse to do, so she could give Tait the gun. Think.

A door opened farther into the house, and footsteps came toward her. She dropped the rag and swung around in time to see a well-dressed man in black snakeskin boots and an expensive three-piece suit walk into the room. He stuck out like a sore thumb amid Berringer's ragtag group. The railroad owner?

He drew himself up short. "I didn't know we had a guest."

Frank snorted. "She's just Trinity's wife, Mr. Markham. The bitch said she'd show me a good time, but I think she lies."

Markham's gaze raked over her body. "What's your name?"

"Don't pretend innocence. It's unbecoming," Melanie

said, turning around. "You know who I am, and if I'm not mistaken, you've been in cahoots with the judge for a long time. He blackmailed me—at your request, I'm sure—to get your money back and arrest Tait."

"And you couldn't even do that right," Markham sneered. "You're a low-down snake, and I hope you rot in hell for what you've done."

His eyes narrowed to slits. He drew back a hand and slapped her. "Why aren't you tied up?"

Frank jerked and shot him a glare. "I was just getting to that."

She had to keep them talking—the longer they did, the longer she'd have her hands free.

"Markham, I'm surprised that you'd hire someone like Kern to do your dirty work. I thought you'd associate with a better class of people, you being a big businessman and all." Melanie was happy to find her words had struck a chord. Markham's face became a mask.

He whipped a straight-backed chair around and sat. "I'm not too particular when I need a job carried out. Kern's a little too rough around the edges for my taste, but unlike you, he's done everything I asked."

Melanie tried to think of something else. "Begging your pardon, Markham, but why *are* you here in this nasty place?"

"I've waited a long time to watch Trinity die. The surroundings don't really matter." He leaned back in the chair and crossed his legs at the ankles, lacing his fingers across his belly. "My turn to ask the questions. Why did you marry a dirty, stinking outlaw? You have beauty, brains, and gumption. You could've gained Trinity's trust without tying the knot."

Melanie shrugged and answered softly. "He gave me something I wanted my whole life."

"What's that?"

"Self-respect and a home." And he'd given her both without knowing how deep the yearning went into her soul. And now she had his love as well. She swallowed. "May I have a glass of water?"

Markham had but to look at Frank, and Kern's son stomped into the other room. Melanie stared hard at the dark shape that was Tait.

Had he gotten his feet free yet?

The railroad owner followed her gaze to Tait. "If he hadn't blacked out, he'd be dead now, but we wanted him awake when he took his final breath."

She turned to ice and kept silent.

"At first, I thought Kern might've killed him, but when we cut him down from the tree, we found he was still alive. We decided to wait until daylight to finish. It's more fun when you can see everything."

Melanie licked her dry lips. "I know Kern and you have plans for me come morning, so I have a last request. One moment with my husband to say goodbye?"

"Guess it won't hurt. It is the custom for the condemned. But don't play games with me, Melanie. I guarantee you won't like the result."

Careful not to make any sudden moves, she crossed the room and knelt beside Tait. She reached under her skirt and tugged a gun out of the strap holding it. "I only have a moment. Are your feet free?"

"Almost."

"Good." She slipped the gun to Tait.

Tait quickly hid his hands and the gun behind his back.

"What are you whispering about?" Markham rose and brought the lamp closer. The protective shadows fled.

She took Tait's stubbled face between her palms and struggled to hold back tears. The words flowed from her heart. "Thank you for taking a chance on me. I'm sorry I wasn't a better wife."

"You were perfect. I'm sorry I wasn't more understanding and patient." He kept his hands hidden behind his back.

Markham gave her shoulder a shove. "Enough. Get back to the other side."

She pressed her lips to Tait's, not minding the blood on his mouth. Then she lifted her head and struggled to keep her voice from quivering. "I knew from the minute I saw you that you were the one for me. I love you, sweetheart. If our lives end here, wait for me at heaven's gate."

"I'll look until I find you."

~∞~

Tait shook back his long hair and closed his palm around cold steel. The familiar feeling washed over him. The gun made all the difference. Now they were on his playing field.

He only had to finish untying his feet and he'd get Melanie out of here before Kern had a chance to implement any of his plans. The thin walls hadn't muffled Kern's threat to burn her alive. From the past, Tait knew it wasn't idle chatter. Cold terror swept over him.

Where were his boots? He didn't relish having a gunfight barefoot, but if that's the way it had to be, he'd not complain.

He waited, barely breathing, for Markham to take the light before he went back to work on the bindings around his feet.

A few more seconds…the rope finally gave way.

Frank Berringer stomped back with a cup of water and handed it to Melanie. He didn't bother to hide his loathing for Markham. "I'm going outside. Pa's not gonna be happy."

"He knows who's calling the shots," Markham returned with a sneer.

Melanie glanced toward Tait, but her gaze didn't linger. He knew she was curious about his progress but trying not to draw attention to him. He was ready.

Tait wondered at this woman he'd married. She'd shown uncommon courage to ride into Kern's hideout with two guns and a knife on her person, knowing full well what Kern had done to Lucy and Claire. His heart burst with love for her. If they lived through this, he'd do his best to show her how much she meant to him every single day.

"What are you doing over there?" Markham grabbed the lamp and strode to him. "Hope you're not thinking to escape. I got your wife now, and I'll kill her if you try anything."

From a sitting position, Tait drew back his legs and kicked

Markham, knocking the lamp from his hand. "This is what I'm doing, you sorry piece of shit." He threw himself on top and stuck the gun to his enemy's head, dislodging a perfect strand of hair that fell across Markham's forehead.

The lamp smashed, spilling oil across the floor, flames licking at the rough floor planks. Flames began to grow. They had to get out. Tait got to his feet, yanked Markham from the floor, and held him firm. "Melanie?"

"I'm here, Tait." She appeared at his side, a pistol in her hand. "What do you want me to do?"

"We've got to get out of here. This wood is like tinder, and it'll go up in nothing flat." He met her gaze for only a moment. "Stay behind me. We'll march out with Markey here in front. When we get outside, fire your gun for the signal and find somewhere out of the way to hide."

"You won't get far, Trinity," Markham promised. "We'll hunt you down."

"Shut the hell up. You get no say in this. Ready, Melanie?"

"Lead the way, sweetheart."

Tait emerged from the blazing house with Markham's hands raised high. Kern was waiting, his gun drawn. "What did you do, Markham? You dumb fool! I oughta kill you myself."

"I had no choice, Berringer. They tricked me," Markham whined.

"I'm afraid I got no choice either. Nothing personal." Kern fired a bullet into his boss then quickly released another round of ammunition at Tait.

Tait threw Markham's limp body to the side and grabbed Melanie's hand. He fired off a shot at Kern as he dove against the side of the house. The jar aggravated the wound on his side, pain tearing through him as he huddled low to the ground.

"Cover me, Melanie." He stretched out and grabbed Markham's foot. Using all his strength, he pulled the dead man over.

Melanie kept up a steady stream of bullets, firing at whatever moved while he tugged Markham's boots off and slipped them on. They were a little big without socks, but close enough.

The wall was warm to the touch. They only had a minute or two more before the inferno would consume everything. He had to find Melanie a horse and get her away from the danger.

He was scanning the compound for options when their men charged in, guns blazing. Fire totally engulfed the house now, providing plenty of light for the battle.

Kern's clan scrambled, and those who found horses leaped into the saddles. In all the chaos, Tait lost track of Kern.

"Run to the trees and stay there," he said to Melanie.

She clutched his arm. "Where are you going?"

"To finish this. Kern's running. I can't let him get away."

"Let Jack or one of them take care of him."

Tait's eyes blazed. "He didn't kill their families. He killed mine, took my niece. This is *my* justice to dole out."

"All right." She released her hold. "Go."

His battered body screamed in agony. He took shallow breaths and circled the fighting, shooting at anyone who got in his way. The acrid taste of gunpowder stood thick on his tongue as he made his way around the burning house to the corral. The animals were going crazy with fear as flames and live sparks filled the air.

There, by the corral! Tait recognized Kern by his bald head. Tait fired but didn't know if he'd hit him because at that moment all hell broke loose.

The house exploded with a loud blast, shooting flames high into the midnight sky. The force pitched Tait to the ground, and a scream tore from his mouth. Pieces of jagged iron from the cookstove fell about him, and kerosene fumes went up his nose.

Part of the blazing wooden roof landed on Kern, trapping him underneath. Screams of agony and pleas for help filled the air.

When the projectiles settled, Tait used all his strength to get to his feet, gripping his weapon. He stared at the horrible sight, Kern's clothes in flame and his lower half pinned by the rubble.

"Trinity, help me. Pull this off!" Kern begged. "Help!"

The smell of burning flesh filled Tait's nostrils and coated the inside of his mouth. He knew seconds counted, but he couldn't take that step. Maybe he'd go to hell for it, but this felt an awful lot like justice—for Lucy, for Claire, and for Becky.

"Sorry." A bullet whizzed past Tait's head. Crouching low, he whirled and fired. The shooter went down.

Pain stabbed his ribs, nearly taking his breath, and sickening nausea flooded his senses. Another shot hit the ground by his feet, kicking up dirt. Though in agony, Tait kept shooting, driven to rid the world of the evilest family he knew.

When he swung back around, Kern had gotten to his feet and was fully engulfed in searing flames. "Shoot me, Trinity!" Kern screamed. "I can't stand this!"

The man seemed too far gone for saving, so it was a surprise when Kern fell to the ground and began rolling around in the dirt, desperately trying to put out the fire. From the corner of Tait's vision, a man ran toward them.

Tait faced the new threat while Kern's agonizing screams behind him almost drowned out the roar of the burning house. Chaos lay everywhere he looked. The dark figure who had been running toward him dove to the ground and fired.

Tait fired back and barked, "I'm riding out of here, and no one is going to stop me. Draw or get out of my way."

When the man raised his gun, Tait shot him.

The sudden lack of noise behind him made him whirl. Kern stood, his weapon pointed at Tait. He'd managed to smother the flames of his burning clothes, but they were nothing but blackened rags. He breathed hard, but he was still able to get enough air to taunt. "You're hurt, Trinity. I'm betting you're woozy, and I know your ribs are killing you. You may not be as fast a draw as you were a few days ago."

"Don't waste time. I mean for this vendetta to end right here. Right now."

"The big bad Tait Trinity, burning for justice." Light from the roaring fire shone red on Kern's blistering face. His lips curled in a sneer. "Do you know where Melanie is? Are you sure she's safe where you left her? Might oughta check the ashes."

The words sent doubts careening through Tait. He wasn't sure of anything. Still, Kern would use every trick he could think of to get into his head. A bead of sweat trickled down Tait's back between his shoulder blades. He kept his gaze tight on the man who'd robbed him of the people he'd loved.

"I'll see you in hell." Tait fired, shooting the gun out of Kern's grip. Kern cursed, cradling his hand, and Tait leveled his pistol. Tears rolled down his face. "This is for Lucy." He sent a bullet whirling into Kern's leg.

Cursing and screaming, the man went down to his knees.

"This is for our baby."

The bullet entered Kern's arm. "Stop! Stop! I'm sorry."

"Too late." Tait took aim again. "And this is for Claire and Becky."

The bullet struck Kern's heart, and blood flew from his chest. He fell to the ground.

Another shot rang out—not from Tait's gun this time. Tait dropped low and whirled. Melanie stood five yards away, the red glow of the fire tangling in the strands of her hair, smoke curling from the barrel of her .45.

Frank Berringer lay sprawled in his own blood.

Melanie stumbled to Tait and gently placed her palm over his gun hand. "That's enough. It's over, Tait. We won."

His hand went limp and the gun fell into the dirt. He took her in his arms and held her, shuddering, his face buried in her hair, soothed by the faint scene of wild honeysuckle.

Behind them the house still gave off enormous heat. The gunfight was winding down, and they'd see what was left once the smoke cleared. But for now, maybe this was the heaven's gate that preachers spoke of. In a way, it felt a lot like heaven. He only knew he'd found the woman of his dreams and he wasn't letting her go.

Thirty-six

"CAN YOU THINK OF EASIER WAYS TO GIVE ME A HEART ATTACK, Tait?" Jack walked slowly toward them, a big grin covering his face. His ruddy skin reflected the red glow of the fire behind him.

When he got close enough, Tait clasped his hand. "Thanks for not listening to me, brother."

"You look like hell."

"Better than dying."

"A darn sight better than that." Jack's gaze dropped to Tait's feet. "Nice boots."

"Markey didn't need them anymore. Never had any made of snakeskin before." Tait looked into the eyes of his best friend and knew—Jack would have gone all the way to the gates of hell and beyond to try to save him. And Tait would do the same for him as well. Nothing would break their bond.

Tait put his arm around Melanie who was holding the edges of her ripped bodice together. He drew her against his bare chest, wishing he had a shirt to cover her with. Maybe he could find a blanket. "Jack, ridding Texas of this vermin was a team effort, and my wife risked more than probably anyone. But next time you let her ride into a hornet's nest, you and I are going to fight."

Melanie gazed up at him, her dimples deepening. "Sweetheart, don't be angry at Jack. I had to do a lot of talking to convince him. And I'd do it again in a heartbeat."

Tait grunted, knowing she meant every word. "How's Becky? Is she really all right?"

"The little darling is fine, just worried about you. She'll be happy to see you."

Relief swept over him. He tightened his arm around Melanie. "I say we go get some sleep. I need a doctor, a bath, and to lie next to my wife."

Sam and Clay strode up to join them. "Glad everyone's in one piece," Clay said. "Hate to say it, but I never expected to see you alive, Tait."

Tait grinned. "Makes two of us."

Sam glanced at the broken bodies of Kern and his son. "They have a lot of holes in them." He exchanged a glance with Tait and gave him a nod. "Clay and I just completed an assessment of the dead, and I think we got every single one of them. We can come back tomorrow and haul them into town. Some might have prices on their heads."

Now that everything was over, Tait's legs buckled underneath him, and he dropped to the ground. Pain rushed through him, and he struggled to draw breath.

"Sit right there while we get the horses, sweetheart." Melanie left for a moment and came back leading a pretty buckskin. Kern wouldn't be needing horses anymore. Not where he'd gone.

She helped Tait stand, and he pulled himself into the saddle with a groan. They rode double with her behind, holding him upright. He didn't remember much about the trip. The next thing he knew he was falling into a bed that had the softest sheets he had ever felt, and Jack was following Clay out the door.

"Just sleep, sweetheart." Melanie lay down beside him and covered them both with a quilt.

His world righted, and he pulled her close, grateful to live one more day.

◦≈◦

Melanie opened her eyes at dawn and stared at Tait, his head on the pillow next to her. With tentative fingers, she touched his long hair and then his stubbled jaw. He was bruised and bloody and desperately needed a bath, but he was alive. And he was hers.

Unshed tears burned as she thought of how easily Kern Berringer could've stolen his life. She would probably never know the details of what he'd gone through in Kern's clutches, but that was all right. It was enough to know that he had given himself over to save Becky.

She'd let him sleep for now, but sometime this morning she'd bring the doctor to look at him. Then they'd have a better timetable of when they could leave for Hope's Crossing.

With a soft sigh, she rose quietly and dressed. She had to check on Ava and her father and find out if Judge McIlroy was truly dead. Lots to do.

Melanie leaned over Tait and placed her lips to his before quietly slipping out. She met Sam and Jack at the stairs. "Morning, gentlemen. We had a short night."

"That we did," Sam agreed. "I'm heading out to see if I can locate the rotten sheriff and find McIlroy's body."

"Good luck."

"Care to wager the sheriff is long gone?" Jack asked.

"Please don't say that, Jack." Melanie shot him a frown. "I want him behind bars."

Turned out, they didn't have to worry. Virginia met them outside the hotel. "If you're looking for our former sheriff, Quitman's at the mercantile. Mac tied him up and is standing guard over him. He tried to break into the store and either kill us or take Ava. Not sure which."

The news sent surprise washing over Melanie. Her father? The man who had made a habit of running away from problems. Would wonders ever cease? "And McIlroy?"

"He died from your gunshot. I doubt anyone will say too many words over him."

"I'm sorry it came to that. He gave me no choice." The world did seem a better place without him. Melanie hugged Virginia. "I'm glad Mac rose to the occasion. How's Ava?"

Virginia smiled. "Much better today. Her head is clearer. Doc thinks she'll be up and around later this afternoon."

"That's excellent news!" Melanie beamed, her heart overflowing. Tait, Becky, and Ava were safe and recovering. Kern and McIlroy were dead, and the rotten sheriff was going to jail.

Life could look so bleak one minute and blind a person with its radiance the next.

Virginia glanced across the street. "Becky was a little angel. When the news came in with the riders that Mr. Trinity was free, she was all smiles."

"I can't wait to see her. That reminds me. I need to send a telegram to the boys." Melanie stepped across to telegraph good news to the twins then went to the mercantile with Sam. Jack headed to the café for breakfast with a promise to take Tait to the bathhouse later.

Becky came running with arms outstretched when she opened the door. "Mellie!"

Melanie picked her up and gave her a long hug. "I'm so happy to see you, and I'm glad you're smiling."

"Wuncle?" Becky pointed in the direction of the hotel.

"Yes, honey, he'll be along in a while. He's just tired."

But she didn't fool one bright little girl.

"Him hurt."

"He'll be all better soon." Melanie kissed her cheek and handed her to Virginia. "Wait here for a minute and I'll be back."

Melanie followed Sam to the back of the store. Mac sat there, a gun pointed at Quitman.

The man raised his head when Sam ducked under the low beam and stepped into the room. Quitman brimmed with arrogance. "It's about time. I want this man arrested." But when he recognized who he was ordering around, color suddenly drained from Quitman's face.

Sam straightened. "I take it you know who I am."

Quitman nodded.

"You're under arrest. Stand up." Sam helped him up and handcuffed his hands behind his back. "You're going away for a long time. You're a shame to your profession."

"I should've kept riding when I had a chance."

"But you didn't." Sam gave Melanie a nod. "I think this concludes things."

On the way out the door, Quitman sneered at Melanie. "Me and McIlroy almost got away with it."

"Almost doesn't count in anything except a game of horseshoes. Your problem is that you underestimate women. Give us a cause and we'll bury you." She turned to Sam. "I gave McIlroy a fourth of the money, and Mac can take you to the rest. We buried half before coming into town. I'm assuming some is still on the packhorse." Then she stepped over to the storeroom to see Ava.

Her sister wore a big grin, her eyes much clearer. Color had begun to return to her cheeks. "Melanie! I'm glad you're back." Ava sat up, self-consciously patting her chopped, reddish-brown hair the judge had butchered. "I'm feeling more like my old self. By tomorrow I'll be back to normal, at least according to Doc."

Melanie sat on the side of the bed and drew Ava into a hug. "That's great news." She leaned back for a good, long look. "You're amazing, Ava. I don't know how you hung on."

"I knew you'd be back and that gave me strength. You always keep a promise." Tears filled Ava's eyes. "My hair is gone, and I'm missing a tooth. I feel so ugly."

"You're beautiful. Your hair will grow back, and you'll be as ravishing as ever."

Ava sniffed. "You always make me feel better."

"I'm heading to the café. What would you like me to bring back?"

"An egg and a fluffy biscuit."

"You got it, sis. Be back soon." Melanie collected Becky. "Let's go eat."

Becky's face lit up and she clapped. "Eat."

That was indeed a sign that things were looking up. Melanie ended up getting food enough for everyone and took it back to the mercantile. Then she bought some clothes for Tait and headed back to the hotel.

Tait was sitting on the side of the bed, his head in his hands. His bruises looked ten times worse in the daylight, with his ribs, back, and midsection almost solid purple and black. Though the sight brought instant tears, she held them back and gave him a wide smile, holding up the new shirt. "I thought you might need this in case you feel up to a stroll. Becky's wanting to see you."

"Give me a minute to wash." He glanced down. "I have so much blood on me I'll scare her to death."

"Let me help." She laid his shirt on the bed and went to the water pitcher, finding it full. She filled a ceramic bowl and reached for a cloth. "Lay back."

"Yes, ma'am." His groan told her how much the request cost, how much the slightest movement was excruciating.

She started with his face and moved down to his chest. Dirt had mixed with the blood before it dried, and it took several bowls of water to get him clean.

Tait sighed. "Did you know that you can lull a man right out of his senses?"

Happiness surged inside. "You don't say?" She helped him turn over, and he let out deep groans with the movement.

"I'm living proof." He breathed heavily. "I can't wait to be able to make love to you."

Melanie gently washed his back, biting back tears. As stove-up as he was, it would be a while. "I'll hold you to that, cowboy. I need to get the doc here to check you out, but we should consider staying here for at least a week before we head home."

"Might not be a bad idea to rest up. Don't need a doctor though."

"Sorry, but I disagree. We need to know how badly injured you are."

"Hell! You'll just waste the poor man's time."

"I doubt he'll complain." She sponged the blood from the gunshot wound in his side. Dr. Mary's careful stitches were all busted out. Another reason for the doctor.

Tait looked around. "You never told me how you happened to be in Canadian. You were supposed to stay with the boys."

Melanie told him about the telegram from the judge that had started her whole wild ride. "After my father accepted that the money wasn't his to take, he actually turned out to be pretty helpful."

"Imagine that. I'm sorry you had to do that by yourself though."

"I'm not. It toughened me up, made me realize I'm stronger than I thought."

"Lady, you have a lot of guts, and I'm proud you're my wife."

A warm glow filled her. "You have a way with words, sweetheart." She pressed a kiss to his back, between his shoulder blades. "By the way, Jack said he'll take you the bathhouse later."

"Good. I can use a long soak."

When she finished washing him, he got to his feet with considerable effort, and she helped him into the clean clothes and his fancy boots. "My, my. I've never seen a more handsome man."

"You probably say that to all your admirers." He buckled on his gun belt.

"How did you guess?" She raised on tiptoe, clung to his shirt, and brushed a kiss across his lips.

"I'm wise to the ways of women. Shall we?" He reached for his hat.

"Lean on me, sweetheart. We'll take our time."

As it turned out, crossing the street took a while. Men and women alike came out to say how glad they were he'd made it and to thank him for getting rid of McIlroy and the Berringers.

At last they made it to the mercantile, and Becky came running. "Wuncle!"

He sat down in a chair and pulled her into his lap. She frowned and patted his cheeks. "Hurt?"

"I'll be fine, honey. Don't you worry."

"Love you."

"I love you more. Do you miss your brothers?"

"Uh-huh. Home."

"That's right." Even though he had to be starving, he sat there holding Becky until she squirmed to get down.

Melanie brought him a plate and a cup of coffee, and he set to work, not stopping until every morsel was gone. Jack and Clay stopped by to let him know that they were going back out with Sam Legend to clean up the mess at Kern's place. Then she helped Tait back to bed and went for the doctor.

Not long after, she stood quietly at the end of the bed while Dr. Levi completed his examination. The man's face remained expressionless, not giving any indication of his thoughts. It seemed to take forever, but she wanted him to be thorough.

Finally, he glanced up. His voice was quiet. "You're a very lucky man, Mr. Trinity. By all rights, from the sheer number of deep bruises I see, you should have multiple broken bones. But other than bruising and that hole in your side, you're in good shape."

"Thank you, Dr. Levi." Melanie went weak with relief.

"Your thick stomach and chest muscles kept the man from breaking your ribs. That's all I can figure." Dr. Levi wagged his head in disbelief. "To satisfy my curiosity, can you tell me a little about your ordeal? What caused most of these bruises?"

Tait's face tightened. He shot Melanie a look. "I don't intend to talk about it."

"I understand." The doctor pressed further. "It's just that this is very unusual and something to share with my colleagues."

"All right. They tied me upside down from a thick tree branch, and Kern began slamming into me with a board."

Melanie swallowed a cry, turning her head so Tait wouldn't see her distress. This was hard enough for him, and the flat tone in his voice said it was anything but cut-and-dried. His pain must've been tremendous.

A smile transformed Dr. Levi's face. He smoothed his white goatee. "Of course. Now it makes sense. They never got a solid hit because you were swinging back and forth. Well, my friend, I'll say it again. You're a lucky man. I'll restitch that gunshot in your side. Keep it clean and bandaged until it heals. I prescribe a week's rest before you leave town. Each day that goes by you'll feel less sore."

Watching the doctor sew Tait back up and put a gauze bandage in place, Melanie gave thanks to God for watching over him. Her knees went weak, and she gripped the iron bedstead, her gaze on the man who filled her world, the man who loved her in good times and bad.

At last Tait stood and slid his arms into the shirt. "Appreciate it, Doctor."

"Don't mention it." Dr. Levi put his stethoscope into his bag. "Whatever you've been doing, keep it up. All of my patients should be so healthy." He glanced at Melanie. "Your sister should also recover just fine. She's much better. A week of rest will do her good too."

Melanie put her arm around Tait's waist. "Dr. Levi, I owe you a great debt."

"It's my pleasure."

When the door shut behind the doctor, Melanie grinned up at her husband and teased. "I have no idea what it is that you've been doing."

"Do tell. But if I wasn't so sore and in desperate need of a good soak, I'd test out a theory. Those dimples are driving me crazy." He lowered his head and kissed her soundly.

Thirty-seven

THE HORSES SEEMED TO SMELL HOME. TEN MILES OUT, THEY started picking up the pace until they were almost in a full-out gallop the rest of the way to the entrance of Hope's Crossing.

Tait had never felt so good to be back. Riding in front of him, his arm around her protectively, Becky glanced up with a grin. "Joe. Jesse."

"Yes, honey. Your brothers will be so happy to see you."

They'd barely ridden through the opening before Joe and Jesse raced toward them like a pack of wild wolves. "You're home, Becky! You're home!"

Becky clamored to get down. Tait lowered her to the ground by an arm, and she was immediately engulfed by her exuberant brothers. Joe swung her around and whooped and hollered. When he set her down, Jesse picked her up again.

Tait gingerly dismounted. He still hurt from head to toe, but it wasn't as bad as it had been at first. The week's rest had been good for him in more ways than one. His gaze found Melanie, riding in a wagon with her sister, and warmth seeped down into his bones. Frustration that he'd been unable to make love to her had built over the week they'd stayed in Canadian. Now that they were on Hope's Crossing soil, he meant to do something about that.

Once the kids had sounded the alert, the whole blasted town came running and yelling fit to raise the dead. Tait grinned. He hadn't thought they liked him that much.

Melanie climbed from the wagon, ducked around the kids, and took Tait's elbow. "This is quite a reception."

"It's our town, and these are our people." He shook Ridge's hand. "It's good to be back. Anything happen while we were gone?"

Ridge pushed back his black hat. "You mean except for the

twins sneaking out to follow you and a hailstorm pounding the heck out of everything?"

"Yeah, except for that."

"It's been pretty boring." Ridge moved aside to let others welcome them home.

Tally juggled little Dillon. "I'm happy to see everything turn out well."

Melanie put an arm around her. "Come and meet my sister. She's going to stay here with us, at least for now."

"Oh good. We can use another at our tea parties, and we have plenty of handsome bachelors waiting for a pretty single lady to come along."

Tait stared after the two ladies walking arm in arm, then headed toward the hotel, anxious to wash the trail dust off and rest.

"Hey, you're going the wrong way!" Travis Lassiter yelled.

"What do you mean?"

Ridge grinned and slapped his back. "You don't live there anymore. We finished your house for you while you were gone and the furniture you ordered arrived, so we moved you in. The women even made curtains for the windows."

Tait stared in shocked silence. He glanced into the men's faces, and each nodded. Thickness blocked his ability to speak. Melanie's eyes held tears as she took her place again by his side.

He blinked hard, overcome by emotion. "I don't know what to say."

"I do." Melanie met his gaze and threaded her fingers through his. "We both deeply appreciate your kindness. Thank you so much. This is the only homecoming I've ever had, and nothing will ever top it."

❦

Melanie helped get Ava settled in at the hotel for now. Although she'd much improved, the trip had taken a toll on her sister.

After they'd unpacked what few things she'd brought, Ava

pushed her toward the door. "Go take care of those kids and that handsome husband of yours."

"Are you in a hurry to get rid of me? Do you have plans to meet someone already?"

Ava laughed, her blue-green eyes twinkling. "Even I can't work that fast." Her face grew serious. "You were right about this town. In all the places I've traveled, I never knew any like this existed. It's more like a welcoming family than a group of strangers. I can see why you stayed."

Melanie hugged her. "I hope you'll settle down here. There is nowhere better."

"I don't have any skills other than cards, and there doesn't seem to be much use for that."

"Never fear, sister. Things are always changing. I heard from Clay Colby that a businessman is looking for an opportunity and may open a bank here. With your uncanny ability with numbers, he'll probably want to hire you right away. Unless the man is a complete idiot."

"I'd love to do something using numbers." Ava squeezed her. "That sounds wonderful."

"In the meantime, you could tutor some of the children who lag behind on their sums. Mr. Denver the schoolmaster is unmarried, you know."

"Stop, Melanie. There's more to life than marriage."

"I know. But finding that special someone sure makes things a lot more interesting." Melanie couldn't think of anything she'd rather be than Tait's wife and mother to his niece and nephews. At least for now.

That night after the kids were asleep in their new beds, Melanie lay with Tait, listening to the sounds of the house. Each board seemed to whisper its happiness in being able to shelter them from the storms.

The light of the lamp on the bedside table allowed her to see the board below the window that she had nailed into place. It seemed like an eternity since that day. So much had happened, but she remembered the joy that bubbled inside her to add her own stamp to their house.

She snuggled against Tait, loving his naked body touching hers, even if it was still awfully discolored. "I'm so happy I could die. This is beyond my wildest dreams."

He kissed the top of her head. "It's sure something all right."

Surely he'd get his pardon now. He had to. Everything he'd done had been for a reason, and he'd given every cent left of the railroad money back. As one of the women had said, these men had to find justice for themselves. There was no other law and they shouldn't be punished for surviving.

"I know you're probably tired and still sore."

"What are you asking, Mellie?" His deep voice roughened, the sound making her stomach do funny things.

She raised on an elbow and traced his mouth with a fingertip. "I want you, Tait. I need what you can give me, but I can wait until you're up to it."

Smoldering desire in his silvery eyes sent delicious goosebumps over every inch of her. "We don't have to wait, Mellie."

"I never thought I'd find a man like you." She drew light circles on his chest and stomach. "Fact of the matter, I didn't think men like you existed in the world."

Tait chuckled. "I sure hope not. I'd hate to think there are two of me."

"Go ahead and make fun, but you know what I mean." She pressed a kiss to the hollow of his throat where his pulse beat.

"I couldn't resist." He laid her back on the pillow and loomed over her, his long hair falling across his face. He nibbled behind her ear, his husky voice feathering across her skin and awakening a desire like she'd never known.

"My darling Mellie, I was dead, and you brought me back to life. You must've seen something worth saving, but God only knows what it was."

"I saw a future." And oh how bright it looked now. Tears filled her eyes to think how easily it could've all vanished.

He slid his hand down her body, throwing aside the covers,

moving across her skin like a whisper. He left a trail of kisses across her collarbone and along her ribs, making promises as he went. "I'm going to make slow, passionate love to you. I have a lot of making up to do."

His kiss held desire, hunger…love.

"I'm yours, my darling, forever and always." Melanie closed her eyes and let the warmth wash over her. She'd waited a while for this. The nights she'd spent alone had been long and painful.

"My wife. You're so beautiful. You excite me in ways no other ever has." His touch burned her skin, branded her, sent every thought from her head and made her forget everything except what he was doing to her body. He planted kisses over her flat stomach and moved lower.

She ran a fingertip across his back and firm buttocks. "Tait." The word was full of pleading.

The path to her breasts was painfully slow, and there he cupped first one then the other.

Just when she thought each caress would spark a fire, he took a nipple between his thumb and forefinger and rolled it around. Heat rushed from her core, leaving her gasping. She pushed herself against his hand, gently caressing his chest, his thick neck, down his bare muscular arms.

Shivers of anticipation rushed over the length of her. She loved every inch of her Texas outlaw. And when he stared at her with those quicksilver eyes, she wanted to melt into his body and become a part of him.

He flicked her nipple with his tongue, hard and fast, before closing his mouth around it, enveloping her with moist heat that threatened to drive her over the edge of a wide abyss. Sucking, seeming to draw every part of her into him. Her body thrummed with need and demanded the fire be quenched.

The ache inside grew until she thought she could stand no more. She strained, gasped, reaching for the elusive reward.

While he was busy with his mouth, his hand moved to the center of her being, his fingers gently pushing inside the wet folds.

Her heart pounded, and waves of pleasure rushed over her, pushing her higher.

Hot.

Pulsing.

Wondrous joy.

Tait moved on top and filled her. She gasped at the delicious sensation.

Yes!

Their bodies joined, they soon hurtled beyond the realm of space and time. Blinding white pleasure engulfed her and she floated, losing all sense of the things that grounded her.

Her bones had turned to liquid and she didn't want to move.

Breathing hard, Tait dropped next to her, one arm across her belly, and she knew he would always be there to provide a tether. Something to hold her safely to him. Together they'd faced joys and sorrow, the highest highs and deepest lows, life and death, and through it all had won.

Melanie lay still, wanting to stay in that perfect place of beauty and happiness where bad things could never touch them.

But such a life would be boring and dull. Without the storms, you wouldn't appreciate the sunshine. A person had to experience it all to fully live. She knew more hard times would come and she'd be ready when they did.

For now, she was in Tait's arms, safe and loved.

His forever wife.

❧

Two weeks following their return, an early-morning knock came at the door. Shaughnessy grinned. "I have a letter for you, Mr. Trinity."

"Just Tait will do." He took the envelope and drew out a single piece of paper with the governor's seal at the bottom.

"What is it, Tait?" Melanie appeared at his side. "Bad news?"

His head was swimming. He put an arm around her to grab hold of something before his legs went out from under him. "It's a pardon. My slate is clear." He picked her up and swung her around. "I'm a free man!"

She clung to him, laughing.

"That's good news, sir." Shaughnessy turned to go.

"Wait." Tait stuck out his hand. "Thank you for delivering this. It wasn't your job."

The telegraph operator took his hand. "It came in on this morning's stage, and I helped sort the mail. I knew you'd want it right away."

Tait pressed a silver dollar in his hand. "You're a good man, Shaughnessy."

"I'll say." Melanie kissed the man's cheek. "You don't know what this means to us."

Shaughnessy said goodbye, and they shut the door. The kids clomping down the stairs sounded like a herd of wild buffalo.

"What's going on?" Joe asked.

"I got a letter. I'm no longer wanted for any crimes."

Jesse pushed around his brother. "Can we celebrate?"

Melanie rested a hand on his shoulder. "Yes, we can. We'll have a party."

The last to make it down the stairs, Becky grinned and clapped. "Me happy."

Tears filled Tait's eyes. He clasped a fist over his racing heart. "I'm free. I'm really free. I never thought to see this."

Later that day, they left the children playing under watchful eyes, and Tait took Melanie's hand and escaped to the bluff overlooking the town. They sat in their favorite spot, gazing down on the place they loved and the special people who filled it. Melanie's sister Ava walked with Nora, Rebel, and Tally, laughing at something one of the ladies had said. Ava was already fitting in as though she'd lived there forever.

Tait wasn't too sad that Mac had stayed behind in Canadian. Even though he'd proven his worth, Mac had rambling feet and would always follow the smell of money.

"We did it." Tait put his arm around the woman he'd love until the day he died. "Only I'm still not sure how." He was silent a moment. Sam had laid out a list of things he had to send the governor, but he hadn't done it yet. "I was supposed to have written the governor and pleaded with him to pardon me, but I got too busy with things after our homecoming."

Melanie glanced up, her dimples peeking out. "I wrote him, sweetheart. This pardon is my gift. Maybe it'll make up a little for my deception when I married you."

"More than amends. Leave the past where it is and don't speak of it again. No more keeping score. From now on, all that counts is the future. I love you more today than yesterday, Mrs. Trinity." He lowered his head and claimed those beautiful lips.

The kiss could've scorched ten miles of fencerow, and it put a glow in his heart that lasted the rest of his life.

Author's Note

Dear Reader,

I trust you're enjoying this Outlaw Mail Order Bride series. You know, outlaws were the original bad boys and those kinds of men even now really make my heart race. They aren't afraid to take chances. They thrive on danger and live on the edge between life and death. Like outlaws of old living where there was often no law to be found, my men also take justice into their own hands. Guns settle disputes and the quickness of a draw is the only way to survive.

Of the published books to date in this series, I think you'll find this one quite different. However, different keeps things fresh.

I've never written a book like this where deception, although for the right reasons, plays such a central part. Lady gambler Melanie Dunbar agrees to marry outlaw Tait Trinity purely for selfish reasons. She's being threatened with prison unless she pulls off a miracle. The task she takes on is a doozy, and it's anyone's guess if she can come out on the other side in one piece.

However, Tait, an outlaw and wanted man, is no better.

After finding himself the sole guardian of twin nephews and a niece and totally out of his element, he takes the advice of a friend and sends for a mail order bride he'd been halfway interested in. He has in mind for her to take on the care of the children, but she's not having any of being a nanny and flat tells him so.

Yet despite Tait's and Melanie's flaws and initial motives for becoming a couple, they find themselves changing and the marriage, which starts out rocky and unsure, becomes rooted in deep respect and love—the kind that doesn't fade.

Life is like that though, and it pays to never give up. If you do, you miss the reward. When one thing doesn't work, be willing to try something else. Just don't quit. Maybe you're dealing with problems and not sure which way to turn. I've been at that crossroads quite a bit, but I take a page from Tait and Melanie and keep moving forward. I pray you will too. Always look to the future, not behind, because that way is blocked. We can't go backward.

Happy reading!

Linda Broday

Read on for a glimpse into
the exciting world of
Harvey Girls and Cowboys
in Anna Schmidt's *Pathfinder*!

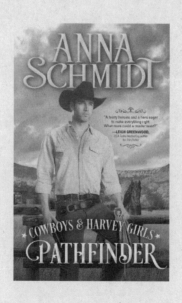

Chapter
1

Juniper, New Mexico, Winter 1903

"Miss Elliott! A moment please." Aidan Campbell, manager of the Palace Hotel, hurried toward Emma. They had worked together for several years now in the Harvey Corporation, and Emma took pride in knowing he held her in high esteem. That respect came in spite of the fact that they had shared a brief romantic relationship, one Emma had broken off. Since that time, Aidan had been overly formal in his dealings with her.

Aidan handed her a telegram he'd clearly just received. "Read this," he said. Given his smile and obvious excitement, Emma had to assume this was good news.

```
MY DEAR FRIEND CAPT MAX WINSLOW
AND COMPANY COMING TO JUNIPER
STOP ARRIVING TODAY BY PRIVATE
TRAIN STOP MAKE THEM WELCOME
STOP
```

It was signed Ford Harvey. Ford was the son of the company's founder, Fred Harvey, and the heir apparent to the empire of hotels and restaurants his father had built.

"Well," Emma said, handing the telegram back to Aidan. "One does not say no to Mr. Harvey or his son, but really, Aidan, a military company here in the hotel? The other guests will surely wonder what brought this about."

Aidan's eyes bulged. "You have no idea who Captain Max Winslow is?"

"Should I?"

In his excitement, Aidan dropped all hint of formality. "Emma, he is a famous former army hero as well as part owner and star of the Last Frontier Wild West Show—a show that is coming here to Juniper for the winter. It's bound to be a boon to business."

Emma chewed her lower lip. Housing and feeding a bunch of soldiers was one thing. In her opinion, doing the same for a troupe of theater people would be far more challenging. According to everything she'd heard or read, such people could be quite rowdy, and their moral standards were questionable as well.

"How many are in this group?" She hoped raising the practicalities of the relatively small number of rooms available in the hotel measured against the number of performers might give Aidan pause.

"Only Captain Max, his leading lady, and the troupe's manager will stay here. The roustabouts, livestock handlers, and other members of the cast and crew will have their own quarters on the grounds."

"The grounds?"

"The area the town council has leased to them for setting up the show just outside town."

"None of that was covered in Mr. Harvey's telegram," she noted.

Aidan sighed. "Are you so busy managing the dining room and counter and playing mother hen to the girls you haven't time to read the paper?"

"The *girls* are young women we rely upon to maintain the high standard of decorum and service for which we are known," she reminded him. "They are the face of this and every other Harvey establishment." She pressed her palms over the starched front of her pristine white apron as she stared at the tips of her perfectly polished black shoes. She rarely challenged Aidan in this way. He was, after all, her superior. "I apologize. It's just that…"

"We'll make it all work out, Emma," he said, lowering his voice. "We always do. Alert your staff, and I'll see to getting rooms set up." He glanced once again at the telegram. "No time given, so we need to get ready." He motioned to his assistant at the front desk before turning back to Emma. "I'll reserve a table for the captain and his costar and manager to use whenever they choose. You should appoint your very best waitress to serve them." He started toward the desk and hesitated. "Better yet, *you* should serve them. No one better." He hurried away.

Emma bristled. She already pulled double duty as the manager of the dining room and more casual counter service as well as housemother to the waitresses. Harvey Girls always lived on-site, in this case on the top floor of the hotel. They were expected to set an example of ladylike manners and morals as well as abide by strict rules and curfews. There was always at least one who thought she could ignore the rules, meaning Emma had the added role of disciplinarian. She had her hands full already, and now Aidan expected her to wait on these show people in the bargain?

Fortunately, she had established the practice of meeting with all the waitresses just after the morning breakfast crowd at the counter thinned and before the dining room opened for lunch. They were waiting now in the dining room. Emma mentally counted heads as they lined up so she could make sure their uniforms—a black dress covered by a bibbed white apron—were spotless and their shoes polished.

Trula Goodwin was missing.

Emma sighed and glanced at Trula's roommate, Sarah.

"She's got another of her headaches, Miss Elliott," Sarah murmured. Two other girls rolled their eyes.

"And did this headache come upon her around two this

morning by chance?" She saw Sarah's eyes widen in surprise. "Perhaps as she was creeping up the kitchen stairs, past my door?"

"It was…later," Sarah stammered.

Emma had discovered that letting these young women know she was aware of infractions of the rules worked miracles in terms of making them think twice before crossing that line. Still, Trula continued to test the boundaries, and Emma had given her enough warnings.

She tapped her pencil against her lower lip, pondering how best to handle the situation. In the distance, a train whistle sounded—the 9:05 freight train. She would give Trula until noon tomorrow to pack her things and decide her destination. Of course, that would leave them shorthanded at a time when that was the last thing she needed. But they would manage.

She forced a smile and faced the girls. "Ladies, we have some special guests arriving perhaps as soon as later today. My understanding is that they will be with us for some time. Has anyone heard of a Captain Max Winslow?"

The girls gasped in unison, and their eyes widened with excitement.

"He's the one on the posters all over town," one girl announced as others turned to one another with animated smiles.

"I saw his show when I was in training in Kansas City. He is gorgeous," a second waitress said.

Emma cleared her throat to regain their full attention. "Apparently, the entire company will winter here in Juniper, although only the captain and two others will be staying here in the hotel. The point is, Captain Winslow is a personal friend of Mr. Ford Harvey, so we all need to be at our—"

A tap on the closed double glass doors interrupted her lecture. Emma turned as the door opened halfway and possibly the best-looking man she had ever seen in her life stepped into the room. Behind her, she heard the girls whispering and giggling nervously.

"I apologize, sir, but the dining room does not start serving until…"

He removed his hat to reveal thick waves of black hair, a face tanned golden, deep-set eyes beneath the ridge of his forehead, and a nose that might have seen a fight or two. He moved toward her.

"Max Winslow, ma'am." His eyes were gray, almost silver, and he was standing close enough that she could not help but notice the fan of thick black lashes that framed them.

"It's miss," she said, her voice a raspy whisper. Behind her, a few of her girls tittered and were shushed by others. "Miss Elliott," she added primly, finding her full voice.

"Well, Miss Elliott, I'm mighty pleased to meet you. I stopped at the front desk, but no one was there, and I heard you talking to these fine ladies and…"

"Your train is here?"

"Ah, that answers the question of whether or not we're expected. I don't take the train if I can help it. I came on horseback. Diablo's tied up right outside there. The others will be along later tonight after they tear down from our last performance and load everything and everyone on the train."

Several of the girls broke ranks and hurried to the window to look outside. "He's gigantic," one of them murmured.

"He's marvelous," another added.

Emma wondered if they meant the captain or the horse. She gathered herself and looked up at him—at least six feet of him with broad shoulders that filled the cotton chambray shirt he wore, a shirt stained with perspiration and dust from his journey. "I'll go find Mr. Campbell, the hotel manager," she said. "I'm sure he has a room ready for you and—"

"No need to fuss, Miss Elliott." He stepped toward the girls at the window. "If you ladies could direct me to the livery, I'll get Diablo settled and then come back." He flashed a smile, and Emma thought at least two of her waitresses might swoon. This was getting out of hand.

She cleared her throat. "The livery is just to the other side of the railway station," she said and, with a sweep of her hand, indicated the door. "I can have Tommy, our bellboy, take care of that for you if you like."

Once again, she had his full attention, and that smile was now aimed exclusively at her. "I reckon I'd best take care of it. Diablo can be a little touchy when it comes to who handles him." He had reached the dining room doors. He swept back the hair that had fallen over his forehead and tugged on his hat before tipping two fingers to the wide brim. "Ladies," he said, glancing at the group of waitresses. "Miss Elliott," he added with a slight bow.

And then he was gone. As soon as the doors clicked shut, the girls started to babble like a brook sprung from its winter bonds.

"He's even better-looking than his posters," one girl said.

"He's downright adorable," another sighed.

"I heard him and Rebel Reba are sweethearts," a third chimed in.

Emma couldn't help herself. "Who on earth is Rebel Reba?" she asked.

The girls froze and stared at her, much the same way Aidan had when she hadn't known who the captain was.

"She's the captain's costar," one explained.

"She's as good as he is with a six-shooter," another added.

"And she's beautiful besides." Trula stepped in from the kitchen, tying the sash of her apron as she joined the others.

Emma ignored her. "Let's get back to business, ladies. The captain and his party will have this table available at all times," she instructed as she pointed to a round table near the double doors. "They are not to be disturbed by staff or other guests." She saw Trula grin. The table she'd indicated was one Trula served.

"Mr. Campbell has asked that I serve our special guests," Emma added, and Trula's smile faded. "In the meantime, we have our regulars from the train due to arrive soon, so that will be all. Prepare your stations. We have a busy day ahead." The girls turned away. "Trula, my office, please."

About the Author

Linda Broday resides in the Panhandle of Texas on the Llano Estacado. At a young age, she discovered a love for storytelling, history, and anything pertaining to the Old West. Cowboys fascinate her. There's something about Stetsons, boots, and tall rugged cowboys that gets her fired up! A *New York Times* and *USA Today* bestselling author, Linda has won many awards, including the prestigious National Readers' Choice Award and the Texas Gold Award. Visit her at LindaBroday.com.

Also by Linda Broday

Bachelors of Battle Creek
Texas Mail Order Bride
Twice a Texas Bride
Forever His Texas Bride

Men of Legend
To Love a Texas Ranger
The Heart of a Texas Cowboy
To Marry a Texas Outlaw

Texas Heroes
Knight on the Texas Plains
The Cowboy Who Came Calling
To Catch a Texas Star

Outlaw Mail Order Brides
The Outlaw's Mail Order Bride
Saving the Mail Order Bride

Texas Redemption

Christmas in a Cowboy's Arms anthology

Longing for a Cowboy Christmas anthology